JOHN LEE JOHNSON:
INTO THE
PITS OF HELL

LAMBERT GOES HOME

CONN HAMLETT

abbott press

Abbott Press books may be ordered through booksellers or by contacting:

Abbott Press
1663 Liberty Drive
Bloomington, IN 47403
www.abbottpress.com
Phone: 1 (866) 697-5310

ISBN: 978-1-4582-2196-4 (sc)
ISBN: 978-1-4582-2195-7 (hc)
ISBN: 978-1-4582-2194-0 (e)

Library of Congress Control Number: 2018908837

Print information available on the last page.

Abbott Press rev. date: 8/7/2018

This book is dedicated to the Kennett, Missouri high school graduating classes of 1959, 1960, and 1961. We acknowledged that God was God, we had school pride, and we loved each other. We still do.

CHAPTER 1

The nattily dressed James Stevens entered his new office in Austin, Texas, with a bounce in his step. He was of medium height with slicked-down brown hair and a relatively handsome face. He sported a pencil-thin mustache and a prideful look; that look came from being the recipient of a serendipity. He had left Pennsylvania for Galveston, Texas, in December 1864 with hardly a cent to his name. He had carried only his carpetbag filled with a shaving kit and a change of shirts when he left the ship and was met by a one-horse hansom that carried him to a high-dollar hotel. There, he was met by an agent of the former brigadier general Frank McGrew. The saturnine agent handed him an envelope with $500 and a detailed note on what his agenda was. He immediately set up residence in the hotel. His rent was graciously ignored by the hotelier.

The next month, he moved to Austin, where he visited the state legislature daily. He took copious notes and made the acquaintance of those whose names were on the list he had received in Galveston. He frequented parties in Austin and became an integral part of the social network there.

He noticed that most of the legislative body was composed of what native Texans called scalawags—Southerners who worked with the Union—and carpetbaggers—Northerners who had come South to take advantage of the vacuum of leadership. The Union army had its headquarters in Austin, and Confederates who had taken the oath of office or had served the Confederacy in some capacity were being treated as personae non grata and were disqualified from holding office.

On the orders of Frank McGrew, who was orchestrating all this from Philadelphia, Stevens ran for a seat in the state legislature and won 167–2. Stevens had no idea that it would be that easy, but he was thus a Texas legislator with the status he needed to fulfill the his ever-vigilant and demanding patron's orders.

McGrew was sending Stevens telegrams with political chess-like moves almost daily from his elaborate headquarters in Philadelphia. James knew firsthand about his benefactor's acidic hatred of the South, but the general especially had the most vitriol for Texas and Tennessee. He made it clear in his long missives that he expected Texas to be treated as a conquered province rather than a defeated state.

He laid out a plan that at first puzzled the young carpetbagger, but Stevens eventually saw a pattern to this madness. McGrew wanted young Stevens to garner as much power as he could to eventually bring about the death of a man named John Lee Johnson. Young Stevens kept this objective private; he put all correspondence under lock and key in his new safe. But as he augmented his wealth and power, he knew the time was at hand to make a decisive move against this mysterious, unseen, West Texas personality. The more he pleased Frank McGrew, the more money and power were within his grasp.

The first order of business for the young Pennsylvanian was to hire an armed escort—someone who had a reputation for taking orders and keeping his mouth shut. He had made a lot of friends among his Northern interlopers walking the halls of the Texas legislature, but he had also created a great deal of enemies among the Texas natives. But with his grandiose schemes, he needed much more than a guardian. He needed a killer, someone who could control a gang of ruthless men who would do his bidding. After much investigating, he settled on the most feared man in Austin—T-Dilly Whitaker.

T-Dilly had come from a louche background. His family had been thieves; its members were considered the worst of the trash even by neighboring trash. During the war, he had initially served in the

Confederate Missouri brigade and had fought in the Wilson Creek battle under General Sterling Price.

After the first day of battle, he had been playing poker with some of the artillery crew and had been caught blatantly cheating. One of the offended soldiers reached for a knife in anger. T-Dilly pulled his navy Colt and cold-bloodedly shot him in the face. When the others recovered from their shock, they attempted to wrestle T-Dilly to the ground. He adroitly escaped their grasps and killed two others. He belligerently made his way to his horse, cussing and threatening other outraged soldiers. He leaped into his saddle and galloped to the Union lines, whereupon he joined the Union command under General Lyons.

Not long after that, he was caught cheating at cards again and pulled iron; he shot a Union soldier and had to escape. As he rode away, he came to the conclusion that he was a sorry card player and a lousy cheat but one who still liked to play and cheat. However, he had pretty much run out of options and decided to flee to Texas.

When he arrived in Texas, he decided against changing his name. No one there cared about his past or gave a tinker's damn about the war effort in Missouri. When the Union army had for all practical purposes quelled Confederate resistance in Texas, the state suffered a void in leadership; it was reeling from the impending loss of the war and broke into disparate factions. T-Dilly suddenly became a necessary commodity. He hired out his talents as a gunman to anyone wanting revenge on anyone.

With a reputation for dealing death and being loyal to the money, he soon caught the eye of Stevens. He quickly became Stevens's main man who systematically and promptly eliminated his boss's adversaries. The populace knew that was Stevens's doings, but they had neither proof nor the power to stop him. With the heavily elected radical politicians in the majority and in his corner, Stevens began a reign of terror against the old-guard Texas secessionists. Native Texans nervously began keeping their political views to themselves; they knew that a critical eye from Stevens or T-Dilly meant death. T-Dilly, the main executioner, was renowned and feared all around Austin. An unfriendly warning or visit by him was tantamount to a death sentence.

In early April of 1865, T-Dilly and his five henchmen arrived in Austin after a grueling ride to and back from Chihuahua, Mexico, an unusual mission Stevens had adamantly ordered them to undertake. Although they endured but nonetheless enjoyed the trip, they were puzzled by it. They were hoping for a clarification when they reached Austin.

The five rode up to the new office of Representative Stevens but remained in their saddles until they received a nod from T-Dilly that they were dismissed. They pulled their tired mounts out of the loose formation and rode toward the saloon a block from the Texas State capitol building.

T-Dilly enviously watched them ride away as he wearily dismounted. He loosely tied his roan and stood straight to get the kinks out of his legs. He stood an inch over six feet. He was broad shouldered and had a tanned face shadowed by the wide brim of his dusty, beige range hat. His blue eyes were lifeless, and his dark spade beard gave him the look of someone no one should fool with. With considerable spur music, he stepped up on the wood plank porch and headed toward his boss's door.

Stevens had watched them ride up through his spacious office window. He leaned back in his chair and puffed on his long-nine cigar. He mindlessly dusted off specks on his suit's lapels. He had been anxiously awaiting the arrival of T-Dilly with the news he was hoping to hear that would catapult his career. The fleeting but pleasant thought of representative today, governor tomorrow gave him renewed energy. He was looking forward to sending a telegram to McGrew, his generous patron. He knew the general was definitely interested in this plan to rid the earth of John Lee Johnson.

Behind him was a new portrait of himself he had commissioned a local artist to create. The painting was hanging slightly off plumb from a screw high on the wall. T-Dilly opened the door and entered; his eyes were on the somewhat tilted painting. He glanced at his boss and back up at the portrait. Stevens puffed some more blue smoke and ran his fingers over his lapels of his new suit. "What do you think?"

Unaware that his boss was talking about his new suit, T-Dilly said, "You're crooked, boss."

Stevens straightened in his chair with his cigar now perturbedly postured in the corner of his mouth. His eyebrows beetled over his flashing eyes. His stony response definitely caught T-Dilly's ears. "What did you just say, T-Dilly?"

T-Dilly realized he had misconstrued what his boss wanted him to see. He quickly remonstrated with his palms out in a submissive posture. "The picture, boss, the picture, not you."

Stevens turned and saw what T-Dilly was alluding to. He smiled at the mix-up, stood, and straightened the picture. Mollified by T-Dilly's explanation, he sat and indicated with a quick nod for his henchman to do likewise.

"T-Dilly, after we talk, I got some money for you and the boys." Stevens leaned closer with his eyes fixed on the deadened eyes of his right-hand man. "But first things first. Did you and the boys go to Chihuahua?" T-Dilly nodded. "And you did see El Toro de Sanchez?"

T-Dilly nodded again. Puzzled and slightly annoyed by such direct and what he considered unnecessary questions, he reached for a cigar in his shirt pocket. He took his time lighting it and tossed the match into a metal can next to his chair. "I did all that you asked." He paused to take two hearty puffs. To satisfy the demanding stare he was receiving, he answered, "That El Toro de Sanchez is one hell of a man." He slid his cigar to the edge of his mouth mirroring his boss's cigar placement. Seeing that Stevens wanted more, he continued. "He's an animal. He's about six four and weighs every bit of three hundred pounds. The thing about him is that he just keeps movin' forward no matter what his opponent does."

Stevens smiled broadly. "I can't tell you how happy that news makes me."

T-Dilly dwelled on Stevens's overly enthusiastic statement. He gave a slow, hesitant, and exaggerated nod. "He fought some Creole from New Orleans." He continued to puff. "For the first ten minutes, it was an even fight." His eyes had a faraway look as he remembered the unbridled brutality. "But that Mexican never let up. He just kept on comin' and punchin.'" T-Dilly added weight to his thoughts. "There ain't a man alive who can beat him especially in that pit."

The pit he was referring to was a ten feet wide, deep, and long rock quarry in black magma less than a hundred feet from the Chihuahua Desert in the small town of Sanchez, Mexico.

Stevens's smile broadened. "Can't be beaten, eh? Oh, I like that."

T-Dilly studied on what seemed such a lingering, obsessive subject. He wondered why in the hell his boss was consumed by this Mexican fighter.

He started to ask why but chose not to appear impertinent. He pushed his hat up and met his boss's stare with his own. He exhaled a thoughtful smoke cloud. "He's the most man I ever saw if that's what you mean." He knew there had to be a reason why Stevens thought that fight was so important. He had made a three-and-a-half-week hard ride to Sanchez. He even bet on the big Mexican. But he was still puzzled why his boss was obsessed with this unusual assignment. He sat silently hoping Stevens would solve the mystery.

Stevens broke the stare. He smiled slyly. "You ever heard of a man named John Lee Johnson?"

T-Dilly tilted his head in thought. He squinted his eyes as if to jostle his memory. He shook his head. "Can't say I have."

"Well, this John Lee Johnson fellow is from Baileysboro, Texas … over in Bailey County. You're going to go there to arrest a woman."

T-Dilly almost did a double take at the change of direction the conversation had taken; Stevens had seemed so intent on this John Lee Johnson but had switched courses midstream. T-Dilly's eyebrows shot up. "Arrest?"

"Yeah, arrest." Stevens's crooked grin became wider. "You ever killed a woman, T-Dilly?" Upon seeing T-Dilly shake his head, Stevens said, "Well, you might have to."

T-Dilly did not want to disappoint his boss. "Never killed a woman, but I've killed some sissies before."

Stevens shook his head in a good-natured, jocular way. "Those sissies don't count." When T-Dilly gave him a blank look, Stevens continued. "Would you kill a woman?"

"I'd hate to kill a good lookin' woman."

"But would you?"

T-Dilly reluctantly nodded. "Yeah, but it would cost you an extra hundred dollars."

Stevens leaned back in his chair and approvingly joggled his head. He studied on T-Dilly's words and leaned forward again. "What about if she was ugly?"

T-Dilly shrugged. "I'd kill her and maybe give you fifty dollars. I never cared for ugly women." T-Dilly knocked some ashes off his smoke. "This Johnson fella you mentioned livin' over in what you said was Bailey County. I gather he's involved in all this palaver."

Stevens ignored the remark and let a knowing smile slide across his face. "Twenty miles outside that town lives the woman in question. Her name is Duchess Thompson. At the same time you arrest her, I want you to set up a bank robbery in Baileysboro. You hire some low-level gang to do that. You're not to be involved in the bank robbery at all. That will keep the local yokels busy while you take Duchess to Hawkshaw. I'll handle the rest."

Stevens saw he had T-Dilly's attention though he appeared mystified. He saw no need to withhold the information he knew T-Dilly wanted. "We're going to charge the old gal with helping General Sibley." He perceived that T-Dilly had no knowledge of whom General Sibley was. Stevens exhaled a blue smoke ring. "General Sibley was a Confederate general who was fighting in New Mexico. He lost a big battle in New Mexico or thereabouts. He tried to escape the Union forces. This woman, Duchess, and her husband, who at that time was alive, hid the general in a storm cellar. She later got him across Texas to Louisiana in a covered wagon." Stevens's grim smile became even more twisted. "The State of Texas will charge her with aiding and abetting a known enemy of the government."

T-Dilly's impassive eyes suddenly took on a discerning look. "You ain't goin' to be able to hold her, boss." He pushed his hat brim up farther. "Not on that charge …" His tone trailed off. "Not in this state. Even with Union occupation."

Not losing his ragged smile, Stevens replied, "You just do what I say, T-Dilly. I'll handle the law."

T-Dilly knew the matter was closed, but he felt compelled to ask one more question. "Speakin' of this John Lee Johnson feller, why don't you just send me to Baileysboro? Hell, I'll just call out this John Lee Johnson and kill him and get it over with."

Stevens's smile morphed into a thoughtful mien. "T-Dilly, it's not that you aren't good enough." He saw that his words satisfied T-Dilly's enormous ego. He thoughtfully rolled his cigar between his thumb and index finger. He decided he might as well square with his segundo. "We want this John Lee Johnson fellow to fight El Toro de Sanchez. If you just pulled iron on him and killed him, that would be fine, but if you were unsuccessful, it would ruin my whole plan. Taking Duchess Thompson and holding her on a trumped-up charge will force him to accept our demands to fight the big Mexican. We'll promise to let her go if he goes and actually fights the Mexican. We'll offer to drop the charges against her and not only that—we'll put up an outrageous bet that will be hard for him to refuse as an extra incentive." He saw that he had piqued T-Dilly's interest.

"He'll probably accept the offer. On the trail to Mexico, I want you and your men to make an effort to kill the big bastard. I have a friend who thinks you'll fail in your effort." Stevens smiled confidently. "I got more confidence in you than he does. Even if he escapes your attempts, he still has to fight the man. But I'm counting on you making life miserable for him before he gets there." Stevens's smile evaporated as his face became very serious. "It's a win-win situation for us regardless." He leaned in to accentuate his message. "It's imperative that he die one way or another, T-Dilly."

T-Dilly frowned. He removed his smoke from his mouth. He let his vision dwell on the cigar in his hand as a reference point as he mulled over Stevens's words. He had noticed that Stevens had used the word *us* but did not think it included him. Also, Stevens had referred to his "friend" earlier. He had suspected for some time that someone much larger and much wealthier was behind his boss. It was not that he did not respect Stevens. He just suspected that the huge amounts of money they had at their disposal were coming from someone higher up the totem pole. Stevens had come far in a short amount of time, but there was no way he could be buying confiscated land and paying his and the others' salaries just by being a crooked Texas congressman.

Second, it riled him some that Stevens considered it necessary to go through all this rigmarole to kill John Lee Johnson. It sounded like a lack of faith in him. He reasoned that he did not know the whole truth. But still, he sat confused and wondering why someone would rather work his way through such an elaborate plan to do something that seemed awfully easy to him. He shrugged it off. He figured he would kill John Lee Johnson on the way to Mexico and be done with it.

Seeing his words had taken some effect, Stevens rose and pulled a yellow packet obviously filled with greenbacks from his pocket. He tossed the large envelope to his right-hand man. "After you pay the boys and you go get some sleep, meet me tomorrow morning at six in the hotel dining hall. I'll fill in a lot of those loose questions you have floating around in your brain."

T-Dilly looked at the folder bulging with money. He relaxed his stern visage and nodded his satisfaction. He still had questions but knew they could wait till morning.

Buoyed by T-Dilly's pleased look, Stevens said, "Besides your salary, inside the folder is a detailed plan of what you're supposed to do and when. T-Dilly, I have great respect for you. Just do what I say and you'll be a rich man sometime this summer, savvy?"

T-Dilly figured that all the loose ends would be cleared up at breakfast. He rose, gave a businesslike nod, and quickly departed to heavy spur music.

CHAPTER 2

It was early May in West Texas. The yellow and beige landscape dotted with mesquite trees moved with the wind. The mild sandstorm was more of a nuisance than anything else, but it was bad enough to keep the rider coming over the bald knob scrunched up to avoid the sudden rushes of abrasive sand.

The large man in the saddle with his hat tilted low had some age on him. It was obvious that he had been at one time in his younger days a well-built, handsome man, but his face was seamed with deep lines. His blue eyes peeking out from the shadow of the brim were sad. They were orbs that had seen a lot of sorrow, eyes that had seen too many bottoms of shot glasses and too many bad poker hands, eyes that had recognized but overlooked the false smiles of many sporting girls. He had awakened in too many beds not remembering his lovers' names. He remembered getting around that by calling them honey and sweetheart until he could get dressed and leave.

After he had exchanged his money and time for fleshly entertainment, he invariably found himself feeling emptier and lonelier than before. Those thoughts seemed to linger as he moved his blaze-faced sorrel through the ankle-deep sand.

Occasionally, the rustling wind would ruffle his hat brim and expose what used to be blond hair but was then more white. He realized he was old and running out of time. That made his mission even more critical. He would not be denied. The occasional singsong of wind served as a monotonous backdrop as he made his way to his destination.

He straightened a bit when he recognized a familiar landmark in the desolation. He cut his sorrel toward a worn path that most would have missed. He pulled up and watched the sand being strewn across the beige trail. It reminded him of sand pouring in an hour glass. In this tableau of browns, yellows, and ochres accompanied by the shifting sand, he suddenly felt time. Loneliness pressed down on him. That act of nature was a reminder of how fragile he was and how quickly time had gotten away. He made a clucking noise that ol' Ben recognized, and he began to trot down the road Lambert had once traveled twenty years previously. His throat tightened. His chest—empty for so many years—was again filled with a mysterious feeling, one akin to hope but not quite.

When he topped a small sand hill, he saw the skeletal remains of his old ranch house. Only one wall was standing. He saw the sun-silvered, warped front porch where he had whiled away the hours years earlier. All that remained of the barn were the sunbaked pieces of wood that peeked above the mound of soft loam that mostly covered it. He reluctantly inhaled and shifted his vision to the left. He saw a forlorn cross tilted over a small mound. He became cognizant of the wind again; he heard its lonesome whine in the background. His sad eyes took in the drifting dust clouds just beyond the small stand of mesquite. That veil of dust in the background made his arrival at the gravesite all the more depressing.

He reined up but stayed in the saddle for a long time. Tears formed in his eyes and were soon streaming down his lined face. He walked ol' Ben closer before he dismounted. He reached behind the cantle of his saddle and into a canvas bag looped over the back. He pulled a tall, ornate cross from it along with a large wood mallet. He walked to the grave and removed his hat. He looked sadly at the tilted cross that simply said in fading letters, "Here lies Portia Lambert. She died a good woman in the year of our Lord 1845."

He felt the full weight of lost years in that lonesome and forsaken tableau. He knelt and felt a heaving in his chest that erupted in a soft wail. He did not care if he cried. He wept deeply as he placed his palms on the soft soil. He knew Portia could not hear him, but he knew God could. He involuntarily wept for her because he loved her and missed her.

He pulled the old cross from its shaky moorings and placed the new marker in its place. With heavy strikes from the mallet, he drove the new cross deep into the soil where the old one had stood. The new standard stated the same thing the old cross had expressed. He wiped his tears and stood, still hatless. He looked to the sky and saw clouds scurrying across the expanse. His eyes searched the sky as though he were seeking God. He knew He was there even if he could not see Him. He held up the old grave marker in his hand as if to catch the Almighty's attention. Words formed in his brain and poured out as he sought a purgation from all he felt. "Lord, I ain't the only man that has lived a wasted life." He paused to collect his thoughts. "I ain't the only man that has regretted it." He stood thoughtfully as he listened to the whistle of wind. "But all I ask is that you'll give me the chance to make it as right as I can."

He donned his hat and glanced at the sand-strewn grave. "Portia, my dear wife, I'll be back before the year's out. I'll bring you some flowers, and hopefully, I'll have some good news for you."

Four days later, G.W. Lambert rode into Baileysboro, Texas. At first glance, the town seemed like a typical West Texas cow town. Before he rode much farther into the community, he saw that the village had some vitality. He saw buckboards here and there and a fancy buggy parked in front of a store. It was obvious that Baileysboro was alive and burgeoning with financial health. He studied on that fact as he nodded to the wandering waddies riding past him as he continued to peruse the town. When he was two buildings past Chili Davis's Livery Stable, he heard the happy sounds of a rinky-dink piano. He surmised correctly that a saloon was up ahead.

G.W. knew his foreman was most likely in the saloon waiting on his arrival. His foreman, Fred Malone, had been sent to Baileysboro several days in advance. Since Lambert did not frequent saloons anymore, he steered ol' Ben toward the hotel veranda and its two chairs. He slowly dismounted, gave his faithful horse a sizable drink at the water trough, and tied him to the hitch rack. He moved to one of the empty chairs, sat wearily, and stretched out his legs. He dusted his hat and tried to slap some alkali dust from his coat. He caught sight of a familiar face anxiously peering down the street at him from one of the open saloon batwings. Malone, a stout gent, departed the saloon and walked his way. Though he was ambling along, he had a particular bounce to his step, a sign he had been successful on his mission. As he drew closer, the soft smile on his round face cinched the deal; he had accomplished his goal. He nodded more fully when he approached Lambert and took the empty chair to his left. "Good to see you, boss."

Lambert nodded but focused his vision on his dusty boots. "It's good to be seen, Fred." He paused and turned to his foreman. He did not feel like rushing anything because he was exhausted. But on the other hand, he had not come to Baileysboro to take a nap. "What did you find out about our man?"

Fred leaned forward and placed his elbows on his knees. "Well, it took some doin', but I found out he's working at a ranch about a four hours' ride from here." Fred sighed. "I went for two days and played a whole lot of bad poker and heard nothin'. I naturally asked nothin', but finally, I heard a bartender talkin' about him last night. I didn't have to ask a question. He went on to say he was a hell of a good man."

"Keep talkin'."

Fred nodded and pulled a cigar from his vest pocket. He struck a match, lit his smoke, and languidly tossed the match into the street. "He's workin' for a man named John Lee Johnson."

"Never heard of 'im."

Fred took a heavy drag on his smoke. "Well, you'll hear about 'im." He exhaled smoke and continued. "I can guarantee you that."

Lambert looked at Fred's thoughtful profile. "What in tarnation is that supposed to mean?"

"Well, I rode out there this mornin' and saw him with my own eyes. John Lee Johnson that is. When I saw him, I had to look twice. He's the most different man I ever saw."

Lambert continued to slap at his britches and send puffs of dust into the air. "Different you say?" He sighed. "I knew a man who lived in Roxy, Texas, who talked to hisself and answered hisself. He was different."

Fred knew Lambert was tired. He usually was not so short with his remarks. Fred turned more fully to Lambert. "Boss, he's one of the biggest and most powerful lookin' men I ever met. I tried not to stare at 'im, but he's got these muscles." He held up his arm and pulled on his shirt fabric above his bicep. "And he's is just ... I can't think of the word."

"Brawny."

"Yeah, brawny." Fred sighed. "I couldn't think of the word."

Lambert leaned back in his chair satisfied he had done a decent job of dusting himself off. "So he's big and strong, but what type of hombre is this John Lee Johnson?"

Fred scratched his face as he mulled over the question. "He was cordial to me. I pulled into his ranch, and he invited me to eat at the cook shack. He asked me how I was doin' and if I was lookin' for work." Fred sighed as he flicked some cigar ashes out into the street. "I told 'im no, that I was just passin' through. I noticed that he was nice to everyone, but when he gave an order, the hands jumped to it. But to answer your question, I liked him."

"You never let on why you was there, did you?"

Fred gave a pained look somewhat perturbed he had been asked the question. "I may be dumb, boss, but I ain't plumb dumb."

Lambert realized he had been too curt with his question. He patted Fred on the shoulder. "You did good, Fred."

Fred nodded. He was satisfied with the compliment. "But he's there." He paused and took a drag off his smoke. He gave a sideways look to catch Lambert's reaction. "That's the man we're lookin' for. I saw 'im with my own eyes." He had nothing else to say. He just stared straight ahead.

Lambert sighed and straightened in his chair. He asked for the directions to the ranch, and once he felt he had them down pat, he gave a contented grunt. He reached in his coat pocket and pulled out a bulging, yellowed envelope. "Here's a thousand dollars. I want you to spend another night here. We'll get up early and get things goin.' I want you to ride to the ranch, get the boys, and head down to Angel Rivas's place along the Rio Grande. He's got a thousand head of mossbacks down there." He nodded as though he approved of the deal he had made a month earlier. "He'll charge you a dollar a head for those critters. You pay 'im and drive that herd up to Roy Rawlins's place and he'll give you five dollars a head." Lambert wearily ran his large hand over his face. "You know where to store the money. When I get back, I'll settle up with you and the boys."

Before Fred could reply, they saw a sight that stifled any other comments they might have had—Irvin Pendly and Butter Bean Baker were riding down the street side by side. They were well known, despicable characters. Fred gave a quick look of disapproval at Lambert and received the same in return. Fred muttered low as he leaned forward with his elbows on his knees. "Well, looky here, boss. What in the Sam Hill are two of the sorriest creatures on the earth doin' in Baileysboro?"

Lambert kept his eyes on the two men as they were almost even with them as they trotted down the street. "I don't know, Fred. I thought they were in Austin these days working for that carpetbagger congressman."

Irvin Pendly turned his narrow head and caught sight of Lambert and his foreman. He gave a sneering smile accompanied by a slight nod in recognition. He mumbled something to Butter Bean, who quickly turned and took a gander at the two men. He did not bother to acknowledge them. As they rode past, Lambert's eyes narrowed. "Whatever they're doing here, it ain't for no good reason."

Fred nodded with a groused expression. "Probably here because of that Yankee representative." He sighed. "That James Stevens fella who came here from Pennsylvania back in sixty-four. He shore in hell got rich fast."

Lambert snorted sarcastically. "Way yonder too fast. The way I heard it, he stepped off the boat in Galveston broke as Job's turkey and in six months he was one of the richest men in Austin." Lambert shook his head in disgust. "There ain't no doubt about it. Some Yankee nabob back East supported him … helped him run for state congress. Since Confederates and secessionists weren't allowed to vote, he won it easily. He's been chasin' Confederates ever since and legally robbin' the state since he got here with some of the slickest, most illegal schemes a man can think of."

Fred shook his head in dismay. "Best of my recollection, he's got a man named T-Dilly Whitaker doin' all his dirty work."

Lambert sighed. "Well, someday, that Stevens fella will get what's comin' to hisself." He paused. "And T-Dilly too."

They gave overt looks at the outlaws' backs as they rode past toward the saloon. They gave disgusted looks and tacitly rose to enter the hotel.

The next morning before first light, Fred Malone headed toward Lambert's ranch and Lambert rode due West toward the Johnson ranch.

Sand Burr Rogers, who had spent the whole night with John Lee Johnson and several select members of the crew painting the interior of the immense barn, stood sleepily outside that barn cinching the saddle on his paint horse. The sun was well over the horizon as his bloodshot eyes acknowledged the orange rays sending heated tendrils slithering through the distant mesquite. He could have stayed at the ranch and slept and no one would have objected, but that was not his way. He had been recently promoted as the ramrod of the eastern-range day riders, and he took that responsibility seriously. He had been given a bump in salary, and he intended to do his job. His crew had left half an hour earlier, and he made ready to head their way.

As he dropped the stirrup fender from the saddle cradle, he caught sight of a rider coming down the road. He took no particular notice of the man at first, but since the man appeared to be riding directly toward him, he gave him more attention. He did not look like a regular brush popper. He rode a fine-looking sorrel with a high-dollar saddle and bridle. His clothes although dusty were not the garb normally worn by a grub rider. He surmised him to be in his quick perusal either a rancher or a lawman; he looked a mite old to be seeking work. The older rider, who was then close enough to make eye contact, was headed his way. Sand Burr sleepily leaned on his saddle awaiting to discover the purpose of the visit.

Lambert rode up and removed his hat; he gave it two swats to remove some dust. He ran his hand wearily through his white-blond hair and looked at Sand Burr, who stood bemusedly observing him. Sand Burr drummed his fingers on the bowl of his saddle and nodded friendly enough. "What can I do for you?" He started to say "old timer" but held off on that familiarity.

Lambert replaced his hat and sighed. "I'm lookin' for work."

Sand Burr gave a soft grin. "Hell, man, I figured when a man got your age, he'd be more likely settin' on an orange crate cussin', scratchin', and chawin'."

Lambert returned a smile. "I tried that already. It shore didn't pay very well."

Sand Burr thoughtfully nodded. "What's your name?"

"Name's G. W. Lambert, but most people just call me Lambert."

Sand Burr observed him more closely. He could tell that Lambert might have had some age on him but that he was still salty looking. He tried not to make it obvious, but his mind was clicking. He knew sitting in the saddle all night and trying to find lost calves in the mesquite was a younger man's job—not that of someone far from his prime. Nagging him also was why a man his age was seeking work. He delayed his decision by looking and meeting the insistent blue eyes curiously studying him. "My name's Sand Burr."

Lambert nodded and gently smiled. "I don't reckon I've ever met a man named Sand Burr before." He paused and gave a faraway look.

Sand Burr returned a wry grin. "Well, don't reckon we can all be called Lambert."

Lambert did not take offense. He let his eyes settle on Sand Burr and sighed as he let his eyes wander longingly to the cook shack next to the large barn. He returned his gaze to Sand Burr and sighed. "Guess not."

Sand Burr had caught his glance toward the cook shack. He had just eaten, but he figured Lambert might have been hungry but was too proud to ask. He decided he would take the initiative so as not to hurt Lambert's pride. He figured if a man came to the Johnson ranch looking for work, he might not be exactly riding around with a full wallet. "I tell you what, Lambert, let's go eat. I'll have ol' Archie fix me and you up some eggs and coffee." He paused as he nodded at Lambert's sorrel. "You're hired by the way." He wryly added, "But after hearing all you have to do, you might want to saddle up and ride out of here."

Lambert had a good idea that Sand Burr had probably already eaten. That act of kindness caused his respect for the young cowhand to grow immeasurably. As far as saddling up and riding away, he knew that was then impossible. He dismounted and tied his mount alongside Sand Burr's horse. He and Sand Burr gave each other a satisfying nod. It appeared it was a done deal that the job was his and that he was accepting it. Sand Burr rubbed his full stomach and said, "Glad you could stay and eat before we head out."

Lambert nodded. "Well, I'll force myself to eat since you seem hungry." They both knew the other was lying; they exchanged droll smiles.

CHAPTER 3

One hour later in Baileysboro, Seth Johnson shut the door to his hotel room and stood in the hallway. He was five eight, and he had blond features, thoughtful blue eyes, and a handsome, clean-shaven visage. He wore a wide-brimmed beige hat that showed some weather stains. The well-worn frock coat that befitted him showed that he was a man who worked indoors, but those who knew him knew he loved the outdoors. He was the president of the Baileysboro Bank, and his longtime partner, Floyd Maccabee, was the vice president.

His eyes were purposely narrowed. He had a problem. He had recently adopted four orphan girls, and by Texas state law, he was required to have a wife before the adoption would be considered legal. Therefore, the four waifs were staying with his legendary cousin, John Lee Johnson, and his wife, Martha, until he could find a suitable mate.

Each day, the mail brought letters of proposals or interest from women as far away as Chicago and St. Louis. How these women could have found out he was seeking a wife when he never advertised that was a mystery to him. Some were timid letters trying to touch his conscience with the plight of lost angels looking for their way and seeking someone to love and hold them. Others were more bold overtures—relating how they would complete his mission with a passionate and loving relationship. He took his first step down the hotel aisle toward the balustrade that would lead him to the lobby. Each thoughtful step was accompanied by the *ching* of his silvery spurs. His thoughts were wearied with those lovelorn missives plaguing him along with the knowledge that he would once more be tied down in his canicular office and humped over his desk all day long agonizing over some ranchers who were in arrears with their notes—ranchers he liked. He had a hard time dispensing justice with mercy. He dreaded each footstep toward his self-imposed jail.

He gave a perfunctory nod to Chester Dowdy, the gaunt lobby clerk. Chester, who stood there guardedly, gave a big howdy wave back. Chester knew that the Johnson family owned the hotel. Though they were easy to deal with, he knew his bread and butter depended on his service. He worked very hard to earn their respect by his work ethic.

Seth realized how hard Chester intended to please, so he made it a point to praise him for his diligence. Seth stopped abruptly realizing he might have been too absorbed in his own thoughts to recognize the sensitive clerk properly. He went over and pointedly shook Chester's hand. As he left, Chester beamed with pride. Seth had made him feel important.

Seth stepped out on the warped, wooden boardwalk. He stood beneath the new wooden veranda. He let his eyes move up and down the street. He saw a few riders moving already down the arenose way. He heard a rooster crowing somewhere in back of the buildings. He watched as old man Talbert emerged from an alley. He was recovering from a drunk. He did not know why the old man drank so much, but he imagined that life had overwhelmed him. He grimaced at that fact and looked to his right as he began walking toward the bank.

He saw that Floyd had his horse already hitched to one of the two hitch racks in front of the bank. He smiled wryly. He had met Floyd in the Nations sometime back. Floyd was three-quarters Choctaw, but he looked more Mediterranean than Indian. While Floyd lived in the Nations, he had married a much younger woman. She had cheated on him with every young buck she could find. Floyd, good-hearted and understanding to a point, had overlooked her faults because he felt his age had made him inadequate for her. But convinced by Seth that he was only lying to himself, he left his faithless wife and departed with Seth as they embarked on what later turned out to be many adventures and misadventures.

On that particular journey, they saved a recluse living deep in the hills from being stung to death by yellow jackets. As a reward, he had given them a sack of what appeared to be wagon washers. They had taken the ersatz reward without much comment figuring the old man was daft. They carelessly tossed the sack of washers onto the back of a packhorse, wished the old man well, and took off.

They were astonished later to discover that the washers were in fact pure gold that had been painted gray to disguise their nature. As they returned from their project, they stopped once more to check on the old man. Finding him dead, they gave him a Christian burial. They also found that he had hidden an additional cache of $50,000 worth of those wagon washers in his wall. They figured he had worked somewhere in a treasury mint and had figured out a way to purloin the coins and by chance had settled in the Nations. They scrubbed the coins of the gray paint and had converted them into the biggest bank in North Texas.

When Seth opened the door to the bank, he saw the pie-faced Merle Tadlock, the head clerk, plinking coins into the till behind the iron grill. Seth walked around the grilled, two-clerk station and saw Floyd leaning over his desk sorting through what looked like a dossier of legal papers. Floyd glanced up, gave him a quick smile, and handed him a stack of lovelorn letters that had been set aside for him. "Maybe you'll find a winner in there today, amigo." Floyd's attention then quickly went back to the matters at hand. As Seth took the bundle of letters permeating with whiffs of perfume, Floyd looked up once more and sighed. "One more thing. Lola Crawford just came by. She said her daddy wanted to talk to you as soon as possible."

Seth gave a concerned look. Lola's father was the town's Southern Baptist preacher. He had no idea why he needed to see him since he had been to the Baptist church only twice and had gone to sleep both times. He thoughtfully walked to his office holding the letters and wondering about Lola. He looked over his shoulder at Floyd while pondering that Lola comment. He caught sight of Floyd's hidden smile as he opened his door and went reluctantly to his chair.

He dropped resignedly into his chair and tossed the congeries of letters aside. He heard a feminine voice coming from the clerk station. It sounded like Mrs. Elspeth Delray, one of the two largest depositors in his bank. She had over $10,000 in her bank account, and he liked keeping her happy and confident. He heard her request to see him. He tossed his hat over the stack of envelopes. He was not sure a depositor would take confidence in a man receiving all those proposals of sorts coming from all over creation.

He heard her footsteps and then a gentle knock on the door frame. She walked in his office with a nervous smile. Mrs. Delray was a handsome woman—auburn hair, blue eyes, buxom figure, full lips, and an engaging personality accompanied by a ready wit at times. She seemed overly timid that day, however. In the past, she had been full of confidence and friendly sass, but that day, she was somewhat demure. She shut the door, which was unusual. She nodded at the chair in front of Seth's desk. "May I?"

Seth, mystified by her unusual behavior, sat motionless for a moment. Then catching that he was being rude, he quickly jumped to his feet and pointed at the chair with alacrity. He sensed that maybe something was wrong with the bank service; he was concerned. "You can have my chair if you want, Mrs. Delray."

She shushed him with a quick flick of her wrist and sat in the proffered chair. He noticed her eyes taking in his in a bolder way than she had ever utilized before. He also noticed a thin line of perspiration above her upper lip. He sensed she was nervous and trying to hide it. Seth felt lost in the moment. He sat abruptly and leaned forward with his hands on his desk in anticipation of being bawled out or told she was closing her account.

She inhaled and leaned slightly forward. "Seth, we need to talk."

Seth swallowed. He knew it was bad. She was going to close her account. "Mrs. Delray, if me or Floyd have said someth—"

She again shushed him with a flick of her wrist. "I'm perfectly happy with my account." She smiled slyly. "This is the best bank in our part of the state. I'm not here because of my account."

Seth ran his hand over his face as he tried to regain some composure. He fought the impulse to start talking; he feared he would say something gauche. He just sat there looking at her comeliness. He gathered Mrs. Delray was at least fifteen years older than he was, which would have made her about forty. But all in all, she was a very attractive woman.

She clutched at the reticule on her lap and as if drawing on some reservoir of strength, she leveled her eyes directly at him. "Seth, I have known for some time that you're seeking a wife." She pursed her lips and inhaled deeply. "This is not easy for me to say being older than you and a widow for ten years, but I find you vastly attractive." She dropped her eyes as though relieved she had said the words. She gathered her strength. "I want you to call me Elspeth, not Mrs. Delray. And I want to know if you consider me marriageable material."

Seth looked at her trying not to show shock. He felt like a man who noticed a rope on the ground and did not know if he had found a rope or had lost a horse. He knew this was quite an outreach for her. She was a former school mistress and presently the owner of 20,000 acres of prime ranchland. Fortunately for him as his mind raced on how to handle this situation, she continued. "I realize that I have a little age on you."

Seth swallowed as the number fifteen flashed in his brain.

She looked more fully into his face. "But I could raise those girls and give them a good education." She paused and ran the tip of her tongue along her upper lip. "And I have been married before and know how to please a man." That statement brought a rush of color to her cheeks. She momentarily averted her eyes.

Seth tried his best to hide his large swallow. He knew he was in a serious bind. He did not take lightly the courage it had taken this refined woman to open her heart to him. He liked her. But he did not love her. He had lived long enough to know there were many women he could live with, but he was looking for the one he could not live without. He let his eyes move to meet Elspeth's. "I think you would make a marvelous wife …" He started to say "Mrs. Delray" but caught himself in time. "… Elspeth. I think it's my time to talk." Seth knew if he did not play with the truth some, he could damage her pride. He liked and even admired her. He sighed as he leaned forward and looked into her eyes. "What I'm goin' to say is just between you and me …" He took in a lungful of air and said with touching affection, "… Elspeth."

She gave him a lingering smile as she moved in closer to meet his gaze more intimately. Seth looked both ways as though he were looking for eavesdroppers, which were of course nonexistent. He wiped his face with his hand nervously. "Floyd," he stated and inhaled again. He nodded as though he were finally ready to relieve himself of longtime, pent-up knowledge. "Elspeth, Floyd's in love with you."

Her eyes opened wide with a sudden realization she had never entertained. "Floyd?"

Seth reached across the desk and took her hands. "Elspeth, it would break his old heart if me and you got married." Since Seth had stretched the truth that far, he went further. "Elspeth, nothin' would please me more than to court you." He paused for effect. "But Floyd has carried a torch for you ever since he met you."

Elspeth tilted her head as to ascertain the sincerity of what she was hearing. "We are talking about Floyd?" she asked as she gave a backward nod indicating the unseen Floyd bent over his desk.

"Yes, that Floyd."

Her eyes seem to dilate. "You say he's in love with me?"

Seth sighed and nodded. "You stay on his mind, Elspeth."

"Isn't he an Indian or part Indian?"

"Not enough to matter. Just enough to make him a good tracker."

Elspeth sighed, gave a bewildered look, and rose. "You have given me food for thought, Seth." She paused and nodded. "After all, he's the vice president of the bank."

Seth held up a finger as though she had made a good point. "You darn right. Everyone knows he's the brains behind all this." He spread his hands wide as though he was paying homage to Floyd's prowess.

She walked around the desk and gave Seth a peck on his cheek. She patted his arm and then through slit eyes said, "Maybe you were too young for me after all." Her eyes and thoughts took in the possibilities of Floyd.

She opened the door, gave a quick approving but departing look at Seth, and walked up to Floyd. He glanced up at her in surprise. In the past, Elspeth had been all business, but that time, she had an amorous look in her eyes. She leaned down and kissed Floyd on the cheek … a noisy kiss. She patted him on the shoulder. "So very nice to see you today, Floyd."

He numbly nodded in shock. He gave a suspicious "Nice to see you too" response and watched her walk out the bank with happy feet. Floyd turned in his chair and gave a quizzical look toward Seth's office. He entertained the notion of pushing aside his paperwork, going in to see his best friend, and getting to the bottom of the weird greeting he had just received. But the overpowering pile of work caused him to just let out a throaty "*Humph.*"

He caught sight of Seth leaving his office, and he gave a half-hearted effort to halt him, but Seth pointedly walked past him so brusquely that he just shrugged it off and returned to his work. He knew Seth was headed to see Pastor Crawford. Floyd's eyes narrowed because he felt on the surface that the pastor could possibly have wanted to discuss some matter with Seth. But in the back of Floyd's mind, he also perceived that Lola Crawford could possibly be up to some shenanigans.

Lola Crawford was approximately twenty. She was blonde with hazel eyes; she was very buxom, and she had a pretty face and kewpie doll lips. She was also very aggressive when it came to men. She fell in and out of love quickly. Floyd had been on some long buggy rides with her in the past and had taken it in stride when he learned several other men in town had done the same. He felt she was not only capricious when it came to men but was also way yonder too forward. He feared for Seth thinking that any talk with the pastor was mere subterfuge. He figured that Lola was getting into the desperate stage and that marrying a man like Seth might cover up her last two years of indiscretions with the promise of being rich as another incentive. He feared for his partner.

Floyd sighed as he picked up an overdue mortgage and looked over the particulars. That arrears note was alarming in that it was held by a minister and his wife. What alarmed him was that previously, they had been very faithful with their payments. He frowned as he pushed it aside deciding on what tack to take. His eyes moved to another deed held by the bank approximately in the same area. That particular document was owned by a rancher who was making payments like clockwork. And that rancher had a beautiful daughter, Patricia, who was the envy of many men for miles around. Floyd laid the groundwork on how to escape the bank for a while and help find Seth a suitable mate.

Meanwhile, Seth was walking back toward the hotel with his eyes on the modest Baptist church at the end of town. He really did not have time for a conversation with Pastor Crawford especially since they had had only minimal contact. He had no idea what in the world they could even discuss. He knew the minister did not like most words that ended in *ing* especially cussing, dancing, and carousing and other words including poker and strong drink, many things that Seth liked. On the other hand, he liked the pastor and even his dowdy wife, Eugenia. But he worried about Lola. She was spoiled and man-crazy. He was not sure her father even wanted to talk to him, and he was not sure how he could circumvent being waylaid by Lola if she was there. He was a bit chafed even thinking about the whole silly talk business.

He reached the church and walked around to the modest, white parsonage. It had several cottonwood trees around it and a small brook in back. He knocked on the door gently hoping no one would answer. But it creaked open, and he saw the compelling, slit eyes of Lola Crawford. She reached through the opening, made it wider, and pulled him through the doorway. Seth allowed himself to be pulled in not wanting to create a scene. He dutifully doffed his hat and tried to look as impassive as possible, but he pretty well knew the pastor was miles from the scene and he had just been pulled into the spider's web of one Lola Crawford. He let his mind race about how to escape this siren's lair. He pretended to let his eyes move over the top of her head as if trying to spot her father.

Lola observed his eyes as she moved closer. She got uncomfortably close and ran her fingers up and down his lapels. "He's not here, Seth." Her voice was thick. Her eyes were feral. Her pupils were dilated. Her lips were moist and provocatively posed. "You know why you're here, Seth. You undoubtedly have known for some time that I have been so greatly attracted to you."

Seth's mind was racing. He knew he had to get out of this silken trap as gracefully as he could. He managed to croak, "No, Lola, I don't know why I'm here." He stretched out the words *at all* to an almost comical level.

She cynically snorted and moved in closer. She took her hands from his lapels and laced them loosely around his neck. "I've waited for you all my life." Her eyes narrowed as he felt her breath inches from his face. "I've been in love with you even before I met you."

Seth knew she had been reading some books by Sir Walter Scott or some other sappy author. Hoping to cool her zeal, he asked, "I shore could stand a cool drink of water."

She cocked her head to one side and studied him. A sly smile moved across her face. She did not connect with the idea he was trying to untangle himself from her clutches. Rather, she concluded he was very moved by her and needed water to cool his ardor. "Seth Johnson, forget that water and just hold me and protect me against the world."

Seth resisted the temptation to raise his eyebrows at such flowery and obviously practiced words. Oblivious to his stiff stance, she unlaced her chubby arms from around his neck and encircled his waist with them. She squeezed him hard and said with all the admiring emotion she could muster, "You are so strong, Seth, so very strong."

Seth's eyes were wide. His breath was shallow. "You're hurtin' me, Lola."

She gave him an incredulous look. "What?"

"I ain't all that strong." He lied.

She continued to squeeze as she disavowed his words. "I've seen you lift a keg of nails from a flatbed wagon, Seth."

"Yeah, but it was heavy … and I breathed a lot." He decided to go all out. "I ain't strong at all. I got some health problems that I can't talk about with a decent woman."

She clung tightly and ignored his words. "Seth, I need you to protect me against all the wolves here in town. I want someone to love me for me and not just my body. I want a man to notice the sun kiss my hair and my country-girl smile. I want to laugh and love and share everything with my man, my hero."

Seth's eyes were moving quickly right and left in concert with his brain. He decided to try a new approach. He pushed down on her arms to break her anaconda stranglehold. "Listen. We gotta talk, Lola."

The urgency in his voice caused her to release him, but her lips were only inches from his, and he felt her body close against him. She huskily breathed, "Let's talk." She sighed with such emotion that Seth thought she would attack him on the spot.

"Lola, we have us a problem."

The word *problem* caused her to move back a few inches, which gave Seth momentary respite. She however was zeroed in on his lips and eyes. Her eyes relentlessly bored into his. She whispered, "What problem, dearest Seth?"

"Well, it's like this, Lola. Floyd's madly in love with you."

Lola moved back with eyes narrowed. She thought Floyd had perhaps revealed too much about their buggy ride. Her predatory eyes suddenly took on a worried and thoughtful look. "What did you just say?"

Seth sighed with relief. He started nodding quickly to jostle his wits. "It's true, Lola. Floyd is madly in love with you."

She stepped back and gave a pensive, side-to-side shake of her head. She looked at Seth and then over his head as if she were concentrating on some far-off perspective to make heads or tails out of what had just been said. Her voice took on a disbelieving tone as she asked, "Floyd?" But she repeated his name with more conviction. She turned from Seth and looked out the window at nothing. Her voice dropped a register as she said in a monotone to herself, "Floyd's in love with me?" But it was not a question; it was to her a declarative truism. She dropped her face into her hands. "You're right, Seth. I knew someday he would recognize he couldn't live without me." She grasped her hands and shifted her body side to side as if she were eight again. "I'll have to think on this, Seth." But she did not think very long. "He has some age on me, but love is eternal and transcends age."

Seth nodded; he was going along with this unusually smarmy chain of thought. He secretly hoped the pastor would go through Lola's library more carefully and remove all those prurient romantic novels. He managed to say as he backed to the safety of the door, "I've got to go, Lola. If I get back late after comin' to see you, Floyd'll have a fit."

She dumbly nodded as she watched him exit. Seth walked away from the cottage and made his way briskly to the bank. He felt like whistling, but he was sobered by the thought he had boxed old Floyd into two romances. He thought about that for a minute and began whistling anyway.

He was surprised when he saw Lola riding her father's mule past him. She was punching the old critter hard down the town drag. He incredulously touched both sides of his face as she skidded the mule to a sudden stop in front of the bank. He slowed his walk and swallowed. He had known she was impulsive, but he had no idea she would have swallowed the bait so arduously and quickly. Seth winced as he watched her leap from the bareback mule to the ground while holding a small vase of flowers.

Seth shook his head in disbelief. He decided he would go to Big Willard's saloon for a while and have some pickled eggs and maybe a beer. He knew Floyd's ears would be shooting steam. He knew he would be given the devil by his old friend.

Seth left the saloon after an hour and took small steps toward the bank. He nervously inhaled with each stride. When he reached the bank, he halfway closed his eyes in dread of the scolding he would receive. He took a deep breath and headed toward his office.

Floyd peeked over the mountain of paperwork on his desk and the newly placed vase of flowers and gave Seth a humorous and sarcastic look. When Seth averted his eyes, Floyd watched him walk by. He grated his chair back and followed Seth into his office. Seth sat and looked at his old friend with dread in his eyes. He just knew old Floyd would chew on him verbally.

Floyd took the chair Elspeth had taken earlier. He pulled a cigar from his vest pocket and took his time lighting it. His eyes never leaving Seth. He leaned forward and placed the match in a crude can on the desk. "Seth, you gotta quit siccing women on me." He took a heavy draw on his cigar, exhaled, and smiled. "Look, my good friend, we've been through a lot, and we can get through this." He paused and leaned back in his chair. "There's a rancher named Barnwell who borrowed some money from this bank the very month we bought the bank. He pays like a charm, and on top of that, I've heard he's got a daughter named Patricia that's not only a looker but has the all the virtues of Southern womanhood."

Seth, relieved that Floyd was not going to bawl him out, leaned forward with interest. Seth's eyebrows suddenly furrowed. "How in hell am I gonna meet this Patricia without it being awkward?"

Floyd smiled and tapped the side of his head as though he already had a plan. "We got some preacher who's in arrears and who lives fifteen miles from this Barnwell fella." He smiled. "We go bill collectin', and we can just …" He dramatically paused. "… happen to be passing Mr. Barnwell's ranch and pay our respects to a good client who pays his bills."

Seth liked the plan, but a sudden practical thought burst out. "You think Merle can handle the bank while we're gone?"

"Merle's honest. He may not have people skills, but his pencil is always correct and the till always adds up."

Seth sighed. "Yeah, maybe we can pay Woody to set in the lobby with a greener over his legs to discourage would-be robbers."

Seth's chain of thought suddenly returned to romance. His eyes widened as he considered the possibilities of meeting Patricia Barnwell and getting out of the confines of the bank. "When can we leave?"

Floyd sat up straighter and shrugged. "Let's get us some supplies today and leave tomorrow at ten."

Seth rubbed his hands together and let his eyes move to the ceiling. "I can't tell you how much I'm lookin' forward to this already."

CHAPTER 4

That same morning at five, Martha Johnson and her daughter, Sally, a young mirror of her mother, climbed up into the seat of the long-bed wagon. In the bed of the wagon lay her husband, John Lee Johnson, who had taken the time to hitch the mules even though he had painted their immense barn all night with seven of the day crew. His large frame was stretched almost to the end of the long wagon. Martha knew she had to get to town quickly because Duchess Thompson, a relative, wanted to see him at the sheriff's office. She had sent him an urgent note imploring him to meet her at nine that morning.

John did not know why she was so adamant, but he was not one to overlook such a beseeching request. Therefore, he was trying to rest while his beloved wife made ready to drive the team into Baileysboro to get their two-week supply of food. He felt Martha's eyes on him, but he did not want to expend the effort to look up. He heard the laughter of his adopted daughter, Sally, as she had rarely seen her usually indefatigable stepfather so exhausted. Martha snapped the reins, and the wagon lurched forward. John scrunched around to accommodate the jostle and soon drifted to sleep.

Six miles ahead on the sandy road to Baileysboro and encamped under a scraggly hackberry tree along the road were J.D. Rysinger and his gang.

They were mounted and discussing the prospective bank robbery. Although it was not yet hot, the tree served as a good place to powwow and go over the plans. J.D. was a lanky individual with a tall-crowned, discolored hat. The brim stretched out shading his grimy, whiskered face. He had a faint scar running down his jawline, and his gravy-green eyes were concentrated. He was not an ugly man, but the hard lines that had chiseled his face gave him a fearsome look. He was known for his meticulous planning. He rarely failed in pulling off successful bank robberies. He was not adverse to killing either; he deemed it at times necessary, and at other times, he shot someone just to put the fear of God in those who might be tempted to resist the robbery. This ruthlessness created a certain respect and fear even among his own men.

His eyes panned his gang as he silently scrutinized them. To his immediate right was Punkin' Head Hicks. He had an overly sized head—he had been born a water baby. Any hat he wore was never large enough. The one he was wearing had been an immense display hat in the window of a store. Though it had never meant to be worn, he was wearing it. The crown shot up ludicrously, and the brim extended forever. His large head and face and his jack-o'-lantern mouth with irregular teeth caused the public to perceive him as a frightful monster and somewhat of a dimwit, but he was far from that. He had been J.D.'s right-hand man for over a year.

Next to him was J.D.'s brother, Adrian, a shorter and less-imposing version of his brother. He wore a hat similar to J.D.'s. He idolized his brother. While J.D. verbalized his plans, Adrian smoked and scratched himself and let his mind drift back to his and J.D.'s younger, formative years. Their father, a brutish and irascible man, had often beaten the hell out of them for little reason if any. He recalled that on one particular day after an extended drinking spell, their pappy had become especially groused by the lack of money and the perceived sassing of his wife. J.D.'s tentatively taking a biscuit without asking had set in motion a series of events that affected their lives forever. The father grabbed a razor strop and began cussing a blue streak with the intention of tanning J.D.'s hide. J.D., tired of being abused, knocked the living Hades out the old man, and when his mother tried to intercede, he knocked her cold too. Adrian remembered vividly that J.D. had told him to get his hat and gun. They climbed on the only horse they had and took off. Thereafter, they joined various marauding gangs of other young men who had been brought up by the hair of the head as they had been. But in each case, J.D. became the leader. He did the planning and showed the most fearless "I don't give a damn" attitude, and soon, he even had older men wanting to be under his hand.

To Adrian's right was Red Farmer, who was nondescript in most ways. He had red hair and wore a typical cowhand's hat. He rode a grulla adorned with well-worn tack and never had much to say. He was not a man who used bad language or drank. The problem with Red was that he made it too obvious that he did not like the way J.D. handled women or the callous way he took human life. What kept Red in the gang was that Red did his job; he could handle his army .44 and was even better at covering a trail. But his facial expressions at times irritated J.D. especially when J.D. was roughhousing a woman or when he decided to kill a bank teller just for the hell of it. On several occasions, J.D. had spotted Red giving him disapproving looks, and that did not go well with J.D. But at that critical moment, he had no choice but to use him.

To J.D.'s left were the Jarrett brothers. Toby Jarrett was quiet, surly, and of medium height. His dipped and stained hat's brim shadowed an unhappy but youthful face. He was adequate with his .44 and took orders well. He did not like how J.D. treated his mentally deficient brother, who was on the outside with his horse toenailed in. J.D. called him Dummy. Dummy, or Timmy as he was called by Toby, sat with a vacant look on his face. His hat was oversized. It sat on his ears, and that made him look ludicrous, but he was good at holding horses even under duress, he rode like hell when a bank heist became heated, and he never did anything stupid to endanger the gang. Blighted with twilight intelligence, he nonetheless managed to pull iron and fire back when the citizenry came out with weapons blazing. He never talked back or gave anyone any trouble. He withstood the withering looks of J.D., who at times while distributing blame made him the fall guy. When J.D. cut loose on him, Timmy would cringe and look toward his brother for encouragement.

J.D. decided it was time to talk strategy. He pulled a cigar from his cotton vest and placed it thoughtfully in the corner of his mouth. He languidly struck a match, and the sizzle caught their ears. He tossed his match aside, took a few puffs, and nodded as if to unleash the words in his brain. "Here's the plan. Punkin' Head, you and Red come in from the east. Don't ride side to side. Me and the Jarretts will ride in from the west. Toby, you and Dummy will tie up and saunter toward the door. When I enter the bank, you boys stand on each side of the door. At that time, it won't matter if those townies know we're robbing the place or not. I'll go in and take over. And I plan on killin' anyone that gives me trouble."

He took a long drag off his smoke, exhaled, and turned pointedly to Punkin' Head. "You'll peel off and go to the back door of the bank. I shore in hell don't want no surprises from the backside." He frowned as he leaned forward to get a better look at Red. "Red, you align yourself to handle the sheriff's office." He paused as he reached into his pocket and pulled out a crude town map that pointedly displayed the town jail. He handed it to Punkin' Head, who handed it to Red. "When we get finished, we head east where we should have some help."

Punkin' Head was surprised. "Who's the help?"

J.D. did not take exception to the question. "Some hombres named Irvin Pendly and Butterbean. I've heard of Irvin. He's legit."

Punkin' Head pushed his sumptuous hat brim up as a concerned look crossed his face. "Why are those jaspers helpin' us, boss?"

J.D. puffed as he thought. "I'm not shore. Good question. If I was guessing, which I am, I thank they are using us as a …" He could not think of the word. He moved his hands around trying to come up with the correct term.

"A diversion?" Punkin' Head asked.

J.D. sighed and nodded. "Well, something to distract, I reckon, for something they're doin'."

Punkin' Head rubbed his jaw. "How did you meet these yahoos? And how did they know we was goin' to rob the bank?"

J.D. shrugged and shook his head. "When they hanged Russell House two weeks ago, you might recall the Texas bank robber, a man from Austin, got in touch with me while we was just north of here. He said that since Russell House was now dancin' in hell, he had a message for me. He told me he and some others wanted us to rob the bank in Baileysboro on this particular date and gave me the time. He said his boss didn't want any of the money. He just said do it and hit the trail to the Nations. And on top of that, he would even help us make our getaway." J.D. again shrugged. "I ain't got the foggiest what they're up to. I just know I shore in hell like robbin' and gettin' away. I met with this Pendly fella three days ago, and I damn guarantee you he ain't no lawdog." J.D. gave a crooked smile. "I thank he works for that T-Dilly Whitaker fella that works for that carpetbagger Stevens."

Red jerked his head when he heard the names Stevens and T-Dilly—two names any good Texan and Southern sympathizer would hate. He straightened himself afraid that J.D. might have caught his disgust. Red had ridden for two years for John Bell Hood and the Texas Brigade. He had been wounded in late '64 and had returned to Texas. He had at first done ranch work but later decided to ride the owlhoot trail. However, even among the sorry individuals he had dealt with, Red had heard nothing but bad about Stevens and T-Dilly Whitaker; they had soured themselves with most of the people of Texas. He just knew the carpetbag sewage that had filtered into Austin had ruined Texas. Red relaxed his countenance. He purged his mind of the two names. He exhaled and concentrated on the bank robbery. He knew he needed money, and if they pulled off a successful robbery in Baileysboro, that would be his ticket to extricate himself from J.D.

The gang knew it was too early to head directly to Baileysboro, so they remained in the saddle and just whiled away the time by smoking and cussing. They heard wagon wheels. J.D. started to make a head motion to get the others to retreat into the mesquite less than a quarter mile behind them, but he took a gander down the road and saw an attractive woman driving a team. He let out a soft wolf whistle and urged his horse farther into the road.

Red inwardly groaned. He pursed his lips and steeled his expression. All they had to do was pull back their horses into the thickets of mesquite and stay hidden and no one would be the wiser. But he knew J.D. had a woman problem. The way J.D. aggressively treated women broke his code. J.D. never took no for an answer; he thought every woman who ever met him fell immediately in love with him or should have. Red had a different idea. He knew J.D. was an impossibly narcissistic man. His psyche could not stand the idea that a woman could possibly thwart his irresistible advances. Since the beginning, this animal streak of his had caused the young gang the majority of their problems.

Martha was smiling and handling the team well as she trotted them down the tawny sand road. She and Sally, her ten-year-old daughter, were talking about the four adorable orphan girls. They were wondering when Seth would find the right woman to marry. Sally was reaching into her food basket for a dried apple when she saw the riders up ahead. Martha caught Sally's alarmed expression out of the corner of her eye and looked ahead. She inhaled when she saw a rough-looking man partially blocking the county road. Her eyes took in the other men gathered around the roadside hackberry tree. She slowed her team and began worrying about how she could get by. The sand to the left of the road would bog her down, and the tree on the right would hinder her. She thought about just snapping the reins and gutting her way through. But the rapacious-looking individual had just spurred his horse directly in her path.

As she pulled closer, she slowed her mules and hoped against hope the men would pull back and let her pass. J.D. took a slow drag on his cigar and nodded in that irritating way of his as though he had some insight no one else could fathom. When she stopped, she gave him a withering look, which intrigued him.

J.D. turned his horse directly toward the heads of the mules while his men sat by wondering what mischief the bandit chieftain had up his sleeve. J.D. doffed his hat and shifted his cigar to the corner of his mouth. "Howdy, pretty lady. Where is one of the prettiest women I ever met goin'?" He replaced his grimy hat and gave her a lusty smile.

Martha groaned inwardly and looked at her daughter, who was nibbling on her dried apple. Martha shrugged and figured she would try to be civil. "We're in a hurry." She paused as she took in the other men, who seemed intent on what was being said but were otherwise passive.

"Well, hell, you ain't in such a hurry that you can't meet good ol' J.D. Rysinger."

Martha gave him a pained look and remarked more pointedly, "I really am in a hurry." She wanted to say more, but she could tell by his churlish look that he had no intention of letting her pass. She await his next move.

J.D. removed his cigar and let his eyes zero in on the smoke in his hand as though trying to find a focal point for his thoughts. He commenced once more his infernal nodding. "Tell you what I'll do. You give ol' J.D. a kiss and I just might haul off and let you pass."

Martha was not shocked or surprised by that, but she was appalled, and her expression betrayed that. She knew anything she said would be misconstrued or twisted, so she just sat there.

J.D. did not like to be ignored, and the woman was acting as though he were of no consequence. He slid his vision to Sally, who also looked at him as if he were just a minor annoyance. Although he had intimidated many women in the past, at least they had the decency to act fearful of him. These two, obviously mother and daughter, acted as though he was just a nuisance.

J.D. gave a look around his shoulder to his men. "Seems like the pretty lady and her snooty daughter thank they're too good for me." He nodded some more and dismounted. "I thank good ol' J.D. will just go get some mornin' sugar." He gave Martha a salacious look. He handed his reins to Punkin' Head and walked toward Martha's side of the wagon. He removed his cigar and ran his shirt sleeve over his lips as though that would make his breath spring fresh. "Now, highfalutin' lady, you're goin' to get the kiss of your life."

As he got within a foot of her, Martha looked him in his eyes. "Listen, whatever your name is."

J.D. proudly nodded. "J.D. Or some call me sweet J.D."

Martha nodded mockingly. "Okay, J.D., let me give you some really good advice. You turn your sorry carcass around and get on your sorrel and head off to whatever toilet you crawled out of and just stay there."

J.D. replaced his cigar. His lusty eyes morphed into cruel slits. "Lady, there ain't a man or woman alive who can talk to J.D. that way." His mouth took on cruel lines. "If you and that pretty brat want to live, you'll just crawl out of that wagon and show ol' J.D. a whole lot of affection and remind me all over again on the fact that I'm a fine figure of a man."

Martha's face took on anger. "Mister, I am a married woman. You touch me and you'll be sorry." Martha's voice raised an octave when she repeated, "Just go on and go your way and you'll be okay, but if you persist in this nonsense, you're going to get hurt bad."

J.D. snorted. "Married, eh? Well, hell. Bein' married don't matter to me. I don't want to marry you, lady, just have some fun."

Martha sighed and looked at Sally, who sat there with a faint Mona Lisa smile on her face. Sally finished her apple, nonchalantly smacked her hands together, and looked at J.D. "My father is in the back of the wagon."

J.D. sniffed irritatingly. He was surprised. "What is he doin' in the back of the wagon?"

Martha deadpanned, "He's dozing."

J.D. gave a lascivious wink to his men and returned his gaze to Martha. He laughed mockingly. His men chuckled lustfully. Emboldened by his men and his own arrogance, J.D. crookedly smiled. "He's dozin,' eh? Well hell, I just might get some sugar from him too." That remark got a rousing Greek chorus laugh from his men—except Red. "Just let me go see this dozin' gent."

Martha again deadpanned, "That would be a bad idea."

J.D. laughed lewdly. "Yes, for a husband who dozes while his wife takes up with good ol' J.D. I think it's a hell of a good idea." He gave Martha a smile that exposed his heavily nicotine-stained teeth. He could not see the inside the bed for the tall side boards, so he walked toward the tailgate of the wagon as he whistled insouciantly. He pulled out the metal holding pin and lowered the tailgate with a dramatic thump. J.D.'s sneering smile quickly vanished.

John Lee Johnson rose up from the bed of the wagon like a phoenix. J.D. stepped back with his cigar barely balanced on his bottom lip. His eyes opened wide exposing red capillaries that ran to his pupils. He saw a man the likes of whom he had never seen before. He took in the sterile gray eyes, the handsome face, and the thick neck corded with ropelike tendons and powerful shoulders that were a yard wide. John's shirt, smeared in barn paint, was unbuttoned, and his thick chest seemed to be molded in heavily striated, bronze bands of muscle. J.D. caught sight of his arms that should have belonged on a pagan god. His wide-open eyes took in the heavy weaponry that seemed to be everywhere around the giant's waist. John slowly slid toward the end of the wagon and agilely leaped down to the road. He grabbed J.D.'s dirty shirt with his left hand and pulled him in close.

His gray eyes met the wary, gravy-green ones up close and personal. John's deep voice came out sibilant through his gritted teeth. "Sweet J.D., is it?" He whirled J.D. around with effortless ease so he could keep his peripheral vision on the mounted hooligans who were watching all this through astonished eyes. John jabbed his fist in successive, quick, meat-smacking pops into J.D.'s face. John released the bandit leader, who collapsed semiconscious to his knees. J.D. wobbly tried to get up. He was holding his right eye, which was puffed up and bleeding. John delivered a hard right hook to his solar plexus that sounded like boat paddle hitting a full cotton sack. J.D. went airborne and slid two feet in the sand.

Punkin' Head reached for his sidearm, but just as his fingers reached the grip, he heard a gunshot and felt his sumptuous hat go sailing over the lowest hackberry tree limb. He removed his hand quickly from his holster and sat there stunned. His small, porcine eyes widened, and his small mouth made an irregular elliptical shape on his oversized face. His misshapen teeth exposed by the small orifice made Punkin' Head's mouth look like some primordial wormhole. His eyes moved warily side to side sizing up what in the hell had just happened. He clasped his saddle horn and hung on tightly as he turned two shades of pale.

John's eyes settled on Red Farmer. He knew Red from their days of riding with John Bell Hood and the Texas Brigade. He did not ask why Red was riding with this trash; he knew. It was obvious that somewhere along the way, Red had taken the wrong trail. But John did not dwell on that. He looked at the saddle on J.D.'s sorrel. He surprised the four men not only by giving his attention to Red but by calling him by name. "Red, I want that bridle and saddle. You dismount and take care of that matter. I ain't goin' to take his horse, but for all the trouble he's caused, I'm claiming his gear." He shrugged his powerful shoulders and pointed to the stretched-out, unconscious J.D. "You tell that piece of …" He glanced at Martha and Sally, who were listening intently. He decided on another choice of words. "You tell J.D. that if he wants to press charges against me for takin' his saddle, go see the sheriff." John smiled wryly. "Or come see me personal like."

Before Red could respond, Punkin' Head raised his hand very much like a primary grade student. "You care if I get my hat?" John did not answer, Punkin' Head took that as a yes. He dismounted and walked to cautiously to his hat, put it on tightly, and remounted his horse with anxious eyes on John.

Red waited until Punkin' Head was back in the saddle. He lithely hit the ground and did as John bade. He deftly tossed the saddle and bridle over the tall side boards and gave a pronounced and respectful nod to John. He pointed at J.D. "What about him?"

John looked briefly at J.D. and then back at the four outlaws. "I want you to take him with you now. You can tie him over his sorrel, or one of you can ride double and hold onto him." He looked intently at Red. "It's real obvious you birds have not done or are lookin' to do any serious labor." He gave them a studied, squint-eyed inspection. "But if you're thinkin' about robbin' the bank in Baileysboro, I strongly suggest you think otherwise."

The outlaws continued to look at John like owls. When they did not respond, John said, "You get goin' all of you. If I see you on this road again, I'll be unfriendly."

Punkin' Head, not fathoming how John could have been more unfriendly, joined Red on the ground and picked up the limp J.D. They situated him on the saddle in front of Adrian. Punkin' Head made a bridle with a strand of rope securing J.D.'s sorrel. It had enough tether to be pulled. He handed the free end to Toby. He nodded shyly to John that they were ready, and they trotted away as fast as they could without losing the hapless J.D.

Punkin' Head gave a motion with his head to Red to join him at the head of the men. Red rode up. They separated themselves from the others so they could palaver. Punkin' Head gave a cagey look mixed with a newfound admiration for his comrade. "You got any ideas, Red, on how we're goin' to handle this?" They rode another thirty yards. Red did not respond. Seeing that he would have to carry the conversation, Punkin' Head said, "You realize J.D. won't be able to handle this. Damn, he got the holy hell beat out of him."

Red nodded knowingly. "Yeah, well, it's like this, Punkin' Head. We gotta tell him he got sucker punched."

Punkin' Head gave a puzzling look toward his compadre and nodded. "What you're saying is that we make him think that he got whipped unfair?"

"That's what I'm sayin'."

"Wonder if he don't believe us?"

Red grumbled, "Then it means we ain't goin' to rob no bank." Red saw the bend in the road ahead. He turned around in his saddle and did not see the Johnson wagon. "Let's pull off the road up ahead and try and get his head right. Punkin' Head, you got to convince ol' J.D. that he got waylaid and make him believe it."

Punkin' Head thoughtfully nodded with hesitant pauses. "I reckon. But all of us know including ol' J.D. that he got his ass whipped and whipped bad."

Red gave him a withering look. "You want that bank money or not?"

Punkin' Head gave another begrudging nod. His estimation of Red's common sense rose considerably. He looked back again searching for the infernal wagon. When he did not see it, his vision took in his comrades riding behind. He raised his arm to get their attention and pointed to a small opening in the mesquite grove ahead that trailed off the bend from the caramel-colored road.

They rode into the cut briskly and dismounted. Punkin' Head pulled the semiconscious J.D. from his brother's horse and gently placed him against one of the larger, scaly mesquite trees. He grabbed a canteen proffered to him by Toby, tilted J.D.'s head up, and poured a small amount of water into his mouth. J.D. accepted the water and reflexively wiped his lips. He kept his eyes shut as he began to slowly twist. His right eye was swollen shut, and blood leaked from the socket. His other eye opened slowly and tried to focus on the faces staring at him. He reached for the canteen and gulped half a pint of water. He handed the canteen to Punkin' Head and let his eyes pan across the men staring down at him. He winced when he saw Dummy looking sad at his current state. He did not want that stupid bastard feeling sorry for him. He did not bother asking what had happened. He knew he had just gotten his ass kicked. He felt a sense of shame and embarrassment, but he decided to wait and assess how his men interpreted the fiasco.

Punkin' Head gave a furtive look at Red to garner some courage. Punkin' Head knew he would be selling a bill of goods that would require some embellishment. When Red gave him the okay with an imperceptible nod, Punkin' Head nodded in return. He began what he hoped would be an image-saving talk with his boss. He straightened and handed Toby his canteen. "Boss, you just got sucker punched by a stranger back there."

J.D.'s mind began racing. He looked at Punkin' Head to ascertain his sincerity. His good eye continued to pan his men to see if they agreed with Punkin' Head.

Punkin' Head gave a quick look to Red hoping he would chime in to lend credence to his statement. Punkin' Head tossed a quick finger in Red's direction. "You can ask Red. That bird ambushed you."

J.D.'s eye moved over to Red, who pushed his hat up and knelt to look J.D. in the face. "Boss, you and me have had our differences, but they ain't a man alive who can whip you in a fair fight." Red looked up at the eyes of the men who were peering at him and listening intently. It escaped J.D. that they were giving edgy looks out of the corners of their eyes; that was not how they remembered the fight. However, the look Red was giving them sparked an epiphany, the gist being that they had better damn well agree with what was being said. All of them besides Dummy began nodding their approval of his words.

J.D. slowly moved his eye over his men. He noted that his sorrel was sans saddle and bridle. He gathered that the big man had taken his gear. He gave one more look at his men and sent up an arm as a signal for them to pull him up. Several hands pulled him slowly up as he groggily positioned his feet. He put a hand on the tree. "He had his day, but I aim to kill that bastard."

Since he was not sure that his men really believed he had been hit unfairly, he cut off further comment on the fight. He gingerly touched his closed eye and sighed. "I gotta have me an eyepatch or I'm goin' to lose this eyeball. I'll ride Dummy's horse into town." He gave a challenging look at Toby, who wisely remained passive. "When I get to town, I plan on lookin' up the sawbones and get me that patch. I want one of you birds to go to the saddle shop and get me some gear while I get tended to," he snarled.

Red inwardly smiled seeing that J.D. had accepted their view of the fracas. He liked how he was taking charge again. "I'll take care of the saddle and bridle business," he said. "Punkin' Head will lead the boys through town to get a quick look-see while I get your gear. Punkin' Head and the boys will wait about a mile down the road." He continued trying to add to J.D.'s confidence. "There, you can tell us how the robbery's to go down." Red knew that deigning J.D. with the success or lack thereof of the imminent bank robbery would inject some pride in his bruised ego.

J.D. sighed and shrugged. "It throws off the plan, but I reckon we don't have much choice."

There was an uncomfortable pause waiting on J.D.'s further comments that never came. They took this cue to saddle up quickly. They pulled out of the mesquite opening looking warily for the wagon they knew was not far behind. They galloped down the road leaving a heavy dust cloud.

CHAPTER 5

Four hours later, Sheriff Henry Nelson, a rawhide-thin man, was seated behind his desk cleaning his Sharps rifle. He was waiting on his young deputy, Woody, who was trying to coax the town drunk, Elias Talbert, out of one the alleys between the hotel and bank. He gave a quick look over his shoulder when he heard the aged Dr. Baker enter the back door of the jail. Henry thought it odd that he would enter that way and gave him a backward, thoughtful, and raised-eyebrow look. "I owe you money, Doc?"

Doc Baker gave him a quick smile at his attempt at humor, but his features sobered rapidly. "Sheriff, I got an idea that you might have a problem."

Henry pushed his Sharps aside and turned his chair to give the doctor his full attention. He knew the town physician was given to humor occasionally, but he realized he was dead serious at the moment. "What are you talkin' about?"

Doc Baker went to the window and looked up and down the street. He ran his finger under his nose as he marshaled his thoughts. "A man came into my office just fifteen minutes ago. He claimed he'd been kicked in the face by a horse. He demanded an eyepatch." He continued looking out the window turning his head this way and that to see better. "Trouble is, Henry, he'd been clocked by a man, not a horse."

The sheriff canted his head. "Maybe he was embarrassed, Doc, and made up the story. Who knows?"

Doc Baker turned from the window and sighed. "He's not a rancher. He's not from around here. And on top of that, he had some money." The doctor qualified his remark. "Not much money, but to me, he had all the looks of someone probably riding the owlhoot trail, you know what I mean? He's sorry looking." He looked pointedly at Sheriff Nelson. "I think he's in town to rob the bank."

The sheriff, fully engaged by the comment, rose. "Where's he now?"

"He headed to the saloon, but he never got there." Doc Baker tossed a finger toward the window. "I saw a man come out from the alleyway on horseback leading a sorrel horse that the man I attended to mounted. They rode like the devil himself was after them heading east." He sighed. "That might sound normal, but I had a strange feeling about him. The man I worked on was edgy and anxious and looking at his turnip watch all the time." He gave another thoughtful look at the sheriff. "I have this sixth sense he's up to no good."

Sheriff Nelson walked to the window and nodded. "East you say?" He paused and shook his head in thought. "That's not equal to robbin' a bank, but on the other hand … better safe than sorry."

Woody, the tall and angular deputy sheriff, entered with the drunken Talbert in tow. The sheriff said, "Forget Elias, Woody. You go down to the bank and warn Seth and Floyd there might be a threat." He rubbed his jaw in thought. "Tell 'em to look out for a man wearing an eyepatch."

Woody looked at the drunken man and helped him to a chair in front of the sheriff's desk. He gave a confusedly quick look to the sheriff and town doctor. "Threat?"

The sheriff quickly answered, "Possible bank robbery."

Woody's eyebrows raised, but he did not ask further questions. He shot out the door slamming it behind him. Once on the boardwalk, he took a gander down the street. He did not see anything suspicious, but he double timed it to the bank.

Red and Punkin' Head headed into Baileysboro from the east. At first blush, Red did not see anything out of the ordinary, but he took note of the fact that no one was on the boardwalk—no activity of any kind. Red's eyes concernedly narrowed when he saw the lack of horses tied to the hitch racks. Suspicion entered his mind.

Red glanced at Punkin' Head, whose eyes mirrored those of his compatriot. Punkin' Head muttered out of the corner of his twee mouth that something seemed haywire.

That unsettling premonition coursed through Red the more he rode. He felt like yanking his mount around and galloping off. What kept him from following his eerie premonition was that he saw J.D. and the Jarrett brothers riding toward him from the west; they did not seem troubled at all. Red garnered some courage from their appearance. He inhaled and gave himself a mental pep talk. He needed the money. He knew this successful robbery would enable him to rid himself of J.D. Rysinger. He chanced a quick look over his shoulder. He knew Adrian was stationed east of town to serve as their rearguard in case things blew up in their faces. He looked frontward to see that J.D. and the Jarrett brothers were haphazardly spaced and seemed bold as brass.

Red swallowed and pulled his hat down tighter on his head. His eyes panned the side of the street where the sheriff's office was. Seeing nothing, he raised his sights to the roof line and then to the other side of the street. He saw nothing. What was missing was the vitality that he had detected earlier when he and J.D. had made their way out of town.

Punkin' Head's breathing became heavier. He blamed his anxiety on a natural feeling he always had when the gang attempted a bank robbery. When he saw Chili's livery stable, the first building on his left, he peeled off. He rode in a determined canter around the building and made his way to the back of the bank. Red veered to his right some but still on the main street. He had to get a view of the bank from the other side of the street, but he positioned himself so he would have a good view of the sheriff's office. He kept his horse trotting briskly. When he was even with J.D. and the Jarrett brothers, he pulled up, dismounted, and tied his horse.

J.D. did not meet his eyes, but the Jarretts cast a quick, nervous look his way. They dismounted with celerity and tethered their horses at the bank's two hitch racks. J.D. grabbed two saddlebags from Toby's horse and stepped up on the boardwalk purposefully. He entered the bank and saw the pie-faced teller, Merle Tadlock, behind the iron grill station looking downward as though checking the till. J.D. walked saucily toward him with spurs jingling. When Merle raised his head, his eyes met the patched eye; the good one was stonily glaring at him through the oval, iron-grilled aperture. J.D. placed the saddlebags on the wood panel in front of him and pushed them through the opening. "Fill 'em up, fat boy."

"Is this a robbery?" Merle's voice quavered.

J.D. growled, "You must be a damned genius."

Merle, drenched in fearful sweat, ducked behind the oak panel barrier at the base of the metal cage. "He's here!"

J.D., taken aback by this sudden turn of events, drew his army .44 and looked around with his good eye to see what in the hell had just happened. He was temporarily rattled by a back office door bursting open and a short, muscular man extending a revolver at him. J.D. fired a quick round toward the door and hit its edge. The flush hit sent wooden splinters shattering into a woodsy cloud and leaving a jagged door scar.

Seth flinched at the shot and the resultant shards but recovered to fire a round that ricocheted off the grill sending sparks. His second shot tore off the bottom of J.D.'s ear.

J.D. cussed and grabbed his bloodied ear but kept up the shooting. He was further muddled when an older man opened the broom closet behind a desk and cut loose with a roaring round that zinged past his head.

Behind the bank, Punkin' Head was standing beside his horse with his pistol pointed up when he heard the shooting. He knew that was not a positive sign. He knew resistance was going on, and that usually meant a robbery was going sour. He was mounting his horse to escape when he saw an outhouse door thirty feet from the bank's back door open. A skinny deputy pointed a rifle at him. Punkin' Head's small eyes widened in apprehension. He fired several rounds at the deputy and created several jagged bores in the outhouse door. Woody, hunkering from the unnerving close shots, dove from the outhouse and hit the sand momentarily discombobulated. By the time he regained his concentration and before he could he level his seven-shot Spencer on the big-headed man, Punkin' Head was spurring his horse around the bend at Chili's livery stable.

Woody cussed his bad luck. He quickly got up and gave chase. He ran down the alley toward the front street, where he hoped he could get a shot off at the weird-looking man. He heard several thunderous shots that were reverberating from the front street. He guessed the were coming from inside the bank and outside on the boardwalk.

Ten feet from the end of the alley, Woody pulled up short. He saw a troubled young man pointing a gun at him. Woody felt a shot buzz by his head. He reflexively ducked and fired his seven-shot Spencer from hip level. The shot nailed the robber high in the chest. Dummy's pistol flew out of his hand as he was knocked backward. The young outlaw was flat on his back with his hands stretched out. He started crying all the while puling for his brother. Woody raced to him, knelt, and looked at Dummy's boyish face streaked in tears. He heard his quivering voice clearly even with a heavy rivulet of blood running out of the corner of his mouth.

Standing by the doorway of the bank and unaware of his brother's condition, Toby Jarrett focused on the commotion in the bank. Alarmed by the disastrous turn of events, he leaned into the doorway and hastily fired at Seth and Floyd; that gave J.D. a chance to escape. As the two bandits bounded off the boardwalk still firing their weapons into the empty, blackened doorway, they backpedaled into the street toward their horses. Toby looked around and saw his brother lying supine with arms extended. He knew Tim was dead or dying. He stifled his tears and started to bolt toward his brother, but J.D. grabbed him by the back of his shirt and angrily shouted, "He's dead, dammit! He's dead! Let's get the hell outta here while we can." Toby shook off the offending hand but reluctantly relented. He tearfully joined J.D. as they hastily mounted and thundered down the dirt street.

Red, on the other side of the street, saw that things had gone bad. He felt an obligation to protect J.D. and Toby as they made their getaway. He watched with relief as the skinny deputy stooped to check Dummy. He knew he could have shot Woody if he had had a mind to, but he just could not bring himself to perform a cold-blooded murder. Knowing he had a modicum of time, he focused on the sheriff's office. Red stepped from the wall with his .44 fully extended toward the sheriff as he burst out of his office door. The sheriff, standing with his legs wide apart for balance, was blasting away; orange flames were jetting from the bore of his weapon.

The sheriff paused to draw a better bead when he heard Woody from the mouth of the alley shouting a warning about Red.

The sheriff jerkily turned to face Red, who had him in his sights. Red was squeezing on his trigger when he recognized Sheriff Nelson. Once more, his conscience overrode his job description. He respected Henry Nelson. He uncocked his weapon, pulled his gun off, and was hurriedly holstering it when Sheriff Nelson saw him. The sheriff did not recognize Red and fired a shot that hit Red in the chest. Red staggered sideways and slowly fell backward. He crumpled against the wall of a building and slid down to his haunches. He painfully sat there knowing he would not be robbing banks anymore.

Sheriff Nelson futilely fired again at the escaping J.D. and Toby Jarrett. However, he did manage to catch sight of the unusual-looking Punkin' Head and another man in the distance. He growled that he had been too slow to act and had allowed some of the varmints to escape. He made his way to the man he had just shot. As he grew closer, he recognized Red. It dawned on him that Red could have killed him but for some reason had not. He holstered his weapon and knelt by the dying Red Farmer. He said apologetically, "Red, I didn't recognize you."

Red nodded wanly. His thoughtful eyes were on some indistinct point in space. "That's okay, Henry. I shouldn't have been robbin' banks noways."

Sheriff Nelson asked him if he wanted water. Red shook his head. He slowly gloved off the blood leaking from his lips. Red sighed. "I got thirty dollars in folding money in my back pocket wrapped in a sock." He leaned his head against the wall. "I want to pay for my burial, and if there's any left over, I want you to have it." He paused and sighed. "I ain't got no kin."

Sheriff Nelson, troubled and moved by Red's sad admission, did not know how to respond. He took in a lungful of sad air and pointed at the fleeing bandits. "Red, who are those hooligans you were runnin' with?"

"J.D. Rysinger and his brother, Adrian."

"J.D.'s the one with the eyepatch?"

Red weakly nodded. "John Lee Johnson beat the hell out of 'im because he insulted his wife."

Remembering his conversation with Doc Baker, he asked, "I reckon that's why he's wearing an eyepatch."

Red nodded weakly.

Sheriff Nelson knew Red was laboring to remain alive. He remembered before the war that Red had ridden for several nearby cattle spreads. He remembered he married a young woman named Delores who had died of typhoid fever a year before Red took off to join John Bell Hood's Texas Brigade. He would try his darnedest to find her grave and bury Red next to her. He placed a hand on Red's shoulder to show that although he was the law and Red was the outlaw, he commiserated with his misfortune.

A forlorn Woody walked up to them and heard the tailing end of their discourse. Woody jerked a thumb over his shoulder toward the dead outlaw stretched out across the way. He sadly recounted what had happened and how shocked he was that the robber had been a mere kid.

Sheriff Nelson sadly shook his head. "Woody, you're goin' to see a lot things in the law business that'll affect you for the rest of your life." Sheriff Nelson studied Woody's hangdog expression. "He have any last words?"

Woody nodded and looked at his boots. "He asked for his brother, but just before he died, he said he wanted some candy."

Sheriff Nelson's eyebrows went up. "Candy?"

Red, hearing their conversation, feebly muttered, "His name was Tim Jarrett. J.D. called him Dummy." Red closed his eyes momentarily working through the sharp edge of pain. "He was a dimwit. But he was a good kid. He just had nothin'."

Sheriff Nelson rose and looked across the way. He spotted Seth, Floyd, and Merle walking toward him. He looked at Woody. "Candy, huh?" He shook his head in dismay and awaited the banking staff. He looked down at Red and saw he had died. The sheriff steeled himself and took another lung of air. "Damn. What a life we lead."

Before he could justify talking to the bank employees, he ordered Woody to go to the saloon and get as many men as he could to give chase to the four thieves, who were raising dust on the horizon. He discussed the attempted bank robbery with Seth, Floyd, and Merle. As Woody was quickly crossing the street, he saw Martha Johnson and her daughter steering a large wagon down the street. Martha said something over her shoulder, and John Lee Johnson rose and looked at the dead man known as Dummy lying partially in the street. Martha, two buildings down from the mercantile store, hauled up and set the brake allowing her husband to exit the wagon. He caught sight of the sheriff and the bank cadre. He stood and shook off the effects of sound sleep albeit with the kinks commonly caused by sleeping uncomfortably in a wagon bed.

Before John Lee could get very far, he was beckoned by a familiar voice behind him. The man who hailed him had recently exited the saloon. He apparently had been watching the wild activity in the street but had remained purposely in the background. He had a mission to accomplish—to deliver a message to John Lee. Sergeant Joe Brewer nervously looked both ways, and upon catching John's full attention, he gave a cautious pull of his hand indicating he wanted a private parley with the big Texan.

Brewer circumspectly stiffened as he heard the boots and spurs of determined men exiting the saloon. Trying to remain anonymous, he backed to the wall as Woody and a half-dozen cowhands ran off the boardwalk and fetched their horses. Sergeant Joe warily watched the posse get their directions and restively await the sheriff's instructions.

John studied on the sergeant's behavior realizing that Brewer would not be in Baileysboro unless it had been important. He was a federal man. He had ridden with John into the Nations seeking Sabbath Sam, and John had the highest respect for the sergeant. He postponed his meeting with the huddled men who were awaiting him across the street.

Before turning to give Joe his full attention, he caught sight of the dead Red Farmer lolling against the wall of a millinery shop. That view of his old comrade saddened him. He felt that Red's life could have been different. He looked at the alley close to him and took in once more Tim Jarrett's supine body. He surmised correctly that the robbery attempt had been a dismal failure. He watched his wife and stepdaughter step down from the wagon. He heard their gasps at the morbid sights of dead men as they made their way to the store.

Joe Brewer stepped off the porch and headed into the alley. John followed him suspecting correctly that Joe had something important to say to him and did not want to be seen by the public.

When they were halfway down the alley, Joe stopped and cast furtive glances both ways. He pulled a packet from his vest pocket and handed it to John. He nervously said, "Before we go any further, your cousin, Duchess Thompson, ain't here. That was a trick to get you into town. If you misunderstand what I'm tellin' you, you can refer to the papers."

John, puzzled by his secretive behavior and the knowledge that someone would go to the trouble to send him a note in the guise of a cousin, gave him his full attention.

Sergeant Brewer, who was usually a jovial man, was stonily severe in his demeanor. "John, I was sent here by Lieutenant Bragg. I can't be seen. As soon as I talk to you, I got to head back to Austin. If I'm seen with you, it's as good as a death sentence."

John knew he was referring to Lieutenant Bragg and several others who watched out for his interests.

Brewer grimly ended that prelude and began full steam. "Your cousin or your mother's cousin, Duchess Thompson, has been arrested by a man named James Stevens and his right-hand man, T-Dilly Whitaker. While this bank robbery was takin' place, they, that is, Stevens's gang, rode to Duchess's ranch and took her captive. They're headed to Hawkshaw, Texas, where she's to be held until you get there."

John was thunderstruck. "Why would they do that, Joe?"

Joe gave a cautious look. "I think I know. But I'm runnin' out of time, so what I'm goin' to say to you may be a jumbled mess." He again nervously cast looks in both directions and sighed. "They're charging her with aiding and abetting an enemy in time of war, but the upshot is that they want you to fight a Mexican down in Chihuahua. They figure holding a relative gives them a chip forcing you to see things their way. I reckon they want the sport of it, and also, it'll give them a chance to kill you before they get there."

Joe nodded at the packet he had just given John. "Please read this before you go to Hawkshaw and follow the directions to a T."

Before John could respond, Joe gave in to his anxiety and walking briskly down the alley to the back of the buildings. John thoughtfully gazed at his retreating back until Joe cut around the corner of the saloon. John listened to his hasty retreat. He heard his horse gallop away in what sounded like a southerly direction. John briefly dwelled on his foreboding words while glancing at the packet in his hand. He wearily inhaled. His eyes moved toward the mouth of the alley leading to the street. He knew his beloved Martha would soon return from the mercantile store and would divine that trouble was ahead—that he would be gone again. He knew he must forgo meeting with the sheriff and the bank crew. He started trudging toward the street. He could presage another weary trek, another death struggle. But each step he took stoked his anger. He would face this new challenge and give it his all. By the time he reached the street, his gray eyes were smoldering in anger.

After getting the details of the robbery and cursory descriptions, the sheriff left his banking friends to hail the posse before they rode out. He gave them a brief description of J.D. Rysinger. They impatiently listened; they gave him annoyed *You're wasting our time* looks. He gave them a quick wave to get going. They slapped their reins and galloped down the street. He wistfully watched their backs as they headed east. The sheriff turned and caught sight of the man in the alley talking to John. It was obvious that the stranger did not want to be seen. Sheriff Nelson surmised that he was probably informing John that someone was gunning for him. He sensed it probably was the former Union brigadier general Frank McGrew. The sheriff watched surreptitiously for a few moments. He saw the man quickly leaving John and head toward the end of the alley. The sheriff reluctantly took his eyes off the scene. He walked thoughtfully to his friends awaiting his counsel.

The sheriff had been correct. Fifteen minutes later, Martha saw John standing at the tailgate of the wagon rather than across the street with the sheriff and friends. She knew something was up. She could read his eyes; she knew he was vexed. She stood by as John and several clerks loaded the wagon.

Sheriff Nelson made no mention to his banking friends about the covert meeting he had seen between John and the stranger in the alley. They were focused on the bank robbery, but their eyes moved to the big Texan as he helped stack supplies in his wagon across the street. They knew that something bad other than the bank robbery had transpired since he had arrived in town. They had seen him go into an alley, but the man who resurfaced from the alley was not the same man who had been sleeping in the wagon as he entered town. They received a perfunctory wave from John, but he made no move toward them. Although none was afraid of approaching him, they sensed that it was not the time to do so. Rather than forcing the moment and hailing him to join them or their joining him, they kept talking about the gang that had attempted the robbery.

They watched with concern mixed with curiosity as John, now driving, turned the wagon around. Martha and Sally matched John's stolid posture. The sheriff and the bank staff perceived that something was up and that it was not good.

Sheriff Nelson looked around the faces leaning in to catch his point of view concerning John's unusual behavior. He cast a narrowed-eye look at the broad back of John as he watched the big fellow snap the mules into a faster pace. "Boys, I got an idea that that General McGrew fella has stepped on his toes again."

They all knew who McGrew was. It was common knowledge that the former brigadier general's hate for John knew no limits. Seth pushed his hat brim up. "You'd think McGrew would know better by now."

CHAPTER 6

S and Burr and Lambert had been on the range about four hours. It was obvious from the get-go that Lambert would be a good hire. He did things instinctively well without being told, and he mixed well with the crew. He did not give advice without being asked, and though he was knowledgeable, he did not come across as a know-it-all.

Shorty Tate, a stocky rider whom Lambert had not seen, rode up and skidded to a dust cloud–raising stop. He looked with concern at Sand Burr. "We done got us a situation, Sand Burr."

Sand Burr pushed his hat brim up. "What kind of situation, Shorty?"

"This heifer keeps returning to a sand bog that's akin to quicksand." He made an exasperated face. "We've pulled her out twice, but she just turns around and goes back in." He spread out his gloved hands and agitatedly shrugged. "Each time she goes back in, she sinks a little lower. I got an idea that she'll sink low enough to cover her head the next time and that's all she wrote."

Sand Burr looked at Lambert. "You got any ideas?"

Lambert sighed and looked at Shorty. "When she gets that low in the mud, you can't rope her horns." He shook his head. "You'll pull her horns out. She'll bleed, and later on, the blowflies will kill her." He took in a thoughtful lung of air. "You can't rope her around her neck either when she's that dug in. You'd just choke her to death."

Shorty looked at Sand Burr and back to Lambert as though thinking, *Who in the hell is this stranger?* Shorty shook his head in dismay. "You done told me a whole lot of things I cain't do. Can you tell me what I should do?"

Lambert sighed. He realized he was an interloper. He gave a big smile to the skeptical face perusing him. "Do you have anyone who can make coyote sounds?"

Shorty nodded and forked his thumb at himself. "I can."

Lambert leaned over with both hands on his saddle pommel. "You go hide so the cow can't see you and start making all those coyote noises. She'll probably get restless when she hears them sounds. If she ain't too tired, she'll struggle to get out of the bog. When she comes out some, two of you circle ropes around her just behind her front legs. Make sure it's two ropes. Then you tie some tether ropes to the ones tied around her chest. And have two riders nearby to pull her away from that mud hole and take her where she can't see it. Have the riders circle her around counterclockwise a number of times, and then pull her to the herd again. And then circle her around counterclockwise several times again. As stupid as she is, she'll be disoriented and stay with the herd most likely."

Shorty looked dubiously at Sand Burr hoping to receive a dubious look in return. Sand Burr nodded in the direction Shorty had just come from. "Git goin' and do what he said."

Shorty, seeing the stranger had some clout with Sand Burr, nodded his respects to both men. He turned and galloped away.

Sand Burr gave Lambert a side-of-the-face look. "You shore as hell know a lot about cattle."

Lambert did not deny it or claim the praise. He just looked straight ahead and remarked, "You ever noticed that all the animals God declared was clean to eat are all dumb as hell?"

"What do you mean?"

"Well, God in heaven in His wisdom made all the clean animals dumb as hell so we wouldn't feel guilty about eatin' 'em. All the unclean animals are pretty intelligent. Speakin' of unclean, a damn pig is pretty smart … can do just about anything a dog can do. So when you kill one of those smart, unclean animals for food, it should bother you." He paused and lifted a finger. "According to the Bible, a cow is a clean animal. To show you they're dumb, I knew a man who milked the same cow for nine years. He claimed she knew her name, but I never believed it. He would hold out a bucket of grain and say, 'Bossie, come here.' Well, Bossie would come because of the bucket of grain, not because she knew her name. Yesiree, they're plain stupid. I ain't ever knowed a cow who knew her own name."

Sand Burr put his fingers under his chin as he thought about that. "Well, ain't a deer one of those clean animals? They seem pretty smart to me."

Lambert shook his head. "I shot at a blacktail deer last year. Missed him but sent a groove over his rump. He never returned to that valley where I shot at him, but that ain't intelligence. That's just instinct. In his little pea brain, he associated that valley with pain."

Sand Burr continued to rub his chin. He was thinking of Lambert's advice to Shorty. "You know something? I've been a brush popper for several years now, but have to confess to you that I ain't ever heard about makin' coyote noises to spook a cow from a sinkhole."

Lambert gave a wrinkled smile. "I ain't neither, but if he thinks it'll work, maybe it just might get the job done." He sighed as he rubbed his jaw. "Hope is a mighty powerful medicine."

Sand Burr wanted to pursue the conversation, but he heard thudding hooves coming from the trail that led to the ranch house. He turned to see a flush-faced rider named Fletcher rawhiding his mount with slapping reins. Fletcher reined up and breathlessly stated that there was trouble at the house. He told Sand Burr that he was needed pronto.

Sand Burr realized that John had set off to Baileysboro and apparently had not made it back. It was not a shock to be wanted at the ranch headquarters. He had been summoned more than once to head to the west range and help put out brush fires or help move the western range herd to the shinry grass on the northern boundary. However, he was surprised at the rider's vehement appeal. Sand Burr gauged it was an important matter. He heard Fletcher mention something about Texas lawmen, but he was too impatient to hear him out. He waved a quick goodbye to Lambert and his fellow cowpunchers in the distance. He told Fletcher to exchange horses with another rider and trail him back. He quickly turned his roan and began riding at a steady clip to the Johnson headquarters.

When Sand Burr pulled into the ranch yard, he spotted four men wearing badges stolidly mounted and fronted by obvious angry cowhands. These cowhands were the night-shift riders who had had their sleep rudely interrupted, and they were not happy about that as well as what was being said and how it was being said.

Unbeknownst to Sand Burr, these hombres had ridden bold as brass into the open yard, roused the bunkhouse, and had assembled all the Johnson employees they could find. They told them to assemble and keep their mouths shut or get arrested.

When the obvious leader of the band caught sight of Sand Burr's arrival, he raised his hand for the murmuring to cease. Sand Burr rode closer and saw the slender, imperious man better. He had his horse situated in front of his three cohorts. He had a sloped, black-brimmed hat that shadowed his almost colorless blue eyes. His severe features included a crooked, thin-lipped smile that reminded Sand Burr of a rattlesnake's grin.

Irvin Pendly pushed up his hat brim. He never lost his supercilious expression as he looked Sand Burr sneeringly up and down. Sand Burr endured Irvin Pendly's condescending looks for as long as he could. He sighed and exasperatingly asked, "What can I do for you?"

Pendly straightened in his saddle and spat to the side. "I like a man who don't waste his time or mine."

Sand Burr's irritated expression was his only response. He was trying to mentally piece together in his mind what was transpiring. His eyes panned the predatory-looking gents who were positioned slightly behind this curly wolf who was doing all the talking.

Irvin once more gave his serpentine grin and in a low, minatory voice said, "You tell your boss when he gets here that he's to be in Hawkshaw in five days. On the fifth day, he better be at Sheriff Doby's office at high noon." Irvin paused as though he savored saying the words. "Or Duchess will be taken to Austin to stand trial." He let the words settle in before he continued. "Tell him to bring twenty thousand dollars or just stay home." He leaned back in his saddle and sneered at Sand Burr. "You got that, buddy boy, or do you got wax in your ears?"

Sand Burr nodded nonchalantly. "I got wax, but even with wax, I know ass braying when I hear it. Why don't you wait, whatever your name is, and tell him yourself?"

Irvin did not like Sand Burr's insolent tone or his message. He straightened in his saddle and gave Sand Burr a baleful look. "You're talking to an appointed law official of the Texas legislature. I don't give a damn for your attitude." Irvin's face was flushed. He look to the left and right indicating he wanted his crew to get ready to draw on the hostile cowhand and the restless hands standing belligerently before them.

Irvin's men knew that was not what they had been ordered to do. They gave each other glances, but they knew Irvin was impulsive and would do whatever he wanted even openly ignoring orders from T-Dilly.

Sand Burr said, "You look like lowlife to me, mister. If you want to arrest me, well, hell, just go for that gun."

Irvin's eye began a nervous tic as he concluded it was time to send the smart-mouth Sand Burr to the Promised Land.

A hard, stentorian voice rang out from behind the four supposed lawmen. "You go for that gun, Irvin, and I'll back-shoot you if I have to."

Irvin's face changed. Anger moved to concern. His focus was no longer on Sand Burr. He slowly reined his horse around. He recognized Lambert, who had an unwavering Spencer carbine aimed at him. He snorted his contempt not only for Lambert but also for the whole yard filled with lowlife cowhands. He had already calculated how he and his four men could come out in a ranch yard filled with bad-tempered men. But with Lambert behind them and foolhardy enough to pull that trigger, that changed the equation. With a calmer mind, he recalled he had been instructed to use no violence. He knew a shootout would be tantamount to being fired and pursued by the same boss he was working for. Irvin inhaled and slowly edged his horse back to Sand Burr. He nodded curtly and snapped, "You do like I say, savvy? Tell your boss exactly what I said." He said over his shoulder, "I ain't forgettin' this, Lambert." Getting no response, he continued. "You done stuck your nose in the wrong damn place."

Lambert was impassive. His carbine was still aimed at Irvin. Irvin, knowing he had played out his cards, abruptly pulled back on his reins and backed his horse from the confrontation. He gave Sand Burr one final, menacing look, and he and his men galloped away. He and his men headed due east before taking a sharp right at the corral and heading south.

Sand Burr's eyes slid to his right as he watched the supposed deputies ride swiftly away. He looked at Lambert with puzzling admiration as the older man placed his rifle in its scabbard. He thoughtfully looked around at the irritated cowhands. "Ya'll go back to sleep." He apologized for something he was not responsible for. "I'm sorry about all this mix-up."

The men grumbled about the deputies and the loss of rest. They liked Sand Burr and knew it was not his fault. They threw up their hands as if to say "Apology accepted."

Lambert rode up to Sand Burr and watched the departing deputies. Their eyes met, and Sand Burr gave him a faint smile. "You're pretty damn handy, Lambert."

Lambert did not respond. He let his vision go to the dust still wavering in the distance from Irvin Pendly's departure. "That man that was doin' all the talkin' is Irvin Pendly. He works for a crooked carpetbag congressman. I don't know what your boss has done, but it ain't a good sign that Irvin and them illegal lawmen were here."

Sand Burr looked at the distant dust cloud of the ersatz lawmen but slowly moved his vision to the ranch road. He stated evenly, "My boss never does illegal things. He's the most honest man I ever met. I ain't got the foggiest what those bastards are up to, but he's the wrong man to cross."

Lambert evaluated what Sand Burr said; it seemed to go hand in hand with what his foreman had told him. "I ain't ever met this John Lee Johnson fella."

Sand Burr let a thoughtful smile slide across his features. "Well, Lambert, you're about to." Lambert gave him a puzzled look. Sand Burr nodded toward the ranch road from that led from Baileysboro. "He's in sight. And if I was any of them gents who's got a burr in their saddle about him, I would just quietly ride away and find a rock to hide behind."

CHAPTER 7

Seth and Floyd decided to leave town a day early. They figured that the disastrous failed robbery news would discourage in the short term at least any attempts to rob the bank. They hastily put things in motion. They gave Merle his instructions and checked with Sheriff Henry Nelson about the loan of his deputy to stand guard most of the day at the bank. They walked out of the bank to a waiting wagon fronted by two waiting mules.

They almost felt liberated from the punctilious bank duties and the seemingly endless paperwork. They checked the supplies in the wagon. They had enough food and provisions for a month though it was an eleven-day round trip at the most.

Seth smiled. He liked the idea of going to see Frank Barnwell under the ruse of bragging on his sparkling credit but at the same time checking out his wholesome and attractive daughter. By just dropping by, he would not appear to be an intrusive suitor, and he would see for himself if she were all Floyd said she was. If he found her not his type, he could gracefully just ride away no worse for the wear and with Barnwell no wiser.

Floyd too was thinking of a love match between the nubile Patricia Barnwell and his best friend. However, he was nagged by the thoughts of J.D. Rysinger too. Not too many men would forget part of their ears being shot off and who had shot them off. He figured that if Rysinger escaped the posse, he might want to exact revenge. He caught Seth's eye and warned him of that. Floyd, known for being laconic, sent an outward sweeping hand motion that said that the bank robbers were still out there. Seth's face sobered. He acknowledged Floyd's words immediately by dispensing the romantic thoughts circulating in his head. He pragmatically checked his sidearm. He nodded to Floyd; they were on the same page. He gazed at the ragged mesquite horizon.

Seth climbed up to the seat and grabbed the reins. He watched Floyd take his place as the passenger. Seth gave a curling smile when he saw his valued friend pull up his ten-gauge shotgun and place it over his knees. He also had a Sharps .52 under the tarp in the wagon bed. Seth snapped the reins and headed toward Roxy, Texas.

J.D. and his remaining crew had pulled up a mile from Baileysboro and squared their horses toward the town they had just left. With his left ear bleeding profusely, J.D. borrowed a ragged towel Toby had in his saddlebag and tied it around his head much like someone with a toothache would do. As he sat there mulling over a plan of action, Punkin' Head, with his twee features scrunched on his moon face, looked around and asked, "Where's all the help we was supposed to have, J.D.?"

J.D. frowned. He was unhappy about the fact that Pendly had lied to him and was irritated that Punkin' Head had the nerve to call him out on it. J.D. chose not to give Punkin' Head the satisfaction of an answer. His good eye opened wider when he saw dust in the distance and realized that a posse was barreling toward them. He gave orders. "Let's separate and meet ten miles south of here at that road junction that takes you to Tuckerville."

His three companions saw the billowing evidence of the distant posse. They gave curt acknowledgement to J.D. and galloped their separate ways.

As he rode adroitly through the mesquite, Punkin' Head began to have second thoughts about J.D. Rysinger. There had been a time when he considered J.D. one of the shrewdest men he had ever met. He had overlooked his womanizing and occasional irrational outbursts because he planned robberies well and was a natural killer. When he shot someone, he did not sit around getting teary eyed thinking of the victim's family or entertaining lingering pangs of conscience. He just shot 'em and forgot 'em.

But when he saw J.D. get his ass kicked by John Lee Johnson, and later on, when he and Red had to rebuild J.D.'s confidence after that fiasco, it began to eat on Punkin' Head's faith in ol' J.D.

Moreover, after the disastrous bank robbery attempt and J.D. getting the lower part of his ear shot off and losing two men—one of which was Red Farmer—because of poor planning, Punkin' Head felt unsettled. He had watched J.D. tie that dishrag or towel around his head to stop the bleeding and saw him sitting in the saddle with the bad eye striking a ridiculous pose like a man who had just gotten out of a dentist's chair. He concluded that unless J.D. decided to give up some of his private loot to keep him and the others around, he just might have to ditch J.D. Rysinger.

He had an idea that J.D. would try to finagle him and the others to seek revenge on that banker who had shot off part of his ear. That meant riding around trying to ambush the man just for defending what was rightfully his and his depositors. Punkin' Head deduced he would hear J.D. out. If it were not to his liking, he might just try to usurp the gang and head back to the Nations. He had learned long ago that robbing banks was profitable but that revenge did not pay very well. Punkin' Head had exactly ten dollars in his pocket. He knew that when that money was gone, so would he.

The deputies found the tracks where the gang had stopped. Their collective hearts dropped when they saw individual tracks leading from the mass of scuffed earth. They instinctively realized they did not have a ghost's chance of finding the whole gang. They hung their dejected heads and glanced at Woody, who also knew the jig was up. He could pick up one set of departing tracks and follow it, but if the bandit lost them, they might be thirty miles from town. It was not lost on him that this posse was a hastily put together group of cowhands. Woody knew the ranchers would probably overlook one day of county-appointed duty but would complain like hell over two or three days of service especially if they came up empty.

He took some heart in the fact that the bank holdup had been unsuccessful. He hoped that Sheriff Nelson would be understanding enough and excuse him for trailing the gang by himself. He circled his horse pondering his course of action. He took one more forlorn look at single sets of tracks leading off in four directions. He exhaled and signaled for the posse to follow him back to Baileysboro.

Toby Jarrett watched the deputies returning to Baileysboro. He had dismounted and hidden his horse in a thicket of mesquite. He had removed his hat and crawled close to the trail. He knew it would be suicide to ride into Baileysboro. With depressed thoughts of his brother on his mind, he cried himself to sleep stretched out on the warm sand. He awoke and found it to be in the late afternoon. He was edging back to his horse when he saw Seth and Floyd pass by in a wagon. He recognized them, particularly Seth. He remembered seeing the muscular banker laying down a steady fire at J.D. He was shocked to see the two bankers out in the open and surprised they would be leaving town so late in the afternoon.

He watched them pass. He noticed they did not have any sense of urgency. He knew that J.D. would be very interested in knowing that the man who had shot half his ear off was moseying down a trail that would fork north to the Nations or south to Finleyville and Roxy. He knew he had to go to the meeting place fast and deliver this information. He boldly arose and sprinted to his mount. He threaded his way through the heavy copse of stunted trees and found an opening he urged his horse through.

Seth and Floyd rode for twelve miles making occasional small talk. At the fork, they headed toward Roxy. Things of the past entered their minds. Seth and Floyd had had a bad encounter with the House family in Roxy a month earlier. They had four orphan girls in the back of the wagon when the evil House family had trailed them from Roxy to Finleyville. Fortunately, the four waifs were saved by hiding out in Ray Hobbs's barn in Finleyville. Seth and Floyd had managed to kill most of the House family with the help of a reformed gunman named Hondo Goodrich.

Usually, Floyd and Seth exchanged light banter when they traveled, but that time, even freed from the confines of the bank, the air seemed thick with an aeriform tension. Seth knew it was more than the responsibility of finding a wife and legally raising the four orphan girls as his own. He knew that the violence of the bank robbery attempt had blighted what would have been a pleasant trip. He also had a nagging recollection of the rage in the eyes of the man whose name he discovered was J.D. Rysinger after conferring with the sheriff.

"What you thinkin' about, Floyd?"

Floyd looked behind. "You know what I am thinkin' about. Same as you. I'm thinkin' about that damned J.D. Rysinger."

Seth nodded. "I didn't think ol' Woody would corral that bunch of yahoos." He corrected his words thinking that his assessment of Woody was too harsh. "Not that Woody ain't good enough."

Floyd looked forward and nodded. "Woody said they split up and headed in four directions." He sighed. "This is not the first bank those bandidos have tried to rob. If we hadn't been warned by Woody, they might have been successful."

Floyd sighed. "I got in mind that we'll see that J.D. fella again."

Seth compressed his lips in thought. Then he abruptly changed the subject. "Something's got John upset. Did you see that look on his face back in town?"

Floyd nodded and looked over at the slow-moving countryside. "All things being equal, we should've stayed and found out what the problem was." Floyd raised a finger. "But a woman like this Patricia Barnwell won't last forever."

"What have you heard about her?" Seth asked.

"Well, she helps out on the ranch and goes to church and has no steady beaus that I know of." He paused. "She's supposed to be beautiful too."

Seth smiled. "Well, I shore like all those things. I like character, but I'm still young enough to appreciate beauty too." Seth's face sobered as he thought about the four wonderful little girls who were depending on him to make a home for them. "If the girls had a wish for a good mother, I reckon we all would prefer a good lookin' mom rather than one not so good lookin'."

Floyd gave a complimentary chuckle, but his face transitioned to a sober look. He did not want to ruin Seth's moment of thinking about a prospective life mate. He tried to mask his expression by pretending to be studying the countryside.

They made camp after dark and ate sparingly. The next morning, they began again and rode all day with few breaks. They remained taciturn; they wordlessly worked in tandem taking turns driving the mules and handing the other a dipper of water from the keg behind the springboard seat. Seth, who was driving, pulled up for no reason. He pulled two cigars from his vest pocket and handed one to Floyd. They lit up. Seth tilted his head to Floyd. "Maybe this'll make us feel better, Floyd."

Floyd sighed and exhaled a stream of blue smoke. "Life can be troublesome, but a good cigar irons out a lot of blues."

Seth sighed. "You ain't still sore about me siccing Lola and Elspeth on you, are you?"

Floyd let a slow grin spread across his coppery complexion. "Hell no. I would've done the same to you I reckon." Floyd's smile faded. "You know what's eatin' both of us, Seth. We both got this premonition that since that J.D. got his ear partial shot off that he's got a mad on for both of us."

Seth took a heavy drag on his smoke and pensively exhaled a stream of blue. "It would be such a pleasant ride to go see this lady, but seems like every Eden has its serpent."

Floyd soberly nodded. "What I'm about to tell you, you may want to discount, but since we've faced dangers before, maybe you won't. You can attribute it to my Choctaw blood or just a God-given intuition, but I can feel J.D. Rysinger behind us."

Seth glanced at his companion. He and Floyd had had many adventures and misadventures together, but one thing he had learned during those many dangerous sojourns was that when Floyd had one of those feelings, it was wise to pay attention. He did not verbally say he believed him; that was tacitly understood. Seth, with Floyd's admonition circling his brain, pulled out his army .44, checked the loads, and holstered it. "What do you suggest we do, Floyd?"

Floyd turned and looked at the trail behind them. "I can feel his miserable hide followin' us now. I believe he'll catch up with us tonight. When the sun is sinkin' and you can find and see an arroyo, pull up and make a fire—a fire that will simmer all night. You make two bolsters, and I'll hide the mules in the gully and stand guard. You go where you want, but let me know where you are so we won't shoot each other."

At twilight, Seth saw a deep enough gulch to hide the mules. He reined up and set the brake. They worked liked a well-trained team. Seth made a reflector circle for the campfire with some rocks. He placed a metal tripod above the circle. He waited till it was a tad past sundown before starting a fire with copious mesquite twigs. He placed two sticks of green oak gathered from the wagon bed at the sides of the shallow fire pit. He left the coffee pot in the food box on purpose. He did not want it shot up if Floyd was right or burned up if Floyd was wrong.

Floyd watered and fed the mules and led them down into the arroyo. He had a blanket over his shoulders like a poncho. He carried his trusty Sharps .52 over his shoulder. He had a hand full of beef jerky and a canteen of water. He found a boulder to sit on close to the lip of the gully. He could see the campsite from there, and he could stabilize his aim on the boulder. He saw Seth making two blanketed bolsters that looked passable in the dark. Seth threw a blanket over his shoulders and headed to a rounded, sandy drumlin. He carried two seven-shot Spencer rifles. He turned and hailed Floyd before continuing. Receiving an acknowledgment, he went over the hillock and took his position.

Four miles back, J.D. and his remaining gang pulled up. J.D.'s one good eye was focused on the strong wagon track. His victorious grin was visible even in the gloaming. J.D. was unable to wear his hat due to the towel around his head. Punkin' Head watched him react to knowing his quarry was up ahead. He looked at his hatless head and the ridiculously oversized bandage and understood Red's disdain of their boss a hell of a lot better. J.D. was letting his pride override his judgment. He was more interested in some useless revenge than making money. Even if they were two bankers on a journey, that did not mean they had any money on them. Punkin' Head's eyes surreptitiously scanned his associates to catch a hint that someone might be thinking as he was. He caught Toby Jarrett's eyes, and for a second, they seemed to connect. Toby pulled his eyes away but took a second glance at Punkin' Head, who returned a knowing look and nodded slightly. Punkin' Head saw Toby's slight, sarcastic smile. He knew he had his first comrade.

J.D. laughed out loud as though he were trying to purge all those bad things that had happened since he had entered Bailey County. His laughter sounded puerile and hollow to Punkin' Head. Illuminated by the soft purple light of sun's afterglow as it sank past the horizon, J.D. pointed toward the tracks that followed a vanishing point over the distant hill. "Boys, when I get my revenge, we can head to the Nations and make us some money." When he did not receive the reaction he had expected from his remaining three gang members, he said, "That son of a bitch shot my ear off, and there ain't nobody can get away from me when I got my hate on." Still not receiving any feedback from his cronies, he looked at his brother. "Ain't that right, Adrian?"

Adrian vigorously nodded in an attempt to generate some spirit. "Damn right, J.D."

J.D. looked at Punkin' Head and Toby to see if Adrian's enthusiasm had fired their zeal. Punkin' Head and Toby nodded in affirmation, but their nods lacked the heart of times past. J.D. sensed that he needed a triumph to regain their confidence. He leaned back in his saddle with his hands on his gun belt. "When we find 'em, I want ya'll to stand back and let me kill 'em." He paused dramatically and jabbed his chest with his thumb. He added in a stentorian voice, "Me. Not any of you. Me."

Roused by his own words, he pointed toward the trail and spurred his horse. The others galloped after him as though they were reluctant sailors following Ahab.

It was one hour later and dark when Seth heard thudding hooves. The riders pulled up when they saw the glow of the campfire; they quickly dismounted. They tied off their mounts, and J.D. held out his hands for the others not to go farther. He pulled his army. 44 from his holster and ran its cylinder. He holstered his weapon with a particular finality. He removed his spurs and began walking softly down the sandy road. He did not want the *chink-chink* of spurs spoiling his stalking. He kept his eyes on the soft glimmer of fire as he mentally rehearsed what he would say and do. Anger and confidence swirled in his chest. He eased off the road following the wagon tracks. He began walking slower with his eyes moving in the darkness. He felt that if he could not see them, they could not see him. He edged closer to the outline of the wagon. He inched his way along side of the wagon bed and peeked around the corner of the driver's box at the two soogans spread about six feet apart.

He pulled his .44 out making a slick leathery sound. He looked back and forth at the sleeping bags trying to determine who was who. He moved with a certain boldness to the one on his right. He clicked the hammer back as he pointed it at what he thought was the foot of the victim. His voice broke the quietude. "All right, banker man, wake up and meet the man who's goin' to send you and your filthy lucre to the devil."

Getting no response, he fired a roaring shot into the sleeping bag. His twisted smile dissipated quickly when there was no yelp or cry. He warily began to backpedal toward the safety of the wagon. His eyes took on a crazy look of someone who realized he had been tricked. He cautiously backed up with the knowledge that he was visible in the flickering yellow light and the understanding that he had to get out of it pronto.

Two rifles made their unique reports. Floyd's Sharps grazed J.D.'s neck. Seth's Spencer nailed him in the hollow of his left elbow. J.D. made a piercing cry and staggered back. Reaching the shadowy bulk of the wagon, He took off running as best he could. He was fighting pain and tears as he reached the safety of his men. Adrian lifted him onto his sorrel, and the gang gave concerned looks toward the distant campfire. With a certain trepidation, they soon were galloping back down the same road they had come.

J.D. was humped over his horse begging his men to cut through an opening in the bordering mesquite that he saw in the wan moonlight. Many hands pulled him from his horse and laid him on the ground. Punkin' Head struck a match and hollowed his other hand to reflect the light. His tiny eyes broadened considerably. "Damn, J.D.! Your left arm looks like hell." Adrian did not know how to express it, but he pointed to J.D.'s triceps, which had rolled up like a window shade. Seth's shot had severed the tendon at his elbow, and his triceps had been released.

Punkin' Head stood and told Toby to make a fire. "We got to cauterize them wounds or J.D.'s goin' to die."

Adrian growled low in his chest. "I'm gonna go back and kill those varmints for what they did to J.D."

Punkin' Head grabbed his elbow. He realized Adrian was acting on false bravado. "You'll just get what he got." He made a quick, derisive motion to J.D. "Why don't we heal up your brother and then we'll make our minds on what to do."

Adrian abruptly pulled his elbow from Punkin' Head's grasp and gave him a disapproving, hard look. He felt that if J.D. was down and out, it was up to him to make decisions, not Punkin' Head. But when he looked at Toby's cold, withering look, Adrian realized that he had little say and that Punkin' Head was calling the shots. He nodded his acquiescence when he felt the heat of Punkin' Head's stare. He realized the new pecking order quickly. He slunk off trying to maintain some self-possession and immediately began looking for the makings for a fire to cauterize J.D.'s wounds.

Floyd and Seth came in from the shadows and tossed some more twigs on the fire. In the increased light, they saw the blood on the ground. Seth shrugged, "Well, one or both of us tagged that turd."

Floyd stepped around the wagon following J.D.'s scuff marks. "I gather his men are down the road."

Seth sighed. "They don't seem too hep on attackin' us."

Floyd nodded and shrugged. "I think that was that one-eyed fellow." He pensively looked off into the umbra. "Hell, he's runnin' outta body parts to shoot."

Seth was too tired to grin. "I'll stand first guard. Drag that soogan away from the light and try and get some shuteye."

Punkin' Head bent down and listened to J.D. moaning. "J.D., I got to burn that wound. If I don't, you're gonna bleed to death."

J.D.'s one eye opened wide in pain and anger. "Just do it and do it good. But do it the hell now!" He went back to groaning and cussing.

Adrian had started a fire and laid a nine-inch Bowie on the circling rocks with the blade in the fire. In fifteen minutes, Punkin' Head grabbed an extra saddle blanket in his gloved hand and pulled the hot knife from the orange flame. His small eyes looked at the writhing J.D. "Adrian, give your brother a slug of that red eye you got in your saddlebag, and be ready to pour a big dose on that wound in the crook of his arm. Be ready to pour some more on where that ball went out near his elbow as soon as I cauterize it."

Adrian nodded. He grabbed a brown bottle of cheap whiskey from his saddlebag and walked quickly to his brother. He gently held up his brother's head and coaxed him to open his mouth. He gave him a snootful, some of which ran down his chin and jaw. Punkin' Head turned fully to his supine boss and moved with alacrity to him. He grabbed J.D.'s left arm and pulled it to see the wound better in the light of the campfire. He laid the blade to the wound, and the sizzling flesh and J.D.'s animal shrieks and profanity broke the solemn silence. That action was followed by a liberal dosing of whiskey.

Punkin' Head turned J.D.'s arm around to see the exit wound and laid the other side of the knife to it. J.D., having passed out, was lying back as if dead. Again, Adrian doused the burned flesh with the hootch. Adrian gave a start when he saw his brother not moving. Punkin' Head assured the anxious Adrian that his brother was not dead. "The pain just shut down his body."

Toby and Adrian looked at the unconscious J.D. and then to Punkin' Head as if for directions. Punkin' Head gandered at J.D. He took note of the bandage around his head, his eye patch, and his mangled left arm with muscles rolled up near his deltoid. He did not want to play his cards yet about ousting the boss, so he just nodded as though he were feeling sorry for J.D. "When he wakes up the mornin,' we'll get him in the saddle and take him someplace where he can heal up."

Punkin' Head's explanation satisfied Adrian but left hope in Toby's eyes that soon they could get shed of the insufferable man who had ruled them with an iron hand. Toby took note that J.D. Rysinger did not look all that tough at that point. He still burned inwardly about how he had treated his mentally deficient brother. He doubted J.D. would ever effectively lead anyone again at least for long. He was a wounded wolf in a pack of wolves who always demanded stronger and better. He was already looking to Punkin' Head for strength and common sense.

CHAPTER 8

John Lee held Martha's hand as they made their way down the road from Baileysboro. Most times when they went together in the wagon on supply day, they did a lot of laughing and sharing. But that day, they talked quietly fearing their concerns might upset their daughter, Sally.

John caught sight of Sand Burr and an older man on horseback by the side of the road near the ranch house. When he came even with them, he reined up, looked at Sand Burr, and shot Lambert a quizzical glance. He initially wondered why Sand Burr was not on the eastern range but overlooked that fact as his mind shifted to the bigger picture.

Lambert, who had been told about John Lee Johnson, almost disbelieved what he was looking at. He was stunned at the man's massive physique. He looked as though he had been transposed from Homer's *Iliad* or *Odyssey*.

Sand Burr introduced Lambert to John and vice versa. John gave a cordial nod and received one in return. John did not tarry long on familiarities. He said, "Sand Burr, I want you to get two saddle mules ready to leave at first light with two mules to pull. I want to take you with me. We need to be in Hawkshaw at noon in four days."

John did not tarry or give further information. When he received Sand Burr's businesslike nod, he snapped the reins, and the wagon began to rumble down the road at a brisk pace.

The hands moving around in the yard saw the wagon approaching and formed a queue to remove the supplies. When the wagon was braked, the busy cowhands knew what went to the cook shack and what went to the house. John, Martha, and Sally did not shirk their duties. In fifteen minutes, the wagon was empty.

Normally, John and Martha would have gone to bed at nine, but they stayed at the kitchen table until midnight with Martha going over each line that Lieutenant Bragg had sent him in the extensive missive. In times past, she had cried when he had had to leave, but that time, she was almost defiant to the external forces that beleaguered her husband.

"John, I want you to go and save sweet Duchess. She's never harmed anyone, and as far as helping General Selby to Louisiana, why not? It was a time of war." She looked at John, who sat with an inscrutable look. "I love you, husband. I fear for you, but I know you well enough to know that maybe they should fear you too."

John sighed. "I know what I'm supposed to do by heart. Let's go to bed. I'd like to hold you some before I have to go and do what I have to do."

The next morning, John hugged Martha in the hallway. They whispered their love for each other over and over. She held his face. "Go now … but come back to me."

He nodded. He could never promise her he would come back, but he could promise her he would do the best he could. He inhaled a heavy breath and walked down the hallway trying not to look back.

When he reached the door, he heard his stepdaughter's voice from the shadows of the large living room. She was in her morning gown. She reached up, and he bent over to embrace her. He saw tears in her eyes. She spoke very formally as if she had practiced the speech. "My dearest father. I want you to know that I love you for making my mother so happy. I love you for making my life so rich with love and attention. Our worlds are built around you, Father. I want you to save our cousin, Duchess. I want you to return, but if you don't, dear Father, please give them all the hell they ever asked for."

John's eyes crinkled as he suppressed a smile. He released himself from her hug, grasped her shoulders, and gave her a confidant nod. He looked down the hallway to the milky outline of his wife hugging the wall and then back to the expectant face of his child. "You both give me all the reasons in the world to come back to." He did not correct her for using the word *hell* but knew he might need to curtail her hanging around the cook shack so much. He released her shoulders and walked out the door to embark on a dangerous mission.

In the barn, Sand Burr and Lambert had completed stocking the war bags and provision sacks with supplies. They loaded two pack mules with the provisions and cinched them down. Sand Burr had saddled up the big, nine-hundred-pound mule for John, but he was surprised to see that Lambert had saddled another mule for the journey. Sand Burr asked, "Why are you saddlin' yourself a mule, Lambert?"

Lambert did not look him in the eyes. "I plan on goin' along."

Seth sighed. His eyes turned quizzical. "Lambert, I want to ask you two questions." He paused in order to get his words right. "Why do you want to go? And what gives you the right to go?"

Lambert's eyes locked on Sand Burr's. "I ain't got that long to live. It's necessary for me to go." His voice trailed off. "It's just necessary." When Sand Burr did not respond but kept a steady stare at him, Lambert continued. "I mean you and your boss no harm … far from it." His eyes watered with emotion. "But you got to let me go with you. I can't tell you all the reasons, and I hope you respect that … but I need to go with you."

Sand Burr felt Lambert's soulful emotion; his words pulled at his heart. He knew he could not say no. He nodded. "Well, if it's like the last time I was with John, there's goin' to be …" He hesitated and pointed to the barn walls as though he saw the horizon. "… hell out there."

Lambert said in a low but emotion-filled voice, "I've been living in misery, boy. Just maybe I can redeem myself to God and some other folks."

Lambert's vehement response puzzled Sand Burr. But he had said it so convincingly that he knew he could not say no to the man, who seemed so damned determined.

When John reached the maw of the barn, he was pleased that Sand Burr had everything in order. He looked questioningly at Lambert. Before he could say anything, Sand Burr explained that Lambert was going with them and that he was a good cook and farrier.

John said nothing; he respected Sand Burr's judgment. As John mounted his big mule, he listened as Sand Burr informed him of Pendly and all he had said. He listened patiently to news he had already received from many others. But he nodded as though it were the first time he had received it. Seth and Lambert mounted their mules and grabbed hold of the tether lines to the pack mules. They departed silently out of the barn and into the warm morning.

Sand Burr and Lambert were riding side by side behind John as they traveled due south. Sand Burr turned to Lambert and said out of the side of his mouth in a low, hushed voice, "You can cook and take care of mules cain't you?"

Lambert gave him half a smile. "Yeah, shore I can."

"That shore in hell didn't sound too confident."

Lambert smiled. "I'll try to stretch the truth better next time, Sand Burr."

Four days later in the Hawkshaw county jail, Sheriff Dan Doby sat behind his desk nervously drumming his chubby fingers. He was a corpulent man. He wore a wide-brimmed hat with an extraordinarily tall crown. His ruddy complexion was flushed with anxiety and irritation. To his right in the first of three cells sat Duchess Thompson wearing a black dress and with her hair piled up high. She was a handsome woman for being in her early fifties, and it was obvious to anyone that she did not deserve to be in jail. He looked at the wall clock and knew the insufferable James Stevens and Judge Harold Roy, recently appointed to the Texas supreme court, would soon return after having breakfast at the local café and visiting the bank.

Sheriff Doby knew the charges against Duchess were trumped-up, flimsy charges that in prewar Texas would have been dismissed or never considered in the first place. He wondered what would happen when Stevens told John Lee Johnson face to face about the conspiracy indictment, but he was sure the prideful Stevens would be shaken when he met the big Texan.

He asked Duchess if she wanted some water or food and received a short, negative headshake. He offered her again his apologetic regrets about her forced confinement. She turned her head and nodded that she understood he was not a fault. "That Stevens fella's goin' to be in for a surprise. The word is goin' around that he if finds some ranch worth havin,' he finds a way to connect the owner with supportin' the Confederacy, confiscates the land, and it goes up for public auction … which he then buys."

Doby had heard the same report. He knew he was on a short leash himself with the arrogant Yankee bastard who had taken over his town even in his short visit. He knew he had to watch what he said to Duchess, but his curiosity got the better of him. "Why's he in for a surprise, Duchess?"

"Because I gave all my land to John Lee a year ago. He takes care of me and allows me to call the ranch my own even if it's not. He's the most upright man I know, Sheriff Doby, even if he's a relative."

Doby glanced at the banjo clock on the wall again and figured if he were going to ask, he better do so. "You got that in writin', do you?"

The Duchess confidently smiled. "Oh yes—one copy in Baileysboro at the land office, and another in Austin, which apparently Representative Stevens didn't check. And one copy at the Baileysboro bank in the safe, and one here in Hawkshaw at your bank." She gave a tight smile. "With so many courthouses burnin' down—I just wanted to be safe."

Doby smiled and nodded in admiration of such sage judgment. He chanced a comment on Stevens and the carpetbagger judge Stevens had brought with him. "I bet they know now. They've been at the bank all morning. I had no idea that you were that far thinkin,' ma'am."

"Oh, I'm not that far thinkin,' Sheriff. I got sick some time back and thought I was goin' to die, and John's my closest kin. So I chose to let him have my property ahead of time. James Stevens will never see the day when he can call my ranch his own."

Judge Roy, an older man who was spare in physique, sported large, fluffy muttonchops and wore a tall stovepipe hat. His eyes edged toward his companion, James Stevens, as they walked out of the Hawkshaw bank. "I've got some questions to ask you, James."

Stevens, who had no idea that the widow Thompson no longer owned her ranch, reluctantly nodded.

"I noticed you put fifty thousand in the bank for some sort of enticement for John Lee Johnson."

Stevens nodded. "That I did."

Judge Roy's expression morphed into concern. "Is that the same fifty thousand the general told you to buy land with?"

Stevens, still inwardly fuming about finding that Duchess Thompson's land was no longer an option, stepped down from the boardwalk and stood stock still on the edge of the dirt street. "Judge, we need to talk."

Judge Roy, who was considered Stevens's equal in the eyes of the former brigadier general Frank McGrew, stood patiently waiting for Stevens's explanation.

"The general has left some options for me to make decisions about. He wants John Lee Johnson dead pure and simple. He's wanted this from the beginning. I took it on myself to withdraw the fifty thousand from the bank in Austin and transfer it here for a very good reason. I have to have some bait to draw in this John Lee Johnson. When I offer him our money for his twenty thousand in a bet on the fight in Chihuahua, he probably will like the odds and go for it. He can't whip this Mexican, and to boot, it's a winner lives and loser dies battle in that pit. When the Mexican wins, which he will, you and I will split Johnson's twenty thousand and put the fifty thousand back in the bank in Austin." He cockily added, "No one the wiser except you and me."

"But what if he wins and you lose?"

Stevens absentmindedly dusted his coat and chuckled. "Then I'm in serious trouble."

The judge exhaled. "We're in serious trouble, young man. The general will know I was complicit in this matter."

Stevens gave a confident smile, but in a brittle voice, he replied, "Let me handle this, judge. I know what I'm doing."

Judge Roy gave a troublesome look at Stevens. "Did you notice the banker saying that if John Lee Johnson didn't have the twenty thousand, he would put up the money himself?"

Stevens drew a cigar from his coat pocket and took some time lighting it. He flicked the match aside and laconically stated, "I noticed."

The judge thoughtfully pursed his lips. "If a banker is willing to put up his own money even after hearing about this El Toro de Sanchez, he must have a whole lot of confidence in this Johnson fellow."

Stevens, chagrined about the line of questioning along with how the Widow Thompson's ranch had slipped through his hands, defensively listened to the judge's words and pensively smoked.

The judge, receiving no response, continued. "You're putting our futures on the line based on the testimony of T-Dilly that this Mexican will defeat the Texan."

Stevens eyebrows arched in anger. He irritatingly exhaled a stream of blue smoke. "Judge Roy, I respect you, but you and I have never laid eyes on this John Lee Johnson. So please reserve your judgment. I don't give a damn what the banker thinks of a local tough guy. He still has to fight a man who has won ten straight damn fights in a ten-foot-deep pit."

The judge, mollified by his words, nodded curtly. He pulled out his pocket watch, checked the time, and looked at the sun to verify of sorts his calculations. "He should be pulling in in about an hour."

Stevens pointedly nodded at the judge's coat. "You have the contract?"

The judge, piqued at the condescending and unnecessary question, gave a *harrumph* and replaced his pocket watch brusquely.

Stevens gave a quick wave to his five gunslicks across the street. These dour figures began traipsing across the way to escort him and the judge to the jailhouse. It was unnecessary to display such a show of force, but Stevens wanted to intimidate the locals and especially John Lee Johnson if he had the temerity to show.

The Hawkshaw citizens were indeed cowed by such distinguished but hated governmental figures and the hard cases guarding them. From behind store windows and over saloon batwings, many fear-filled eyes scrutinized the unusual assembly. Some dull eyes did not understand the import of the visit, and others just liked to observe something different.

The five bodyguards stopped at the door of the sheriff's office and let Stevens and the judge in. Doby kept his head down when they entered. He was an old-time Texan and realized that the protocol he had established with the rangers and prewar politicians had gone out the window. He understood by Stevens's and the judge's actions that he was to kowtow to their whims and demands without question. There had always the threat since he first met them that his job hung by a thread.

Stevens looked at the coffee pot on the stove and grunted at the sheriff, who had his head down stacking wanted posters. Doby sighed and grated his chair back. Without being told, he walked to the stove and poured two cups of coffee.

Stevens sneered. "I hope to hell that coffee is not that jailhouse coffee that's been through the grounds three or four times."

He and the judge sat in cane-bottom chairs on each side of the doorway. Doby ignored the acerbic comment and handed each man a tin cup of java. He managed civilly to say, "Don't have any sugar. It's not in the town budget."

Stevens snorted. "Hell, if you didn't steal everything, you might have some."

The judge smiled taking great pleasure in the sheriff's discomfort. He sipped his coffee and nodded approvingly. "You think this Johnson fellow will be here?"

Doby mulled over the question. "When he finds out you've pressed charges against Duchess and are holding her against her will, hell, yeah, he'll be here."

Stevens took umbrage at the sheriff's impertinent words and started to excoriate him as he done the last four days. But Duchess spoke up. "You two Yankees don't belong down here. You both are goin' to regret botherin' me, and you shore in hell will regret crossin' John Lee Johnson."

Stevens studied Duchess as she primly sat behind the bars. "If I were you, you old crone, I'd just keep my mouth shut." He added with all the vinegar he could manage, "You're in enough trouble as it is."

The Duchess studied Stevens and gave him an enigmatic smile. She turned and lost herself in thought.

The metronomic ticking of the clock filled the quiet room. Stevens occasionally glanced out the window or at the judge, who was smoking a Cuban cigar. He wanted to get this matter over. He was anxious to get a look at this figure he had been plotting against. He looked forward to whittling him down to size verbally.

The sound of mules broke the silence. Stevens glanced at the wall clock. It was ten minutes to the hour.

The door opened. Cherokee Charley, the half-breed leader of his five watchdog men, stuck his head in. "He's here, boss!"

Stevens noted that Cherokee Charley, normally nonchalant about most things, seemed spooked. It was not like Cherokee Charley to be so verbally demonstrative.

Cherokee Charley, sporting a high-crowned black hat with a feather, quickly shut the door. Stevens heard jingling spurs and boots grating on the wooden porch. For the previous four days, his men had been bored. He noticed that whoever this John Lee Johnson man was, he certainly had his men's attention.

Five minutes earlier, John and his two companions had made their way into town. Sand Burr, due to prior instruction, directed his mule to the bank as John and Lambert made their way to the sheriff's office.

Before John and his small crew were spotted, Cherokee Charley, Butter Bean Baker, and the others were preoccupied with passing a bottle of whiskey and cussing for no reason. They were cloyed and tired of Hawkshaw with its confined pleasures. They were prepared or at least thought they were ready to meet John Lee Johnson. They had been commanded to disarm him and admonish him about the accepted protocol—calling James Stevens Representative Stevens.

John and Lambert rode up to the hitch rack, which lodged only the sheriff's horse. John saw the five men eyeballing him and spreading apart. He observed Cherokee Charley opening the door and announcing he had arrived. Cherokee, unable to take his eyes off Johnson, cast wary eyes to his compadres, who were returning the same look. Cherokee tried to swallow without gulping. Johnson looked like a man cast in hard brass. He noticed his neck with the huge cords of muscle covering his mastoid area. The ripped shirt of the big Texan displayed a chest chiseled in muscle. His arms were bigger than most men's thighs. John and Lambert never took their eyes off the group of five as they dismounted and tied up. Lambert loosened his sidearm and stayed a few feet behind John. His eyes moved left and right at the men situated on the ends.

Cherokee held out his hand to halt the advance of the two men. Once more, he checked to his left and right to make sure he had the full support of his gang. "Hold it right there, stranger."

John kept moving forward followed by Lambert. Cherokee's hand was on the massive chest of the big Texan. John stopped and gave Cherokee a steady, minatory look. Cherokee looked into those unfeeling gray eyes as he nervously licked his lips. He again looked left and right to ascertain if he had the support he needed. Gathering courage, he said, "You're goin' to have to drop your weapons before goin' any farther. After droppin' your weapons, you may enter." He took in a lung of air and continued. "You must address Representative Stevens as Representative Stevens or be in danger of being charged with contempt … a jailable offense."

John grabbed Cherokee Charley's hand and began twisting it. Cherokee Charley tried to pull his hand away, but it was ensnared in a steel vice. John kept turning his hand. The other gang members were shocked. They watched cautiously but were afraid to act. Charley whimpered as he began to walk on the tips of his toes. John stopped long enough to ask, "What's your name?"

Charley painfully eked out his name. John disarmed Charley and handed his .44 over his shoulder to Lambert. John phlegmatically stated in the deepest voice Charley had ever heard, "Now let's start all over again. Did you tell me that I had to disarm?"

Charley, almost fainting from the pressure of his wrist, nodded yes. But as the pressure intensified, he shook his head no.

John gave a mirthless smile. "That's what I thought you said, Cherokee Charley. Now how am I supposed to address this Representative Stevens?"

Cherokee Charley wanted to say, "Representative Stevens," but he knew based on the unbearable pressure being applied that he might need to readdress that. He knew that if John twisted his hand another fraction of an inch, it would break. Tears were running down Cherokee's face as he literally danced on his toes. "Any damn thing you want to."

"Does that include 'Your royal turdness'?"

Cherokee could just nod. John released his wrist and tossed him backward with such force that Cherokee landed on his back. He grabbed Butter Bean, who had been beside Cherokee all the while. John's fist sank almost six inches into the blubbery midsection of the bandit. "That's for not helpin' your friend in a time in need." Butter Bean fell to his knees on the wood planking and puked his guts out. John turned to the other three, who were backing up as though they were confronted with a male lion and were armed only with peashooters. "Now you other three." John paused as if to collect his thoughts. "Go somewhere where I can't find you when I leave here. If I see you, I'll kill you on the spot." He sighed. "We all know you're goin' to try and waylay me on the trip to Mexico, so if I kill you now, it'll mean just less trouble later on."

One of the three, someone with green teeth and a week's worth of whiskers, managed to croak out, "Can we take Cherokee and Butter Bean with us?"

John ignored the man and his fruitless question. He had said and done all he wanted. "All right, Lambert, let's go in and see this turd."

When the door opened and Representative Stevens saw John Lee Johnson for the first time, his jaw dropped. Stevens was undergoing a strange experience. He looked at the Herculean physique and shuddered. Johnson was fearsome. In all his jaded life, Stevens had never seen anyone remotely resembling the big Texan. Everyone in the room seemed dinky compared to this powerful being.

Judge Roy's eyes appeared almost on stalks as they perused the compelling man. Once the initial shock stopped, the judge looked charily over at Stevens.

Doby kept his head down grinning inwardly but keeping a composed face for the dignity of his office. He had seen John's effect on people in the past. Realizing the air had been sucked out of the room, he drummed his chubby fingers on his desk. He caught John's glance and nodded affably.

John gave the sheriff an abbreviated nod and walked to Duchess Thompson's cell. She jumped off the cell cot and extended her hands lovingly to her cousin through the bars. "Oh John, so glad you're here." She wanted to say, "Please get me out of here," but she refrained because she felt it might compel him to do violence to the two interlopers who had arranged her arrest. He gently placed a hand on her cheek. He did not say anything, but Duchess knew he was angry about her confinement. Ever since childhood, John could hold himself in check. He was still the same, but he was just more dangerous.

He did not say anything to Duchess. He turned to Stevens and the judge. He walked slowly to the seated Stevens and stopped a few feet away.

Stevens was trying his best not to swallow. He did not want that audible gulp betraying his fear. But he was afraid. He wanted like hell to jump up, bolt through the door, and run back to Austin. But he put on his best face. He managed to look over at Judge Roy, who appeared to be as uncomfortable as he was. Stevens also took into account that his men—his security blanket—were nowhere in sight through the dirty window. He gave a quick glance at the sheriff, who seemed preoccupied with other things, but he noted that the sheriff's expression was of a man inwardly gloating.

Stevens did not know what to say, so he said nothing. John inhaled a deep breath that held in his anger. He knew that beating the hell out of the crooked representative would endanger him as well as his federal friends working behind the scenes in Austin. He said in that deep voice that seemed as though it came from some subterranean cavern, "All right. I'm here." Although John was remembering the facts his friend, Lieutenant Bragg, had sent him, he made out as if he were using the information Pendly had given Sand Burr. "According to your man Pendly or whatever his name was, it was necessary for me to place twenty thousand in the Hawkshaw bank as my bet. I just have. I gather you have deposited your fifty thousand that you'll bet against me."

Street gave a tentative nod.

John observed Stevens and took his nod at full value that he had indeed deposited his money. "I'll go fight this fellow in Chihuahua." He paused as though he did not have the information when in actuality he did, but to mask any suspicion that Stevens had a leak in his organization, he feigned ignorance. "When do I have to be there?"

Stevens puffed on his cigar to get the quavering out of his voice. "June fifteenth at high noon," he said with a curling smile. "The twenty thousand you placed in the bank is just your personal bet with me." Stevens garnered some courage. "You still have to bet another twenty thousand in Sanchez as your ante money to fight El Toro."

Sand Burr and the fluffy bank president entered on the tail end of Stevens's remarks. The bank president, Flavius Jeffers, had seen John when he had brought in the Russell House gang sometime back. Jeffers nodded to Stevens and the judge. He gave a quick wave to Doby and extended his hand to John. "John, I couldn't help but hearing about the money needed to bet in Mexico. You have over five thousand on the books already at my bank." His face took on an almost glow as he added, "I'd like to bet fifteen thousand of my money on you. So when you decide to take off, you're good to go."

John expressed his thanks to the banker and turned to Stevens and the judge. "Get out them damn papers and let me sign 'em." He said over his shoulder to the sheriff, "Go get a notary and have all the papers properly notarized." He pointed at Stevens and the judge. "I don't want to give these two jokers any wiggle room."

Stevens did not like the tone of the conversation and the fact that he was not calling the shots, but he remained silent. He especially squirmed when he was called a joker. He had serious doubts running through his mind. He had the former brigadier general Frank McGrew's blessing about killing John Lee Johnson, but he did not have the general's okay about using the fifty thousand as bait. He knew the general wanted him to use his own or others' money. Seeing John in the flesh had changed the whole paradigm. He sat there wishing he had allowed T-Dilly just to ride to Baileysboro and kill the big bastard in the first place, and then there would be no need for a second place.

Doby started to rise from his chair when Jeffers halted him with a palm out. "I'm an official notary. Have been since eighteen sixty." He looked at the judge. "If you'll get out the papers, we can all sign them. I'll notarize them and place them in my safe."

John halted the judge from pulling out the papers with his outstretched hand. "If Duchess is not allowed to leave, there ain't going to be no fight."

The judge looked relieved as though it was a way for him and Stevens to save face, get the general's $50,000 back to the bank in Austin, and scheme to kill Johnson later.

The judge looked on incredulously as Stevens suddenly became emboldened. Stevens stood and looked John full in the face. "Do I have your word of honor that you'll still go if I let her go?"

"I'll go. But it must be put in those documents that she's not to be charged again."

Stevens, gaining more confidence that he would not be crushed by the big Texan, replied in an oily voice. "If you aren't there by June fifteenth at noon, your twenty thousand is mine."

"I'll be there."

"You seem very confident."

"If I weren't confident, I wouldn't go."

Stevens grinned sarcastically. "Have you ever heard of El Toro de Sanchez?"

John did not reply. He was tired of the conversation. He watched the judge pull the papers from inside his coat. John snatched them and began reading them. The judge wanted to remonstrate but merely shrugged when John gave him a look. The judge quickly borrowed the sheriff's pen and dipped it in the ink bottle on the desk. He added the codicil that Duchess would not be charged with any crime. John took his time reading the added wording and finally nodded his approval. "Let Duchess go now and I'll sign."

Doby received the high sign from Stevens. He pulled out a set of heavy keys from his desk drawer. He walked smilingly toward her cell and turned the tumblers with a heavy metallic sound. She grabbed her reticule, left her cell, and stood behind John. She avoided looking at Stevens fearing he might change his capricious mind.

Doby received his bottle of ink and the pen with a dull nib from Judge Roy. The sheriff nodded at his writing equipment and said, "It writes big, but it writes."

Stevens signed, followed by John and Roy. It was witnessed by Doby, Lambert, and Sand Burr. Jeffers dated the document, pulled a metal clamp from his pocket, and notarized it. He asked Doby to walk with him as protection to the bank to get it into his safe.

Stevens and Roy gave the banker a severe look for the veiled insult, but they remained silent. The whole proceeding had not gone as Stevens had wanted, but at least he had the Texan headed to Mexico. He had to find a way to stop him before he got there. He had a feeling that the Mexican was John's equal but certainly not his superior. He decided not to depend on the fight; Johnson was the most dangerous man he had ever encountered. Stevens placed his coffee cup with a hard-tin finality on the sheriff's desk and gave Doby a severe look. "Sheriff, after June fifteenth, when I come back to get my money, you best look for another job."

The sheriff did not acknowledge Stevens's words. He kept his head down and sent a wish heavenward that Johnson would beat the living hell out of El Toro.

Stevens and the judge sneered and left the sheriff's office. They stepped out on the boardwalk seeing neither hide nor hair of their crew. Stevens shook his head in disgust. He nudged the judge, and they walked to the livery for their buggy. The judge said out of the corner of his mouth, "Why did you let his cousin go? He was ready to back out if we didn't. We could have taken the money back to Austin and found another way to kill that big bastard."

The humiliation Stevens had felt in the presence of the big Texan was more than he could live with, but he did not mention that to the judge. He simply said, "We got him where we want him, judge."

The judge raised his eyebrows expressing his doubt but knew it was time to be silent. He compressed his lips and kept walking. Up ahead, he saw Cherokee Charlie sheepishly looking out the barn maw. He had his head down; he looked shamefaced.

Playing the good politician, Stevens said nothing to Cherokee Charlie and his men. He decided to verbally lash them later. The judge, still out of earshot of the guards, asked, "You coming back tonight to rob the bank and burn the building down?"

Stevens snorted. "You got to be joshing me, judge. If we robbed that bank and took the safe in a wagon back to Austin, we would be hounded all the way by these stupid county sheriffs." He sighed in derision at the judge's question and stated superciliously, "Not even I could pull that off."

Reaching the barn, Cherokee Charley barked a command, and one nondescript gang member drove the buggy out of the barn. Stevens and the judge climbed up and in, and they and their escorts departed Hawkshaw in a rumble of hoofbeats.

CHAPTER 9

Seth and Floyd were approaching the road that led to Roxy. Floyd sat slightly bent over from his wagon seat looking at his homemade map. "Seth, I figure we need to go check on that minister who's in arrears first." He folded the map after believing he had it committed to memory. "Take a left to go to Roxy, but after another six miles or so, take a right on what probably will be more of a trail than a road."

"What's the story on the minister besides not paying his bills?"

Floyd reached for a cigar. His eyes narrowed as he considered Seth's question. "According to the records, he paid right on time up until three months ago. Now, nothing."

"Is he married?"

Floyd nodded but suddenly realized Seth could not hear a nod. "Yeah, on the papers he signed for the previous owner of the bank, he listed a wife named Yvette. His name is Carlton, Reginald Carlton."

"Sounds like a back-east dude."

"Probably is."

More than an hour later, Seth spotted the trail. He turned the team, and they encountered some sand bumps and depressions making for a rough ride.

Floyd pulled his map out again though he thought he remembered how far they still had to go. He pursed his lips. "It's another two hours. It'll be on our left about half a mile from the trail."

It was approaching dusk when they saw part of the adobe house to the left. He turned the team down the sand way for an even more turbulent ride. The wagon jittered and jolted the two riders. At last they pulled in front of the house, which looked partially burned.

Floyd spotted a paint horse that looked bone skinny in in the round-wood corral fence. He looked at the hundred-gallon water tank in the corral that held water, but it was obvious that the horse had not been fed in days. Floyd shook his head in disgust. "Anyone who would treat a horse like that needs to be shot."

Seth nodded. "Why don't you go see if you can round up some food for that paint. I'll go in the house and see if I can find any evidence where that scamp and his wife have taken off to."

Floyd gave him a skeptical look and eased off his seat as Seth set the brake. Seth figured Floyd's skepticism was probably justified. He stood facing the adobe structure. At one time, he imagined it had been a very costly building. The area he imagined as the kitchen was burned badly, and only half the house remained unharmed. He saw that the roof still covered about two-thirds of the dwelling but was badly burned in spots. He walked slowly to it reckoning it would be a waste of time. He thought about forging entering the place, but he heard a soft moan. He looked both ways in case it was an animal. Not seeing anything, he walked in. The place had no door. He saw that the stove was badly burned and that the flames had apparently caused some the roof over the kitchen and the dining area to collapse. Clumps of adobe detritus were everywhere.

Seth shook his head at the amount of destruction. He dismissed lightning as the culprit; it did not have the signature markings of a lightning strike. He looked for some sort of accelerant that might have spread the fire and saw a can of coal oil just beyond the doorway lying on its side in the yard. He nodded knowingly. He heard the moan again. It was not an animal or his imagination; it was the moan of a woman or child. He moved to the undamaged part of the house. As he walked through an elaborate, curved doorway, he noticed an open door to a bedroom. He walked softly to the doorway and saw a young blonde woman lying face-down on the bed. She was partially clothed in a blood-soaked dress. The hem of her skirt was hiked up exposing more flesh than she probably would have shown normally. Seth eased up to her to not alarm her. She was beautiful, but it was obvious by looking at her flushed complexion that she was in great pain and had passed out. Seth placed his hand on her temple. She was burning with fever.

He felt he needed to do what the old country doctor back in Arkansas had done when confronted with a fever-ridden child. He stripped her clothes off, picked her up naked as a jaybird, and walked briskly through the house and out the door to the water trough in the corral.

Floyd, who had just fed the horse, was looking for a shovel to rid the corral of horse manure when he saw Seth with the naked woman. He forgot about the shovel and made his way to his partner to get the scoop on what the hell was going on. Floyd caught up with him as he was making ready to give her a quick dip in the tank. He knew what Seth was going to do, and it had his approval, but when he saw an exit wound in her lower abdomen, he said, "She's been shot, Seth."

Seth stopped and looked where Floyd was looking. When he saw the two wounds, he shockingly stated, "The hell you say!"

"Go ahead and dunk her and get her in the house. Get some clothes on her, ones she ain't been wearin'."

Seth held her over the tank and was ready to immerse her up to her head. He stated just before he pushed her under, "Small caliber, so it probably wasn't some hombre like J.D. Rysinger."

He held her body under the water for a good ten seconds. Even in her unconscious state, she gave throaty noises of protest and feebly fought the sensation with resisting hands. Seth hurried her back to the house with Floyd in close pursuit. Floyd went around him getting the directions to the bedroom over his shoulder from Seth. Floyd found a chest and pulled out a pair of men's long flannel underwear. Seth found a towel near a washbasin and dried her off. They got her into the oversized underwear as if getting a pillow into a pillow case. Floyd suggested they find other bedsheets and pillow casings. While they looked, Floyd said that bed clothing soaked up fever and she would require new sheets and pillow casings daily.

They found a lantern in another room and enough coal oil to last them the night. They had the young woman under a light sheet lying with her head on a pillow they had discovered in another bedroom. Floyd piled the sheets in heap just outside the bedroom. He left to take care of the mules and check on the paint horse.

Seth spent the night in a chair by her bed and awoke the next morning. Yvette's inquisitive eyes were on him. Her sleepy eyes were a mixture of blue-green … hypnotically elegant. She sensed that the man in the chair was not a threat. She closed her eyes and went back to sleep.

Floyd had awakened earlier and had brought in two poultices from the wagon. He asked Seth to pull down her underwear top. Yvette was so deeply asleep that she weakly resisted but soon drifted into a twilight state between consciousness and unconsciousness. Floyd put the poultices on the entrance and exit wounds and pulled up the flannel underwear to grant her some decency.

Floyd nodded as he felt her forehead. "She's goin' to be all right. Her fever is almost gone." He soberly looked down at her and nodded as though considering what to do next. "I'm going to make a soupy broth. I looked at the stove. It's damaged, but I can make it work. She's gone days it seems without food. I think she's been workin' through the pain and drinkin' water, but she needs nourishment."

"How are we goin' to get her to eat, Floyd?"

"Well, it's like this. I'll make some beef jerky broth, and you'll put some on her lips. When she feels the broth on her lips, she's goin' to lick it off because that's human nature."

Seth nodded at the sage observation. "I reckon we can give it a go."

Later, Seth sat at Yvette's bedside and pasted some broth on her lips. At first, she did not make a move to lick it off causing Seth to wonder whether she had enough strength and was conscious enough to do what Floyd had predicted. Just as he was about to take the broth away, he saw her tongue snake the soupy moisture off. He smiled, put more there, and saw it disappear. She ate half the bowl, and Seth finished the rest.

Floyd leaned in the doorway; Seth told him she had eaten half a bowl. Floyd looked pleased, but that look transformed into a thoughtful mien. "Since we need to heal this young lady, I reckon one of us needs to go into town and get some supplies. She can't live on broth … at least much longer. She's goin' to need something more solid, and I'm not shore she can eat what we have in the wagon. She needs some canned goods and some greens."

Floyd volunteered to go because he felt he knew hay better than Seth. The small amount of hay stored in the lean-to loft had mold in it, and Floyd had burned it earlier that morning. Seth determined that Yvette needed some sheets and towels. And they needed more coal oil for the lamps. Armed with a long list of what they needed, Floyd harnessed and hitched the wagon and departed to Roxy.

Around ten o'clock, Yvette's eyes opened as she shifted her head on the pillow. She felt the strange clothes on and peeked under the edge of the cover to see she was wearing her husband's underwear. Her eyes immediately went to Seth, who was sitting in a cane-bottom chair with a high ladder back. He had fallen asleep. She eased her hand out and touched his arm. His eyes blinked, and his vision shifted to her. She was one of the prettiest women he had ever seen: tousled blonde hair, perfect nose, pouty lips, and beautiful but questioning eyes. Her voice was honey Southern. "Who are you?"

He introduced himself. She stared at him curiously for a while. "Why're you here?"

Seth did not want to tell her that he was there collecting bills. He ran his tongue over his lips as his mind raced. "Well, we were passin' through, and we saw that paint that looked like he was starvin' to death. We stopped, and I heard you groanin'."

She averted her eyes. She felt the two poultices on her body and knew they had doctored her. She felt a blush fill her peach-like complexion. The thoughts of being undressed by a stranger flustered her, but she instinctively knew she had not been violated by the kind and gentle man. Still, she felt a rush of embarrassment.

Seth saw that she was discomfited by her situation and decided to take control of the conversation. "You've been shot, ma'am." He knew her name was Yvette, but he chose to keep that a secret.

She lay back on her pillow almost obstructing her eyes from sight. Seth sighed, but he chose not to play games. "I gather it was probably your husband."

She did not respond. He could barely see her eyes blinking as she was thinking of what to reply. Seth said, "Me and Floyd think he shot you and set the place on fire."

90

"Who's Floyd?" she asked in a voice partially muffled by the pillow.

"He's my friend who treated your wounds and placed those poultices on you."

Yvette realized being coy was no longer necessary since Seth had figured out most of the tragic facts. She rearranged her head to see Seth better. "Where's Floyd?"

"He's gone to town to get some supplies and you some better food."

Yvette sighed and ran her fingers through her blonde hair. "Pardon my manners, Seth, but all this has been a shock to me. But thank you and Floyd for savin' me."

Seth nodded. "I have to admit, ma'am, you were in bad shape."

She softly exhaled. "My name is Yvette, Seth. I knew there were people here aiding me, but I felt too weak to say or do anything."

Seth leaned forward with his hands on his thighs. "You want to tell me what happened?"

She thought about the ramifications of a confession, but she liked Seth, and after some consideration, she figured it might be best if she shared her plight with him. "Reginald …" She paused realizing that Seth would not know his name. "… my husband, bought this spread one and a half years ago. He was sponsored by our church to preach to the Indians. But witnessing to the Indians was a whole lot easier talkin' about back in Tennessee than actually doin' it here in Texas."

"So that didn't pan out?"

Yvette face registered her disgust. "No. He tried maybe a couple of times, but he was so discouraged that he just stayed around our place here or rode into Roxy. He didn't know that I knew it, but he was sendin' letters back to Nashville that he was having great success. And they in return were sending money to us regularly."

"So he was lyin'?"

Yvette shamefacedly nodded.

"How did you find that out?"

"By accident, he left one of the letters from an elder in his coat pocket. They were braggin' on him for things I knew he hadn't done. I just put two and two together."

"Is that why he shot you?"

"No. That was another matter."

Seth waited for a moment; he saw she was struggling to confront the truth. "I'll not pry further if it's that painful."

She shrugged as though she thought she had gone that far and might as well finish the matter. "Earlier this year, we were in Baileysboro, and the doctor there—named Baker I believe."

Seth nodded to her that Dr. Baker was indeed the town doctor.

"He told me that considering how long Reginald and I had been married, it was obvious that I was barren." She placed her hand to her lips to stifle a sob.

Seth sighed. "So that upset him."

She nodded. She kept her hand over her mouth to keep her from crying. After a few seconds, she composed herself. "Yes, he was never the same after that." She stayed silent as the past came rushing back. "He spent more and more time in Roxy and would never take me with him. I stayed here sometimes for a week or so without seein' him."

"Was he drinkin'?"

She shook her head. "No, he's not given to alcohol. I'm not sure of what he was doin.' I just know that five days ago, he rode in and asked me to fix him dinner. I didn't have much to fix since he hadn't bought anything in a while. But I fired up the stove and was goin' to make some potato soup when I guess he shot me from behind. I knew I had been shot. I fell down like I was dead. I knew if I didn't, he would probably shoot me again." She fought through her tears. "I smelled him pouring coal oil all over the place. He even poured some on me. I watched him strike a match at the doorway, and flames went up everywhere. When I saw him leave, I crawled to the safety of this side of the house, took my clothes off, and crawled under the bed. I had enough strength to walk and take care of myself for a spell, but later, I got a fever and collapsed here." She covered her face and sobbed. "You and your friend saved my life."

After she cried herself out, she sheepishly stated, "Now if you'll excuse me, I need to go outside."

Seth knew she was needing to answer a call of nature, so he modestly nodded in assent. He asked if he could help her get outside. She gave her thoughtful, nodding assent and extended her arm. He helped her out of the room. She indicated that she could make it on her own, and he released his arm. She staggered around the house using her hands to steady herself. She looked like a baby bear walking in bulky underwear.

Seth waited by the front door. When she returned, she gave him her arm, but it had taken all her strength to walk, so he scooped her up and carried her to her bed, where he modestly covered her. She observed him briefly from the top of the coverlet but slowly drifted back into slumber. He looked at her from the bedroom doorway. He felt guilty because of his growing attraction to her. He also sensed she had an attraction to him, but she was married whether her husband was worth a damn or not. He knew he was playing with fire. He decided to go to the corral and shovel the horse manure that had infected the paint's hind feet.

Floyd pulled his team to a stop in front of the trading post. He had been in Roxy before but was surprised at how much larger it was than only a month or so previously. Besides the buildings that had been there in his first visit, he saw a church on the outskirts of the town, a small saloon, and a sheriff's office. He marveled at how quickly the community had burgeoned. He set the brake, stepped down, and entered the store. He was surprisingly recognized by several citizens inside.

Across the street, Toby Jarret peered over the batwings of the dinky saloon and caught sight of Floyd. Toby had been sent to Roxy to get some whiskey and cigars. After purchasing the items, he was reluctant to return to the hideout. He had spent some time looking over the batwings for any good-looking women passing by. But upon seeing the coppery colored banker that he and the other gang members had called an Italian, his eyebrows shot up. He knew it was imperative that he remain in the shadows and trail the banker back to wherever he had come.

He returned to the zinc-topped bar and ordered another whiskey. He tossed two bits on the counter and tossed down his drink in one gulp. He made a face, wiped his lips, and went back to the batwings.

After fifteen minutes, Floyd returned to his wagon. A clerk helped him load what to Toby looked like two weeks' worth of goods. He sidled out the batwings and stood on the small, uneven wood porch. He watched Floyd drive out of town. He went to his horse, quickly mounted, and began trotting after the wagon as it headed west.

Floyd sensed he was being followed. He pulled back the side of his summer coat for better access to his army .44. He would occasionally

93

turn around to take a look-see, but he never saw anyone. Nonetheless, uneasiness gripped him all the way to the Carlton spread. Floyd had a feeling that he and Seth would have a return visit from J.D. Rysinger.

Two days later, J.D. rose from the stained, crumpled bed at his old home place, their hideout. He took a heavy slug of whiskey and ran his hand over his whiskers. He sat on the edge of his bed and addressed his three remaining gang members. "Boys, here's the deal. I got a hundred dollars for each of you when we kill them damn bankers. If you stick with me and see me through, I got some more money for you." He took another heavy draught and said with solemn vow, "You boys can take that to the bank."

Toby had already told them the whereabouts of the bankers. But Punkin' Head, who at that point had only five dollars left, was determined to keep the promise he had made to himself. When his five dollars gave out, he would be gone. He knew Toby would go with him, and he had a suspicion Adrian would also go. This mysterious money cache of J.D.'s seemed farcical at best, but the promise of a hundred dollars caused Punkin' Head to stick around a while longer to see it out.

Chapter 10

Ten miles outside Hawkshaw around a mesquite fire, a morose James Stevens stood uneasily with the judge as he mulled over the dreadful meeting with John Lee Johnson. Over twenty-five handpicked men stood quietly affected by their boss's sour disposition. T-Dilly Whitaker knew that Stevens had been unsettled by that meeting and that he was nettled at how Cherokee Charley and Butter Bean had been humiliated. T-Dilly was waiting for Stevens to give him the high sign that he wanted a private parley.

He did not have to wait long. Stevens met his eyes and gave a slight toss of his head. T-Dilly unobtrusively pulled himself out of the circle of men and slowly moved toward the judge's buggy at the periphery of the fire. Stevens's absence from the circle drew interest and a certain trepidation from some of the men—especially Cherokee Charley and his crew. They kept the two men in mind as they covertly watched them huddle.

"What gives, boss?"

At first, Stevens silently cogitated what action he should pursue. "T-Dilly, you've never disappointed me."

T-Dilly realized those words were the preamble to what he really wanted to say. He watched as Stevens's downcast expression become even more sour. "I've never met this El Toro de Sanchez, and I've taken your word that he's unbeatable." He paused. His voice rose above the vocal range of confidentiality. "But I've met this Johnson fellow, and to be perfectly frank, he scares the hell out of me."

T-Dilly's eyes widened. In all his days, he never would have thought the haughty, self-assured Stevens would make an admission like that.

T-Dilly made a thoughtful moue with his mouth. "What you're sayin' is that you want me to kill the bastard."

Stevens's slight nod became more pronounced as his qualms took over his expression and actions. "I've never met a man I wanted dead more than him."

T-Dilly suddenly had an epiphany. John Lee Johnson had dominated Stevens, and Stevens could not stand being relegated to the junior-boy rank. He realized that Cherokee Charley and Butter Bean had suffered a loss of face, but Stevens was the one who was out of sorts. He had always commanded and demanded the alpha position, but he had taken a lick to his ego. T-Dilly realized the only way Stevens could recapture that edge was by Johnson dying. But also in the back of T-Dilly's mind, he knew the $50,000 bet was working on him too. What once was a sure thing in his mind had become a real risk.

T-Dilly figured that since he had not faced the big Texan, Stevens was counting on him to balance the accounts so to speak. He reached for a cigar and languidly lit his smoke. "Boss, why don't you go back to Austin and get a good bath and just take it easy. I'll fix Johnson's wagon for him before he gets to Mexico."

Stevens exhaled a sigh of relief. He gave a thankful nod. He remained speechless for a moment, but then, he released his other ruminations. "T-Dilly, I don't like Pendly. He gets on my nerves. He doesn't take orders worth a damn, and he thinks too highly of himself."

"You're sayin' you want him in the heat of the battle when push comes to shove with this Johnson character?"

Stevens gave a knowing smile. "T-Dilly, you take care of matters. If you kill Johnson and whittle Pendly down to size, come July, you'll get a sizeable bump in salary, my friend."

T-Dilly exhaled a satisfactory cloud of smoke and nodded approvingly. "I'm countin' on that." He reassured his boss. "I'll not fail on any count."

The next morning, Stevens and the judge departed to Austin guarded by five of the men T-Dilly had appointed. T-Dilly took into consideration that he had twenty men including himself to kill Johnson. He called his men together to lay out the plan he had devised with Stevens. He made sure that his holster was tied to his leg and that his .44 was ready to make a hook and draw if he received any back talk from Pendly.

T-Dilly looked at the semicircle of men who were focused on him, but he let his eyes move to the sullen and seemingly always irritated Pendly. "I want you boys to eat and have some coffee. I want Cherokee Charley and his men to go with Pendly and set up an ambush for this Johnson fella." That implied that Pendly would be calling the shots. He paused and looked Irvin squarely in the eyes. "That'll be six of you—that should settle the matter once and for all with this bastard who has everyone spooked." To T-Dilly's surprise, Pendly acted as if the assignment pleased him. He did not cuss or moan or want someone else to take on the chore; he just nodded agreeably.

In reality, Irvin was happy to be away from T-Dilly even if he considered Cherokee Charley and his crew to be worthless; at least he would be in charge. He had in mind the bonus promised to the man who brought the big Texan down. He wanted to see the look on T-Dilly's face when he accomplished the deed. Before he and Cherokee Charley's group headed for a quick cup of java, Irvin asked T-Dilly, "Where you gonna be, T-Dilly? After we kill that jaybird, we'll need to make contact with you."

T-Dilly jovially answered, "Me and the boys will be in that cow town Boscoville. We'll wait for you and then head to Austin with the good news."

Irvin mulled over T-Dilly's answer. He wondered why they just did not bullrush this Johnson fellow and get it over with. But he knew T-Dilly did not like him, and he suspected T-Dilly was putting him on the firing line on purpose. Irvin returned a smile to T-Dilly but inwardly cussed him. He congenially tipped his hat and made his way to the breakfast fire.

That same morning, Johnson hugged Duchess and watched her climb up into the town banker's buggy. The banker had loaned her the buggy and had graciously paid two of the town's deputies to escort her home. She was accompanied by Sheriff Doby's wife and daughter. The deputies were to stay for a few days to make sure she was safe.

John nodded his approval at the arrangements as her entourage rode out of town. He figured Stevens's crew realized she was of no further value and would leave her alone.

John, the sheriff, Sand Burr, and Lambert heard the rattle of a wagon rumbling into town surrounded by Sergeant Joe Brewer and fifteen federal men. They had come as instructed in the papers given to John in Baileysboro. They had come to take his wagering money so he would not have to worry about it as he journeyed to Mexico. Sergeant Brewer, not as secretive as he had been in Baileysboro, led the wagon up even to the sheriff's office. Apparently, someone had tipped him off that Stevens and the judge had left.

The sergeant nodded in greeting to John, the sheriff, Sand Burr, and Lambert, who stood under the roof that shadowed the sheriff's office. The sergeant barked an order, and three of his men and the driver turned the wagon aside and headed toward the bank. "Howdy, John. Glad you got shed of Stevens. As you know, we'll take your betting fee to Sanchez, and me and the boys—and that includes Lieutenant Bragg—have raised an additional forty-five thousand to bet on you. So rest assured we're guarding this money with our lives."

John smiled tightly. "That's a hell of a lot of money you soldier boys raised."

"Yeah, well … but if you win, it's enough to grubstake us for a long damn time." Sergeant Brewer returned a broad smile. "A lot of the boys you see here rode with you when you had the showdown with Sabbath Sam and the twenty-one." He nodded as if to add to his words, *We believe in you.* Sergeant Brewer, knowing that John was inherently modest, did not wait for John to respond. He nodded again and gave an order. His men quickly moved to the bank to do their business and head to Mexico. They had chosen to go their own way and not have John ride with them for strategic purposes.

John watched them head to the bank, but then he looked at the horizon beyond the town. He knew he would face the Stevens gang probably repeatedly all the way to Sanchez. He remained expressionless as he nodded for his two companions to mount their mules. He rode toward an alley that separated the saloon from the dry goods store. He was dutifully followed by Sand Burr and Lambert. Once they reached the back of the stores, they trotted their mules due south.

They rode for eight hours before taking a break. They ate briefly and rode deep into the night. Sand Burr and Lambert were exhausted and relieved when the indefatigable big man called a halt. They watered and fed the mules, and John took the first watch.

In the twinkling firelight, Lambert stretched his weary body under his saddle blanket. He turned to the sleepy Sand Burr. "Is he always like this?"

"Yep."

He mulled over the terse answer. "You think he's worried about fightin' that Mexican?"

"Nope."

Lambert sighed and shook his head marveling at the faith Sand Burr had in John. He gave himself an *Oh well* smile, rolled over, and went to sleep.

They kept up their rigid, straight-ahead, disciplined ride for seven days. On the eighth day, they rode over a sand-swept hill and saw an unusual sight. A man on the dark side of middle age with sparse hair was tied upright to a mesquite tree. He was stark naked and looked like he might have been there for two or so days.

Normally, Sand Burr and Lambert followed John, but seeing the naked man, out of curiosity, they rode up even with John flanking him. John sat there for a moment trying to figure out how the man had gotten himself in such a fix.

Before he asked the man any questions, John looked at the hoof marks on the ground. He ascertained it was probably six men. His eyes followed the tracks until they merged and left a trail leading south.

The man, sunburned on his shoulders and chest, attempted to lick his crusted lips. It was obvious that he was suffering from thirst. But even in his great need, he stared above their heads never making eye contact as if to preserve what dignity he had left.

John leaned forward, his massive fists on his saddle horn. "You look like you're in a heap of trouble, mister."

The man let his eyes fall on John and the others. He unsuccessfully tried to lick his lips again. He nodded ruefully and deadpanned, "Yeah, you could say that."

"What happened here?"

His voice was more of a croak. "I was robbed. They took everything I had."

John still made no move to help him. "You know who they were?"

The man tried to shrug his shoulders but was too weak to do so effectively. Once more, his vision went back above John and his associates' heads.

John kept looking at the trail and at a distant hogback that loomed on the horizon about two miles away. He nodded to Sand Burr, who dismounted with a canteen in tow. He pulled a knife from a sheath on his boot and cut the leather thong bindings holding the frail arms of the man to the tree. The man collapsed to one knee and accepted the canteen as though it were the Holy Grail. He took several hearty gulps, and then, feeling he might have drunk too much, looked sheepishly at Sand Burr, who gave him an okay nod. The man gulped another two big swallows.

John looked down grimly at the man. "What's your name?"

"Ollie Tuggle."

Lambert dismounted and looked into his war bag. He pulled out a pair of long, red-flannel underwear and gave them to Ollie. "These are my extras. I figure you can use these."

Ollie looked shamefaced. "I'm beholdin' to you, mister." He staggered to his feet and awkwardly put on the underwear. Since Lambert was larger than Ollie, the drawers looked droopy in the rear and gave him a comical look.

John said, "Let's make camp here and talk about all this before we head to that hogback." The way he said *hogback* indicated it was more than just a geological formation; the word portended ominous danger.

Sand Burr and Lambert looked at the distant, crooked skyline of the linear ridge of rocks in the distance. They had not initially thought the ridge was anything more than a landmark, but their trust in John caused them to think of it differently.

Sand Burr started a fire. He set up the tripod and shortly had coffee going.

John and Lambert unsaddled and unpacked the mules. After tethering them, they gave them some water and a handful of corn.

They were drinking coffee, and Sand Burr gave Ollie a few dried apples to curb his hunger. John was looking at the rocky ridge in the distance. Soon, his gray eyes settled on Ollie. Ollie met his look with one of his own. "You must be that John Lee Johnson feller."

John nodded.

"I heard 'em talkin' 'bout you."

"That so."

Ollie nodded. "They told me if you came along to tell you they was waitin' on you." Ollie sipped coffee. "They said you was big."

John did not respond to that. His mind was on the important matter at hand. "How many are there?"

Ollie shrugged. "I reckon about six." He let his eyes move up to the sky as though seeking external help. "Yeah, believe it was six."

Lambert asked, "Ollie, what in the hell were you doin' out here in the first place?"

Ollie gave a downtrodden look and shook his head in dismay. "It's a long story."

John kept his eyes moving; he was calculating how to get to that ridge without being seen. But he again focused on Ollie. "Well, get to tellin' why you're here."

Ollie blinked at the command. He had had in mind to keep that a secret, but the compelling gray eyes bearing down on him caused him to sigh and relent. He leaned back on his haunches cushioned by the voluminous drawers.

"Well, it was like this. I was working on a ranch over close to Finleyville, Texas. But about a month and a half ago, I decided to go to the barn dance in Roxy. I'd been savin' my money … wantin' a good time. I had a nice pinto and a good kak and bridle—I had it all. I walked into that barn dance with slicked-down hair and a bath that mornin.' I was dancin' and drinkin' some of that hard lemonade. I was feelin' like a new man.

"It was then I met Inez Schmidt. She was purtier than a new pair of spurs." He paused. "Well, maybe a tad heavy." He shook his head as if to clear his mind. "But anyways, we started dancin', and, well, to be honest, we was dancin' pretty darn close … real close. She told me she wanted to get some air, which I took for she wanted some spoonin.' We went outside for a walk, and we ended up in a toolshed next to the barn. Once we got in the toolshed, we got to kissin' and carryin' on a whole lot more. Pretty soon, we was doin' more than kissin' if you get my meanin'." He paused. "Well, we did it."

Sand Burr and Lambert glanced at each other.

Ollie was oblivious to that. He continued. "When we got through, Inez told me that since I had seduced her, at least I should have the decency to ask her to marry me." Ollie rubbed his chin. "That sounds funny now because it seems like she was the one who attacked me." He shrugged. "So there I was in that toolshed with that blue moon shinin' through the slats, and there she was with her skirt up to her hips. I guess I was filled with romance and such—I hauled off and asked her to marry me. I thought I was just humorin' her since that was all she asked for—a proposal. I had no idea she was really wantin' marriage." He swallowed and sighed.

"But when I proposed, she grabbed me around the neck and said, 'Yes!' I didn't know what happened next. It was such a blur, but that very night, we ended up in front of a justice of the peace, and he married us on the spot." He sighed and shrugged. "I went to the dance lookin' for some hard lemonade and ended up in the silken web of matrimony."

There was a moment of silence, but Ollie was not through. "When we was goin' home—to her home, she mentioned that her former husband, Hootie, had passed on. I thought on her words as we was ridin' along … I thought on them a whole lot.

"It was mornin' when we got to her small ranch. I met her mom, Birdie, who was sickly and mean as a snake, and her brother, Otto, who had a bad back and couldn't work. Inez fixed me a big breakfast and gave me a list of things she said 'we' needed done. I can tell you boys that that first week, I repaired the barn roof, dug a new well, and repaired the front and back porches.

"I had to restack the hay in the loft, milk the cow daily, and gather up the eggs in the hen house." Ollie paused and shook his head in disgust. "Her brother never turned a tap, and her mother always told me to wash my hands no matter if they was dirty or not. She hardly took notice of me except to tell me to wash my hands." He sighed as he recollected her acerbic words.

"This went on for better of a month. I would get up at five and work till seven." He shook his head as all that labor came back to his memory. "And I wasn't gettin' much romance at night either if you know what I mean.

"The last night I was there, after workin' like a dog all day, I told Inez I wanted to get, you know, romantic. She told me to go clean up at the stock waterin' trough and she would be waitin'. Well, I go clean up and come back in the house and she's sound asleep. I heard her mom snoring in the next room and her brother doin' the same in the living room. All sleepin' good after not doin' a thing all day.

"I got to thinkin' about what she said about that husband named Hootie and how he had passed on. I came to the conclusion that he hadn't died and gone to heaven. He just got tired of the work and passed on—as in takin' off. I decided I couldn't let ol' Hootie be smarter than me, so I went into the kitchen to where Inez kept her money in a fruit jar. I took thirty dollars and left the rest. I know I deserved more, but I wanted to be fair. I packed up my belongin's in a war bag, went to the corral, and saddled up ol' Dan, my pinto. I took off and just decided to head to South Texas to punch cows for a friend. I reckon I was on the trail for about nine days.

"I woke up early two mornins' ago when I heard a lot of horses gatherin' around me and a whole lot of gosh-awful laughin'. There was this hombre named Irvin Pendly hurrahin' me. He jumped down from his horse and beat the hell outa me for no reason at all. They took my horse, clothes, all my gear, and tied me up to that mesquite tree over there. They all took turns hittin' me and cussin' me." He paused and raised a finger. "They told me that a big man named John Lee Johnson probably would come along and untie me. They also made it plain that I was to pass on that message to you." He consciously looked at John. "They said they was goin' to do the same to you."

John ignored the message. His eyes were focused on the distant ridge.

Sand Burr drolly asked, "Wonder what's goin' to happen to Inez Schmidt?"

Ollie worked his mouth around cogitating the matter. "I reckon she'll go to that barn dance and find another husband. I imagine she'll tell the new guy that ol' Ollie passed on."

Some smiles passed around the campfire, but John wordlessly dismissed himself. He went to his saddle on the ground and pulled a collapsible telescope from his saddlebag. He eased to the tree to which Ollie had been bound. Through the branches, he panned the hogback and its foreground for an hour. Satisfied about his plan of action, he socked the telescope together and returned it to his saddlebag. He returned to his friends and sat.

As he drank coffee, he said, "Sand Burr, I want you to make a campfire that'll shine all night but not too big. One that's too big or obvious might spook our friends that we're up to somethin' or tryin' to trick 'em. I want them to think we're here. When it gets ten o'clock tonight, I want all of us to saddle the mules and get the pack mules ready. We're goin' to walk single file down that trail." He pointed at the pathway the Stevens gang had taken. "I estimate when we've walked three hours or so we'll come upon an arroyo I spotted. There's enough rocks along the lip there to shield you boys. We'll find a crook in the arroyo that'll serve as a blind to hide the mules, and hopefully, the edge of the gully will be high enough that they can't see 'em."

He laid out the rest of his plan and told them to get some sleep. He did not have to tell them twice. Sand Burr and Lambert threw out their saddle blankets and found some canvas for Ollie to use as a bed covering. John did not sleep with them; he went about an eighth of a mile away and made his bed.

They snoozed until ten. They did not have to be awakened when it was time. They were already up when John appeared in the darkness. He nodded his approval, and they began to walk down the same trail the outlaws had taken. They were walking in single file with Ollie in the rear pulling the two tethered pack mules. The only noises were the cicadas and an occasional desert owl.

John kept up a steady pace. By the silver-blue glow from the rustler's moon, he found the arroyo he had spotted earlier. They went down into it until they reached the place with some boulders evenly spaced above and beyond the lip of the ravine. John showed them where to place the mules. He took his mule and disappeared from sight.

Sand Burr, used to John's way of doing things and knowing the plan, took his disappearance in stride and made his way to the far left. He laid out his seven-shot Spencer, leaned against the dirt incline with his blanket wrapped around him, and waited for dawn.

Lambert was not used to John's habits, but he did as he was told. He was beginning to trust the big man. He took the far right using the boulder there as his aegis. However, Ollie, who was now armed with one of Seth's spare pistols, did not like it a damn that big John was no longer around. He was placed squarely in the middle just the way John had laid it out. He fussed to himself mentally but made no noise. He did not want to be the reason to draw those dreadful bullies down from the ridge.

When the early sun painted the clouds a salmon color, the three men became alert. John had told them to be on the lookout for some of the Stevens bunch who would ride out of some of the cuts in the ridge close by. He was counting on the gang being focused on the site where they had seen the campfire all night and would expose themselves too soon.

Cherokee Charley was leading the first group. He came down the cutaway in the ridgeline first. He was leading three men, and Butter Bean and another greasy gent were veering off to box in the campsite from the opposite side.

Sand Burr drew a bead on Cherokee Charley. His Spencer made its unique report—a crackling reverberation off the hogback. The shot hit Cherokee Charley flush in the left shoulder causing a large halo of blood splatter. The impact of the shot caused him to lose his hat. Cherokee Charley was falling to his right when he caught his balance. He painfully used his right hand to pull his horse around and galloped back to the safety of the ridge. His men did likewise just as John had predicted.

It was not long before the gang was back to their preassigned positions and firing down at Sand Burr. It was obvious they were bent out of shape about being fooled and having exposed themselves. A voluminous cacophony of gunfire erupted from their hidden positions. All Sand Burr could do was hunker down and wait it out. His boulder showed heavy gunshot pock marks with rock shards splintering and spraying the air.

Lambert, seeing puffs of gun smoke along the ridgeline, began a series of calculated shots. That caused him to draw his fair share of attention from the gunmen. Like Sand Burr, he was shielding his eyes as shots ricocheted off the boulder fronting him in mind-bending buzzes and metallic whines.

Some of the shots sent heavy plumes of sand into the air from the lip of the protective gully. He remembered that John had told them to hang on for thirty minutes. He was desperately counting on that promise.

Lambert and Sand Burr managed to get off some shots, but they noticed that Ollie was not shooting at all. It rankled them that he was rolled up like a ball with his gun hidden somewhere in his cocoon of red drawers.

Lambert shouted for him to start firing up at the ridge. Ollie shouted back that he was not a good shot. Lambert told him that it did not matter if he was any count at shooting—just do it—but if he did not start shooting, it was likely the gang would come down off that ridge, and being outnumbered, they would all be killed.

Ollie reluctantly stood up and fired around the boulder only to fall to his haunches and cringe. Both Sand Burr and Lambert saw that Ollie would not be much help.

The firing from the ridge continued in a steady barrage. Sand Burr and Lambert were doing enough shooting to keep the outlaws honest but at great risk. However, Ollie's shots were sparse and not very well aimed. Lambert felt like verbally chastising him, but after taking time to deliberate, he decided it was no use scolding him. He took into consideration that Ollie was just a cowhand and probably had never shot at anything other than a rattlesnake or rat. He concluded it was up to him and Sand Burr to hold them at bay.

The volume of gunshots was increasing, and Lambert was becoming uneasy about holding the position for the full thirty minutes. He reasoned that since the outlaws had the high ground, they could spot movement more easily and be protected more easily. Lambert sighed. He knew they were not playing out of the same deck as were the infernal killers. At that moment, he pulled out his pocket watch, gave it a critical look, and wordlessly mouthed a silent prayer that the big man would be on time. He snapped his watch cover shut knowing that if he or Sand Burr were to be wounded or killed, it would be all over.

Lambert saw the crown of a hat moving above the skyline. He rose and took a quick shot at the target. He realized he probably had not hit the man, but it would make the skulking bastard have second thoughts about sneaking down the incline and finding a better spot. Lambert was peeking around the boulder to see if he could get another credible shot when he heard a rifle concussion. Ollie gave a soulful yelp and fell with his back to the gully. Lambert licked his lips thoughtfully as he observed Ollie. It appeared Ollie had been tagged by that shot. Lambert did not relish running the gauntlet of gunfire, but he knew he had to reach his new friend or not be able to live with himself.

He holstered his .44, took a deep breath, and began chugging away with his head bent down to get to Ollie. Several shots zinged mighty close, but he made it and sat breathlessly down beside Ollie.

Ollie had his eyes heavenward with a mournful look on his face. "Lambert, I don't have long to live. I've been gut shot. I can feel the blood runnin' down my body. I reckon this is the end of the trail for old Ollie." Fueled by his own sad words, he began to whimper. He had incipient tears in his eyes. "Oh, sweet Jesus, I'm comin' home."

Lambert sighed. "Ollie, before you go see Jesus, I got one question to ask you."

Ollie lolled his head to one side; his lugubrious expression was altered some irritated by the neutral intonation of Lambert's voice. He tearfully whined, "What?"

"Does that gut shot hurt?"

Ollie's tears were flowing. "How can you ask me a stupid question like that just before I cash in my chips?"

"Well, does it?"

Ollie gave him a blank look. "No. Guess I'm numb is why."

Lambert nodded. "Well, I've seen several men get gut shot in my life, and to my best recollection, they bled."

Ollie let his eyes move up again and stared at the clouds. "I'm bleedin,' Lambert, damn your soul."

Lambert leaned with his back to the same dirt wall Ollie was occupying. He drolly countered, "What I'm tryin' to say, Ollie, is that they bled red blood."

Ollie cocked his tear-stained eyes at Lambert. "What're you tryin' to say?"

Lambert sighed and met Ollie's stare. "Your blood is yellow, Ollie."

Ollie glanced down. He saw that he was not gut shot or bleeding. He had wet on himself. His sorrowful expression quickly transitioned into shame. He looked down once more and back at Lambert.

Lambert realized it was not the time to reprimand him. He quickly rose, put his hand on top of his hat, and skedaddled back to his original position with several gunshots coming right on his heels.

Ollie, feeling the deepest opprobrium, jumped up and began a staccato of gunfire. He shot recklessly and often. He wanted desperately to regain his manhood and rid himself of shame. Sand Burr, who was not cognizant of the situation, was amazed at the sudden infusion of bravery Ollie was displaying.

Blackie Jensen, one of the riflemen on the hogback, felt the air furrow of those shots whizzing by. He turned to Butter Bean Baker, who was forty feet away. He yelled, "I tell you, Butter Bean, that's that John Lee Johnson shootin' behind that middle boulder down there."

Butter Bean considered his words. "What makes you think so?"

Blackie replied, "That son of a bitch can shoot. It has to be him."

Butter Bean nodded. "Well, just let me train my rifle on that big bastard."

He and Blackie laid down a heavy fusillade on Ollie's protective boulder. After emptying his rifle and putting in a new tube, Blackie shouted to Butter Bean that he was going to slide to his left and see if he could get a better shot. As he moved from boulder to boulder trying to pick a pathway to the ledge of the ridge, he suddenly was snatched up by two strong hands from the shadows of a looming boulder. While in the process of being grabbed, he lost his rifle and found himself looking into the fierce face of John Lee Johnson. He felt like a rag doll suspended in midair by the big man. John placed him down and coldcocked him with a savage punch to his face. Blackie, knocked backward, teetered on the skyline edge and fell screaming down to the rocks below.

Lambert saw the man falling spasmodically and jerking his body in midair. He saw him crash on the smaller boulders beneath the skyline. At first, he was flummoxed. He thought perhaps one of the owlhooters had made a misstep, but as he looked to his left down the line, he saw Sand Burr waving his hat—the signal they were to stop firing. It occurred to him that John was on top of the ridge with the Stevens bunch. John had told them that when they knew he was on the ridge to stop firing so they would not hit him. They did not have to worry about Ollie; he had run out of ammunition and was sitting glumly with his back to the gully wall.

Butter Bean had been firing consistently, but when he heard the ungodly scream, he paused and rose from his protected position to see better. It was hard to fathom that a man could scream that loud and much less Blackie. He saw the man seemingly molded from metal aiming Blackie's rifle at him.

John pulled the trigger. The bullet hit Butter Bean in the forehead. He collapsed in a bloody mess with his rifle clattering beside him. John quickly moved to him and removed what money Butter Bean had in his pocket. He tossed the corpse over the ledge.

Lambert watched Butter Bean's body fly in the air and settle soddenly on the detritus below. The way the man was falling indicated he was dead. He sighed and shook his head all the while marveling how the inexorable, big man was taking care of business.

Green Hodges, known for his green teeth, was firing away oblivious to the sudden rifle silence to his left. He was taking aim when he felt a pistol bore on the back of his head. His green-tooth smile changed into a comical lip transformation that looked like a vertical ellipse. His gravy-green eyes moved to the edges of their sockets. He said his words as though hoping they were heard over his shoulders. "You wouldn't kill a man who reads the Bible, would you?"

John pulled the trigger. Green Hodges's head burst like a melon. John rolled him around, got to his pockets, and found fifty dollars. He grabbed him by his belt loop and the top of his shirt and tossed him over the ledge.

Sand Burr watched another body fly over the top and crash on the rocks. He laid his rifle aside and pulled out his pocket knife to clean his nails. He concluded that if the crooked outfit stationed above knew what they were in for, they would throw up their hands and go screaming off the mountain. He heard some desultory rifle fire from the top, but it was less and less. He allowed himself a small grin of satisfaction knowing that the boss would shortly end the matter.

Cherokee Charley was the first to pick up on the lack of firepower coming from their lofty position. He was seated with his back to a boulder. He was bleeding and in great pain, but through his narrowed, pain-filled eyes, he ascertained that the big Texan was in their midst. He croaked out to Dough Boy Jackson, his nearest gang member, that if he had any sense, he would make a run for it.

Dough Boy looked at Cherokee Charley as though he were speaking to a daft man. "Have you lost your cotton-pickin' mind, Cherokee? We got them waddies pinned down just where we want 'em." Dough Boy laughed in derision and shook his head at Cherokee as though Cherokee had lost his nerve. As he lifted his Spencer to fire down at the men below, he heard a noise to his left. His squinty eyes embedded in his fat face slowly moved to their edges. He reacted as though he had seen Lucifer himself. He swung around with his rifle pointed at the big man, but he caught three successive pistol slugs that drove him a step back each time until he collapsed close to Cherokee Charley's feet.

John stooped and went through his pockets and found twenty dollars. He grabbed the stocky Dough Boy by his boots. He wound up and circled his body around much like a discus thrower. He hurled the chunky body far off the ledge. It landed with a *thunk* on the jumbled rocks below.

John walked like a predatory lion to the hatless Cherokee Charley, who was leaning back with a disgusted look on his face. Cherokee's shoulder was profusely bleeding, and his face was pale—not his healthy, coppery complexion. He looked up at John and nodded. He turned his head aside as in resignation and said in a pain-ridden voice, "Go ahead and kill me—I shore in hell you would."

With discerning eyes, John moved closer. He looked at Charley's wound. The hole in his shoulder was raw. "I reckon you would, Cherokee, and I still might just kill you." He paused as he thought about Cherokee's words. "At least I like your honesty."

Cherokee, not really understanding, at first looked off and remained silent. Then he decided he wanted to talk. He leaned forward to be better heard. "I'm a killer, a whoremonger, a sorry-ass individual, but I ain't a liar."

John nodded as he looked around. "Where's the horses? Do you have Ollie's horse with you?"

Cherokee shrugged. "They're down the incline—'bout where you're standing but down about two hundred feet in a rock cove of sorts. Pendly's got your friend's pinto."

"Where can I find Pendly?"

"Hell if I know, but if I was guessing, he's in a cantina at a crossroads two miles south of here."

"If I let you go, what are your plans?"

"What you're askin' is if I'm gonna head to Irvin or Stevens and join up with them and keep tryin' to stop you from gittin' to Mexico."

"That's what I mean."

"If you let me go, first thing I gotta do is find a doctor and get this shoulder seen to. After that, I'm headed to the Nations." He paused. "But I shore in hell am not goin' to join back up with any of the Stevens bunch. I don't care for Pendly. I don't care for T-Dilly Whitaker. And I shore in hell don't like that Yankee bastard Stevens."

John held out his hand but not for a handshake. Cherokee Charley handed up his .44. John emptied it and handed it back. Without being asked, Charley handed up his rifle, which John kept. He grasped Cherokee's hand and pulled him up. "Get your horse. Leave the others. Get the hell to the Nations."

Cherokee nodded humbly. He did not say thank you. He knew it would be awkward for them both. He wearily began descending the incline. When he got to the gang's makeshift remuda, he took only his horse as requested. As he rode away, he gave thanks for his good fortune. He also knew he never wanted to meet John Lee Johnson again.

At the bottom of the incline, Ollie shucked his fouled underwear and was standing stark naked again. Lambert gave him a disgusted look. "Ollie, I shore in hell am tired of seein' you naked."

Ollie stood. Partly shamefaced and partly vexed, he retorted, "You think I like standin' around naked?" He muttered under his breath for a moment. "But I ain't goin' to walk around in stained drawers."

Sand Burr looked at Ollie's nakedness curiously and then to Lambert for an explanation. He received just a blank look. Lambert would not violate a matter of confidence.

They retrieved their mules, and Ollie wrapped the canvas top he had slept under around him. They made small talk until they saw John riding a claybank gelding leading three saddle horses and two packhorses as he rode down the arroyo toward them. John had picked Green Hodges's claybank gelding because he gauged him to be able to carry his weight over a long distance.

When John saw Ollie standing with a canvas top wrapped ridiculously around himself, he gave a puzzled look. He pulled up and handed the tether to the five horses to Lambert. He looked at Ollie once more and pointed to the area where the late Blackie had landed. "Ollie, go over in that area and find a guy dressed in black. He's about your size, and he's fully clothed. Besides, he's still got his gun belt and weapon."

Ollie, chastened by the command, shamefully began walking toward the area to find the late Blackie.

John told Sand Burr and Lambert his plans and what he wanted them to do. He told them twice; seeing that saying it a third time would irritate more than educate them, he nodded, and they nodded back.

He quickly saddled up and galloped due west. When he saw a cut in the ridgeline, he turned his mount and headed south to the crossroads he was faintly familiar with.

The stark, adobe cantina sat just off the crossroads. The wind was blowing sand, and the sky was filled with the warp and woof of cross-current winds accompanied by swirling dust. Two horses were tied to an uneven hitch post with their heads down in a protective posture from the capricious and abrasive wind.

The sun sat in the sky like a fried egg. Garish yellows and reds streaked through the scudding clouds. John Lee spied the building and made out that one of the two horses was a pinto. He rode solemnly toward the wind-whipped structure. The big claybank thudded the sand with a heavy, plangent sound. As he grew closer, he saw the batwings of the cantina were moving in the wind.

He edged his mount between the two other horses and dismounted. He looked around at the forlorn environment. His attention went back to the batwings. He caught sight of an oleaginous face looking at him over the tops of the swinging doors. The face disappeared. He heard some Spanish.

He knew enough of the language to know someone had just been warned about something. He stepped up on the crude boardwalk a few inches off the ground. He walked to the batwings as he heard the dreary whine of wind in the background.

Inside sitting in a dark corner was Irvin Pendly. He had had a premonition that the crew assigned to him would fail. He left Cherokee Charley in charge on purpose. He wanted the glory of bringing down John Lee Johnson, and he did not want to share the spoils of victory with idiots. Irvin reached for his small, clay mug of milky pulche. He took a sip and nodded his approval. The bartender interrupted him to warn him about a big man riding up. Irvin's thin face shaded by the filthy, black hat brim became thoughtful. He pulled a cigar from his front pocket and languidly lit it.

John entered slowly—he pushed the right batwing open and let his eyes adjust to the dark interior. He entered and faced Pendly. The bartender's oily face showed his discomfort. His brown eyes moved quickly from the big Texan to the deadly Pendly. His heart raced as he tried to decide to head through the beaded portiere just behind him or see this fatal showdown. He decided to stay. He looked at the massive gringo with a chiseled physique and an overpowering presence. He looked at the thin man with the serpentine smile—the dead eyes of a person with no conscience or fear.

John walked up to Irvin's table. Irvin took a drag off his cigar and exhaled a thin blue stream of smoke. Irvin's voice broke the silence. "I'll get to you momentary, big man." He emitted a small chuckle. "I still got me some drinkin' to do before I kill you."

John's foot shot out and kicked under the table top sending the table flying and toppling close by. Irvin's pulche vessel went flying with it, but some of the liquor splashed on Irvin's face. Irvin stood. The nervous tic began as his anger rose. "I ain't ever seen a man so damned eager to die, big man."

The bartender stood transfixed at what seemed to him for five minutes but in fact was five seconds at most. Irvin went for his .44 with uncanny skill, but he was late. John's two navy Colts were already jetting orange flames in the dark umbra and barking death. He kept firing. Irvin kept convulsing as he staggered back as each thudding pistol ball tore his insides up.

Irvin fell on the floor with some life still in him. His open eyes filled with shock that he had failed and was dying. John walked up to him and stood over him. He looked down with impassive gray eyes and said, "I never like killing a man—never have. But in your case, it was a damn pleasure."

Irvin coughed up blood. His eyes turned glassy and then dull as his spirit left him. John effortlessly pulled the thin man up by his belt and went through his pockets. He discovered over $200. He dropped Irvin's body with a callous thud.

The bartender looked nervous. He had no idea that anyone could beat the notorious Irvin Pendly. He also knew that the big man had heard him warn Irvin. His oily features began to mix with fear sweat as droplets of perspiration drooled down his face.

"Señor, I meant you no harm."

John ignored him He started toward the door. The bartender tried to hail him by saying the word *señor* repeatedly. John slowly stopped and gave him a steady but irritated gaze.

The bartender swallowed and said, "If you give me a dollar, I will bury him."

When John shook his head no, the bartender dropped the price— "'Two bits por favor."

John was ready to leave when a young Mexican girl burst through the beaded portiere. She called to him. He turned his tree-trunk neck and saw a thin child about the same age as his Sally. She looked as if she had not been eating steadily. She had tears in her eyes. The embarrassed bartender tried to shush her with tender hands, but she ignored her father's bidding by saying in a childlike plea, "Señor, we need the money."

John turned to face her. He walked with faint spur music to her. He laid a kind hand on her cheek. He looked at her sad eyes. As he studied her, he heard the whipping, lonesome wind in the background. The needful girl entrapped in such a forlorn tableau touched his heart.

He glanced at the downturned look of her father and back to her plaintive eyes. He suddenly straightened. To the small Consuela, he looked eight feet tall. He reached into his pocket and pulled out a leather pouch. He counted out $50 in gold coins and stacked them neatly on the counter.

The tearful bartender remonstrated that it was too much. John looked at father and daughter with thoughtful eyes. He reached into his leather pouch and added $20 in coins to the pile. He nodded at the child and patted her head. He turned and left. He went to the hitch post. He mounted his horse, grabbed Ollie's pinto by the reins, and rode quickly away.

The bartender and his child walked to the batwings and watched him disappear into the sandy winds.

Consuela opened the right batwing and stepped out on the gritty porch to capture the fleeting image of the big man. In Spanish, she asked her father over her shoulder, "He is not an angel, is he, Father?"

Her father, still behind the batwings, looked at the splayed, dead body of Irvin Pendly with two leaking holes in his chest and two in his abdomen. His eyes moved back over the batwings. He shrugged. "No, Consuela, he is no angel." His eyes moved behind him as he looked at the stacked gold coins. "And he is no devil." He gave a confused look and then returned his gaze over the batwings. "I do not know what he is. I am glad the frightful man came our way, but let us hope he does not come this way again."

CHAPTER 11

A fter two days of recuperating and eating Floyd's cooking, Yvette was up, walking around, and spending a lot of time with Floyd and Seth. She enjoyed their humor and kindness, but she especially relished the times she and Seth were alone.

After an early supper, Yvette suggested to Seth that she would like to walk to the corral and watch the sun go down. Seth could tell by the manner she said that that she wanted him to accompany her. He realized she was in a thoughtful mood as they walked along. He felt she was troubled by having been betrayed by her husband, but he also knew she was confused about the growing attraction between the two of them. He was beyond having beginning feelings for her; he knew beyond doubt that he loved her.

He did not have to intuit that she was reciprocating those feelings. She found ways to touch his arm and shoulders when they were alone. Each time she touched him, he yearned for more. In the last few days, he would catch her glancing at him, and at times, she would catch him looking at her. But they knew they had to keep their emotions in check.

The dying sun sent generous orange rays that emphasized the light colors and made the dark colors more vivid. Yvette leaned against one of the corral posts and let her blue-green eyes move to the horizon. After a few moments, her eyes narrowed in deep concentration. Her question surprised him. "Seth, is your wife pretty?"

Before she had asked that, he had also been watching the interplay of the orange sun on the beige and brown countryside. His head whipped to meet her inquisitive eyes. He ran a disturbed hand alongside his face. "I ain't married, Yvette." When she did not respond, Seth caught a soft smile of relief that briefly appeared and just as quickly disappeared as if she did not want him to see her reaction.

Seth suddenly remembered that Floyd had mentioned his daughters Denise, Julie, Sherry, and Teresa during the noon meal, and he gathered that she had assumed he was married. Seeing that she was receptive to his bachelorhood, he laid out the situation that had resulted in his becoming the father of four. He left out the part that he and Floyd were going to buy a bank safe, but he did give her the details they had encountered when they visited Finleyville, Texas, several months earlier. They had found the town burned down, including the Methodist West Texas Orphan Home. He told her about the four surviving girls and how he had come to love them. After telling her about the adoption, he informed her that he could not legally claim the four waifs as his own until he was legally married.

She gave a genuine concerned look. She asked him to tell her about the four girls. He took his time and gave her twenty minutes' worth about them—their appearances and personalities and how much he wanted to give them all the love and security he could. He repeated their names though Floyd had mentioned them earlier.

This prompted her to ask another question, one he had been dreading. "What do you and Floyd do?" She waited for his response, but when he did not answer fast enough, she asked, "I mean, how do you make a livin'?"

Seth did not want to tell her he was a rich and successful banker. On the other hand, he did not want to lie. He rubbed his chin thoughtfully as he considered a proper neutral answer to placate but not mislead her.

Fortunately for him, Yvette came to her own conclusion. It was as though she had a revelation. "You got to be fix-it men."

Seth gave a half-hearted nod. "Well, we fix things all right." In a lower and droll voice, he admitted, "Sometimes, we get ourselves in a fix."

Yvette's eyes suddenly became quiet. A troubling thought entered her mind. As much as she resisted it, her eyes misted over. "You'll be leavin' soon, won't you?"

Seth never wanted to leave her. The thought of not being with this gentle woman was more than he could stand. He knew it could be possibly harmful for him to admit that to her—not only to her but also to himself. He inhaled and tried to steel himself. He knew the best thing he could do was some nonverbal communication. He pulled her to him in a gentle hug. He did not answer for a long time; he felt her heave. He knew she was trying to stifle her sobs. He lovingly placed his hands on her back.

She slowly withdrew and covered her face with her hands. "I'm so sorry, Seth. I've no right to do that to you after all your kindness." She inhaled trying to infuse herself with some self-possession. Her face took on a thoughtful expression. "I have no right to pull you into my worries. Maybe I can sell the place and move back to Tennessee." Her tearful eyes opened in a sudden, gut-wrenching realization. "Oh gosh, Seth, I don't even own the place. And I'm not shore Reginald's been makin' the payments."

Seth avoided that remark about her and Reginald's financial status. He looked into her eyes as he took her hands in his. "There's no way in hell you're staying here, Yvette." He let his eyes move to the adobe house beside them. "Almost half of the house is gone. You wouldn't stand a chance if someone came along with bad intentions. You're comin' with us when we pull out."

His reassuring words gave her another tearful reaction; she rushed into his arms and circled his neck. "Oh Seth! Why couldn't I have found you earlier in my life?"

Her words echoed in Seth's brain down to his heart. Seth knew Floyd had been watching them from the window and in all likelihood would give him a good talking to later. But what Seth really wanted was to hold onto her in an hour-long embrace. He wanted to pull her to him and kiss her and totally reveal his love for her. But instead, he took a breath and resisted the impulse. He too wished he had met her before. He just knew he was glad he had met her, and he was anxious to embrace the present and possibly the future.

Later, after a meal of beans, potatoes, and cornbread, Yvette cleaned the table and Seth received a certain look from Floyd. They walked out to what had once been the porch and a good distance from the oily kitchen light that was painting the ground yellow. When they were out of earshot of Yvette, Floyd said, "Listen, I ain't so old that I don't appreciate love. I ain't blind or deaf, you know." Floyd didn't wait for Seth to respond. "If you want this girl to be your wife, go to Roxy and find out about her husband."

Seth nodded. "I reckon you're right, Floyd." He paused and looked up at the sparkling stars— like diamonds scattered recklessly across black velvet.

Floyd gave him a soft smile. "One thing, Seth. You still need to go see Patricia Barnwell." Floyd paused as he reached for a cigar. "If you don't, you probably won't ever regret it, but just remember the saddest words in any language are 'I wished I had.'" He paused as he took a strong draw off his smoke. "Regardless, you'll have seen her."

Seth mulled over Floyd's statement but did not respond to it. He shrugged. "Give me a cigar."

Floyd handed him one and struck a match. They lit up and took several thoughtful puffs. "Seth, you got to go see the town marshal and get the lowdown on this Reginald Carlton. I think you know what to do after that."

"Except kill 'im."

Floyd nodded. "Except kill 'im."

Seth sighed as he concentrated on his cigar. "And make shore I see this Patricia Barnwell."

Floyd did not answer right away. "Seth, I know you love Yvette. I don't think Patricia Barnwell is goin' to make a dent in your love, but it shore in hell won't hurt to see her." He gave himself a smile. "Do it for ol' Floyd."

Seth nodded thoughtfully. "You got it, partner." He took a draw off his smoke and sighed. "You and Yvette be careful tomorrow, Floyd. That bastard Rysinger is still out there you know."

Floyd grimaced. "I know. He'll get around to us soon. Take off early to go to Roxy. I'll tell Yvette you've gone to get some more supplies for us for when we all take off."

Seth grinned. "I told Yvette she's goin' with us, but I don't remember tellin' you."

Floyd rolled his eyes. "I ain't goin' to respond to that. I knew she was leavin' with us after the first day."

Seth got up early, hitched the team, and got to Roxy before noon. He had been told by Floyd that the town had grown. As his team trotted down the street, he saw the emporium on his right. He knew what supplies they needed. He knew pragmatically that he should go there first and take care of business, but he directed the wagon to the wooden plank building that served as the town marshal's office. He pulled up, set the brake, and jumped down. He stepped up on the boardwalk and entered the doorway.

Seated at his desk was the town marshal. Seth shut the door and nodded cordially; he received a friendly greeting in return. The marshal was a middle-aged man with a mustache that hung drearily down to his jaw. His range hat was wide brimmed with an impressive crown. His eyes, at first serious, suddenly twinkled with recognition. "Ain't you that banker from Baileysboro that prevented the bank robbery here a few months ago?"

Seth shrugged and modestly replied, "I had some help." He walked up to the marshal's desk and asked to sit in the cane-bottom chair in front of the lawman. The marshal graciously extended his hand. "By all means." The lawman introduced himself. "Name's Gil Tucker. And you be Seth Johnson."

Seth again gave a courtesy nod at the recognition and sat. The marshal, able to divine that Seth was not overly effusive by his terse words and body language, leaned back in his chair. He decided that the young banker was there on a mission, so he changed his demeanor to match Seth's. "I gather you're here on business."

"'Fraid so, Sheriff."

Tucker responded, "I'm not a sheriff. I know you know the difference, but here in Texas, you call a lawman a sheriff if he's over the county. Now he can have the county seat as his headquarters and still be called a sheriff, but if you're just over a town, you're called a town marshal." He gave an affable grin. "What can I do for you, Seth?"

"You know a man named Reginald Carlton?"

The marshal's expression changed from serious to surprised. "Yeah, I know him." He pointed in the direction Seth had come to enter his town. "He's the new minister at the Disciples Church down the street." He paused and wryly asked, "Bein' a banker, don't reckon you're here to be saved?"

Seth gave him a deadpan look. "Not hardly. What else can you tell me about him?"

Marshal Tucker figured that Seth was deadly serious. He pulled a pipe from a desk drawer and took his time tamping tobacco into it. His eyes narrowed as he dwelled on the question. "If you were just somebody off the streets, I wouldn't tell you doodly-squat. But since you're a man of good repute, I'll answer your question. He's friendly enough. He reportedly is a good speaker. He's single and is engaged to a young girl just outside town. He pays his bills and lives alone in the new parsonage just behind the church."

Seth mulled over the marshal's words. "Did he ever own a ranch about five hours' ride out of town?"

"I wouldn't know. I moved here from East Texas about three years ago." He paused and tilted his head up as if to jostle his memory. "But to answer your question, I've never heard he did." The marshal fired his pipe. He shook his match as he was evaluating Seth's question. "Seth, there has to be a reason you're asking me about Pastor Reginald."

"Reginald Carlton is three months in arrears on his ranch. My friend, Floyd, the vice president of the bank in Baileysboro, is out there now. Someone tried to burn the house down." Seth sighed and straightened in his chair. "I think it was him."

Marshal Tucker's eyes widened as he leaned forward to meet Seth's stare. Seth's words were circling in his brain. Questioning words escaped Tucker's mouth. "Pastor Carlton?"

Seth leaned forward so their faces were only a few feet apart. "There's more than just burnin' down his house and bein' behind on his payments. I have a plan if you're agreeable to it. But it'll take you and the highest rankin' official in town to pull this off."

Seth walked the short distance to the church. The trees were filled with birds chirping away. He saw the side door of the church Marshal Tucker had described to him. He went to the door and found it unlocked as Marshal Tucker had told him it would be. He opened it softly. The thoughts of meeting the man who had attempted to kill Yvette would in any other situation have made him anxious, but he was very calm. He reasoned Reginald Carlton should be the nervous.

He walked into the umbra of the church sanctuary. He saw another door just beside the preacher's platform. He started to knock on it, but he heard the unmistakable sighs and moans of lovemaking. His knuckled hand poised to knock fell to his side. He stood there patiently for the end of the primal dance, which he figured would end in three minutes. He shortly heard the mutual yelps and groans of pleasure male and female. He gave it another ten seconds. He heard the rustling of clothes and low-level talking. He knocked on the door. He heard a masculine voice. "Just a moment please."

A pretty, sweating, dark-haired beauty cracked the door and crisply closed it. She came out with head down demurely, not meeting Seth's eyes. She turned her body not to expose the unbuttoned portion of her dress all the while walking sideways through the door Seth had entered. He watched her leave the door ajar, which fortunately fit Seth's plan.

Again, Seth gently rapped on the door. He heard a rustling. The door swung open. It was obvious that the sweaty Pastor Carlton was irritated with the unplanned visit. He was the same height as Seth. He had mousy brown hair that was wet with perspiration. His glasses were askew and slightly fogged up. He looked Seth up and down and curtly asked him the purpose of his visit. He did not explain the hasty exit of the young woman or act as if anything were out of the ordinary. His aplomb at first surprised Seth, but the more he stood there and dwelled on the matter, the more he realized it should not have.

Seth smiled and sarcastically said, "I've come to seek your counsel, but I hope I don't get the same treatment as the young lady."

Reginald was sweating. His features were flushed. The obvious temerity of a perfect stranger caused him to clinch his teeth. He started to explode in anger, but seeing the calm demeanor of the what he considered a cowhand, he refrained.

Seth asked him if he could come in and sit. Reginald ran a hand through his ruffled hair and reluctantly nodded. Seth looked around the room and smelled the afterglow of sex and sweat. He took a handkerchief and wiped the seat of the visitor's chair. That act infuriated Reginald, but again, he restrained himself.

Reginald asked Seth if he would close the door. Seth shook his head. "I will in a minute." He smiled impishly. "The room needs to air out, don't you think?"

The pastor sat simmering and indignantly ran his fingers through his hair once more. He rolled his neck around as though loosening it up. "Who are you?" He wanted to ask, "Who in the hell are you?" but again, caution governed his anger.

"My name is Seth Johnson."

Reginald shook his head as if to say the name did not ring a bell.

Seth shrugged. "Try this. I'm the banker over in Baileysboro."

Reginald straightened up. Seth knew he had his attention. Reginald leaned back in his chair. Seth knew the wheels were spinning his head. Reginald again ran his hands through his sweaty hair. "What do you want?"

"I want to discuss three months of nonpayment on the ranch, Reginald."

Reginald licked his lips and studied on the question. "I've chosen to let it go."

Seth nodded. "That normally would be okay, Reginald, but you see, you tried to burn down the house."

Reginald let out a snarky laugh. "Lightning hit the house. I'm not paying for no lightning strike." He paused and removed his still fogged-up glasses. "No siree, banker man, you can have the ranch with my blessings, but you can't haul me into paying for some act of God." He rubbed his glasses vigorously. The more he thought about being held responsible for burning down the ranch house, the more he rubbed the lenses.

"I found the coal oil can in the front yard, Reginald."

"What in the hell does that prove, banker man?"

"There's coal oil scent all over the kitchen area."

Reginald laughed and waved derisive fingers at Seth. "People spill coal oil in the kitchen, and people light lamps in the kitchen."

Seth's patience was wearing thin on the pastor. He did not like his attitude. Seth leaned back in his chair. "I'm goin' to ask you one more time. Are you goin' to pay for the house?" Seth sighed as he leaned forward to make certain he would get the answer he demanded. "I'll take the ranch back, but you'll pay five hundred dollars for the house."

Reginald scoffed again. "I reckon we'll see how the courts see it, won't we, banker man?"

Seth had waited for this moment all day. He pulled a cigar out languidly and struck a match on the bottom of his boot. He torched his smoke and shook the match dead as though it was part of a choreographed drama. "Well, Pastor Carlton, it's like this—I've got a witness that you burned down your house."

Reginald straightened himself in his chair. He replaced his clean glasses. His eyes seemed magnified as he belligerently leaned closer to Seth. "I guess you're talking about some itinerant cowhand passing by."

"Nope." Seth looked at Reginald through narrowed eyes. "I'm talkin' about Yvette."

Reginald swallowed and sat back in his chair. "You're a lying bastard."

"You didn't kill her, Reginald. She's alive and fully recovered. You should have used something besides a derringer when you shot her."

Reginald's flushed color instantly to a ghostly pale. His eyes moved erratically behind his glasses. He had never brought Yvette to Roxy especially when he found out she was barren. He first planned to abandon her but was afraid she would be found alive and his ambitious plans for himself would be foiled. He finally concluded that he had no choice but to kill her and burn her body leaving no evidence.

He knew Seth Johnson was telling the truth. He felt like a cockroach caught in the sunlight. Reginald grabbed his coat lying rumpled on the side of his desk. He pulled his wallet from an inside pocket. "Five hundred dollars, you say."

Seth thoughtfully looked at his cigar. "Well, Preacher, before I leave here today, I want that five hundred for the house and want you to write a bill of divorcement for Yvette."

Reginald leaned back with the $500 in hand. "If I write out the bill of divorcement or even annulment, who's going to see it?"

"Just write it out—that you're divorcing Yvette. If you don't, I'll see Marshal Tucker and bring Yvette in. You'll be changed with attempted murder."

Reginald suddenly straightened as though he had received a revelation. "How do I know you're not bluffing, banker?"

"You want to ride with me out to your ranch and see for yourself?"

The sudden infusion of bravery left Reginald as quickly as it came. He knew the banker was not running a bluff. He wilted and nodded. "I'll pay you the five hundred and sign a writ of divorcement if we do it out of this town."

When he said these words, Marshal Tucker and the town mayor, who had been hiding behind the door, entered and gave the pastor a baleful stare. Reginald looked as though his heart had stopped. Sheriff Tucker said, "Pastor, you're goin' to jail until we get this matter resolved."

Reginald abruptly slid out his desk drawer and with snakelike quickness pulled up a derringer. He swung the short pistol back and forth trying to cover all bases. "You all stand right there, all of you." His eyebrows arched over his intense eyes. "Hand over your hardware, Marshal." His eyes slid to Seth. "You too, banker man, and don't be cute." He snarled, "I wouldn't mind killing you anyways."

The marshal gingerly slid his pistol out with two fingers and handed it to the nervous pastor. Seth did the same. Reginald stood and placed the two pistols in his belt. He sneeringly ignored the mayor as he carelessly placed his coat over his shoulder. "Anyone who tries to stop me will get shot." His voice rose to an almost irrational level as he glared at Seth. "You got that, banker man?" After giving Seth a brief but withering look, he whipped around the three men and darted out the door. They loosely followed him, but on seeing the desperation in his eyes, they knew he would fire if pressed too closely. They watched him get on his horse and gallop like a madman out of town.

Marshal Tucker turned to the chubby mayor. "If I live to be a hunnert, I don't reckon I'll ever see anything like that again."

The mayor pushed up his hat and mopped his forehead with a handkerchief. "He baptized my nephew last week."

Seth watched the pastor toss his and the sheriff's pistols aside and then gig his horse into a frantic gallop. He observed him becoming a smaller figure leaving a dust trail as he became part of a vanishing point on the horizon. Seth sighed, "He can run, but sooner or later …"

Marshal Tucker shrugged and completed the comment. "He'll get caught. I'll notify the county and the surrounding sheriffs," he said with a mirthless smile on his face. "He shore had me fooled." He rubbed his chin. "He had all of us fooled." The marshal sighed and changed the subject. "Before you leave town, I'll see to it you get your pistol back."

Seth nodded as he thought about what action the maverick pastor might take. It amazed him that the minister thought he had killed his wife but had never gone back to make sure. He figured the vain man thought that he was invincible and that Yvette's body would be burned beyond recognition and be consumed by animals. But what really stuck in his craw was how a man claiming to be a preacher could have been so damned calloused.

As the marshal, mayor, and Seth walked to the jailhouse office, Seth asked where the Barnwell spread was. Before the marshal could respond, Mayor Quiggs pointed at a wagon in front of the emporium. "That's Frank Barnwell's wagon over there."

Seth peeled off from the mayor and marshal and made his way across the street. He saw a stolid man walking out the trading post carrying a sack of potatoes. Seth, feeling he owed something to Floyd and himself, made his way dutifully toward the rancher. He saw Barnwell ardently trying to use each square inch of space in his wagon.

Seth knew by the comings and goings of other customers that they were unaware of what had happened at the church. He decided to let others spread the news; he just wanted to meet Barnwell and possibly his daughter, but meeting his daughter did not hold the same importance it once had. He walked up as the tall, rugged man who was shoving around fifty pounds of potatoes near the tailgate.

Frank Barnwell saw Seth approaching out of the corner of his eyes. He made out enough to know the man seemed friendly and was seeking him out. He stepped back from his wagon and smiled. Seth extended his hand and introduced himself. "Just wanted to meet you, Mr. Barnwell."

Frank nodded. "Oh, the banker from Baileysboro. Nice to meet you, Seth." He firmly pumped Seth's hand. Seth asked if he could help him load his wagon, and Barnwell gladly accepted. In ten minutes, Seth proved the equal of the rancher, and every bit of the wagon space was utilized. As they talked, the rancher pulled his timepiece from his vest pocket and gave a wistful look up and down the street. It was obvious that he was waiting on someone. Just as he replaced his watch, his daughter came out of the emporium behind him holding a new dress over her arm.

Seth could not believe his eyes. She was a beautiful. But the part he could not believe was that she was the same girl who had hastily exited the pastor's office. She flashed a big smile to her father and apologized for being late, which he offhandedly excused. Her eyes slid over by chance; she saw Seth, and her cheeks became crimson. She kept her head aside and avoided any eye contact with him. Barnwell nodded farewell to Seth, and he and his daughter quickly climbed into the driver's seat; he snapped the reins. As they drove away, Patricia kept a rigid straight-ahead look, but as they passed the bank, she took a curious, quick look back. She saw Seth with hands on hips looking directly at her. Her head snapped around, and she sat ramrod straight until they were out of sight.

Seth inwardly sighed. It was another secret that would die with him. He just wondered how Patricia Barnwell would handle the news that her fiancé was married and would be accused of attempted murder. He looked in the direction that Carlton had escaped. He had doubts after meeting him that he would go immediately to seek revenge, but he could not be sure. He walked to the jailhouse and waited inside till a young boy who served as the marshal's gofer came in with his and the marshal's pistols. Seth and Tucker gathered their weaponry and walked out the door together. The marshal wordlessly mounted up ready to depart to the county seat to meet Sheriff George French. Seth, anxious to get his supplies, climbed up to the springboard seat and turned his wagon toward the emporium.

Toby Jarrett had followed Seth into Roxy. For two days, he had the adobe house staked out. He was directed to keep tabs on Seth and Floyd. He had spotted Yvette days before through his telescope. That fact puzzled him. He had had no idea a woman was involved. He had shared that information with Punkin' Head and J.D., but they had seemed uninterested.

He had returned early that morning to his scouting post. From his blind of mesquite trees, he saw Seth hitch up the mules and head toward

Roxy. He followed the banker at a distance; there was no need to take risks, and the wagon tracks and mule prints were distinctive enough. When Seth was approaching Roxy, Toby headed to the backside of the town. He had already surmised that he would be going to the trading post.

Toby hitched his horse to a pump handle behind the bulky emporium. He sidled along the wall. His watchful eyes moved alertly to pick up any snooping eyes that might spot him. From the corner of the large building, he saw Seth's wagon in front of the marshal's office and wondered why Seth would stop there. Later, he was intrigued when Seth walked to the church. His inquisitiveness was further fueled when he saw the town marshal leave his office and gather a chubby man from the land office next door. He saw them slowly heading to the church also. Much later, he saw a skittish, attractive young woman leave the building as though she were in a hurry; she was buttoning the front of her dress especially over her bosom. Not long after that, he saw the town minister exit in hurry waving a small handgun. He watched him gallop out of town gigging his mount like a bandit on the run.

Toby stroked his chin thoughtfully. It was obvious that the minister had had a run-in with the banker and the town law. Toby nodded to himself as he put things together. The minister could prove a useful ally. When the banker, marshal, and chubby businessman were out of sight, he quickly returned to his horse and circled behind the few outlying houses. He made it to the main road and saw the swishing hoofprints of the runaway minister's horse.

Later that night, Carlton was wadded up in a blanket in a small hunting hut near a dry weather creek. He slept with his derringer in his hand. He uneasily rolled over with his bleary eyes peeping open; he thought he had heard something, but he shook it off as a figment of his overactive imagination. But when he felt the cold imprint of a pistol bore on his temple, he knew it was no illusion. He initially thought it was Marshal Tucker, but the unknown voice dispelled that suspicion. "Hand me your peashooter, Preacher. We're goin' for a ride."

As Reginald and Toby rode to the hideout, they began a series of mini conversations. Reginald recognized by the drift of the talks that he was being taken to some gang that had a hard-bitten grudge against the banker,

Seth Johnson. Reginald decided to go along with this train of thought. He indeed resented Seth Johnson. He disliked him immensely for exposing him to the world and preventing him from marrying Patricia Barnwell, but he in no way wanted to kill him. He wanted to kill Yvette. If she were to die at the gang's hands, he would be off the hook and could claim he had been innocent all along. He felt that if he repented for claiming he was single when he was actually married, he might have a chance to redeem himself with his congregation. He felt through charm and fake innocence that he just might reclaim the life he had grown to love. But he knew he should in no way in hell reveal that. He knew if he were to confess it or even hint at it, this mysterious gang he was being taken to would in all likelihood kill him.

As they were riding, he formulated a plan to use the outlaws to his own end. He began to toss out diatribes against the banker. He decided to claim that the banker had stolen his wife and turned her against him. When he discovered that this train of talk was convincing Toby, he had an idea that the rest of the gang might believe him too. His interest in joining this gang intrigued more than frightened him.

They rode into the outlaws' hideout as the sun was dawning. Reginald gave himself a smile as he saw the crude building blushed with the orange sunrise. The house looked like it had once been a home place, but through neglect, it was a wreck.

Reginald saw the gang members emerge from the soft shadows of morning, but he did not smile. They looked like a motley crew that had escaped a cheap circus. When he saw Punkin' Head, he bit down on his lower lip to keep from grinning. He let his eyes slide over to Adrian, who resembled a small dog who looked aggressive but was relying on the other dogs for protection. His vision soon panned to J.D. Rysinger.

J.D. was no longer wearing his eyepatch. He had a blind eye with a hideous, light-blue film covering it. His ear, sawed off by the pistol ball in Baileysboro, was raw and ugly. His left arm was in the dirtiest sling he had ever seen. It once had been reasonably white but was a butternut with weird stains on it.

It was obvious that they were nettled with Toby bringing a stranger to their headquarters. Toby dismounted and asked to speak to J.D. privately. J.D. had a fast rule about bringing strangers around. But after a long talk out of earshot, it was clear that J.D. was amenable to the addition of the new gang member.

Carlton, still mounted, looked on with interest. If they did not kill him for some reason, he relished being a member of this gang. They appeared to be a group of idiots he might be able to control. He watched J.D. nod at Toby. He watched the hideous gang leader walk toward him. J.D. told him to step down. After he dismounted, J.D. introduced him to his new friends. He was then an official member of the J.D. Rysinger gang. They all nodded friendly enough, but he noticed that Punkin' Head was seemingly not fooled by his sense of superiority he hoped he had masked sufficiently. He could tell by the expression of the man with the oversized head that he was being judged as well as scrutinized.

Carlton was given back his derringer and was told by several gang members that he needed some real man's weapons. That hearty advice was accompanied by moronic, gravelly laughter. He gave a soft smile back; he thought it was too much loud laughter for such a small amount of humor, and he felt he was a cut above these swine he had to deal with. He looked at Punkin' Head, who was still observing him. Punkin' Head gave an almost indiscernible nod to himself as though he were reading the preacher's mind. Reginald's face sobered. He knew the freakish-looking man could be his bane if he did not manipulate him.

J.D. called the assemblage into a loose circle. "The day after tomorrow, we're goin' to make our play on the banker." He let a ragged smile filled with lots of yellow teeth slide across his face. "We're goin' to let Toby and the preacher lead us there." He sighed and let his eyes slide to Punkin' Head. "Those of you who doubted you'd get paid the hundred dollars for stickin' with me will be rewarded."

Punkin' Head ignored the dig. He let his small eyes move toward the preacher. He gave a quick finger flick toward the soon-to-be-defrocked pastor. "Him too?"

J.D. gave a thoughtful look up at the orange glow of the burgeoning day. "He'll get half." J.D. laughed a mirthless chuckle as he watched the faces of his gang. "I've always believed that in that old sayin' and bet the preacher agrees with me—'A woman, a dog, and a hickory nut tree—the more you beat 'em, the better they be.'" He looked at the preacher. "That's why I like this turd. He'll get his chance to kill the banker that stole his wife, and he'll ride with us to the Nations and start makin' some real money."

Reginald winced when he used the word *turd*, but he returned a begrudging smile. He thought to himself that these subhumans would eventually do his bidding. He felt Punkin' Head staring at him, but he did not give in to his curiosity to find out for sure. His mind was racing on how he could ditch these bunch of losers if he were able to kill Yvette. He rocked on his heels as he heard J.D. droll on how the plan would unfold and what would happen if the bankers tried to escape by wagon.

CHAPTER 12

T-Dilly walked out of the Boscoville saloon onto the uneven porch. He stood thoughtfully under short wooden overhang and looked over the tops of ramshackle buildings across the street. Beside him stood the outlaw chieftain of the area, Ace Turner.

Ace, as tall as T-Dilly and wearing all black, rubbed his whiskers. He knew T-Dilly was in a bind for time. Ace controlled the whole area but had deferred to T-Dilly since he had arrived. He knew he held only deuces and treys compared to the full complement of powerful cards the powerful gunman from Austin wielded, but he knew T-Dilly was worried about not hearing from some of his key gang members. Ace had been told about this John Lee Johnson fellow though he knew nothing of him personally. But it was obvious that T-Dilly was chafed about the lack of contact and the length of time that had passed.

Ace glanced at the Austin bad boy. "I ain't tellin' you your business, T-Dilly, but it appears that Irvin and Cherokee Charley didn't get the job done." He watched for any reaction from T-Dilly. "I would've thought Pendly would've been able to bring him down."

T-Dilly solemnly nodded. He sighed and fished a cigar from his front pocket. He bit the end off and lit up. He liked Ace, and he decided to confide in him. "The fact that Irvin came up short has me concerned. This hombre

Johnson may be a whole lot tougher bird than I thought. Ace, it's like this. If I kill the bastard, he won't be fighting El Toro. Since I figger that the big Mexican will win, I'll lose money if John Lee Johnson gets killed. So you see I'm in a pickle. Furthermore, I plan on bettin' all I have on that big greaser. But if Johnson gets through and beats El Toro, I'm in serious trouble. So what I need to know before I go any further is if John Lee Johnson can fight."

Ace nodded. "Let me see if I got it right. You prefer that he get through to fight this Mexican so you can make that nest egg to live the good life?"

"Something like that."

Ace reached into his pocket for a cigar. He lit it and exhaled a thin line of smoke. "I think I got part of your answer, T-Dilly."

"How's that?"

"I got a rider named Bobo Sweeney. He ain't never been whipped. Now what your boys say about this John Lee Johnson is how big he is and how tall he is. Well, Bobo is not that big, but he's big enough, and ain't nobody can whip 'im."

T-Dilly dwelled on his words. "Tell me some more about this Bobo Sweeney. If I like what I hear, you and me can do some business, Ace."

Ace took a few quick puffs. "Well, Bobo is about six feet tall and weighs about two hundred and thirty or so. He's beaten the hell out of anyone he's ever faced." He gave a sidelong look at T-Dilly. "I was thinkin' about havin' him go down to Mexico, but I ain't got your kind of money, T-Dilly. I shore in hell can't come up with that twenty-thousand ante."

T-Dilly continued to gaze over the roofs of the merchant buildings across the street. "How much will it cost me, Ace, to get you and Bobo to cooperate with me?"

"You me want to set up a fight between this John Lee and Bobo?"

"I do."

"If Bobo wins, you'll let this Johnson fella go through to Mexico, where he's likely to lose again to this big Mexican, right?"

"Right."

"If this Johnson fella wins, he's the real thing and you'll then know you're goin' to have to kill 'im, right?"

"Right."

Ace said, "Now Johnson has to come through Boscoville. That is, if he wants provisions. He still has a long damn ways to go."

T-Dilly nodded.

Ace thoughtfully examined his cigar. "How much are you willin' to pay, T-Dilly?"

T-Dilly reached in his vest and pulled out a leather pouch. "I ain't goin' to pussyfoot around, Ace. You've been up-front with me from the get-go. Here's five hundred dollars." He painstakingly counted out the money into Ace's hand.

Ace counted the money along with T-Dilly beneath the dinky veranda and nodded approvingly at the count. As Ace placed the last twenty-dollar gold piece in his leather pouch, he said with conviction, "You and me are solid, T-Dilly. I'll take care of things from here." Ace thoughtfully rubbed his jaw. "Why don't you leave a couple of your boys here to see you get your money's worth. I reckon they'll know where you'll be from here."

T-Dilly sighed. "Ace, you're a good man to do business with." He took a slow drag off his smoke. "I'll be twenty miles from here at Lako Springs." He nodded at Ace's earlier suggestion. "I plan on leaving Slick and Lefty here to see how the fight goes."

Ace put away his money and sighed. "You're goin' to have a smile on your face like a rich widow. Sleep tight in Lako Springs."

T-Dilly uneasily nodded. "Well, if Bobo comes up short. I aim to close this Johnson feller's lights."

Ace pursed his lips and let his eyes move over to T-Dilly's profile. "You say this Johnson fella is goin' to go all the way to Mexico and fight this El Toro?"

T-Dilly turned his head. He was puzzled; he thought this matter had been discussed thoroughly. "What're you askin', Ace?"

Ace looked straight ahead. "If he's headed to the Guadalupe Mountains and then across part of the Chihuahua Desert to fight this big Mexican, it stands to reason that he's got that twenty-thousand entry fee with him. Why would he go all that way and not have the ante money?"

"I've heard he has someone takin' it for him."

Ace thoughtfully rubbed his chin. "But you don't know that for a fact?"

T-Dilly gave a pensive nod. "No, Ace, I don't know for shore, and if you want to make a play for it, go for it. The money that is." He paused as he gave his caveat. "But don't kill him just yet. I want to make some money off El Toro."

"That's all I wanted to know."

John Lee and his crew were making good time. One day, they rode their horses to the point of exhaustion. The next day, they rode their mules using the horses as pack animals. They kept up that grueling routine for the next four days.

On the fifth day, John and his men made camp in an arroyo to hide their campfire. John gave instructions on where to hide their horses and mules and where to sleep; he gave them their night-watch assignments. He took off on his own to scout ahead.

Sand Burr made a small campfire and set up his metal tripod for the coffee pot. Lambert was sitting to the side of the campfire with his Spencer rifle across his lap. Ollie was wearing Blackie's all-black outfit including his hat and was walking around like a peacock proudly looking down at his new holster and army .44.

Lambert smiled. "You know, Ollie, with that new outfit, when we ride into Boscoville, you can walk into the saloon like a man."

Ollie vigorously nodded. "You're mighty right." He reached into a pocket and pulled out a small leather bag tied with a thong. "There's forty dollars and some odd cents in here." He gave a big smile. He stuffed his money back into his pocket and joyfully stated, "Good gosh amighty, I might just haul off and dance."

Sand Burr pulled a French harp from his pocket and began playing an upbeat "Yellow Rose of Texas." Ollie began dancing a jig. He worked his hands in and out as his boots pounded the campsite sand. He picked up the tempo amid the laughter of Lambert, who clapped his hands in time.

When the coffee was ready, the dancing stopped and all three poured a cup. Ollie sat close to Lambert and looked over with thoughtful eyes. "You reckon John will let me go with ya'll to Mexico?"

Lambert took on a pensive expression. "I thought you were goin' to go down near the border and work on your friend's spread."

Ollie ignored that question. He sipped coffee and let his eyes drift to the darkening sky. "I don't know if it's because I got shot at with you boys or what the hell it is." His voice thoughtfully tailed off. "But I shorely would love to tag along with ya'll."

Lambert gave him a smile. "If I was you, Ollie, I'd just keep ridin' with us. If you don't bring it up, I don't figure he will either."

Sand Burr walked up and sat on the other side of Ollie. "You got enough money to get married again, Ollie." It was a statement, not a question.

Ollie took no offense at the teasing. "No more marriage, no more diggin' for water, no more fixin' roofs. From now on, I just want to dance, drink hard cider, maybe have a bowl of chili con carne or maybe a fried peach pie." He raised his eyebrows. "And maybe catch a kiss or two."

Sand Burr gave an exaggerated nod. "I like a man with ambition, Ollie. To hell with diggin' for a pump."

Ollie laughed in spite of himself. "I just feel free, and it shore feels good."

That statement was followed by reflective silence. It was broken as Sand Burr retrieved his rifle and headed to his post. "You boys sleep tight."

John Lee Johnson rode the last remnants of daylight. He thought he saw a distant campfire. He doubted it was cowhands. It was hard even for a lizard to stay alive in this barren land much less cattle. He knew very well it could be part of T-Dilly's outfit sending out feelers for him. He decided to ride surreptitiously to the flickering light. He rode to within half a mile of the yellow glow and dismounted. He removed his spurs and headed to the campsite. He used various cacti and low-lying rocks as cover as he crept closer. He heard muffled voices as he got closer. It was obvious they did not have a guard posted; they apparently had enough confidence in themselves to forgo a watchman.

He looked into the twinkling yellow light and saw two men sitting and drinking coffee. He listened and gathered that they worked for a man named Ace Turner. The gist of the conversation was that they were to find him and report to Ace, whereupon they would bullrush him and possibly kill him along with his small crew. Then, Ace and his men would gladly purloin his ante for the big fight.

John Lee learned their names as he remained in the shadows. The tall, lean one wearing buckskin was named Hawk, and the other, who was shorter and stout, was Burke. John saw their horses in the shadows just beyond the yellow light. He knew that if they gave him no choice but to kill them, the dun and the sorrel would be welcomed additions to his growing remuda.

John stepped from the large, solitary boulder that had shielded him and walked into their midst. They sat with open mouths looking at the huge, powerful man. The reflecting light cast shadows that made his pectorals and deltoids look impossibly large. His ragged shirt displayed more iron-ridged muscles than they had ever seen.

Hawk audibly gulped and looked over at Burke, whose eyes were distended. It was as though they were looking at the devil himself. John picked a flat-topped rock close to the campfire and sat. He gave a lingering look at their coffee pot hanging above their fire. "I wouldn't mind coffee." He gave them sarcastic smile. "Pardon my manners … Howdy."

They returned a too fast and nervous "Howdy." After an uneasy silence, Hawk looked at Burke. "You heard the man, Burke. Git him a cup."

Burke swallowed and warily stood. He forked a thumb in the direction of his horse as though he was informing John. "I might have a spare back in my gear."

John's voice sounded as though it came from a ground swell. "Don't be thinkin' about gettin' a hideaway."

Hawk, who seemed desperate to please the ominous man, repeated, "Yeah, Burke, don't go for some damned gun."

Burke frowned at Hawk. He had no intentions of finding a hidden gun, and he resented the ingratiating way Hawk was trying to curry favor with the big man.

Burke returned with a crude clay cup. He handed it to John at arm's length.

John nodded, rose, and pulled the coffee pot from its stand. After pouring a liberal amount, he replaced the pot, took a sip, and nodded his approval. He sat. "I gather you two are lookin' for me."

Hawk worriedly looked at Burke, who was returning the same look. It dawned on them that he had probably eavesdropped on them.

John looked from face to face. He received no response. He took another sip and looked over their heads far away as though contemplating their fates.

Hawk swallowed and pointed at Burke. "He was lookin' for you, not me."

Burke's fat face flushed in anger. "I was not doin' no such thang." He composed himself as he looked at the gigantic man. "We was sent out here to look for you." He ended his statement by saying in a louder register, "Both of us."

John continued to sip his coffee. "I gather you or that hombre you work for think I'm carrying this twenty thousand to fight this man down in Old Mexico."

They gave him sidelong glances; they wanted to know the answer to that statement. John looked at Burke and at Hawk. "I don't have no money like that with me."

Hawk sighed disappointedly and leaned forward with his head cradled in his hands. He knew that drawing his weapon or that a mutual attack by him and Burke would result in either their getting their asses whipped or getting killed. He knew it would be useless to even harbor any aggressive intentions. That left him and Burke at the discretion of the big man. He resignedly asked, "What're you goin' to do with us?"

John consciously swiveled his coffee in the crude mug. His words sent shivers down their collective backs. "That depends on what you tell me." He looked over at Burke, who was obviously scared as hell. "Do you tell the truth?"

Burke looked down and shuffled his boots. "I tell the truth a whole lot."

John's face remained inscrutable. "I want to know about this Ace Turner bird and what he's got up his sleeve for me."

Hawk started talking; he said that Ace wanted John's ante money and would kill him if necessary, but they preferred not to. He said that if things went as planned, they wanted John to fight a man named Bobo Sweeney. John asked about T-Dilly, and Hawk said that T-Dilly had left for Lako Springs but had left two men to witness the fight between him and Bobo. John asked what would happen if he lost to Bobo. Hawk said that in that case, he would be allowed to go through to Mexico unharmed so he could fight the big Mexican and probably lose. Hawk added that T-Dilly and many others in his gang were going to bet on El Toro and emphasized that they planned to bet heavily.

John asked what would happen if he whipped Bobo. Hawk said that in that case, they would try to kill him before he reached Chihuahua. He added that they could not take the chance that John would beat the Mexican.

Hawk finished talking. He looked nervously at John. He sensed the time of reckoning was at hand.

John slowly moved his thick neck as he took in both of them. "I could kill both of you right now, and that would probably benefit me more in the long run."

Burke threw his palms out. "Oh, you don't want to do that."

Hawk shook his head in agreement with Burke. "No, you don't want to do that."

John sighed. He was concentrating on the matter. "Well, you two birds came out here scoutin' me and probably would've took a shot at me at long distance."

Burke retorted quickly, "Well, yeah—long distance."

Hawk, realizing Burke's awkward response might make matters worse, winced as he glanced at John to catch his reaction.

"All right, Hawk. What do you think I ought to do with you two birds?"

Hawk swallowed and nervously shrugged. "I don't know what you're goin' to do, but I know it'll be fair, ain't that right, Burke?"

Burke gave a fake smile and nodded vigorously. "I have no doubt you're a fair man." He gulped and leaned forward as though he had just run a mile.

John mawkishly looked back and forth at the two men. "I'll tell you what I'll do. I'll tie you two over your saddles and send you back to Boscoville."

Hawk vigorously shook his head. "Ace will chew us out and tongue-lash us forever. We won't be worth dirt if you do that to us."

Burke desperately added, "He's likely to kill us to make us an example." He rubbed his chin contemplatively. "Besides, ridin' that long over a saddle could rupture me."

Hawk nodded and snapped his fingers. "I got an idee. Why don't we work for you?"

Burke quickly picked up on the hope they might get out of their pickle with their lives. "Why, me and ol' Hawk could make a fortune bettin' on you against that El Toro or whatever his name is."

John stared severely at Burke. "What in your lifetime have you done that warrants me to consider lettin' you live?"

Burke ran his hand over his face. His eyes were moving back and forth trying to remember something of value he had done. An inspired look came over his face. "I take good care of my horse." He studied on his own words. "And I ain't never hit a woman."

John gazed at Hawk, who realized it was his turn. He started swallowing and rubbing his face. "Well, I take good care of my horse too." He sighed. "Not as good as Burke, but pretty damn good." He exhaled. His eyes were moving around in concert with his brain. "When I was a young and precious boy, I was always good to my grandmother." He paused as his voice took on an almost trembling tone. "I used to pick flowers from the ditch dump and give 'em to her sometimes." He sighed. "I used to go in the kitchen and get her favorite snuff for her when she was churnin' buttermilk."

John nodded as he ignored the cloying remarks and replied with a deadpanned face, "You were a fine grandson, Hawk."

Hawk fingered away an incipient tear hoping John took notice of that.

John tossed the dregs from his coffee mug and handed it to Burke. He stood and beckoned them to stand. Hawk and Burke looked nervously back and forth. "If I let you go, are you goin' to go tell Ace all I said?"

Hawk appeared surprised but also cautious of his answer. "Do you want us to?"

"What about you, Burke?"

"We can't join up with you?"

"Nope."

Burke looked at Hawk and inhaled audibly. "I thank I will just head out and join Turk Larsen's gang over in the next county." He looked over at Hawk, seeking confirmation as he directed his comments to him. "I don't want to answer all them questions to Ace." He paused and added, "No siree, I'm leavin' and not plannin' on comin' back."

Hawk nodded his approval of that. He realized he should have said that instead of asking a question. He turned to John. "Me too. Turk's not a bad guy." He thought on his response and modified it. "Well, he's a bad guy, but not as bad as Ace."

John's vision moved to their mounts. He said matter-of-factly, "Get your coffee pot and get on your horses. When I get to Boscoville, if you're there, I'll kill you pure and simple." He turned and disappeared into the shadows from which he had come.

Hawk and Burke got their coffee pot and tripod and headed to their mounts in record time. Soon, they were riding off. Hawk looked at Burke as they loped their horses along. "We really goin' to join up with Turk?"

Burke said loudly out of the corner of his mouth. "You damn right. I never want to meet that feller again."

Hawk looked over his shoulder as though John were still close by and nodded. "To hell with Ace."

Ace Turner did not sleep well that night. He knew he should have heard from Hawk and Burke. He had expected them back in town at eight that night. He understood they were not his top-level men, but on the other hand, they were not his worst.

The next morning, Ace found himself in the same posture as T-Dilly the day before, standing in front of the saloon. He was peering above the tops of the crude buildings across the street. He pulled his watch out, checked it for the zillionth time, and agitatedly replaced it. When he heard the barkeep open the door behind him, it was the happiest sound he had heard in the previous twenty-four hours. He did not care if roosters crowed or birds chirped or if a smiling merchant waved a good morning to him. He did like a cold beer for breakfast and a good, low-stakes monte game.

He followed the chunky barkeep to the counter. He tossed a dime on the bar top and received a schooner of cold beer. Smitty, the bartender, pulled the dime in and dropped it in his drawer. "What's eaten you, Ace? You look down today."

Ace nixed the remark with a wag of his finger. "Nothin' that can't be remedied."

Smitty nodded at the strange remark as though he understood and began his matutinal duties.

Soon, Ace's crew began sauntering in. His eight-man gang was at that point down to six with the absence of Hawk and Burke. Slick and Lefty of T-Dilly's group joined them. The nonappearance of Hawk and Burke prompted comments. Ace tried to allay their anxiety by telling them they were out scouting. What he did not tell them was that he was worried they had encountered Johnson and came out on the short end.

Ace caught Bobo's eye and nodded; he wanted a private parley. They sat next to the large window apart from the others. He always could depend on Bobo, who would fight at the drop of a hat and drop his own hat. The one thing about Bobo, however, that irked Ace was that he was basically good. He tried to bring out the worst in him but was not always successful. Be that as it may, he laid out his plans for the fight with John Lee Johnson. He pulled out his coin pouch and counted out $100 in gold. He made it clear that if he whipped the big Texan, he would get another $100 in gold. Bobo's eyes widened. His spirits were boosted by the money; he wanted to fight. Ace calmed him to go easy on the beer; he said the Texan had a huge reputation.

Bobo pugnaciously ran his finger beneath his nose. "When does he pull into town?"

Ace indecisively shook his head. "Before long." Ace's following words were a mixture of a command and a wish. "I want you to take him out … as in knockin' him to kingdom come. None of this pussyfootin' around and showin' mercy stuff." Ace waggled his finger and gave Bobo a confident smile. "Don't let me down."

Bobo gave his best smug look; he stood and gave a brave smile to his boss. He walked cockily to his companions at the bar. Ace's eyes drifted to the large window with the curlicue writing proclaiming it was Smitty's Saloon. He figured that his vigilance would change the bad start and ensure a good finish.

Ace caught sight of four well-dressed Mexicans coming through the batwings. These Mexicans were not like the field hands and ranch hands he saw daily around South Texas. They wore expensive clothing, and they appeared to be men who were used to giving orders instead of taking them.

Ace watched them ease to a table in the corner. They perused the saloon. Ace watched Smitty walk over and take their orders. Smitty was no dummy. He recognized quickly that they were men of wealth; he quickly deferred to them with a big smile and a wish to please.

Ace drowsily closed his eyes and fought off the impulse to doze. He took a sip from his schooner of beer and a gander out the window but saw nothing of consequence.

At eleven, a chubby boy of nine and his uncle entered the saloon and took their regular places against the wall. The man, Eugene, had a shock of white hair and wore glasses. His overalls did not conceal his big belly. He carried a fiddle. He sat and rosined his bow. He began to play "Bonnie Blue Flag'" in a fast tempo, which brought about a few cheers from the bar.

The hefty, freckled youngster, also wearing overalls, sat at a contraption with a seat and pedals. He began to pedal, and the ceiling fan commenced turning. Smitty had rigged a system whereby a rod that shot up from the floor turned the fan blades when the pedaling began. The belts that turned the fan were in a crawl space beneath the saloon. The boy, aptly named Tubby, pulled a cigar from his vest pocket and struck a match as he was pedaling away. He appeared comical as he puffed and pedaled. But the blades soon built up speed and began to stir the vapid air. The cooler air was offset by the flies circulating over the fan against the ceiling and the magnifying smells of body odor, gas, cigars, and beer.

The four Mexicans appeared bored as they drank beer, but they were more patient than uninterested. They were indeed very wealthy, but they were not only bankers or ranchero owners. They were bandidos who worked for the El Toro cartel that controlled the three Mexican States of Chihuahua, Sonora, and Coahuila. They had made a fortune betting on El Toro and working with this powerful man. They had come north of their own volition to find more about this mystery man John Lee Johnson.

Enrico Perez was the leader of the four. He had a jaded face, a pencil-thin mustache, and a large, black sombrero covered in silver filigree. He and the others had heard secondary conversations from the bar that the thick gringo named Bobo was to fight John Lee Johnson when he came to town. They had left Lako Springs, where T-Dilly was. He had suggested that this was the next logical place for John Lee Johnson to roost.

Their lassitude was faked in every way. Their interest was very heightened with the anticipation of seeing this next opponent of El Toro's. Enrico whispered to a companion dressed in a brown suit. Miguel Torres nodded at the words, pushed back his chair, and went to the bar. He talked to Bobo for a few minutes and came back to his table followed by the husky gringo. They nodded at Bobo and invited him to sit. He shrugged as though that were an odd request by strangers and Mexican strangers at that. But he sat.

Enrico pulled five large gold cartwheels from his money pouch tied to his fancy, silver-tipped belt and put them on the table. His knowing eyes looked into Bobo's green eyes as Bobo focused on the gold coins. Enrico's accented voice reached across the table. "You are to fight John Lee Johnson when he comes to town, no?"

Bobo's reluctantly raised his eyes from the $100 in gold stacked before him. "Yes, I aim to fight him." He looked at their inquisitive eyes and at the gold. "What's this?"

Enrico leaned back in his chair. He looked at his companions with appraising eyes and let his vision fall once more on Bobo. "If you whip this man named John Lee Johnson, the money is yours."

Bobo moved his eyes around meeting each Mexican's look. "This ain't a bet?"

Enrico shrugged. "No bet. Just a reward if you can defeat this man."

Bobo let a smile ease across his ruddy features. "You just keep that money handy. When he gets here and after I knock his ass off, I'll be wantin' that little extra dinero." He pushed back his chair, nodded his goodbyes to each of the Mexican gentlemen, and sauntered over to Ace. He told him the Mexicans wanted to tip him if he defeated the big Texan.

Ace gave a sideways look at the four Mexicans and let their offer to Bobo circulate in his mind. He nodded at Bobo that he appreciated the heads-up. He gave a sly smile as he watched the burly, tough guy head to the bar. He had briefed his men on his plan of action. All he needed at that point was for the big Texan to show up.

Ace pulled his pocket watch out. It was noon. He thoughtfully put it away, cut his eyes to the ceiling of the boxy saloon, and drummed his fingers impatiently. He was beginning to feel antsy about whether John Lee Johnson was making his way to Boscoville. He was about to rise when he saw an older gent wearing all black enter Smitty's. He knew he had not ridden his horse to the saloon. The only other place he could have hitched up was the livery stable at the end of the small community. The man he was watching stood just inside the batwings but seemed reluctantly bewildered as though searching for someone. Ace scoffingly looked the man up and down. Though he wore all black as Ace did and had a fancy holster and gun, Ace thought the older man was wearing a costume or playing a part.

Ollie spotted Ace and knew by instinct he was the gang leader. He walked over to his table beside the window and nodded affably enough. "You Ace Turner?"

Ace sized him up again before answering. "Yeah. You got a problem with that?"

Ollie shook his head. "I got a friend down at the livery barn that told me to tell you that he's got twenty thousand he needs to hide and wondered if you could give him a hand."

Ace cocked his head as though he had not heard him correctly. "Your friend would not be John Lee Johnson, would it?"

Ollie gave a big smile. "The one and the same."

"And he wants me to give him a little help, you say?"

Ollie nodded.

Ace rolled his cigar around in his mouth as he took on a dark, angry look. He knew he was being baited. The more he thought about it, the angrier he became. "You and your friend …" He said *friend* caustically. "… are looking for trouble." He exhaled a thin line of smoke. "I'm goin' to help your friend with his problem, and after I settle his hash, I aim to take care of you and your bold-as-brass attitude." He took another puff and continued his tirade. "And for comin' in here actin' like you're somebody." He abruptly dismissed his conversation with Ollie. He looked to his gang lined up at the bar. "Shorty, you and Bird Dog go down to the livery stable and help a man named John Lee Johnson hide his twenty thousand dollars."

Ollie watched Shorty and Bird Dog drain their shot glasses, wipe their mouths, and give Ace knowing smiles. They slapped their holsters and walked cockily to the batwings. They gave Ollie a sneering look as they exited.

Ollie watched them leave and looked at Ace. Ollie pointed toward the empty chair facing Ace. "You mind if I set down?"

Ace's eyes became slits. "Get the hell away from me you old bastard."

Ollie shrugged and blithely walked to the bar. Ace watched his back through angrily narrowed eyes. He did not like the insouciance and bravado he should not have had. He watched Ollie drinking a beer and smoking a cigar as though he did not have a care in the world. He heard gunfire. His eyes went to the batwings and back to Ollie, who seemed unaffected by the gunshots. That irked him even more.

Ace gave it about five minutes. When his men did not return, he rose to check on the matter himself. Lambert walked through the batwings. He looked Lambert over and thought he looked old but might still be a problem.

Lambert looked around the room and spotted Ace. He walked brazenly up to Ace and forked a thumb over his shoulder. "I just talked to a gent down at the livery stable. He says he needs more help tryin' to hide his twenty thousand."

Ace's eyebrows shot up like a window shade. His face became red in anger. He stared malevolently at Lambert. "You and that turd ..." He gave a quick flick of his finger toward Ollie. "... are playin' with fire." He postured that he was seconds from going for his pistol. However, when Lambert did not blink or act intimidated, Ace balked. Keeping wary eyes on Lambert, he said out of the corner of his mouth, "Luke, Strawberry, Tate."

The three men stepped back from the bar ready for action. Ace nodded in the direction of the livery stable. "Go down to the barn and take care of that smart-ass that thinks he's pullin' one."

The three men walked briskly toward the batwings all the while giving Lambert a baleful look.

After they departed, Lambert carefully walked backward with the intent of leaving the saloon. Ace quickly pulled his .44 and aimed it at Lambert. "You get your ass over at the bar. Don't make a move or I'll blow your liver out."

Lambert frowned. He had promised himself to avoid saloons and liquor, but he gave that a pass when he saw the ominous bore of that .44. He gave a deadpanned look at Ace and walked to the bar next to Ollie and Bobo.

Ace kept his pistol aimed at Lambert and Ollie, but after a minute or so, he holstered his weapon and sat with his eyes on the batwings. In just a matter of moments, he heard several booming gunshots. Ace jumped to his feet with his hand hovering over his .44. His worried face looked at the batwings and then at Ollie and Lambert. They looked calm as if they were attending a baptism. Their expressions were getting on his last nerve.

The batwings opened slowly. Sand Burr entered and looked the room over. As had Ollie and Lambert, he quickly determined who the boss was. He walked over to Ace and canted his head as though indicating something outside and behind him. "There's a fella down the street that says he needs your help in hiding twenty thousand dollars."

Ace swallowed. His dark, beetled eyebrows suddenly drooped. He said nothing. His nervous eyes were moving in concert with his brain. It suddenly occurred to him that he had vastly underestimated his opponent.

Sand Burr abruptly turned and headed to the bar. He did not act in any belligerent manner that would set off Ace. He ordered a beer and looked over at Bobo, who stood worriedly looking at Ace and the empty spaces where his cohorts had stood.

Sand Burr flipped a dime on the bar top and once more took in the husky Bobo. "You the hombre that's goin' to fight John Lee Johnson?"

Irritated that these upstarts had upset the social hierarchy in Smitty's saloon, Bobo gave Sand Burr an unwavering stare. "You want to take his place?"

Sand Burr nonchalantly shook his head and gave Bobo a sly smile. "But to be honest with you, I'd like to have second crack at you."

Lambert looked over Sand Burr's shoulder. "I'd like a go at you too."

Ollie, hearing Sand Burr and Lambert's challenges, peeked around Lambert and Sand Burr. "I want fourths." He shuddered and went back to drinking his beer.

Bobo slammed his fist on the bar and sent vibrations down the zinc top. "You both are smart-asses. When I get through with this John Lee fella, I aim to work both of you over." He leaned forward and glared at Ollie. "And Grandpa, I'll get to you too."

Bobo, fueled in anger by his own voice, decided to take on all three at once. He stepped from the bar indicating that he was not waiting on John Lee Johnson; he wanted to clean house immediately. He heard Ace's warning voice. His face relaxed, and he returned to his original posture as though Sand Burr and Lambert were nonexistent.

Slick and Lefty, two of T-Dilly's men, were on the other side of Bobo. They had taken quick note of Ace's disappearing men. They gave each other wary looks. They didn't like the odds; they would follow orders and watch Bobo fight the big man from North Texas, but they sure in hell were not going to take sides. They had a damn good idea of what had happened to five of Ace's men, and they had a good idea Ace knew it too.

The four Mexicans were playing cards, but the game was merely a distraction while their eyes moved constantly from cards to batwings hoping to catch sight of Johnson.

Eugene put his fiddle aside. Tubby stopped pedaling. There was little noise. Each bar patron drank quietly. The only noises were the buzzing of flies and the sounds of anxious breathing. They all knew hell was on its way.

A looming outline stood above the batwings. Bobo, who was facing Smitty and the stained bar mirror behind him, could not see clearly but felt the presence of someone at the entryway ... someone standing behind him ... the big man. He turned and nudged his beer schooner away. He watched as John pushed the batwings and entered.

Ace's cigar, which was at first clinched in his teeth, was barely balanced on his lower lip. The four Mexicans who had appeared bored for over an hour were wide-eyed.

Bobo watched the powerful figure almost glide in. He gave out a troubled exhale upon seeing someone who appeared to have been carved from stone. Bobo swallowed and looked at Ace for confidence. Ace looked as though all the blood had drained from his face. Bobo shook his head in a shuddering way as if to shake off his fear. He started walking toward his adversary.

John halted him with a palm out. "I'll get to you shortly, Bobo." He walked to Ace and looked down at the bandit leader. "You want to stand, or do you want me to drag you outta that chair?"

Ace spat his cigar aside and slowly stood, his eyes warily looking at John and at his crew, who stood at the bar like roosting birds. Ace started his hand downward in a hook and draw, but that aggressive action was interrupted when a jab that traveled less than a foot crashed into his face. The sickening sound of smashed flesh permeated the small saloon. Ace's face looked disfigured when he received the blow. A bloody arc of blood surrounded his face as he was knocked backward and off his feet. His body slid two feet. He lay with his arms sprawled above his head, and his boots quivered in quick vibrations. It appeared as though he had been killed by the single blow.

John turned to Bobo. "I imagine you got paid for fightin' me. Do you need the money that bad, Bobo?"

Bobo looked at the either dead or unconscious Ace and then at the powerful man before him. He unclenched his fists and shook his head. He relaxed his shoulders in admitted defeat and walked back to the bar. He slumped over the top of the bar and looked into the stained mirror with vacant eyes. The fact that John Lee Johnson knew his name had disconcerted him.

Slick and Lefty pushed their half-empty mugs aside and walked around the big Texan feeling lucky to exit the saloon. They stood on the porch and out of earshot from those inside. Lefty turned to the swarthy Slick. "Don't know about you, Slick, but the faster I'm away from that devil inside the better I'll feel."

Slick answered, "I heard that."

They soon rode away in a yellow dust cloud.

The four Mexicans saw that there was not going to be a fight. They were obviously disappointed. They rose and followed Enrico, who walked to Bobo. Enrico leaned in close to get Bobo's attention. He insultingly placed the five gold cartwheels in his leather pouch, one clinking coin at a time to make his point.

Bobo saw the mixture of contempt and disappointment in Enrico's eyes. All Bobo could do was exhale. He wanted the moment to pass quickly, but he had no idea what he would do once the big Texan left town. He just knew the world at ten o'clock was a whole lot different from the one at noon.

Enrico gave a blank look at John as he and his friends walked past him. Sand Burr walked from the bar toward the supine Ace Turner. He felt his neck and chest. "He's dead." He searched him and found over $400. He looked to John wondering about the money. John told him to keep it.

Smitty was watching from the bar. "If you give me his gun and holster and horse, I'll see to it he gets a Christian burial."

Ollie asked, "What exactly is a Christian burial?"

Smitty shrugged. "Eugene and Tubby will wrap him in this sheet." Smitty held up a yellowed sheet he retrieved from behind the bar. The sheet had some questionable stains. "Eugene will find a good place at least nine feet from my toilet and dig a grave. He and Tubby will wrap the body and place it in the grave and then fill it in. They'll doff their hats and remain silent for a spell and then come inside and eat some white beans I reckon."

Ollie nodded approvingly. "Well hell, that shore sounds Christian to me."

Sand Burr and Lambert gave each other wry looks.

John was expressionless. He said, "You can have everything you asked for, but we're keeping his saddle, bridle, and the two rifles he has in his scabbards."

Smitty knew there was no need for further dickering. He nodded and turned to Eugene and Tubby. "Boys, I'll give you a dollar a piece to go bury ol' Ace."

Eugene and Tubby nodded and went over to Ace's body. Each grabbed a boot ankle and dragged him across the floor; they headed around the end of the bar to the back exit.

Sand Burr, Lambert, and Ollie began walking to the batwings headed to the livery barn. They knew the plan and wanted to check the shoes on their mules and horses. Once on the street, Sand Burr and Lambert unsaddled and unbridled Ace's horse and confiscated the saddle along with his two Spencers. They made a rope hackamore and tied him to the hitch rack for Smitty.

Smitty grabbed a mop, slopped it into a bucket, and mopped up Ace's blood. Bobo stood stolidly at the bar. He looked around and realized he was the only survivor of the old gang. He sighed and glanced at John, who was finishing off his beer; he seemed about ready to depart. Bobo inhaled audibly several times to build his nerve up. "I'd like to talk to you if you'll let me."

John heard the hint of meekness in Bobo's voice. "I got time to listen."

Bobo moved closer and shrugged in frustration. "Mister, I got no one. No family, no home … nothing." He paused and tried to prevent himself from tearing up. "I wondered if you would consider me going with you." He tapped his hand on the bar top to give himself encouragement. "I'm loyal to the brand."

John nodded. "I'm goin' after T-Dilly. You have any problem with that?"

Bobo shook his head. "If you take me on, I'll fight for you." He paused. "And I don't really care much for T-Dilly."

John gave a half smile. "Get you and your horse down at the livery. We leave in less than an hour."

Bobo could hardly believe his ears. He smiled broadly but sobered it quickly. "I'm on my way now." He proudly slammed his fist on the bar top and headed out.

Smitty stopped mopping and looked at John as he was getting ready to leave. The bartender canted his head in the direction he imagined Bobo was headed. "He was the only one of 'em worth a damn."

John turned to leave; he replied succinctly, "I know."

Lako Springs was a warm-water spring that had once been used by Coronado and his men as they moved into Texas and beyond in the 1540s. It had been a spa for the Indians for centuries before that. In 1865, five whitewash adobe structures constituted Lako Springs—a saloon, a hospital, an emporium, a hotel, and a large administrative house all in a line and facing a high hill with a flat rock exterior. At the base of the hill, the hot springs spouted gurgling water from a rocky crater.

In the hotel, T-Dilly was lying in large metal tub filled with the spring's warm water. Rubbing his neck and traps was a thick, fully dressed Indian woman. If she took note of his nakedness, she never displayed it. T-Dilly leaned his arms down the sides of the tub and made throaty noises as the Kiowa woman used her thumbs and index fingers to apply pressure to those sinews. The bath and massage were interrupted by a knock at the door.

T-Dilly nodded to get the woman to stop the rubdown. He pulled his army .44 out of his nearby holster and leveled it at the door. "Who is it?" he growled.

Lefty announced it was he and Slick. T-Dilly lowered his pistol and told them to come in. They entered slowly and gave a look at the old Kiowa woman and back to the naked-as-a-jaybird T-Dilly. T-Dilly looked back and forth at them trying to read their expressions. T-Dilly impatiently barked, "What time is it? And what happened?"

Lefty and Slick looked at each other. Neither wanted to be the bearer of bad news because T-Dilly considered bearers of bad news just as culpable as the bad news itself. Lefty inhaled and began. "Boss, it's almost six." He took a deep breath and gave out the bad news. "That John Lee Johnson fella killed Ace Martin with a single punch." Lefty shrugged his shoulders and gave out the rest. "Their whole damn gang is dead 'cept one."

T-Dilly swallowed and placed his .44 back in his holster looped over a chair. "What about that hombre Bobo?"

"He was the one that survived. On top of that, he never fought Johnson. I guess he had second thoughts."

Alarmed and angered, T-Dilly stood. Water ran down his body. He grabbed a towel from the Kiowa woman and started drying off hurriedly. "Where's this Johnson fella now?"

"I guess still in Boscoville. As far as I know, he's now runnin' the place."

T-Dilly was thoughtful. "This Johnson fella seems to have things goin' his way." He toweled off some more. "You boys go get some rest. We're goin' to Boscoville and burn every damn building until we run him outta his hidey-hole." He gave a grim smile. "I've had enough of this damn man." He stepped out of the tub and grabbed his shirt. He paused and with a pensive expression remembered Jericho Davis standing watch on Ascension Hill. "Lefty, did you tell Jericho all about what went down in Boscoville?"

Lefty nodded. He was glad he and Slick had informed the lookout about possible strange riders headed their way. "Yeah, boss, he knows all about it."

T-Dilly flicked his fingers at them in dismissal as he pulled up his pants. He said to himself, "That damn Bobo probably has some of my money, and I want it back."

Lefty and Slick turned to walk away as they heard the words they expected. "We ride at midnight."

John left Smitty's saloon, went to the livery barn, and shifted the pack loads onto the mules. He knew Sand Burr and Lambert had checked all the shoes on his horses and mules. He was shifting their ammunition and heaviest weight to the big mule he rode when he noticed his men stiffen. He sensed the reason for their discomfort. He caught their vision and looked at the newly arrived Bobo. John said calmly, "He's ridin' with us now."

They accepted his decision wordlessly, but it was apparent they had reservations. They did not greet or show any outward sign of friendliness to Bobo. Bobo knew it would be like that. He never made eye contact. He realized he would have to earn some trust. He concluded he could not interact with any of the old guard just then.

John gave them the news they knew was coming. "We're pullin' out to Lako Springs as soon as we pack some food and water. I saw those two birds that work for T-Dilly pull out. They got a head start on us. T-Dilly's probably thinkin' we're goin' to take it easy and rest up, but we're not. We're goin' straight for him."

Sand Burr and Lambert exchanged knowing smiles; they had adjusted to his aggressive thinking. Ollie displayed a sad face. He wanted a few more days at Smitty's saloon. Bobo was expressionless; he just wanted to earn his spurs.

Thirty minutes later, they were riding south to Lako Springs following Bobo, who was well acquainted with the topography. The cut he led them through in the steep hills shortened their ride by thirty minutes. It was sundown when they reached the vicinity of Lako Springs. They pulled up and decided to take a break. John wanted to ensure they were on the same page about the attack. He gathered them as they sipped water. He nodded toward Bobo. "We're getting' close, and I need to know the layout of the town. I especially need to know where they keep their horses."

Bobo dropped to one knee and began drawing a rough sketch of the resort. He drew the corral on the west side of the town and went down the line naming the buildings. He suddenly stopped and looked up at the four inquiring faces. "One thing I forgot. Nearly every outfit that goes there has a guard on top of what people call Ascension Hill." Bobo drew the smaller hill, which was just 1,000 feet from the hill that fronted the warm water spring. "This lookout can see for a mile, and it ain't goin' to be easy to get past him. If he sees something threatenin', he usually fires a warnin' shot."

John thoughtfully looked at the rendering in the sand. He let his eyes move over to Bobo, who was looking up. "How well do you know T-Dilly's men?"

Bobo shrugged and honestly answered, "I know 'em all. But they looked down on Ace and me and the other boys." He paused as he considered

John's words and where those words were headed. "You're askin' me if I can ride to the guard and maybe he won't shoot me since he'll know me?"

John shrugged his yard-wide shoulders. "Bobo, if you can make it to that hombre and overpower him, that shore in hell would make it easier on the rest of us."

Bobo looked at each face peering down at him as he was kneeling next to his drawing. He knew that could be the opportunity to earn the respect of his newfound friends. His eyes made the full gamut until they resettled on John's face. "I'll do it." What he did not say was that whoever was standing guard would not be all that thrilled to see a member of Ace Turner's gang. He knew it could be a real possibility that the lookout would just blow him out of the saddle.

But John and his men were thinking the same thing. John knew Lako Springs and T-Dilly had to be dealt with. He did not relish putting Bobo in harm's way, but he had to make the June 15 deadline and could not just swing wide of the town. He realized they would be on his heels the whole way to Mexico. He nodded to Bobo. "If you don't want to do this, just say so."

Bobo shook his head. "I'm a little scared, but I got a hundred dollars in my pocket, and I intend to bet on you in Mexico." He gave himself a brave grin. "Like I said, I'll do it."

John knelt beside Bobo and pointed to the drawing of the corral. He looked at Sand Burr, Lambert, and Ollie. "When Bobo takes care of this hombre, me and him will head to the corral and work east." His eyes went to Sand Burr. "You and Lambert and Ollie start at the eastern end and work toward me." He stood. He was not going to insult them by asking if anyone wanted out. He knew that they were proud men, and though they were anxious and perhaps worried, they did not show it.

Bobo did not have to be told. He went to his sixteen-hand chestnut gelding, mounted, and headed out in a gallop.

As they watched him ride toward the distant hill, the thought that he could sell them out was in their minds. If he did, it would result in a scurried retreat with the numbers on T-Dilly's side. But no one wanted to be the first to bring that possibility up. They saw the hill faintly in the distance. Without being told, they placed their horses behind boulders that dotted their position.

Jericho Davis, the sentinel, was a grungy-looking man. His face was covered in dirt and facial oil. His sloping hat brim covered in alkali shielded his wooly-worm eyebrows and tea-brown eyes. He was dozing when he spotted in the dying rays of the sun a three-stocking chestnut headed his way. Normally, he would have unsheathed his Spencer and shot a round in the air to alert his comrades, but he recognized Bobo. He let a sneer ease across his oleaginous features. After Lefty and Slick had informed him about what had happened in Boscoville, Jericho wanted the opportunity to berate Bobo for his cowardice. After verbally abusing him, he intended to take him to T-Dilly and let the boss deal with him.

Lefty had informed him that T-Dilly had given $500 to Ace Martin who in turn had given some money to Bobo to fight Johnson. Jericho had a good idea that T-Dilly probably would not be in a happy mood that both men had failed. He knew by bringing in Bobo, it would earn him a feather in his cap and some high-grade whiskey for a change.

When Bobo got closer, he recognized Jericho and breathed a sigh of relief. He knew him well. He did not like him. He considered him mean spirited and stupid, but as he got closer to Jericho, he realized he liked that stupid part. He rode up the small, soft dirt incline and settled in a few feet from the leering Jericho.

Jericho was leaning over his pommel with crossed wrists. His greasy face was cast in disdain. He looked Bobo up and down. "Well, well, well. Looky what we have here."

Bobo did not want to spook Jericho, so he acted as though he were not offended by the obvious contempt. "Hidy, Jericho. Good to see you."

Jericho scornfully shook his head and parroted Bobo's words in a girly voice: "Hidy, Jericho, good to see you." He spat to the side and wiped the excess off his lips by the stained underwear sleeve covering his forearms. He straightened up. "You got a hell of lot of nerve showin' up here, Bobo."

Bobo feigned naivety. "What do you mean?"

Jericho's anger rose considerably. "What I'm sayin' is that you showed more yeller than new mustard you stupid bastard." Spittle was flying from his lips. "You got some money you didn't earn!" Jericho suddenly had a revelation. His enraged eyes suddenly softened, "Hand it over, Bobo."

Bobo faked indignation. "I was aimin' to give it to T-Dilly."

That statement stymied Jericho. He licked his grimy lip and studied on Bobo's words. He knew he would never see a cent of that money if he took Bobo as a prisoner to T-Dilly. On the other hand, he reasoned if he killed Bobo and hid his money, he might come back for it later and no one would be the wiser. Bobo knew what was going on in Jericho's brain. He sensed Jericho was going to make a play on him.

Bobo surreptitiously moved his big chestnut closer to Jericho. He knew a showdown was impending and decided to take matters into his own hands and not wait on the grimy lobo. Jericho was still giving him the evil eye. Bobo knew that a gunshot would bring unwanted attention, so he decided to go for broke with his choice of weapons.

But the inching toward Jericho was not lost on Jericho. He jutted out a stained finger toward Bobo and growled, "Hold it right there, pilgrim."

Bobo quickly reached behind and pulled his nine-inch Bowie knife from its sheath in the back of his gun belt. Jericho saw that the line had been crossed and he was reaching for his pistols. Bobo leaped across the small space and caught Jericho under his whiskered chin, and they both tumbled to the sandy soil. They landed with a thud with Jericho on the bottom sending up a puff of beige dust. The impact temporarily knocked the wind out of Jericho. He crawled desperately away from Bobo trying to regain his feet. Bobo struck with his knife and nailed Jericho in the leg, and Jericho let out a blood-curdling scream. Jericho gritted his stained teeth and clawed for his weapon, but the younger Bobo was quickly on him. He and Jericho fought for control of Jericho's army .44. Jericho cursed his fate and Bobo's ancestry as the younger man wrested it away. Beneath his tattered hat brim, Jericho's eyes widened in fear. He saw that he was at the mercy of Bobo. His eyes were focused on the menacing bore of his .44 in Bobo's hands.

Bobo stood and looked down at Jericho. "Yeller as new mustard, hey?"

Jericho knew better than to acknowledge the mocking comment he had made earlier. He gave a big sigh. "What now?"

Bobo wordlessly pulled a rope from his saddle and told Jericho to stand. He tied his arms close to his body and then fettered his legs. "Jericho, you'll see the conclusion to this."

Bobo could faintly see his new friends moving toward him in the purple gloaming. John and the rest soon rode up the incline. Each rider nodded in respect to Bobo. He had earned his spurs. They dismounted and wordlessly, according to plan, began digging and soon had a hole dug deep enough that would fit Jericho up to his chin.

Jericho looked at Lambert as he stood with his shovel at arm's rest. "I reckon that I'm supposed to be in that hole?"

Lambert gave a slow nod. "I reckon so."

Jericho sighed. "What direction should I face do you think?"

Lambert shrugged. "I wouldn't want to face east because of the sun." He ran his hand up to his chin in thought. "I'd face north."

"Why north?"

Lambert drolly said, "I saw some birds out there among that cactus. It'd give you something to look at I suppose."

Jericho sighed. "I do like lookin' at birds. Sometimes, I've shot at 'em, but I don't reckon they minded. I never hit any of 'em."

Lambert nodded. "I'd take a good drink of water before I got in that hole. It might be days before someone finds you."

"How long do you think before someone finds me? Got any idea?"

Lambert shrugged. "Probably two, three days."

Jericho looked in the hole. "If you don't mind, I'll take you up on that water."

Lambert retrieved his canteen from his saddle pommel. He put it up to Jericho's mouth and let him drink his fill.

Jericho asked Lambert his name. Lambert told him. Jericho studied on his answer. He wanted to say he remembered a Lambert whose wife had died and he had become a hell raiser, but when he caught a look from Lambert, he decided to be quiet.

They placed Jericho in the hole and shoveled in dirt up to his chin. He asked Lambert to adjust his hat and scratch his nose, which he did.

John pulled them out of earshot of Jericho and had them set their watches. He wanted the attack to take place at ten. They mounted up and began riding to their assigned spots. John and Bobo pulled their horses and mules on a long tether as they rode due west. They hid their horses in a ravine that was walking distance to the corral that housed the gang's horses. At ten, John and Bobo began walking.

Two guards, one Mexican and the other Anglo, were casually smoking thin cigars and making idle conversation. They were leaning against the wooden poles of the large corral. They were employees of the town and not privy to all the commotion in Boscoville concerning John Lee. The Mexican was strumming a guitar and singing a sentimental song about lost love. The gringo was smiling and occasionally joining in on the chorus. They had just reached the apex of the song with the Mexican hitting a trilling high note. The song ended with the guitar hitting a discordant note. They swallowed and slowly began reaching for the clouds when they heard pistols being cocked and the cold reality of gun barrels pressed against their backs.

John spoke in Spanish for them to drop their gun belts. The Mexican quickly laid his guitar aside, and both unbuckled their holsters. Bobo had the ropes. Using his revolver as a pointer, he trundled the guards into the small office where he and John trussed them up tightly and tied them back to back to a support pole in the middle of the room.

As they were leaving the small, ramshackle building, John put out an arm and stopped Bobo, who thought he had done something wrong. He peered anxiously into John's gray eyes partially hidden in the shadows of his brim. John sensed Bobo's anxiety and quickly allayed his fears. He gave him a friendly slap on the back. "Bobo, you mentioned something today that has given me cause for concern."

Bobo was silent. John continued. "You said the Comancheros ran this town."

Bobo nodded.

"Well, what's the connection with the Comancheros and the Austin bunch?"

Bobo shrugged. "I know they're connected someway, but from what I've heard, they're just workin' together loosely." He knew John wanted him to be brief; he sped up his assessment. "The alcalde of this town works for the Comancheros and takes orders from them. He knows that the real leader of both groups is probably someone higher up than that Stevens hombre. The alcalde is friendly with T-Dilly but makes him pay for stayin' here just like any poor soul passin' through." He paused. "T-Dilly means nothin' to him."

John canted his head in thought. "In other words, you're tellin' me that if we shoot the livin' hell out of T-Dilly's men, that alcalde or whatever his title is ain't goin' to do a damn thing about it."

Bobo gave a tight nod. "I got an idea that whoever loses this battle tonight will end up in a Mexican silver mine—either us or them—courtesy of the Comancheros."

"If you know that, so does T-Dilly's men."

Bobo gave just half of a smile. "Way I see it, boss."

John grunted. Bobo's words confirmed his suspicions. John inhaled. "Well, hell. Let's get this fandango started."

The cantina—what gringos would call a saloon—had no harmonium or rinky-dink piano but did have a female dancer, and they served wine and tequila as much as they did beer. This particular drinking establishment was medium sized. It had rough beams running just beneath the ceiling from which hung sundry metal containers holding variously colored peppers and in some cases flowers.

A self-absorbed guitar player in a dark corner strummed his thick-bodied instrument with slow, heavy chords but then would pick up the tempo with frenzied, facile fingers.

The light that came from the bracketed wall lanterns was muted, yellow, and oily, redolent of an Impressionist painter.

Bellied up at the bar were three of T-Dilly's men. The lithe Lefty was in the middle. To his left was Big Roy, a red-faced man who laughed too much. To Lefty's right was the saturnine Felix Green. They had their backs to the open oval door that led to the street.

Big Roy turned to Lefty. "What time we pullin' out?"

"Twelve."

Big Roy shook his head, "Well, hell. I might as well just stay up."

Felix, who always appeared sour, chimed in, "If I go to bed and don't get my full sleep, I just feel worse."

Big Roy poured a shot of tequila and downed it in one gulp. He wiped his mouth with his sleeve and sighed. "What about this John Lee Johnson feller? How come he's so hard to kill?"

Lefty paused in his answer; he thoughtfully swirled his foam-laden beer. He gave a stern look to his friends. "When I get aholt of him, he won't be so hard to kill no more."

Big Roy looked at him from the corner of his eyes and he cogitated Lefty's words. "How come you didn't kill him when you saw him earlier today?"

Lefty's voice raised a register. "I done told you, Roy, T-Dilly said let him live so he could fight that damned Mexican. And that's the only reason. I was plannin' on kickin' that ass for him, but I knew I had to get here."

Big Roy saw he was getting Lefty riled, so he just nodded and dug for a cigar. But another question just popped out. "You think this Johnson hombre is still in Boscoville?"

Lefty snorted. "Hell yeah he is." He let a sly smile move across his spare features. "Probably sleepin' in ol' Ace's bed."

Felix, who was listening and nodding his approval of Lefty's words, suddenly felt the presence of someone behind him. He lifted his scowling face to look into the large, smoky mirror bracketed on the adobe wall behind the bar. He saw the faint image of an immense man, someone who looked like the embodiment of the Archangel Michael. When Felix uttered a nervous, throaty sound, Big Roy and Lefty looked his way and saw the direction of his eyes. They lifted their vision to the mirror and saw the same frightening sight.

John's deep voice added to the terror. "Drop your gun belts and knives and head to the door."

Lefty, trying to save face after his bragging, said, "Wonder if we don't want to?"

He was quickly turned around by two strong hands as though he were a small sack of flour. His eyes, centered on John's chest, panned up to catch the unyielding flint of John's gray eyes. Lefty gulped. He turned to his left and right and nodded for his pals to unbuckle. Bobo entered with his army .44 extended and picked up their weapons.

Lefty looked at Bobo and back at John. He turned his gaze once more on Bobo and sarcastically stated, "You shore change friends fast, Bobo."

Bobo nodded. "I traded up, Lefty. I reckon you ought to do the same."

When Lefty sneered, Bobo grabbed him by his shirt. "Listen, you turd, if you give me any more lip, I'm goin' to fix your wagon, you understand? Now head out the door and get goin' to the corral. I got to do me some rope tyin'."

Lefty nodded. He rapidly learned trying to maintain his manhood was causing him to lose his manhood. He dropped his pretense of toughness, and he and the others marched meekly out the door into the night with Bobo following.

John perused the cantina for any other possible gang member. When he did not see anyone of interest, he departed the place and took the narrow rock walkway that led to the other buildings.

As he marched past the building used as a hospital, he heard a groan coming through the large, oval, open doorway. He knew he needed to move on down the street, but he could not allow one of T-Dilly's men to fall through the cracks.

His gray eyes scanned to the right. He drew his navy six and entered the dimly lit room. Two candles were giving off yellow light. He made out in the murky glow the outline of a nun sitting behind a tiny wooden desk in a shallow alcove.

His eyes went to the figure of a man on a cot. He was groaning and stirring around beneath his thin cover. John took note that the nun seemed to be shifting around and aware of his presence. He ignored her and walked quickly to the man. John threw back the thin cover, grabbed the man by his underwear top, and pulled him close to his face. The face he saw was an old man's and was painfully thin. The man's eyes opened wide with fear. His toothless mouth gaped in confusion.

John caught sight of the waddling, protesting nurse headed his way dressed in her nun's habit. John looked at her as he let the old man slowly down to his cot.

As she drew near, she pulled up short. John looked like a fierce giant to her. Her eyes perused the massive muscles that looked even more frightening in the wavering candlelight highlighted by black shadows. He seemed to her to be from another world. She composed herself and walked to the cot. Her eyes glared outrage. She started to bless him out in Spanish when she was interrupted by the old man, who had settled back on his stained pillow. As she listened to the elderly man, her hands went up to her mouth to suppress what looked like a cross between outrage and laughter. John looked at her in wonder as he considered her mercurial emotions.

The old man said something else in Spanish. John could speak rudimentary Spanish but could not follow the rapid exchange between the nurse and the patient; he knew, however, they were words of laughter mixed with mild reproaches.

The nurse turned from the patient and introduced herself as Sister Rachel. John introduced himself. She nodded at the elderly man. In a heavily accented voice, she said, "This is Ernesto Lopez."

John gave a perfunctory nod knowing this was eating up his valuable time. He holstered his navy .36. He was looking for any excuse to leave. She sensed that the giant was anxious to depart. Again, her hand shot up to her mouth to keep from laughing. "Ernesto has shall we say been constipated for over two weeks." She paused and looked down with a reproving but kind look at the old man, who was smiling and showing his red maw. She looked into the Texan's inquiring eyes. "He told me to tell you he is no longer stove up. He says you have cured him."

John gave her an incredulous look. He looked at the seemingly happy old gent and back to the twinkling eyes of the nurse. He moved back one step and then another. He shrugged his massive shoulders and gave an awkward nod to them. Since he did not know how to respond, he did not. He left hurriedly back to the street.

After fettering Lefty and his two companions, Bobo took their weapons he had requisitioned earlier and began firing them into the air—sporadically at first and then more rapidly.

On the other end of town Sand Burr, Lambert, and Ollie, hidden behind some auxiliary structures awaiting Bobo's signal, fired their weapons innocuously into the sky.

T-Dilly, who was restlessly tossing and turning, rose on his elbows in his bed. He ran a hand over his whiskers and shook his head as if to clear it. Some of the gunshots that woke him were close by; others were in the distance. He initially thought it was his men acting foolishly, but when he heard footsteps and alarmed voices of his crew running down the corridor of the hotel, he knew he was under attack.

As the cobwebs cleared, T-Dilly hastily slipped on his pants. After he was fully dressed and had his holster on, he heard a frantic knock at the door.

T-Dilly jerked the door back and looked with anger at his right-hand man, Gabe Green. Gabe, big and burly with hard features, was taken aback by T-Dilly's fierce expression. Trying to ignore that look, Gabe forked a thumb over his shoulder. "That damn Johnson feller's in town."

T-Dilly gave him a sarcastic look and asked with words dipped in acid, "You wouldn't josh me now, would you, Gabe?"

Gabe did not answer the gibe.

T-Dilly nodded for Gabe to enter. T-Dilly canted his head toward the open oval window behind him. "Do you know how many men he's got?"

"Not exactly, but Wylie told me he thanks there's about twenty of them."

T-Dilly shook his head. "There ain't no way in hell Johnson has that many men." There was a long pause as T-Dilly listened to the increased volume of gunshots. It was obvious to Gabe that T-Dilly's confidence was waning.

T-Dilly gritted his teeth. He gave an anxious look at Gabe. "Have you heard from Lefty, Big Roy, and Felix?"

Gabe shrugged. "I thank they're dead."

"I reckon Wylie told you that too."

Gabe recognized the sarcasm and remained quiet.

T-Dilly's mind was spinning. His brain was caught between the doubt that it was as bad as Gabe was saying and the uncertain reality he found himself in. His mind was a spinning roulette wheel, but the whirling stopped. He grabbed Gabe by his grubby vest. The information about Lefty and the others suddenly landed home in his troubled mind. "Are you damned shore you're tellin' me the straight of it, Gabe?"

Gabe wobbled his head around indecisively and then nodded as though he had made his mind up.

"And what of Jericho Davis?"

Gabe reluctantly sighed. "He must be dead too, boss."

He released Gabe's vest almost apologetically. "All right. Damn all this to hell," he hissed as he clinched his fists. "Johnson wins the first round." T-Dilly grabbed his hat off the washstand and walked out into the hallway. He reluctantly nodded toward the stairs at the end of the landing that headed down and to the back door. He and Gabe walked briskly down the hallway and down the stairs. Along the way, they picked up a third member of the gang, Leoncio Gomez. The three made their way quickly to the alcalde's stable behind his house. After saddling up, they quickly rode out into the darkness away from the heavy volume of pistol and rifle reports.

The gunfight continued throughout the night. The Austin outfit suffered a few casualties but not enough to surrender. But just before sunrise when they discovered that T-Dilly had been talked into leaving, they began to lose heart. That morning under a white flag attached to a rifle barrel, the remaining stragglers walked out of the hotel and sought terms with John Lee Johnson.

The alcalde showed up just as they were laying their sidearms and rifles on the ground. He was a pure Spaniard, which he extolled from the beginning. Señor Madura, a thin, graying man, appeared with three of his law officials, all beefy Mexicans with black sombreros and armed with Spencers. He introduced himself to John and his men and let it be known that he would take the matter from there. John watched him and his deputies march the prisoners away to a cell in the basement of his large house.

What haunted him was that as Lefty was being shoved into the ranks of the prisoners, he said the men would not have surrendered if they had known the alcalde would end up in charge of them. He was referring to the death sentence of being sold to Mexican miners and working underground for the rest of their lives.

John was mulling that over when the alcalde returned with an oily grin and an extended hand. John weakly shook his hand. Señor Madura pulled a thin, black cigar from the pocket of his black, Spanish-style suit. As he lit his smoke, he kept his eyes on John. "Since you've handed over these vermin to me, you may stay here two nights for free, and that includes everything except for food and drink." He paused as he contentedly smoked. "If you give me their horses and weapons, I will see to it that you have carte blanche, and that includes all the food and drink you are able to consume."

John knew he and his men needed rest. They still had a long journey ahead. But he shook his head about trading the Austin bunch for the two nights. He matter-of-factly stated, "We'll pay our way, Alcalde."

The alcalde did not like that response. He exuded a certain iciness as he nodded. But he was a consummate politician. He traded his true feelings for a patronizing smile. He gave a quick "As you wish" and returned to his house.

CHAPTER 13

J.D. Rysinger and his gang were making their way close to the ranch that Reginald Carlton had once called home. The plan was in place; they would kill the two bankers and let the woman go. J.D. promised to pay each man $100 and the preacher $50 once they had accomplished their objective. They would then light out to the Nations, where J.D. had a dozen places to hide with nearby towns in Texas to rob.

As they were riding at a very quick pace, Carlton kept his eyes straight ahead so Punkin' Head would not be analyzing him. Of all the trash he was riding with, he feared the misshapen man the most. He knew that once he was able to kill Yvette, he could possibly pass it off as an accident to the others. But he knew Punkin' Head would divine his intentions and put him in danger. He thus had two people he wanted dead—Yvette and Punkin' Head.

Floyd, who had cured Yvette's paint horse of foot thrush, was riding the nine-year- old mare gently behind the wagon. Seth was driving the wagon with Yvette close to his side. On the last day they had spent at the abandoned ranch, they had pretty much put aside the pretense of not loving the other. She was nestled up close to Seth as though he were her husband. Seth reacted to her attention.

They looked like two inseparable ticks to Floyd. He was observing all their outward affection with a knowing smile, but his mind was occupied with the more serious matter at hand—J.D. Rysinger. He would frequently pull up the mare, turn, and take a studied gander behind him even in the growing darkness. He was looking for dust or to hear any distant noises. He had recommended that they go the long way around to Roxy rather than the quick way. He had a premonition that they might run straight into the lunatic bandit if they had gone the usual way.

J.D. Rysinger's bunch was close enough to see the Carlton house. In the gloaming, they saw a dim light coming from inside. He drew his army .44 and let his one good eye slide side to side. A wolfish grin spread across his greasy features. He felt good barking out orders once more. "Boys, we caught 'em with their britches down." He then commanded Toby and Punkin' Head to circle the house and approach it from the east.

He watched his two men peel off and start riding wide to box their quarry. When he thought his men were in place, he slapped his reins. He, Adrian, and the preacher started riding down the road at a gallop. J.D. had his mouth angrily snarled. He used his good arm to snap the bridle reins as they grew closer. He pulled out his .44 and cocked it. He intended to use it and show no mercy.

When he got even with the lit doorway, he savagely pulled his horse to a stop and made a fast dismount. He was shouting obscenities as he bolted through the aperture. He saw the coal oil lantern with the glass reservoir half filled with fuel. His good eye then moved to the letter lying on the table close to the lantern.

He picked it up. He gave it a once-over as though he could read. He looked around the house disappointed that no one was there. He quickly handed the missive to the preacher, who took the letter slowly to make sure J.D. knew he was indispensable.

The preacher straightened the page and read, "Dear, J.D. You're an idiot. You ain't a good human being. And you're a worse thief. And as you can now see with your one eye, we ain't here. Floyd Maccabee."

J.D. did not want the others to hear that message. He snatched the yellowed page from the preacher's hands and bellowed, "Damn his soul!" He tore the paper to shreds and threw them on the floor. His good eye moved to the low-level flame of the lantern and secondly to the eyes of the preacher. He snarled, "Well, hell! What are you waitin' for? A damn invitation?"

Carlton smiled knowingly. He slapped the lantern off the table, and it crashed sending oily yellow, fiery tendrils across the floor.

They ran out the door and met Toby and Punkin' Head. They did not have to ask if the banker and woman were there. The preacher hissed to himself but loud enough to be heard, "They're headed to Roxy."

J.D. gave an evil grin. "My thoughts exactly." They mounted up and decided to take the shortcut to Roxy. They wanted to be ready for the bankers when they reached town.

After they had ridden at a steady clip for two hours, they felt the air becoming humid. J.D. gave a raised hand for them to stop. He looked at the roiling sky and cussed. He did not need a damn storm. The heavens began grumbling and continued to do so. A bolt of lightning sizzled across the sky. In the electrical, light-blue luminesce, Punkin' Head gave a disgusted grunt.

J.D., knowing Punkin' Head's usual throaty noises when he was disgruntled, turned with his one good eye crowned by an arched eyebrow. He was ready to cuss him out when in another lightning flash he discovered the reason for Punkin' Head's displeasure. J.D.'s head started swiveling back and forth. He then hissed out the words, "Damn that preacher!" In a trailing sibilant statement, he conceded, "He's gone."

All four bandits sat there quietly mulling over the situation. Punkin' Head broke the silence. "J.D., I got to tell you this—hate to say it, but got to say it. That damn preacher tried to kill his wife. He left her for dead and went on to try and live some sort of other life." He paused. There was dead silence. "Since he failed the first time, he's out to try and kill her again—not those two bankers." His words hit home, but no one said anything fearing a cussing from J.D.

J.D. leaned forward with his hands on his pommel. The flickering blue light from the lightning revealed a face filled with hate. He disconsolately dropped his head trying to fight off another disappointment. "How long have you knowed this, Punkin' Head?"

"Toby went to town yesterday to get some supplies. Ever' one is talkin' about it. I figured you'd want to give the bastard the chance to prove himself, but he was playin' us all."

J.D. did not upbraid Punkin' Head; he knew the man was right. He also knew he needed him more than ever. J.D. kept nodding as though thoughts were zipping around his brain and he was trying to catch one. He turned his mount around and addressed his small group. "You boys go to Roxy. I want you to kill those two damn bankers if they get by me, and then it's over." He made a level motion with his hand palms down. He repeated, "It's over. I ain't so shore that the preacher, damn his soul, can kill his wife with those two bankers standin' guard on her."

J.D. gave another once-over to his men as though gauging their mood. Another crackling flash of jagged lightning threw surrealistic light over the countryside. J.D. took that as a cue. He spurred his horse and began headed back toward the Carlton spread.

The other three watched him ride away. Toby and Adrian turned to Punkin' Head seeking advice. It was obvious to them that J.D. had drifted off the deep end. He had once ruled them through fear, but then, he governed them with the promise of money. However, they were penniless and had little hope in sight. Following two bankers seemed gloomily foolish. The heavy air and the crackling lightning served as the backdrop for their sober thinking. Collectively, they sadly realized there was no money and never was. J.D. was no longer viable. He was something from the past. He had outlived his usefulness to them.

Punkin' Head understood the moment. He sat wordlessly looking at the direction J.D. had gone. He maintained a stoic look letting the others come to the same conclusion he had made weeks earlier. After another heavy roll of thunder, Punkin' Head turned his face side to side to catch Adrian's and Toby's attention. He did. They wanted direction. "Boys, it's like this. I told both of you when I was out of money, I was out of here." He nodded to emphasize his next words. "Well, I'm outta money."

He pulled a cigar from his vest pocket and struck a match. The heavy orange glow dimly illuminated his grotesque features. His voice was low and filled with pent-up emotion. "If we go into Roxy and try to kill those two damned bankers … You realize this is Sheriff George French's county. Do you in your wildest imaginations think we could get away from all them damned deputies? Do you really think we could get to the Nations? These county sheriffs don't have the Texas Rangers anymore, but they shore in hell have each other. They would be on us like a dog on gravy."

He let his practical words set in. He puffed on his cigar and shook his head in disgust at the mess J.D. had gotten them into. His eyes moved in the darkness to Adrian. "Adrian, do you know of any money J.D. has?"

Adrian shook his head. Realizing that no one heard him shaking his head, he said, "My grandfather supposedly had some money, a lot of it, but I'm a thinkin' that was just a family story." He sadly confessed to his two comrades answering Punkin' Head's question, "I ain't seen any of it, and I'm twenty-four."

Punkin' Head looked up at the flickering streaks of lightning. The threatening backdrop and Adrian's admission helped Punkin' Head make up his mind, "Let's go back to the preacher's old house and spend the night. In the morning, let's head to the Nations. We got some friends there who'll give us shelter." He added as he pulled his reins up as to make ready to go. "We can ride like free men all the way to the Nations. That failed bank robbery hadn't caused a ripple with them law dogs."

Punkin' Head gigged his horse, and the three rode in the same direction J.D. had taken earlier.

J.D. trotted his horse for two hours. He passed the adobe house. He glimpsed the road when lightning flashed. The flickering light also revealed wagon ruts. He saw two sets of horse tracks following behind. He figured one of the bankers was riding a horse trailing behind the wagon. He deduced the other horse print had been left by the preacher. He rode another two hours. The rain began pelting him. He heard wet thumps on his hat brim. Occasionally, he witnessed jagged strikes of angry yellow savagely thrusting toward the ground. As he continued his angry search, he saw something ahead that all the earmarkings of Moses and the burning bush.

His one good eye bulged as he drew closer. He saw a mesquite tree burning, but the soft rain seemed to have dampened the flames. Close by, he saw a dead horse. He reined up. The rain was sliding off his brim and soaking his shirt. He drew his pistol and dismounted. He tied his sorrel and walked sideways along the road skirted by mesquite. He paused from time to time to allow the capricious lightning to reveal his position in relation to the dead horse. Once he was close enough to see the horse properly, he saw that it was the preacher's.

He looked slowly back and forth trying to spot the preacher. In a quick, ethereal flash of lightning, he saw boot marks and knew the preacher was nearby. Soaked with rain, J.D. paused by the road trying to determine a course of action. It dawned on him that he wanted to kill the preacher more than he did the bankers. He felt betrayal was more egregious than defending yourself as the bankers had.

He continued to stand stock still until the lightning's glare would reveal where the boot marks headed. He saw them leading into the gap among the trees. Apparently, the preacher knew where his wife was.

J.D. figured the bankers and the preacher's wife had pulled off the road. He surmised that the preacher had seen that the wagon tracks headed through an opening. It appeared that the preacher had dismounted and was sneakily making his way through the prickly branches. He may or may not have known his horse was killed by a bolt of lightning.

J.D. nodded to himself that he had all his enemies clumped together. He began following the boot prints. He would pause until the lightning revealed the tracks. When it became black again, he would pause and wait for the flickering strikes to guide him. He repeated this procedure several times. Up ahead, he thought he saw the outline of a wagon with the bed covered in a tarp. He knew the preacher was close by.

A heavy bolt shot across the black sky. The coruscating afterglow revealed the preacher scrunched behind a patch of weeds. He was holding a Spencer rifle across his chest. What irked J.D. even more was that J.D. had given him that rifle.

Carlton was trying to figure out who was who around the wagon. Although they had a tarp spread wide over the wagon, he thought that Yvette would be in the wagon bed and the two men would be under the wagon. He was lifting his rifle when he heard the ominous click of a .44. His eyes widened considerably behind his somewhat foggy glasses.

He swallowed. He knew it was J.D., but he had no idea how that simpleton could have followed him. He started to slowly turn his head to confirm that it was J.D. when he felt that cold, circular bore on the back of his head.

"Just keep your eyes straight ahead, Preacher."

Carlton licked his lips. His mind raced. His eyes darted side to side in concert with the fears circulating in his chest. "I can explain, J.D."

"I don't want to hear any smooth-sounding words, you Bible-thumpin' hypocrite."

Carlton lowered his rifle to the soggy soil. He inhaled to bolster his courage and slowly turned his head grazing the ominous pistol bore. He rose slowly and turned to see J.D's ugly visage temporarily illuminated by a strobe-like glimmer of lightning. "You need me, J.D."

J.D. angrily shook his head. "I rode off leavin' my men knowin' they're not goin' to Roxy. I've made some bad decisions, but killin' you won't be one of 'em." He increased the pressure on his trigger.

Carlton knew that talking was over. He reached hurriedly for his derringer and heard the pistol's loud boom. He felt a searing pain in his gut that felt like a poker heated in hell. As he was losing consciousness, he fired his derringer. He knew it had landed and where it had landed. He staggered backward before collapsing in the wet sand.

J.D. gritted his yellow teeth. He emitted a few protesting, primal hisses in reaction to the searing pain. He felt faint and nauseous. He staggered back. The Bible thumper had shot him in the knee. Through pain-slit eyes, he took in the preacher's unmoving body. He warily looked at the wagon. He assumed correctly that the bankers would not confuse the shots with thunder. The pain was almost unbearable, but he hopped back to his horse and painfully mounted it. He began riding down the road that would pass the adobe house. But he had no intention of hiding there. He was headed to the only place he knew to run—his old home place.

After hearing the shot and departing hoofbeats, Seth and Floyd crawled out from under the wagon. They had faced danger before, so two gunshots did not rattle them. Tacitly, one went left and the other right. They moved slowly in the heavy umbra, waiting cautiously for the lightning flashes to show them their way. They were soon on both sides of the periphery of trees that led to the cut. They heard a moan. They inched their way to the source of the anguished sound.

Seth saw Carlton. He knelt and lifted his upper body, and in a flash of lighting, he saw the bleeding hole in the preacher's abdomen. He cradled

171

his head. Carlton looked up to see the man he had wanted to kill. He saw another figure move into view.

Floyd knelt and looked at the wound by the flickering night lights. His eyes went to Seth, and Seth returned the look.

Carlton let a mirthless smile move across his pale features made even more gruesome by the spatter of rain. "It was J.D. who killed me." He gave another convulsion and said with a throaty sound of satisfaction, "I shot that bastard in the knee." In a lower, pain-filled voice, he added, "I know I did."

Floyd turned his head to estimate how far ahead J.D. would be then. "Where's J.D.'s men?"

Carlton croaked out, "Hell, I don't know. They're probably getting close to Roxy or hiding." He gave a lurch and gave out a blood-curdling scream. "Oh, sweet Jesus, I'm dying."

Floyd sighed. Though the man had come there to kill Yvette and possibly them, it saddened him to see a man die. "We'll bury you, Reginald."

Carlton convulsed again. "I'd want that." He gave another squeal of pain. He placed his hand over the gaping hole in his stomach. He felt the spreading red liquid. "Would you place a coin under my tongue?"

Floyd's eyebrows went up in surprise. "That's pagan."

Carlton gazed at Floyd. His glasses were mostly fogged over. "Hell, it might as well be. There ain't no God, and there ain't no Jesus." He had another spasm. "There ain't nothing on the other side … Just a big black hole." Carlton exhaled for the last time.

Seth sighed. "You bury him, Floyd. I'll go after J.D."

Floyd shook his head. "You need to stay and take care of Yvette."

Seth placed Carlton's head carefully on the wet sand. He started to remonstrate about who should do what, but when he saw Floyd's determined eyes, he relented. "When the rain ends, we'll take off to Roxy. We'll wait for you there, Floyd."

Seth went to the wagon for a lantern and an iron skillet he would use for digging. Yvette was not cowering under the wagon tarp. She asked if it had been Carlton. She did not cry when she was told it was.

Floyd saddled Yvette's paint. He carefully led the horse to the soggy road. When he reached it, he mounted and began trotting after the old reprobate. Floyd figured it was well after midnight; he knew it would be a long ride, but at least he did not have a hole in his knee.

Floyd saw the road with the help of the crackling flashes of light. He had his Sharps in his scabbard. He had his army .44 in his holster and another in his belt. He was determined to end this misery for Seth and Yvette. He wanted them to have a chance to live happily. He knew J.D. was a rabid dog who had to be destroyed.

Floyd passed the Carlton home. He saw no horses. He figured J.D. was headed to his house. He knew he would have to have help to find that remote place, but he was not going to Roxy until he did.

Punkin' Head heard both horses go by. He and his compadres had hidden their horses in the house. He was sleeping in what had been the kitchen shielded from the rain by part of the roof that was left. He figured that it was either J.D. or the preacher passing by. He listened for further horse traffic. Hearing none, he smacked his lips sleepily and shook his head as though he no longer cared who it was.

Hours later, Floyd saw the sun inching its rays over the horizon. It was still cloudy, but he felt a lessening in the humidity. Up ahead, he saw three men sitting on horseback at the turn in the road that led to Roxy. He was wary until he saw the silvery glitter of badges; that settled his mind. He rode up to them. He saw they were intently observing him. He saw an older man lean over and say something to the other two. They relaxed their postures after that. He reined up and looked at each lawman. He recognized Marshal Gil Tucker by the description Seth had given him. Floyd leaned forward with his hands on his saddle horn. He nodded. "Howdy."

Marshal Tucker said, "You be Floyd Maccabee, right?"

Floyd nodded.

"You probably lookin' for the preacher or J.D. Rysinger?"

Floyd nodded but realized the need for a correction. "I'm lookin' for J.D." He straightened and canted his head in the direction he had just come. He explained what had happened five and half hours earlier. When he got to the part where J.D. killed the preacher, the deputies looked at each other. One pulled out a small writing tablet from a vest pocket and took notes. He was asked about the burial and where it was. Floyd answered with the best description he could.

Tucker shook his head upon hearing about the preacher. "He was one sorry individual, but he's one less problem for us to worry about I reckon."

Luke, one of the deputies, was heavyset and ruddy. He said, "You're one of the two bankers, right?"

"Yes. Me and my pard are from Baileysboro."

Luke nodded as he waited for his fellow deputy, a slender man named Melvin to finish his notetaking. "Well, we work for George French. He's the sheriff of this county, and after hearin' about the shenanigans in Roxy with the minister, we were sent here to find that scoundrel." He paused. He looked downcast as if he hated to relate something. "Sheriff Henry Nelson, your sheriff, failed to send a want to Sheriff French about J.D. Rysinger and that failed bank attempt in Baileysboro." He squirmed in his saddle. "We'd naturally pick that sorry rascal up if we saw him, but he's not first on our list. In fact, he's way down it."

Floyd mulling over the deputy's words. "I'm not shore why Sheriff Nelson didn't send a want on J.D., and yes, I'm disappointed. I was hopin' for a little help."

Luke sighed and shook his head as though commiserating with Floyd. The deputy leaned forward as though he wanted to make sure his words were duly noted. "You ever heard of an outlaw named Turk Larsen?"

Floyd rubbed his chin thoughtfully. "Don't reckon I have."

"Let me fill you in so you won't think we don't care about J.D. Rysinger. The Comancheros are movin' their territory farther east, and they're pushin' outlaw gangs out of their natural territory. The outlaw gangs are bein' pushed up against each other. Turk Larsen's gang was pushed out of its territory and entered the Carson gang's domain. The two gangs had a shootout about three counties south of here. Turk's gang won, but in the process, they killed the sheriff and three of his deputies who were tryin' to do their duty since the shootout happened in their town. Well, hell, every sheriff in West Texas is now after that turd. We got word that he's headed to the Nations and comin' through here."

Floyd nodded. He gave a brave face toward the three lawmen. "Got any information about J.D. Rysinger and where in the hell his house is? I reckon that's where that old hell raiser is headed."

Melvin, the slender, quiet deputy, spoke up. "Long ago, my family lived in Galveston, and my father used to tell me a story about Odell Rysinger,

J.D.'s grandfather, who was an auditor … worked for the government. A few years after the Mexican War, there was somethin' called the Mexican Cession. Our government offered to pay Mexico fifteen million for the land we took from Mexico plus some." Melvin shrugged. "Now, I'm just goin' on what my father used to say. He said that we never paid fifteen million for the land but that the Mexican dictator settled for an amount under the table." Melvin's face became animated. "My father said that Odell Rysinger stole a whole lot of that money and the US government had to make up for what he stole … close to sixty thousand."

Luke shook his head amused at the idea an auditor might steal that much and try to conceal it.

Melvin continued. "They figured he stole it, but he denied it to the day he died. But deny it or not, he couldn't get another job in the whole state. Thus, he moved his wife and grown son to this area and bought five acres where he raised potatoes." He paused. "That grown son was J.D.'s pappy."

Luke asked, "Did they ever find the money?"

Melvin shook his head. "The authorities have been over his place in Galveston a dozen times and at his home near here."

Floyd took in the information, but he figured it was just rumors and gossip. He asked the lawmen if they could tell him where J.D.'s old home place was.

Melvin tore a page out of his notebook and drew a map. He would describe a landmark and get Floyd to nod that he understood. He would then have Floyd repeat it to make sure he had it down pat. "It's probably another four hours' ride from here." Melvin handed the page to the marshal, who handed it to Floyd.

Floyd thanked all three lawmen and told the marshal that Seth and Yvette would be arriving in Roxy.

Marshal Tucker smiled and made what he thought was a joke. "You think that I'll need to put on my justice of the peace hat and marry 'em?"

Floyd nodded solemnly. "I wouldn't be surprised, Marshal."

Marshal Tucker's jocular expression slowly morphed into surprise. He rubbed his face and excused himself from the deputies. He turned his horse and began galloping back to Roxy.

Floyd rode for over two hours. Even with the map, he was unsure he was on task. It took him another hour just to find the identifiable hackberry tree that bordered a narrow, weed-infested road that led close to the Rysinger place. What gave him heart was that he saw only one set of tracks. He did not know where J.D.'s gang was, but he felt one on one, he was a match for the one-eyed bandit.

He rode an additional hour satisfied he was on course. He saw the glorified path that led to a low rise in the distance and took it. He sensed he was closing in on the man who had caused him and Seth such misery. His eyes were searching. He could not see around a bend ahead, but he remembered that Deputy Melvin had said that when he rounded the bend, he would find J.D.'s house and eventually J.D. When he made the turn, he saw a poorly painted white house on a rise. He knew it was the Rysinger abode; it had two scraggly mulberry trees in the front yard as Melvin had told him.

At one time, the house might have been passable, but it was a ramshackle mess. Weeds ran up to the porch. Burlap covered most of the windows. A tilted outhouse sat off to the left, and a dry well was off to the right. Some roof shingles were missing leaving barren wood wet from the previous night's rain. Floyd's eyes caught the small lean-to that sheltered J.D.'s horse. The sorrel was there still saddled in a run-down corral.

Floyd tied off his paint on a low tree limb. He adjusted his pistol in his holster and tugged his hat down. He saw multiple old horse prints. He realized that they had gathered there to plot his, Seth's, and Yvette's deaths.

Floyd walked toward the half-open door above the porch. He moved up the steps with considerable wood stress. He was on the porch. A wasp zipped by him. He looked up at the porch ceiling, over at a corner, and then at a large, grotesque, papery wasps' nest.

He stepped through the door. The house smelled musty and felt hot. Old poker cards were strewn across the floor in the front room. Two empty whiskey bottles had rolled against a wall. Floyd smelled something else … something akin to dry blood and sour flesh.

As he crept closer to the first room to his left, he heard husky breathing. He drew his army .44 and held it vertically. He walked on the balls of his feet as he inched around the corner. He was not prepared for the sight of J.D. stretched out on his back in a filthy bed with sheets that appeared not to have been changed in years. J.D.'s hat and gun belt were on the floor. His mouth was working in and out much like a fish out of water. His face was flushed with fever. His glazed expression turned to clarity when he saw the banker. He gave a feeble smile and swallowed as he tried to talk. He was dressed in soiled, flannel underwear with the leg cloth pulled up exposing his injured kneecap.

"Too late, banker man."

Floyd, seeing no need to use his .44, holstered his weapon and walked up to the bed. He took time to view J.D. more fully. His tousled hair had lots of gray. His damaged eye was covered in a hideous film that looked like a nictitating membrane on a crocodilian. Floyd took note of the old bandit's ear that Seth's .44 had truncated a bit and his arm that hung limply by his side. He discovered the source of the sour smell—J.D.'s putrefying kneecap. It had a gory hole surrounded by dried blood stains and shreds of cartilage. It emitted a foul odor. He saw the wound was in the incipient stages of gangrene.

J.D. watched Floyd back up and lean around the corner as if to make sure no one else was in the house. "There ain't no one here."

Floyd leaned back in and assessed J.D.'s condition. He knew the jaded old buzzard did not have long for this world. He also knew J.D. was telling the truth about no one else hiding in the house. He had been deserted.

J.D. slowly shook his head. "They took off on me."

Floyd knew he was talking about his gang.

"I should've known that Punkin' Head would pull a trick like that."

Floyd had heard the description of the man but not his name when he was palavering with the sheriff in Baileysboro. He was unsure of his course of action.

"Which of them damned bankers is you?"

"Floyd Maccabee."

"Well, if you're here to arrest me, too late. I ain't got long for this world."

Floyd put his hands on his hips and surveyed the room. He saw little there—a faded picture of an old man on a buckled wall and cigar butts here and there. The whole surrounding was depressing. A large fruit fly stridulated by. Floyd sighed and decided he would just leave and let the man die.

J.D., sensing Floyd's imminent departure, raised his good hand. "Don't go, Floyd. I don't want to die alone." J.D. dropped his hand; a tear appeared in his bad eye and slithered down his whiskered face. "I want you to do a readin' over me."

Floyd was taken aback by the tear and the request. "What do you mean a readin'? You mean the Bible?"

"Yes."

Floyd sighed in frustration. "J.D., readin' the Bible over you is like readin' over a goat."

J.D. nodded. "I ain't much, I know. You got ever' reason to hate me." He paused. His sick voice broke. "But sorry or not, I'm made in the image of God. A sorry copy, but still ..."

Floyd gave a small, consenting nod. "You realize I didn't bring a Bible, J.D. I came here to kill you."

J.D. did not flinch. "I want you to read over me and then kill me, Floyd. Just don't leave and let me die alone."

Floyd shrugged. His resolve had been deflated by the words of a dying man. "Where's the Bible?" He wanted to say "in this damn hole," but he thought better of that.

J.D. told him that a Bible was in the kitchen cupboard.

Floyd saw J.D.'s gun belt with his army .44 in the holster at the side of his bed. He hesitated but went to the kitchen and found a faded Bible in the cupboard. Next to it was half a bottle of homemade whiskey.

When he returned, he saw J.D.'s gun and holster still in place. Floyd looked at the fevered, imploring, and intent face looking at him. "You want me to read Psalms twenty-three?"

J.D. shook his head. "Don't know nothin' about that book."

Floyd gave an impatient chuff. "Well hell, J.D., you got to work with me here."

J.D. ran a wan hand over his fevered face. "My grandfather used to read me the Battle of Jericho."

Floyd gave an annoyed expression. "The Battle of Jericho ain't what you read to a dyin' man, J.D."

J.D.'s face clouded up as though he were a child again. He looked as if he would break out in tears at any moment.

Floyd held out his free hand to shush that emotion. "I'll read you the Battle of Jericho."

J.D.'s face returned to normal.

Floyd looked up at the dirty ceiling as if appealing to God. He put his hat upside down at the foot of the dirty bed. He turned to Joshua chapter 1, verse 9, and began reading. He paused from time to time to observe J.D.'s reaction. The old bandit had a dreamy expression as if he were young again and in a place where the trees were always green.

When Floyd finished, J.D. nodded his satisfaction. "Fine readin', Floyd. Mighty fine readin'."

Floyd did not know how to respond. He placed the Bible on the bed and picked up his hat. "J.D., I can't stay."

J.D. nodded sadly. "Kill me, Floyd. Don't leave me like this."

Floyd put on his hat and looked up at the ceiling. "Well, it's like this, J.D. It was easier to kill you before I read the Battle of Jericho to you. It's a mite hard to kill a man after you've read the Bible over him."

J.D. gave a sick smile. "Hell, I like you, Floyd. I ruined my life chasin' a man I got to like … Feature that." But his smile evaporated. "If you won't kill me, hand me my pistol."

Floyd hesitated. He was wary about handing him his .44 not because he felt he would turn the pistol on him but because he thought he would witness a suicide.

"Please, Floyd."

Floyd walked to side of the bed, extracted the .44 from its holster, and handed it to J.D.

J.D. looked at the pistol and then at Floyd. "Will you bury me, Floyd?"

"I'll bury you, J.D." He paused. "You want to be buried where your maw and paw are buried?"

J.D. slowly shook his head. "No. I hated 'em, Floyd. I got a good idea they're responsible for me livin' like I did and now dyin' like I am. Forgive me sayin' them hateful words. You're lookin' at the man who's responsible for his lot in life."

Things went in slow motion for Floyd. J.D. tilted the .44 to his chest and used what strength he had to cock the hammer. The metallic clack was magnified by the silence. Floyd watched the old bandit point the gun to his chest and flex his trigger finger. He heard the concussion. He witnessed J.D.'s body shuddering. He saw blood splatter in thick, red droplets outward. J.D.'s hand dropped the pistol. The silvery weapon slid off his chest and tilted awkwardly between his abdomen and arm.

Floyd inhaled deeply and exhaled fully. He noticed a fruit fly on the ceiling whose monotonous existence had just been disturbed flying in a tight circle and making an irritating sound. Floyd looked at the blank look on J.D.'s face. His half-opened eyes and pained look caused Floyd to lean against the wall. A shaft of light coming through the window revealed seemingly billions of dust mites. Floyd felt he was in the epicenter of the loneliest place on earth. It seemed hidden from heaven itself.

This oppressive environment on top of the suicide he had just witnessed caused him to reflect momentarily. It dawned on him that he had come with hate in his heart and the desire to kill J.D., but at that point, he felt sorry for him. No one would mourn for J.D. He had killed himself and would be forgotten. Floyd was determined to bury the old outlaw and honor his word. He would not take the easy way out and throw his corpse into the dry well he had seen earlier.

He turned to find a shovel when he heard an unusual sound. It sounded like metal ... like metal hitting the floor—*chink*. He looked around once more at the depressing room but saw nothing that would have made that noise. He raised his eyebrows as though he had just imagined hearing something. Then he heard a second and third *chink*.

Floyd bent and looked under the bed. He saw three gold coins. They had come from a large bed box covered in buffalo hide that sat under the soiled mattress.

Floyd got on his knees and in the narrow space between the bed box and the floor edged his way in as far as he could. It appeared to him that when J.D. shot himself, the ball had gone through J.D.'s body and the mattress and partially into the bed buttress. The force of the shot had sent shock waves through some heavily packed coins that rended the hard buffalo leather and allowed the coins to escape.

Floyd grabbed the coins and pocketed them. He stood. He had found J.D.'s grandfather's stolen money. He knew the leather-covered buttress held more money than he and Seth could carry. He wondered how he would be able to load and transport the treasure, but first things first.

He went out and found a flat-nosed shovel in the smokehouse that was meant for scraping, not digging. He reminded himself to buy a spade before he came back. He went outside near the drywell and laboriously dug a good-sized grave. He went inside for a rickety chair that he put in the grave to one side. He went back to digging and finally had dug the grave six feet deep. He stepped on the chair and crawled out of the pit.

He wrapped J.D. in the soiled sheet he had been lying on, grabbed him under his armpits, and dragged him through the house. He did not want to drag him by his feet; he did not want J.D.'s head to bounce on the steps; that did not fit Floyd's code of ethics. He respected the dead even if the dead had been a thief. He buried J.D. and set up a makeshift cross. With his pocketknife, he carved, "J.D. Rysinger—RIP."

Back in the house, he stuffed two of J.D.'s filthy socks into the hole in the bolster to prevent more coins from escaping. He did not want anything of interest to catch the eye of some busybody just passing through. He formulated a plan as he went to the corral and watered and fed J.D.'s sorrel and Yvette's paint. He decided to use the sorrel as his main horse and pull Yvette's.

He left half an hour later knowing he had a long ride to Roxy. He intended to tell Seth about what he had found but then leave Seth there in Roxy with Yvette so they could enjoy some connubial bliss and privacy. He planned to return with the wagon to J.D.'s place without much rest. He dreaded that, but he realized the enormity of his find. It occurred to him that maybe he should notify the authorities even if the statute of limitations had expired. But on the other hand, Floyd reasoned that he and Seth in all likelihood would be pestered the rest of their lives by endless bureaucratic investigations and explanations. On top of governmental snooping, the public knowledge that they held this gold horde would mean they would have to contend with endless outlaw gangs from Texas and the Nations regularly. The salivating prize of Santa Anna's gold in their bank would draw every dishonest swinging jack from all over the Southwest more than willing to risk his life for such wealth. The more he rode, the more it made sense to keep the purloined Santa Anna's bribery money a mystery.

Seth and Yvette left the morning after the deadly altercation between J.D. and Carlton. Seth skillfully maneuvered the mules and wagon out of the miring wet sand just off the road. They decided to continue on the long route; neither wanted to go back past her house. The soft daybreak painted the horizon with thick splashes of yellow and orange.

Yvette sat close to Seth but seemed melancholy. She was turning her head from Seth and dabbing at her eyes. To make sure Seth did not think she was crying over her late husband, she grabbed his arm and cut her unusual blue-green eyes to him. "Seth?"

He turned to meet her look. "I noticed you've been cryin'."

She nodded. "I want to tell you somethings I didn't want to tell you earlier." She pulled her eyes away and looked straight forward. "I knew that Reginald didn't love me after the first month. He wanted a good girl until he got one. To him, the perfect woman was always the next one. When we moved here, he began to spend more and more time in town. He never took me with him.

"Sometimes, he would leave me out at the house a week or more at a time. At night, I would bar the doors and sleep with a rifle next to my bed. I was always afraid and lonely. Sometimes when I got really restless, I would get up, take my rifle, and go to the corral and hug my horse, Rosie. I would talk to her and sing church songs. I would hug myself and walk back to the house looking at stars that no longer shined for me. I would bar the door and go hide under my bed where I had hidden a pallet. When the sun came up, I would look out the windows to make shore I was safe and get up and start another lonely day."

Seth slowly brought the wagon to a stop. He set the brake. He let the reins fall to his feet and turned to Yvette. He placed his hands on her face. "I'll love you and be good to you, Yvette. You won't have to hug horses any longer just because you're lonely. When the nights are cold, I'll be there for you. I ain't a prince, but you'll be my princess. We'll walk through life hand in hand. Nobody wants to grow old, but it's just a fact of nature. I want to grow old with you."

Her eyes filled with tears. His did too. "Yvette, when we get to Roxy and when Floyd gets back … I want you to marry me."

She grabbed him around his neck. "Oh Seth! Yes, yes, yes."

They arrived in Roxy around two that afternoon and drove the wagon up to the emporium. Seth looked at Yvette, who looked wistfully at the goods on display in front of the store. She had only three dresses—two for daily use and one for Sunday service. Seth set the wagon brake, and they climbed down. Yvette, who still had the idea that Seth was a fix-it man, knew her choices would have to be frugal as she went into the trading post. She meekly followed Seth with her eyes moving side to side. It was her first visit to Roxy, and she had not been in a mercantile store since she had left Tennessee.

Seth beckoned Mr. Finley, the owner, who recognized Seth immediately. He praised him again for thwarting the bank robbery attempt over a month ago. Finley, a tall man with leonine but graying hair, came around the counter with celerity, grabbed Seth's hands, and pumped them enthusiastically. "What can I do for you, Seth?"

Seth turned and guided Yvette in front of himself. "We aim to get married, Mr. Finley. She needs a wedding dress and about six other dresses and all the accessories."

Yvette's hands went up to her mouth. She looked at Seth and back at Finley. She was afraid he was going to put the goods on credit. She started to protest until she saw Seth reach inside his jacket. She nearly fainted when he pulled out $200 and handed it to the proprietor. "If she runs out of money, let me know. I'll give you some more."

Yvette impulsively grabbed Seth's neck and began weeping. He gently unwrapped her determined hands and gave her a gentle nod. "You better get started," he said in a higher voice as a reminder. "Get a trunk too—a big one."

Finley took hold of Yvette's elbow. "Let's begin with the wedding dress. You can buy a whole lot with two hundred dollars."

Yvette looked over her shoulder at Seth as if to make sure she was not in a dream. He watched her walk away with the owner. He gave a satisfied nod that things were going well. The look on her face when he pulled the unexpected money out was a memory he wished he could have captured forever. He gazed at her happily looking around like a kid in a candy store.

But as he was basking in the happy moment, the niggling, insidious feelings of Floyd out on the trail turned his happy look into a sober one. When he caught Yvette's eyes, he gave a toss of his head indicating that he was headed to the marshal's office. When she gave a quick nod, he walked out onto the boardwalk. He gave a lingering look up and down the street and headed across the sandy way to the jailhouse.

He went in and saw Marshal Tucker standing at his window. It was apparent he had seen him pull into town. The marshal gave him a worried look. He told Seth all that had transpired with his meeting Floyd at the bend in the road that led to Roxy.

Tucker made his way to the coffee pot on the pot-bellied stove. He beckoned for Seth to join him. They poured coffee and sat—the marshal behind his desk and Seth across him much like the first time they had met.

Tucker informed Seth that if Floyd made it back, it would probably be around midnight. When Seth suggested that he might need to go after Floyd and give him some assistance, the marshal quickly nixed that notion. "Before long, you'd be ridin' in the dark not knowin' where you're goin'. The second reason he went is obvious—he wants you safe to marry that pretty lady you rode into town with." The lawman paused. "What a friend to have."

At midnight that night, Yvette was sleeping in the marshal's house. She had gone to bed earlier and had immediately drifted off to sleep. It had been a long and emotionally taxing day.

The marshal and Seth were lightly sleeping in the jailhouse. The lantern on the wall shed its oily, orange-light on the marshal as he was sleeping in his chair with his boots up on his desk. Seth was lying on a cot in one of the two open cells. The long, excruciating wait for Floyd was measured by the metronomic ticking of the wall clock. Whenever they heard the *clip-clop* of some passing waddy's horse, they would gather hope … only to have it extinguished when the sound became fainter.

But then Seth heard hoofbeats that sounded as though they were headed toward the jail. He turned away his thin blanket and sat up. He slipped on his boots and grabbed his hat. The sheriff, who was in a light sleep, heard Seth's shuffling and what he guessed to be two horses. They kept their eyes on the door, but there was an interminable pause as the rider dismounted and tied up.

The door opened. Floyd entered. He had a tired smile on his coppery countenance. Seth wanted to run and hug his old compadre but went to him with an extended hand. They shook warmly. The marshal stood, gave his cordial welcoming words, and said he would take care of the horses. He inquired about J.D., and Floyd informed him that he was dead. Marshal

Tucker nodded and said he would fill out a form and send it to Sheriff French.

When he left, Floyd looked over his shoulder to make sure he had the privacy he wanted. He hesitated until he heard the marshal moving the mounts around the office to the mule lot. Floyd's cautious expression and precautions let Seth know he had something important to say.

After looking around unnecessarily, Floyd related all he had seen and done. Seth was flabbergasted. When Seth suggested that he postpone the marriage to help Floyd gather the stolen loot, Floyd shook his head sternly. "If we was to get killed, Seth, that little girl would be at the mercy of wolves. After being married to such a cold-blooded bastard, she deserves better than that." He paused and kindly said, "She deserves you, my friend."

They talked about the wedding planned for the next day and how they could disguise Floyd's mission. They decided that Floyd would take off shortly after the ceremony in the wagon on the pretext of going back to the Carlton spread. A lot of people might not pay any attention to Floyd riding out the next day, but Seth and Floyd knew Tucker might find it odd. They respected the marshal; he was no dummy. They realized they would have to utilize subterfuge and maybe stretch the truth a little bit—maybe more than a little bit. They decided he might not connect Floyd's leaving with any cache of gold, but it was up to them to satisfy or divert any suspicions he might have.

The next morning, Floyd got up early. He went without his coffee to Marshal Tucker's house. He rapped on the door; it was answered by a sleepy but beaming Yvette. Floyd removed his hat and smiled. She ushered him into the living room. She was dressed in one of her new, high-necked dresses. He had to admit that she looked beautiful. She greeted him and made the usual small talk but then gave him a questioning look that asked, *Why are you here?*

He almost did a double take as it hit him why he was there. He reached into his pocket and pulled out a polished gold band that was obviously expensive. Floyd had bought it from a wholesaler passing through Baileysboro the day they had left. When he concocted the whole Patricia Barnwell matter, he decided to buy a ring for the bride to give to Seth in case the Barnwell girl was embarrassingly short of money. He handed the ring to Yvette. "When you get to the point of exchanging rings, you'll have one."

Yvette teared up and shook her head in gratitude. "Floyd, do you always think of everything?"

Floyd shook his head. She impulsively came forward and hugged his neck. He paternally patted her back. He released her and said goodbye.

He quickly walked around the mule barn and lot and made his way back to the jail. He walked in and saw that the marshal and Seth were up. Seth stood over in the corner of the cell and was shaving looking into a small, cracked mirror. Floyd nodded amiably at the marshal and made his way to Seth. Seth looked at Floyd in the mirror. "Floyd, you're goin' to have to move. I might shave both of us."

Not getting any jocular response, he placed his razor aside and turned around with soap foam still on his face. Floyd glanced at the marshal out of the corner of his eyes as though he did not want him to hear. "Listen. I took the liberty of buyin' you a weddin' ring to give to your bride." He left out the fact that he had bought it from the same wholesaler who had sold him the gold ring he had given Yvette.

Floyd reached into his pocket and pulled out a glittering diamond ring. Seth's jaw dropped. He reached for it tentatively. "Floyd, do you always think of everything?"

Floyd shook his head.

Seth sighed as he looked at the large glimmering diamond and then at Seth. He knew that he would cry if he did not start shaving again.

Floyd fraternally whacked him on the shoulder and walked to the marshal, who nodded and said, "You're up early, Floyd." Tucker nodded to the coffee pot. "Better load up, banker. You got a weddin' to attend in about …" He looked at the large regulator clock on the wall. "… two hours."

Floyd got his coffee. He rocked on his heels as he cogitated. "Marshal Tucker, I got a favor to ask of you."

Tucker allowed a slow smile to ease across his face. "You want the honeymooners to stay at my place today and tonight?"

Floyd nodded. "You're very perceptive." He got around to laying the groundwork for his upcoming absence. "After the weddin,' I got to go back out to the Carlton place and see what I can salvage."

Marshal Tucker gave him a thoughtful look. "What in hell is there to salvage?"

"I imagine Yvette left some things behind. And I have to make shore what's left of the house can be utilized. I plan on bein' out there all day and part of the night."

The marshal gave a hesitant nod, but Floyd was not sure he had sold him the whole bill of goods.

Since the church carried the stigma of Carlton, Seth and Yvette decided to be married in the backroom parlor of the emporium trading post. Seth was there with Marshal Tucker. Finley had decorated the parlor with some flowers. When a lookout spotted the bride, Finley's dowdy wife, Hortense, began playing Mendelssohn's "Wedding March" on her out-of-tune piano.

All the principals were there including the mayor and his overweight wife. They smiled when Floyd and Yvette entered. Yvette was all in white. The dress accentuated her figure, and her high-button collar captured her incredibly pretty face. Floyd entered with her on his arm but slowly withdrew his arm as they approached the marshal, who was serving as the justice of the peace.

Tucker gathered them in a semicircle and asked who would bequeath the bride to the groom. Floyd spoke up. Marshal Tucker nodded approvingly. He pulled a Bible from under his arm and gave a good account of himself as he read from the book of Ruth. He asked each to repeat the wedding vows he had read. He had a hard time keeping Yvette from hugging Seth, but he managed to move the ceremony alone.

Soon after exchanging rings and each saying, "I do," the marshal pronounced them man and wife. Yvette kept looking at her wedding ring in awe. "Oh Seth!" She would cry, stop crying, and start crying again. Once the marshal calmed her down, he had the bride and groom sign two documents. One of the wedding certificates was going to the county, and the other was for their private records. Texas law required for witnesses to sign, and all present did so, one clerk with an *X*.

Floyd had paid for the small reception that followed. Even some customers in the store made their way back and began eating some of the hors d'oeuvres and punch that was there for the taking.

Floyd impatiently shook hands, kissed the bride, and hurriedly guided Finley to one side. "I need five rain barrels. I want four fifty-pound sacks of flour and a spade shovel, not a flat-nosed one. I need them in ten minutes."

Finley ran his hands through his leonine hair and disconcertedly shook his head. "Floyd, I know you're a pretty smart fella, but rain barrels don't hold flour worth a damn. I got some barrels that are meant to hold flour."

Floyd gave him a level look. Finley met those eyes and shrugged. "All right, I'll have them out on the boardwalk for you to pick up."

Soon, Seth and Yvette disappeared. Everyone smiled and nodded approvingly to each other. Floyd paid Finley and made his way to the mule lot behind the marshal's office. Soon, he had the wagon in front of the store, and Finley and two of his hired hands loaded the goods into the wagon.

Floyd caught sight of Marshal Tucker entering his office. He climbed up to the springboard seat and snapped the reins. He had respect for Tucker. He was not sure the lawman had any thoughts about the purloined loot. And he felt that if the marshal did suspect something, he would not resort to criminal activity to get the treasure. But he understood well that the marshal had heard the same speech that he had heard about Odell Rysinger's theft of some of the gold that had been earmarked for General Antonio Santa Anna. He did not want Tucker suspecting he had found it.

Floyd felt very tired as he picked up the reins. He smiled to himself; Seth had found a quality woman, a keeper. After traveling the first five miles, he fought off the urge to pull off the road and take a nap. He reached for a cigar, gave himself a pep talk, and sent some encouraging cuss words to the mules.

He reached Rysinger's in midafternoon. He looked at the ground and did not see any fresh tracks. He set the brake, tied the reins, and hopped to the ground. He placed the barrels in the corners of the wagon bed with one in the middle close to the driver's seat. He wanted the weight distributed to avoid a broken axle or excessive drag. He opened the tops of the barrels and laid the circular wooden covers close by. He pulled out his spade and headed into the house.

He went to J.D.'s room and removed the blood-spattered mattress. He decided not to burn it immediately fearful that smoke might be spotted by a passerby. He pushed the mattress up against the wall but avoided blocking the sun-warped window panes; he wanted that view open. He pulled a sharpened Bowie knife from its sheath inside his coat. He inhaled in anticipation of what he might find. He started cutting the wooly buffalo hide down the middle much like gutting a deer after a kill. The hide was obstinate but gave way to the razor edge of the knife. When he peeled back the two sides, coins reflected a gold sheen on his face. He swallowed as he looked at a treasure the count of Monte Cristo might have envied. The whole large rectangular bed buttress was filled to the brim in 1840s minted twenty-dollar coins.

He drove the spade into the middle of the cache and carefully walked backward until he reached what had been the living room. He went down the steps carefully to the first barrel and carefully raised the shovel with its heavy load and dumped the coins, which made a crashing sound in its emptiness.

He repeated that routine for hours. He had not lost a single coin. He was exhausted, but he knew he could not give into the fatigue. When it was twilight, he made his last run, and he had filled the barrels to two-thirds of their capacity. He searched for any coin he might have overlooked in the bed bolster. Seeing none, he pulled the empty wooden frame through the door, down the steps, and tossed it next to the dry well. He did the same with the mattress. He doused them with what coal oil was left in a lamp he took from the kitchen. He struck a match and set it on fire. He hurriedly climbed into the back of the wagon and poured flour from the sacks into each barrel until it reached its rim. He pounded the lids down with the spade. He hopped down from the tailgate and glanced over at J.D.'s grave. He nodded his goodbye and turned to leave.

In the fading light, he climbed up in his wagon, set his rifle at his feet, and snapped the reins. He knew it would be a long ride back to Roxy, but he was full of adrenaline. As he drove down the weed-strewn road, the orange flames burning the frame and mattress were crackling behind him making him a silhouette; he feverishly encouraged the team to make tracks.

It was past midnight when he got back to Roxy. He left the wagon with the goods in the barn. He unhitched the mules, watered and fed them, and turned them in the large corral. He reentered the barn, climbed the vertical steps to the loft, and slept soundly until daybreak.

The dawn prompted a rooster somewhere in the near distance to crow. Floyd rose, smacked his lips, picked hay straws from his clothing, and climbed down the ladder.

At that time, he saw Seth coming through the barn maw. Seth had a neutral look on his face. He looked at the barrels positioned in the wagon and smiled. "I see you were successful."

Floyd gave him a cautious nod but turned in the direction of the marshal's office. Before he could ask about Tucker, Seth stated, "We don't have to worry about the marshal's suspicious eyes. Sheriff George French came by and deputized him yesterday afternoon."

"Deputized him?"

Seth nodded. "He's ridin' with about a dozen men after an hombre named Turk Larsen." Seth explained that Turk Larsen was being chased by a mob of out-of-county deputies.

Floyd asked about Yvette, and Seth smiled. "How many times do I have to say she's wonderful, Floyd?"

Floyd nodded. "We need to eat. Let's meet at the emporium and have breakfast. After that, we need to get on our way to Baileysboro."

The three left Roxy at seven and were headed to the burned-out town of Finleyville. They traveled all day and did not see a solitary rider. That night, they camped in a cluster of mesquite and cooked around a low fire. Floyd took his sleeping gear and slept near the road to give the newlyweds some privacy. The next morning after coffee, they began their trek again.

Floyd was driving, Yvette was in the middle, and Seth was on the outside. They had two rifles at their feet. The countryside moved slowly by, each mile much like the last—all they saw were mesquite and weeds poking out of yellow sand.

Around noon, Yvette passed out some beef jerky and dried apples. They sipped water from their canteens. It was a pretty much a normal day for Seth and Floyd but not for Yvette. Her head was always turning this way and that to see everything. She had a big smile on her face. She would hold out her hand to look at her ring, gaze at Seth, and then back at the scenery that was to Floyd and Seth rather mundane. The two men smiled, sadly amused that such a pretty but mistreated woman could find such joy in things they took for granted.

They traveled another mile, and as they were making a turn around a sharp curve in the road, at least seven riders suddenly rode out of a thicket of mesquite. The man who obviously in charge was a large, burly man; his face was covered in whiskers. His wide-brimmed hat shadowed some of his features but not his twinkling green eyes.

He threw up his hand for Floyd to stop. Floyd looked anxiously at his Sharps rifle at his feet but made no move for it.

The burly man rode up to Floyd and looked at the rifles at their boot level. "Put them rifles and what pistolas you have in the back of the wagon … and do it real slow like."

Seth and Floyd sighed and picked up the rifles. They put them and their Colts in the bed of the wagon.

The big man pushed his hat brim up with his thumb. "My name is Turk Larsen. I'm one of the meanest, sorriest pieces of mankind ever made in the image of God." He forked a thick thumb toward his chest and added, "I'm a robber, and …" He comically rolled his eyes up. "… you're the robbees." He ran his finger under his nose as he ruminated. He let his eyes fall on Floyd since he was the closest. "How much money do you birds have on you?"

Floyd looked straight ahead as he deadpanned, "About forty dollars I reckon."

Turk repeated Floyd's words in a sarcastic drone, "Forty dollars I reckon." He sat there with his hands on his saddle pommel. He shook his head in disgust. He asked Floyd his name. Floyd gave it. Floyd asked him where he had gotten the name Turk.

Turk shook his head. "It ain't civil to make day-to-day conversation with a man I'm goin' to rob."

Floyd swallowed and continued to look straight ahead.

Yvette leaned forward. She looked into Turk's eyes, her curiosity piqued. "Well, where did you get the name Turk?"

Turk ran his finger under his nose again. He hesitated about answering, but he liked how she looked and how she asked.

"When I was a boy, my daddy used to go turkey huntin', and he would have me make a turkey gobble." He gave a small laugh. "It always worked."

Yvette smiled and suppressed a giggle as she placed her hand over her mouth. She knew she should be afraid, but she was not.

Turk asked who she was. "My name is Yvette …" She started to say "Carlton" but recovered. "… Johnson." She introduced Seth as her new husband and Floyd as her Dutch uncle.

Turk sighed. "Now look, Yvette, you're a sweet missy and all, but I got to rob someone. Hell, I got to get all the way to the Nations." He sighed and gave Yvette a phony scowl. "You quit bein' so nice."

He turned to Floyd. "What you got in them barrels?"

Floyd resignedly sighed. "Flour."

Turk shook his head in disgust. "You mean to tell me you got five barrels of flour?" He inhaled in irritation. "You must be some sort of idjit. Man, one barrel of flour will usually take on weevils before you finish it, and you've gone and went and bought five barrels."

Turk turned his baloney-sized neck to share his disgust with his gang. "Burke, get up on that there wagon and check them barrels."

Floyd and Seth looked straight ahead with *Oh hell* looks on their faces. Yvette, who had no idea about the valuable cargo, was smiling and taking everything in.

Burke dropped the tailgate and climbed up onto the wagon bed. He took his knife and pried a lid up. He went to another barrel and did the same. He pushed his hat up and shrugged. "They got flour."

Yvette spoke up. "Mr. Turk, have him put the lids back on. We got to get to Baileysboro, and we don't need that flour spillin' and spoilin.'"

Turk nodded to Burke to replace the lids. Turk told Burke to check to see if there was anything else to steal in the wagon.

Burke spied Yvette's new chest and informed Turk of his find. Turk told him to look inside. Burke opened it up and looked for a minute, his eyes going here and there.

"Well, what did you find, Burke?"

"Uh, womany thangs."

Turk voice raised a register. "Womany things? What sort of womany things?"

Burke, nonplussed, held out his hands out palms up. "Well, dresses and, er, frilly type thangs."

Turk exasperatedly shook his head. "Close that lid. You don't want that lady thinkin' you're a prevert."

Burke asked, "What's a prevert?"

Turk answered, "A prevert's a man who looks too long at women's flimsies and gets all shaky."

Burke shut the lid of the trunk with a pronounced *thump*. "I ain't no prevert." He sighed and swallowed and said in a much lower voice to himself, "Not much of one anyway."

Floyd bit his lip. He wanted to pronounce *pervert* for them, but he kept his eyes straight ahead.

Turk asked him what else was in the wagon.

Burke told him that there were foodstuffs and two ten-pound sacks of ground coffee.

Turk snapped, "Well, get the coffee."

Yvette leaned forward. "Please, Mr. Turk. Don't take our coffee. We got a long trip ahead of us."

Turk sighed. "Yvette, you can stop at some mercantile and buy some more." He waved his hands as though including his whole gang. "It ain't likely we can stop at some store and buy stuff. Missy, we got to get to the Nations. We got two posses after us."

Yvette looked sad. She shrugged as though disappointed.

Turk looked at her expression and said to Burke, "Leave one bag."

Yvette smiled, and Turk smiled back.

Turk asked Burke if there was anything else worth taking.

Burke said there was a shovel.

Turk shook his head again in frustration. "Get down from the wagon, Burke."

Turk turned his attention once more to Floyd. "How do you make a livin,' Floyd?"

Yvette again intervened. "They're fix-it men."

Turk leaned back in his saddle and deliberated the matter. "Floyd, you got one shovel and you call yourself a fix-it man?" Turk looked above their heads as though he were trying to make a Solomonic decision. "Floyd, I got to tell you of all the people I've robbed, you have to be the biggest idjit I've ever come across. You store flour in a rain barrels, you ain't got much money, and I now know why. You've been tryin' to make a livin' with one damned shovel."

Turk slowly dismounted. He frowningly walked up to Floyd. He scrutinized him and made a disapproving noise. He cursorily looked at

Seth and eventually settled on Yvette. He noticed Yvette's ring. He made no move for it. He simply nodded his approval. He asked her if she was happy. She nodded that she was. She told Turk that Seth was good to her. Turk respectfully removed his hat. He reached across Floyd and touched her cheek with his gloved hand. It was a gentle touch. He reached inside his shirt, pulled out a roll of greenbacks, and peeled off $200. He took her hand and put the money in it.

She looked at him in wonder. Her eyes opened wide as she sat there astonished. Turk held her hand kindly. "This is my weddin' present, but I have one request of you." He paused. He wistfully said, "You and your husband go and have children. Bring 'em up right and maybe they won't turn out like ol' Turk."

His eyes suddenly turned sad. He slowly withdrew his hand and gave a final stern look at Floyd. "Five rain barrels of flour?" He made a gruff noise. He mounted up and gave a farewell nod. He and his hard cases rode like the devil north.

As the plangent sounds of hoofbeats dissipated, Floyd and Seth looked at each other. Yvette was looking in fascination at the greenbacks in her hands. Seth pushed his hat up and said, "You know, Floyd, I don't believe I've ever seen such a thing."

Yvette looked back and forth at the two men. "Do you two always live like this?"

Floyd and Seth looked past her toward each other. Neither spoke, but each knew that Yvette had no idea of the trial they had just gotten through. Floyd wearily wiped his face with relief and exhaled audibly. Yvette put her money away. "Well, we still have ten pounds of coffee." She patted Floyd's shoulder and kissed Seth's cheek. She turned and thoughtfully looked forward at the caramel-colored road. "I know the money is probably stolen." She exhaled. "But since I can't give it back to the rightful owners, I plan on spendin' it on my four daughters. I reckon that'll square things with God."

Floyd gave a thoughtful smile. He had an idea Seth was smiling too. He had hoped that Yvette was the woman he had imagined, but at that point, he knew she was. He snapped the reins.

CHAPTER 14

John Lee and his men stayed a full day and night in Lako Springs; he paid up-front for the time. He felt he and his men needed the break. He had rested and eaten well, but he was uneasy. It was one thing to shoot an enemy who was trying to kill you, but it was another to have your enemy surrender and then be consigned to a Mexican silver mine that was tantamount to a tomb.

He did not like how the showdown at Lako Springs had gone down. He disliked the oily alcalde, Señor Madura, and he hated the Comancheros much more than T-Dilly's men. He had kept the Austin bunch's weaponry and horses on purpose. He knew what he needed to do though it might appear foolish to the world at large. He had his principles and would not sell out to anyone.

He and his men pulled out of Lako Springs at dawn. They rode down the narrow road bordered by boulders and long stretches of cactus. He kept his gray eyes on the horizon. He knew T-Dilly was out there somewhere, and he instinctively knew the bandit leader must be eaten alive by losing face by abandoning his men and not putting up a proper fight.

After riding ten miles, John told his entourage to hold up. He rode off the road after seeing a large pile of boulders to hide behind. He told them to dismount and keep their eyes on the road they had been traveling.

They did not have to be told why. They had witnessed his sullen face back in Lako Springs. They knew the reason. They all would follow John Lee into the pits of hell. They knew that was exactly where they were headed. They gave satisfactory looks to each other. They knew John would not let the prison wagon pass by without freeing T-Dilly's gang.

They waited patiently and quietly for over an hour. They had become an effective fighting unit. They did as they were told. There was no cigar smoking, no canteen drinking, no farting. They waited in the heat.

They heard noises in the distance—clopping hooves, jingling traces, and a juddering prison wagon. They made themselves invisible. John, who had not dismounted, was on the other side of the boulders. When the prison wagon came even with the tumbled rocks, John rode out and caught the driver by surprise. The driver, a filthy-looking Anglo, pulled up the four-horse team. The three Mexican guards started to reach for their weapons, but upon catching a closer look at the powerful man who faced them, they decided otherwise. They gave nervous looks at each other but slowly moved their hands up to a nonthreatening position.

Lefty, Slick, and other prisoners sat looking out the heavy vertical bars wondering what John was up to.

John gave a toss of his head as the lead guard rode up to powwow with him. "Turn 'em loose."

The guard gave an uncertain look to his compadres, who had heard the command. He started to shake his head, but again, he took in the gigantic frame of the man facing him. He licked his lips. "Señor, you fought these men. Why do you care?"

"I care. Now unlock the back door and unshackle them."

The guard saw and heard John's men walking around the tower of rocks. He shrugged and nodded his acquiescence. He dismounted, and so did the other two guards. They unlocked the heavy, caged doors. As each of the Austin gang members stepped awkwardly down the crude wooden steps in leg irons, he was freed of the steel pinions.

After the ten men were freed, they looked back and forth at John, his men, and the guards. Their former captors also looked to John for further instructions. He told them to turn the wagon around and head back to Lako Springs. The alcalde's men quickly did as they were told. They realized they were heavily outnumbered. They also took into account that the Austin bunch would not easily forget the rough treatment they had endured.

As the empty, clattering prison wagon turned in the narrow road, the nervous driver soon had it straightened out. He gave one guarded look over his shoulder feeling lucky to be alive. He popped the reins. The prison wagon and guards soon disappeared over a humpback in the road. Lefty and his gang members turned their attention to John and his men. They were initially fearful of being executed, but upon looking at the calm demeanor of John, they intuited he had something else up his sleeve.

Lefty looked sheepishly around. He nodded a quiet but cautious thanks to John, but he was not sure he and the others were out of the woods yet. He asked, "What now?"

John folded his large arms across his chest and studied each gang member. "I'm lettin' you go."

Lefty's look of surprise was mirrored by those of his companions. Lefty nervously wiped his face. He was not sure he had heard correctly. He stood and inhaled as though choosing his words carefully. "Lettin' us go?"

John nodded.

Lefty looked up into the cerulean sky. He could not fathom why the big man had saved them from an eternal tomb below ground. Eventually, his eyes came down to look into the appraising gray ones looking at him. Lefty dropped his head and said in humility, "Well, it pains me to say this, but we wouldn't have done this for you."

John said nothing.

Lefty licked his lips and tried to hide the grateful emotion forming in his chest. "I don't want to lie to you. We ain't goin' to go to church after this. We're a sorry lot, and you know it." He took in a lung of air to steady his quavering voice. "But I swear this to you here and in front of God above and my sorry-ass range riders behind me, we won't raise a hand against you ever again." His voice almost broke. "Not sure how, but there will be a day a' comin' when me and the boys will do you a favor."

John saw Bobo ride around a large boulder bringing their horses he had kept. John pointed to the last horse laden with a canvas bag that contained their weapons. John said in his deep, commanding voice, "When you mount up and ride beyond that ridge ..." He pointed to a saw-toothed mountain in the distance. "... you can put on your iron."

Lefty and his gang members lined up. They each walked up to John as he remained mounted, respectfully nodded their thanks, and walked to their horses. They were soon riding off leaving a cloud of dust.

John watched them ride away. He noticed they did not attempt to stop and put on their weapons as he had ordered. His thick neck slowly turned. His eyes took in the crooked road ahead. He did not have to say a word. He was soon surrounded by his men. They wordlessly rode down the trail. They were getting that much closer to the destination where he and his men would meet up with the federal soldiers.

T-Dilly was ten miles ahead. He and two men were concealed in some large boulders high above the road. He had no idea what had happened to his men in Lako Springs. He supposed they had been captured or killed. He knew he should not dwell on that, but he was. It was bothering him that he had allowed Gabe Green to talk him into leaving the battle at Lako Springs. The only thing that would absolve him of that egregious sin would be to kill John Lee Johnson. He knew he had to accomplish that or kiss his job with Representative Stevens goodbye.

He sat with a collapsible telescope in one hand. His Spencer rifle was propped up against a craggy boulder in easy reach. He took periodic looks down the road with his scope, sit, and brood.

Gabe and Leoncio remained silent. They knew T-Dilly was testy, frustrated. They were afraid of him. They could not imagine John Lee Johnson could possibly be more fearsome.

Gabe thought he saw some trail dust in the distance. He caught T-Dilly's attention and silently pointed down trail. Without enthusiasm, T-Dilly reached for his telescope. He had had so many dry runs that he lacked the spirit he had initially had. But when he stretched the scope out and placed the lens on the trail, he began to smile.

Gabe and Leoncio took in T-Dilly's expression and gave sighs of relief to each other. They knew their violent boss had someone else to take his anger out on.

T-Dilly took the scope away and slowly socked it together. He looked at his position and began to plan an attack. His thoughtful eyes became clear. He huddled with his two men and described an ambush. He told Gabe to go to the bottom of the hill and conceal himself. He specifically told him not to open up until he heard his shot. He gave Leoncio the same advice but commanded him to stay south of Gabe's position. T-Dilly watched them leave. He had little doubt that John Lee would die that day.

John and his group were moving at a steady clip. He was riding point, and his eyes were searching the lofty peaks that grew taller with each mile. His gray eyes shielded and shadowed by his dipped brim saw a twinkle to his right about a mile down the road. He guessed correctly that it was manmade; he knew neither mica nor quartz made that kind of sparkle. He realized he had to make a quick decision. If they kept moving at the pace they were maintaining, he and his men would be in danger in a matter of minutes. He did not know if T-Dilly had a Sharps .52 or not, but if he did, he knew that if it was handled correctly, it could nail a man within the range they were in.

He had prearranged his plan. He slowed the gait of his horse and pointed to the left and right. Lambert, Sand Burr, and Bobo went to the right, and he and Ollie broke to the left. They drifted into spaces between large boulders.

Both groups pulled their rifles and dismounted. Sand Burr kept his eyes on John. John gave him a pumping hand signal and a forcible point of his finger. Sand Burr knew he meant that trouble was up ahead on the right side of the road. Ollie had all the packhorses and pack mules in his care, and he did not take that task lightly. He led the horses and mules into a tight alcove of rocks and pulled his rifle out. He watched John moving in and out of rocks toward the appointed destination.

John's sudden action did not deter T-Dilly. He gave a begrudging smile. He admired his intuitive skill. But it spooked Gus and Leoncio. T-Dilly knew this was a showdown. He actually felt a rush of excitement. He wanted a direct confrontation with John Lee. He was tired of hearing about the man's seemingly mythical abilities. He wanted to put the quietus on the big Texan once and for all.

But the action did not start fast. The hot orange sun sat in the sky and seemingly not moving redolent of the book of Joshua, in which the sun stood still. It was not nerves that made sweat stream down T-Dilly's face; it was the hot, dry heat. But T-Dilly relished the tension; he thrived on it. His eyes moved toward both sides of the road.

At the bottom of the rocky tor were Gabe to the north end and Leoncio to the south. They knew the numbers were not in their favor. When John's group did not just ride by but started moving their way through the rocks, they became spooked. They had faith that T-Dilly would pull them out of the fix, but trust in T-Dilly did not stop the sun from beating down on them. They tapped their canteens. They heard a hawk screeching in the hot sky, but other than that—silence.

Gabe Green thought he heard noises about a hundred yards downward on the side Johnson had taken. He slowly raised his head for a better look-see. Sweat dripped into his eyes, which looked furtively this way and that. He heard rocks tumbling as though someone had boot-scuffed some loose gravel. He moved his head up to get a better view.

A loud rifle explosion reverberated among the rock-covered hills and small, craggy mountains. Gabe Green did not hear it; a heavy-grained shot propelled a rifle ball that hit him in the forehead. His head exploded. His body remained upright for a second or two before toppling like a headless chicken in reflexive movement.

Leoncio did not see but feared what had happened. He knew T-Dilly had not fired and was still hidden above him. But if Gabe had been killed as he believed, he liked the odds even less. He licked his lips and decided he wanted no part of this T-Dilly–John Lee Johnson showdown. He slowly began edging backward. He did not want to give the big Texan a shot. When he looked over his shoulder, he caught sight of some large, odd-shaped boulders. He knew he would be home free if he made it to them. He made it barely—a close shot zinged and ricocheted—but he managed to scurry and gyrate his way through an impossible blind of boulders to reach his pinto. He made a running mount and jerked his horse roughly. He headed for Comanchero territory. He wanted to get away from the big man ... and T-Dilly.

T-Dilly did not need a fortune-teller to tell him he was alone, but he did not give a damn. He wanted John Lee. He knew this was the second round, and he sure in hell was not doing very well. He gave himself a pass knowing that he was holding a hand of deuces and treys while the big Texan held a royal flush. He gave himself a consoling shrug. He was counting on a third round. He pulled his Spencer from his peephole in the rock crevice and reluctantly made his way down the rocks. He zigzagged his way almost to his horse when he saw Lambert and Bobo through an open space between two boulders. It was such a flash moment that he did not recognize Bobo.

T-Dilly quickly stepped ahead of where he thought the two men might be. He whipped around an egg-shaped boulder with his Spencer in hand. He caught Lambert flatfooted. When Lambert saw he was in the direct and deadly sights of T-Dilly, he shouted out for Bobo to run. When T-Dilly heard the name Bobo, he shifted his vision to the stocky man running toward him. He cussed out the words "Traitorous bastard!" swung his rifle, and pulled the trigger. The first shot landed one inch from Bobo's head making sparks on the boulder beside him, but the second shot landed in Bobo's torso. Bobo grabbed his chest cussing every second as he fell backward.

But Lambert was not still. He fired a shot that blew off T-Dilly's little finger. Lambert knew he had the bastard hurt, but before he could fire again, he slipped on some pebbles and fell sideways.

T-Dilly, cussing like a sailor and shaking his left hand in pain, jerked his rifle toward Lambert. Before the bandit leader could fire, two pistol shots rang out that saved Lambert and grabbed T-Dilly's undivided attention. Sand Burr was shooting one pistol at a time; the buzz and whiz of shots were close enough to send T-Dilly scurrying for safety among the rocks.

Sand Burr ran after T-Dilly, but it was soon obvious that he would not be able to find him in the maze of boulders. In frustration, he socked his pistols into his holsters and ran to Lambert, who was kneeling and holding the obviously dying Bobo.

Bobo was gasping for air. Rivulets of blood were running from the corners of his mouth. He grabbed Lambert's coat lapel and stared at his new friend. He choked out, "Lambert, don't let that bastard go unpunished." When Lambert did not respond, Bobo implored him, "Please, Lambert, I know your word's good."

Lambert, who did not like making promises but not following through, nodded. "Bobo, I'll get him."

Bobo gave a dying smile and released his hold on Lambert's coat.

Lambert laid him back on the ground and stood. He looked at Sand Burr and took another glimpse at Bobo. He exhaled and shook his head in dismay.

Sand Burr shook his head in concert with Lambert. He felt his anguish. He thought Lambert had made a promise to Bobo that perhaps he could not keep.

In fifteen minutes, John and Ollie showed up. They gathered around Bobo's body. No one spoke for minutes. They knew they could not go after T-Dilly collectively or individually. It would be impossible to track him, and furthermore, they had a good idea he would be heading to the Comancheros seeking aid. What caused them more grief was that they could not spend the proper time to mourn their comrade.

All four men stood bathed in orange rays and radiating heat. Ollie looked at John and let his eyes pan the others. "I admit that when Bobo came onboard, I didn't like him." He brushed away a tear. His voice broke. "But I got to likin' him, and I respected the hell out of him. This dirt's too hard to bury a man in. But I had a Scot for a grandfather. He said in the old country, they buried a man in a cairn when the ground was too hard."

Sand Burr narrowed his eyes. "What's a cairn?"

Ollie inhaled and wiped more tears. "You cover the body in a blanket or tarp and start with small stones and go to bigger ones and build a rock tomb above ground."

John nodded. "Ollie, you tell us what to do. Let's get to it."

In two hours, they had built a conical pile of rocks that resembled an Old Testament burial site. When they had laid the last stone, they stood around with their hats in hands. In a surprisingly good voice, Ollie began singing "Shall We Gather at the River." Soon, all four were singing with wet eyes and chests full of meaning.

When the song ended, they were silent for a good while. They knew it was time to go. It was as if their movements had been choreographed. They all began moving away from the tomb to get the horses and continue their journey.

Twenty miles deep in the Guadalupe Mountains and settled by a small river lay the headquarters of the Comancheros. It was actually a small town. It had all the amenities of any community—bank, hotel, barber shop, horse lot and barn, a jail for offenders, and a medical clinic with a real doctor. The Comancheros had a code among themselves. If any of their members got drunk in town, they were excused as long as they were not belligerent and had not made threats against fellow members. They occasionally had trials, and repeat offenders were given harsh warnings and were fined. In rare cases, a violent man who could not control himself was trundled off to the Mexican silver miners and was gone forever. But for the most part, it was a calm community of highly skilled criminals who were placed in specialized groups—rustling, selling alcohol and weapons to the Kiowas and Comanches, human trafficking, and robbing banks and stagecoaches.

The Comancheros had started as a Mexican organization but quickly were run off or absorbed by the more aggressive and deadlier gringos under the leadership of ex-Colonel Stafford and his military-style associates. When Walter Stafford was captured by a combined force of sheriffs and federal men the previous year and was eventually hanged in Fort Smith, Arkansas, his position was taken over by Pugh Larrimore. Pugh maintained the military efficiency of his predecessor but was more practical and not given to grandiose schemes that had brought about Stafford's downfall.

Five days after T-Dilly's attempted ambush of John Lee Johnson, Larrimore leaned back in his chair in the bank building of the Comanchero headquarters. It was midnight. The coal oil lantern on his desk sent an oily light over his features. Pugh had a large body and craggy, acne-scarred face. His hat brim was wide, and the crown reached up high. His eyes were on the sizeable profits he and his cohorts had made the last month. He was adept at figures, and he was satisfied he was on task even with half the profits going to the former brigadier general Frank McGrew. The surplus, which would be meted out as bonuses to his crew, would keep them happy.

The orange glow of the dim lantern on his desk normally would have revealed a satisfied look, but it displayed a scowl. He should have been happy with the overwhelming profits, but after meeting with Leoncio Gomez, who had ridden in earlier, he was vexed. He had been looking forward to getting a good night's sleep and getting ready in the morn to head to Sanchez, Chihuahua, to watch El Toro beat the living hell out of some sucker who had enough gumption and money to brace him … until he was informed that sucker was no sucker at all but John Lee Johnson.

Gomez had been allowed to ride in because he was well known by the Comancheros. Pugh had a sit-down with him. He thought it would be your basic du jour conversation, but the more he listened, the more irritated and upset he became.

Gomez had told him about Representative Stevens's mission to kill Johnson or have him fight El Toro. Leoncio confessed he and the others remained confused—you killed someone or you did not. Leoncio also informed Pugh about the fiasco at Lako Springs and how T-Dilly had been talked into leaving the resort. He also mentioned how they set up an ambush that failed to kill Johnson.

Pugh had raised a hand for Leoncio to stop. He did not want to hear any more. He told him he no longer was an employee of the Stevens outfit. He advised him to go to the hotel and get some rest. On the morrow, he would be assigned duties as an employee of the Comancheros. He abruptly dismissed Leoncio.

Pugh sat in his chair breathing shallowly. He thought about all the things going his way. He was selling rifles and hootch to the Indians. He was making a fortune in human trafficking by sending white and Mexican males to the Mexican silver miners. He was making top dollar by selling women and girls to the Mexican border town bordellos. He had a special unit robbing banks and stagecoaches. He had stockpiled a fortune for McGrew and the Comancheros. There was enough money to go around, and that made all concerned very happy. He had plans to extend his sphere of influence as far north as the Nations and even into Kansas.

But the more he thought about John Lee Johnson, the more morose he became. He sat and thought and shook his head as though his thoughts were carrying on a conversation and he was a mere bystander.

His melancholy thoughts were interrupted by a knock on his door. Lonzo, his bank employee, stuck his head in and announced that T-Dilly Whitaker wanted to talk to him.

He cursed silently and gave a steely nod to Lonzo, who understood that nod was not friendly. Lonzo disappeared. A very solemn T-Dilly took his place. He walked in shielding his left hand, which was wrapped in a soiled, yellow, and bloodied handkerchief. Pugh noticed that. He nodded to a chair, and the Austin crew leader settled in it. Pugh gave a big sigh, pulled a cigar from his vest pocket, and lit up.

His eyes locked on T-Dilly's. He leaned forward. His eyes narrowed. "Before we begin, T-Dilly, let me make myself perfectly clear. You and I work for the same big boss. As a professional courtesy, I want you to have all the food and sleep you need. But if you've come wanting some men to help you kill John Lee Johnson, forget about it!"

T-Dilly remained quiet. His eyes glinted flint, but he knew he was at the mercy of the most powerful man in West Texas.

Pugh continued. "Here's what I know, and you can correct me if I am wrong. Your boss Stevens hatched up a plan for John Lee Johnson to fight El Toro. But somewhere along the way, he decided for you to kill him. You on the other hand did not kill him thinking you were going to bet on El Toro, make some money, and perhaps go out on your own. But then mysteriously, you had a change of heart and tried to kill him, but I can see that shore in hell didn't work out. I can see by your hand that you must've had trouble with some of his men." A sarcastic smile rolled across his cold features. "I know it must be one or more of his men because if you'd braced John Lee Johnson, you'd be dead."

T-Dilly did not respond. Pugh leaned back in his chair and added more fuel to the fire. "I don't aim to enflame John Lee Johnson. I want him the hell away from me at all times. It tickles me when he's at home and practicing domesticity with his wife and child. I still plan on heading to Sanchez in the morning, and I plan on betting on John Lee Johnson, not El Toro. There ain't a man alive who can whip him or outshoot him. I've had dealings with him before, so I know."

Pugh gave a knowing nod to T-Dilly's hand. "You can go over to the doc's office. He'll see to that hand of yours. You can eat and drink all you want at no charge. Stay as long as you like at the hotel. As a professional courtesy, you can even ride most of the way to Sanchez with me and the boys since we take lots of water and food, but when we get real close, I want you to break away from me and my men and go your own way. I don't want him associating you with me."

Pugh sighed as he withdrew his cigar and contemplated it. "T-Dilly, if you want to live, when the fight's over, you better make tracks to Austin and forget you ever heard of that big devil."

T-Dilly gave a curt nod. He was not used to being talked to as if he were a child. He wanted to ask who the big boss was but did not want another lecture or to be told it was none of his business. He rose smoldering on the inside and departed without saying a word.

El Toro de Sanchez—aka Ramon Avila—was seated outside on his Roman-style patio. Potted plants bordered the periphery. His rancho dwelling was elegant. His house was a mere mile from the edge of the Chihuahua Desert. He was sipping a glass of wine. He usually indulged himself in two glasses and two strong cigars daily. A shock of black hair covered his large head. He had eyes the color of obsidian. Geneticists who claimed there were no such things as black eyes—only dark brown that people called black—had not seen his. He had broad shoulders and an expansive chest. His face was full but not round; it was covered in whisker stubble. He had a scar over one eye and another on his cheek. He sat calmly letting his strength return after a taxing run; he had run four miles in the desert. Each day, he soaked his face in brine water to toughen his skin and lessen the possibilities of cuts. After dunking his face into salt water over and over, he put his enormous fists in the water for fifteen minutes to toughen his skin.

He was awaiting his associates of the Mexican cartel that covered the states of Sonora, Chihuahua, and Coahuila. They were to decide where and how the money would be allocated when he won.

El Toro, as he was affectionately known, was an immensely egotistical man. He was huge and brutal but more important undefeated. Nonetheless, he was much more than a fighter. He was an intellect. He spent hours reading Socrates, Plato, and Aristotle. He pored over Latin and Greek texts. If the internal affairs in Mexico were not in turmoil, he would have loved to study at the university in Mexico City. He was self-made man, and that added to his enormous self-image. He felt compelled to correct people's grammar and considered himself an expert on everything from weaponry to poetry. He felt he was better than the ilk he had to deal with. He had something else on his impressive resume; he was the crime boss of three Mexican states. When he spoke, people listened. As long as he won, he would be at the pinnacle of his power. He had no intentions of losing. He was twenty-eight, and he was anxious to fight and validate his estimation of himself.

He had heard that he was to fight John Lee Johnson on the fifteenth, and that was not far off. He knew nothing else about this man, but he knew he would probably be a good adversary. He trained the same for all the men he fought. But in his mind, this Texan would be another notch in his belt of conquests.

He took a sip of wine and watched his cadre filing down the flagstones in his sandy courtyard. He raised his glass and saluted them.

Enrico Perez always sat to his immediate right followed by Miguel Torres and three others, who always took their lead from the first two. A servant in an expensive shirt with balloon sleeves and charro pants appeared. He balanced five wine glasses on a silver salver. He adroitly placed a sparkling glass of claret on the table for each guest. He quickly disappeared as he knew he should.

El Toro made a toast, and the others clinked their crystal glasses over the round table. El Toro gave them a big smile. He felt good and was looking forward to the fight. As they made small talk, he noticed that Enrico seemed reserved. El Toro, who had great respect for his colleague, gently put his glass on the table. "Amigo pobrecito, what ails you?"

Enrico put his glass down and looked at El Toro evenly. "This John Lee Johnson needs to be killed."

El Toro's dark eyes widened. "What?" He had never heard his longtime companion say something that outrageous. "Enrico, if you have something to say, say it."

Enrico shrugged. "This John Lee Johnson is not like anyone you've ever fought."

El Toro frowned. "And you want to kill him because he is very formidable?"

Enrico nodded. "Si, señor."

El Toro sneered. His ego could and would not accept another man getting that much credit. "Do you really think this gringo can honestly beat me?"

Enrico took his eyes away from the angry eyes he was looking into. "I did not say that, Ramon, but I think in the past, I was a hundred percent sure you would win. But this time, I think it will not be so easy."

El Toro gave a reluctant grin. His ego could not stand this assault. "I am not going to kill a man because I am afraid of him." He became angry. He jabbed his chest with his thumb. "I am Ramon Avila. I can defeat any man in the world." A mirthless smile began spreading across his grim features. "I will kill him in the pit. I will not resort to killing him before he fights me." He finished his wine and put the glass down hard. "I now want to fight this piece of mierda and destroy him before your very eyes. I dare you to speak again of someone so highly in my presence. I will show you when I destroy this piece of trash."

There was an unhealthy silence around the table. Enrico nodded in acquiescence. "You will beat him, Ramon. I just wanted to hear you say it."

El Toro sneered at what he considered empty words and dismissed himself. His ego bruised, he wordlessly walked toward his house.

Miguel nudged his companion. "You made him mad, Enrico. Was that your plan?"

Enrico smiled. "He probably would have won without this talk, but now I know he will win."

The servant returned and filled their glasses. Enrico again toasted. At that moment, he felt El Toro was unbeatable.

John Lee and his men reached the limestone sentinel rock that resembled an obelisk at noon on the appointed day. Beyond that remarkable landmark lay the Chihuahua Desert. There were thirty troopers thinly disguised as cowhands waiting. Lambert and Sand Burr were aware of the troopers trying to jockey their positions to get a better look at the big man. There were two wagons each pulled by four horses standing by with extra horses tethered to the wagons. John saw his friend Sergeant Brewer and several others he had ridden with in the Nations when he was confronted by Sabbath Sam and the twenty-one. He noted that Brewer's men had increased in number since they had last met in Hawkshaw. He had an idea this was done on the orders of his friend Lieutenant Bragg.

Sergeant Brewer sat on his bay, his eyes hidden in the shadows of his wide-brimmed hat. He and John exchanged cordial nods. Brewer moved his countenance to the fierce desert beyond them. "Do you want to sit awhile before we head out?"

John shook his head and nodded toward the desert. "Let's get this over. I can rest later on." John's eyes moved toward the two wagons.

Sergeant Brewer caught the drift of his vision. "One is filled with water and supplies." He gave a small grin and continued. "The other has a Gatling gun and lots of ammunition ... and a whole lot of money."

John nodded and turned his claybank toward the desert. The others followed suit. The Chihuahua Desert had vegetation and animals but little water. Clumps of yucca and mesquite were growing here and there. Gray, jagged mountains served as the backdrop. They began slogging across the ankle-deep sand. They drudged onward even when the sun drearily set. At ten o'clock under a starlit sky, they made camp. Guards were set, and John sat with his back against the wagon spokes and drank coffee. One of the soldiers strummed a guitar. Somewhere, a desert owl hooted, and occasionally, a coyote howled. No one talked. They were exhausted.

At dawn, they began the daunting trek again. That was their routine for five days. On the sixth day at eight in the morning, they saw Sanchez and the black obsidian stone that stood as a marker for the pit John would fight in that day. As they rode closer, they saw words carved into the stone—Los Abismos del Infierno Ardiente—The Pits of Fiery Hell.

They saw striped canvas tents set up on the border of the desert where bankers anxiously awaiting bettors. They saw the brown-tiled roofs of the adobe houses just above the tents that fronted the picturesque town beyond. The largest tent had a long table around which three men were patiently sitting and drinking wine. This tent was the one where the big bettors went. Enrico Perez sat with two bankers on each side. Behind Enrico were four heavily armed Mexican gunmen dressed in typical Chihuahuan regalia—black sombreros, crisscrossed bandoleros, white drill trousers, and high boots adorned with large, roweled spurs.

Sergeant Brewer ignored the smaller tents with oily looking agents staring like buzzards waiting for their next pigeon. He and his men carried their bets in heavily banded boxes into Enrico's tent. A banker on Enrico's right made a gesture, and Brewer's men slid the chests down the long table to the banker. Sergeant Brewer stated that the first chest was Johnson's ante money and the rest contained bets on Johnson.

The banker named Antonio who had sweat on his forehead and pince-nez glasses tilted low on his nose looked at the large chests of money bet on Johnson. It had never happened that way before. In the past, most money was bet on El Toro. He looked once more at the large amount of money and at Enrico for confirmation that the bank would take that large of a wager. Enrico gave a jaded smile and a faint nod. Antonio told them to open the chests. The other banker rose and had the soldiers empty the other large containers. After counting the money, the banker announced it was $70,330.

Enrico's jaded smile morphed into concern. The two bankers turned to him. Enrico knew that was pushing the limits of the financial potential of the two banks he oversaw, but he refused to lose his composure. He nodded—the bets would be matched.

Antonio nodded to the other banker; he disappeared momentarily but returned with four bank employees. They carted four boxes of Mexican double eagles into the tent.

They method they used was to count out the coins to match the bet. They would sack the entire bet in leather bags and then place the leather bags in a larger canvas bag with the bettor's name on it. If the bets were on El Toro, they would tag the betting bag with a tag written in black ink. If the bets were on someone else, they would repeat the same process but write the other combatant's name in red.

The offsetting bets by local Mexicans and some minor leaders of the Mexican cartel helped relieve some of Enrico's anxiety, but not for long. When Enrico caught sight of Pugh Larrimore and his band of Comancheros, he gave a sigh of relief. He had faith that Pugh would bet his usual $20,000 on El Toro. But when Larrimore announced he was betting his $20,000 on John Lee Johnson, Enrico frowned and let Pugh know his displeasure. He reminded Pugh that the Mexican cartel and the Comancheros had an alliance and that this bet was an insult to El Toro. Pugh said that business was business but that he perceived this as all pleasure.

Enrico became sullen and refused to respond. He realized he could end up financially broken if Johnson won. He wished he had taken the time to chance an assassination attempt on the big Texan.

Lambert walked up and laid down $2,000 in greenbacks on John Lee Johnson. Antonio looked up at him and told him he could bet and it would be accepted but at the going exchange rates. He told him that $2,000 in US paper currency translated to $1,600 in Mexican gold. Sand Burr standing by handed over $400 in gold to make it an even $2,000 bet. Lambert patted Sand Burr on the back, and they walked out to a smaller tent to bet Ollie's $40 on Johnson.

After placing the bet in Ollie's name, Sand Burr, who had followed him to the next tent, gave Lambert a biting look out of the corner of his eyes. Sand Burr's voice had an edge on it. "Two thousand is a lot of money for a down-and-out cowhand lookin' for work."

Lambert started to smile but cut it short when Sand Burr did not return the smile. Sand Burr gave him a disapproving look and walked off. Lambert stopped momentarily. Sand Burr's look had cut him to the quick. He knew he could not respond. He took a deep breath to handle the emotional load Sand Burr had put on him. He looked at Sand Burr's retreating back and walked slowly after him.

The betting line was getting longer when John's and Sergeant Brewer's men finished. The bettors' line was over half a mile long for the heavyweights, and the other lines for smaller bets were of similar length.

At eleven thirty, John, who had been resting in the shade of the ammunition wagon, rose and drank half a canteen of water and poured the rest over his head. He shook his head shedding water droplets. The men gathered around him as if he were Moses. Sergeant Brewer said, "Only a few of us can stand around the top of the pit. I'll designate who can stand at the edge." His voice dropped a register as he looked at John. "The loser is generally stomped to death." He looked at his men. "It's not for the faint of heart."

Their eyes moved to the big Texan. If the vivid description of past fights affected him, it did not show. He stoically started walking toward the pit.

A limited number of men from the cartel, the Comancheros, and John Lee's bunch had permission to stand at the edge of the black pit. No one but the bank guards could be armed. John Lee led his entourage to the guards near the pits. He unbuckled his holsters containing his two navy sixes and pulled a knife from a sheath in his boot.

The guard placed his weapons in a sack. Soon, all the Johnson men were weaponless. One surly and proudly nationalistic guard was nonetheless awestruck by the big Texan. He had too much fear to make any remarks as he led John to the edge of the pit, but his expression made it clear that he disdained him.

The pit was a mystery even to the denizens of the area. It had always been there. Legend had it that the Aztecs had carved it out of the impossibly obdurate black magma, but no one knew how they had accomplished that. People in the area believed that it had been dug to hold the Indians of Northern Mexico captive for sacrifices in the Aztec's capital city. It was a perfect cube—ten feet deep, long, and wide.

A large metal pole had been sledgehammered in the rock rim around the black pit. Attached to that pole was a hemp rope ladder that was folded up at the edge. On the other side of the rectangle was a duplicate setup.

John walked to the pit and looked down. He pulled off his scraggly shirt. When he dropped his shirt, the crowd moving in swallowed in fear and shock. They had never seen such a human being. If their reaction affected him, he did not show it. John, who had not seen T-Dilly, was looking for him based on Lambert's description. At the time, he did not care if El Toro had made his appearance.

A smattering of applause announced that El Toro was making his way to the fight scene. He stood shirtless. His body was thickly muscled. Sergeant Brewer studied the men and thought that El Toro had an atavistic body. He looked like a primordial man; he had a primitive, brutish body with a bull neck and wide shoulders. He did not have any noticeable muscular delineation. But it was obvious that he was formidable. On the other hand, John was a lean, predatory jungle animal carved from stone. When he made the most innocuous movement, the muscles that appeared stunned most onlookers.

El Toro looked at John but displayed no emotion. He held up his hands to show John he had no foreign objects that could aid him.

John responded in kind did not dwell on the moment. He whispered over his shoulder to Sergeant Brewer. "Have you seen T-Dilly?"

The sergeant leaned in and said in a low voice, "He's here. He bet four thousand on El Toro. But I can't see him now."

John nodded. "If you see him when I'm in the pit, wave your hand."

Sergeant Brewer admired his nonchalant attitude. John, who would shortly be fighting for his life, was already making plans to put T-Dilly's lights out.

A stentorian voice rang out at noon. It was time to fight. Guards threw the two rope ladders into the pit. He and El Toro climbed slowly down and reached the bottom at the same time. The temperature there was well over a hundred degrees. The black and relatively smooth wall exuded a hellish heat. The floor was somewhat covered in a friable, starchy layer of black dust.

They looked up and saw a square, cerulean sky with silhouetted heads peering down. John identified Sergeant Brewer among all those shadowed outlines. He dropped his head and looked at his opponent. He assessed that El Toro would be one hell of a competitor.

El Toro scrutinized John as he did all his opponents. He had never seen a man with the Texan's physique. He knew John would be a challenge. He wondered how the big Texan could withstand the heat and how he would react when he was hit. He intended to find out.

John knew he wanted to end this fast. He had decided that the heat would drain his strength and that a long fight would be too debilitating and leave him without the energy to find the infernal and elusive T-Dilly.

He watched El Toro moved toward him. He did not hulk or stumble-step. He moved lithely with a peekaboo defense. John Lee had fought a champion out of Nashville who had used that technique. He took note of El Toro's dark eyes peeking through his massive fists. He was being analyzed by rounded magpie eyes.

The noise coming from above grew. El Toro ignored the recognition of the applause and shouts from above. He hooked a right that scythed the air. John ducked and responded with a meat-smacking left to El Toro's side. John noted that El Toro pulled back his right quickly not leaving his arm extended and his body vulnerable. El Toro rapidly returned to his original turtle-shell protection. John realized El Toro was a skilled fighter, not some lumbering novice.

El Toro had felt that shot to his side. He knew this fight would not be like the others. The big Texan looked good. He was good. He had felt the fight would not be a long affair because the heat would eventually melt the big Texan, but he was having doubts about a brief fight. He had always fought aggressively. He liked to be on the attack; that fit his personality. He wanted to keep the pressure on until he caught the Texan. He moved in again bobbing and weaving. John shot out a straight left jab that found its way between El Toro's fists. It jolted and irritated the big Mexican more than it hurt him.

El Toro cut loose with a left-right combination that caught John by surprise but did no damage. The ferocity of the punches from both men stunned the crowd looking down. Even the harmless blows made meat-smacking noises when they landed.

John took note of El Toro's quickness. He decided that if El Toro liked to be aggressive, he would let him be that to an extent. He was analyzing what weaknesses he might have but had found none. El Toro threw another right hook that went high, and the big Mexican got nailed in the side again for his effort.

El Toro did not like that last shot, which hurt like hell. He stepped it up. He figured that his training in the desert would allow him to take the attrition of heat and savagery better than the tall gringo. He moved in again throwing straight jabs. Most of them missed, but some landed on John's arms and shoulders.

John moved backward as El Toro moved forward. El Toro kept up the barrage of straight jabs, which brought shouts from the Mexican cartel crew. John saw he could not retreat any farther or he would be backed into the hot wall, so he circled and countered with swift left jabs that were not doing any real damage but were keeping El Toro at bay. John avoided another barrage of straight jabs and hooked a hard right into El Toro's side again.

El Toro frowned. He had not yet hit the big Texan with a solid shot, and he was somewhat frustrated. He continued his aggression. He looped an unorthodox left hook that caught John on the side of the head. He grunted contentedly knowing he had hurt the big man.

John Lee felt as if he had been hit by a nine-pound hammer. It was the hardest lick he had received since he had fought the Kentucky Squirrel in '64. He shook it off. He knew he needed to keep working on El Toro's body.

El Toro, reenergized by that left hook that had landed, decided to try it again. As he feinted a right jab, he went over the top with another looping left hand. John leaned in low and countered with a hard right to El Toro's abdomen. El Toro's hook only whiffed the air.

El Toro was feeling those blows, but he was willing to take shots to give the coup de grâce. He returned to his peekaboo defense. After John missed on several jabs, El Toro savagely threw that devilish left-handed hook again and smacked John on the forehead. That hurt John. He knew he needed to start pounding the Mexican and stop all this foolishness.

El Toro, brightened by that success, began throwing hooks and uppercuts, but he had overestimated his damage. John found cracks in El Toro's defense. When El Toro started throwing those wide hooks, John countered with inside jabs that were rocking the bandit king.

This style of hit and counter had gone on for ten minutes. They were bathed in sweat. Usually, the fights were over by that point. El Toro decided to bullrush the big Texan and smash him against the black wall that was as hot as a stove. He schemed he would use his razor-sharp spurs to drive him backward before he made his move to shove him against the wall. He lifted his right foot and made a sweeping move with his spurs coming close to John's shinbones. After that swipe failed, John dropped his hands and gave him a disapproving look. Most of the time, that look would have been ignored, but El Toro's estimation of John was high. He curiously dropped his hands and nodded to John that he would forgo that strategy.

Their hands were down; they had the same thought. They rushed each other and collided like two behemoths. Each feverishly tried to get a bear-hug on the other, but their heavy sweat prevented that. They chuffed seeing that strategy would not work.

In frustration, El Toro pulled his fists up and sent a haymaker from hell that barely missed. John countered with another hard body shot that knocked El Toro backward. John moved in with rapid straight jabs to El Toro's face and body; he could tell they were having an effect. John dropped his left hand as he was setting up to deliver his own finishing punch. He was more than surprised when El Toro threw another haymaker. Once more, it landed flush on John's forehead. He saw red stars. For a few seconds, he felt woozy. John had learned long before that from his old friend Big Willard not to let an opponent know if he had been hurt. John smiled though he felt he had been kicked by a mule.

John shot stiff jabs as he tried to recover from the heavy blow. He saw an opening. He threw a haymaker with all the force he could. It caught El Toro between the eyes, and the big man stumbled backward. He tried to maintain his balance but went to one knee. He shook his head trying to unscramble his thoughts.

John moved in. He knew El Toro was in trouble but was cautious. El Toro sprang from his knee with a hooking left hand that brushed John's chin. John went over the top of that hooking left with a right hook of his own. The punch distorted El Toro's face. He staggered to his left and fell on his haunches. He toppled backward. John walked to him and looked down at him. El Toro's eyes were fogged over. He was helpless. John did not want to hit him again regardless of the damn pit's rules. He looked up and caught Enrico's eyes. He remembered seeing him in Boscoville. But he knew he was the de facto boss by his position at the top of the pit.

Enrico, angered by the loss of a fortune and the fact the local hero was lying helpless in the pit, turned his back to John Lee Johnson. Enrico maintained an implacable face as he started to move from the edge of the pit. He chose to wash his hands of El Toro's fate. But when he started to walk away, he caught sight of his comrades, who met him with pleading eyes. He knew for his own sake and the pride of his nation that he could not allow the Texan to kill the local hero. He gave a signal to the guard. The guard gave a sigh of relief and threw down John's rope. It was the sign that he had won.

John climbed up and out. He stood on the edge of the pit and put on his ragged shirt. The guard who had initially shown John contempt was showing nothing but deference to him. He congratulated him unsmilingly as he handed him his weapons.

John spoke his thanks to the Mexican official. He gave perfunctory nods to all the happy troopers who felt compelled to hug and slap him on the back. But his eyes were seeking Sergeant Brewer. Brewer, who was busy collecting money, sent a corporal to tell him that T-Dilly had departed as soon as he had learned that El Toro had been defeated.

Brewer and his men collected their and John's winnings. Some marched the heavy strongboxes to the wagon; others guarded them carrying their rifles in the port position.

Enrico entertained thoughts about sending his men to storm the wagon, but when he saw those rotating barrels of the Gatling gun, he knew he was out of his league. He licked his lips, sighed, and ordered his guards to climb down and help El Toro out of the pit.

After collecting on their bets, Larrimore and the Comanchero delegation also cleared out fast; they were masters of the disappearance act. As they departed, they cast coveting eyes on the chests of money John Lee had won but feared him and the Gatling gun. But even more than those external threats, Larrimore wanted distance between him and the big Texan. He breathed a sigh of relief as he and his men headed out. Each mile that Pugh and the Comancheros traveled away with their money gave him a sigh of relief.

Sergeant Brewer went to John, who was still brooding about T-Dilly's escape. The sergeant tried unsuccessfully to raise his spirits. He congratulated him and reminded him that they would depart as soon as the crew returned with fresh water and supplies.

He was true to his word. When they returned, the corporal said they were nearly ready. They were called together for roll call. When they were dismissed, they went to their assigned positions ready to head back over the Chihuahua Desert. The Gatling gun was highly visible from the back aperture of the canvas-covered, long-bed wagon. As they departed, they saw a thin line of Mexicans lined up to see them go. No villagers waved, and they sure in hell did not wave.

Days later, they reached the border, found a cool spring for the livestock, and made camp. The enormous amount of money in their possession made them edgy. They set round-the-clock guards. The ranchers in the area were shocked to see such manpower around their watering hole. They learned to water their herds quickly and leave.

Brewer had told John Lee that Sheriffs Doby and McFadden would be there the next day along with enough deputies to get them home safely. John hardly cracked a smile upon hearing this news. He had been moody and depressed the whole trip back. Everyone who knew him realized that the money he had won was secondary; that he wanted T-Dilly to pay for the unnecessary death of Bobo Sweeney. He would walk liked a caged lion to the edge of the camp and look toward Austin. He would take deep breaths in frustration, walk back, and repeat the process.

Sergeant Brewer decided to take matters into his own hands. He waited until nighttime and went to where John had his bedroll. He always slept next to the rear wheel with his saddle edged up to the spokes.

John watched Sergeant Brewer move to him. He knew what he was going to say. Brewer knelt and gave a sheepish look to the big man because of his high regard for him. "John, you can't go to Austin and kill T-Dilly. If you do, you'll endanger Lieutenant Bragg and me and all your friends who've helped you behind the scenes. Not only that, the radical pro-Union group that runs Austin and Texas will declare you an outlaw and come after you. You'll lose your ranch ... all you have. I have the greatest respect for you. I don't like talkin' to you like this. But the truth is you need to hear the truth. If you'll be patient, me and the Lieutenant—we'll alert General Levi Brown about the situation, and we'll pursue legal methods to take care of T-Dilly." Upon seeing John's skeptical look, he said, "It'll take some time, but you go on back to Baileysboro and to your wife and let us work on it."

John inhaled audibly and sourly nodded. He did not ask the sergeant if he had his word on that. He respected the man and did not want to insult him. He roughly knew that the sergeant was right. Once more, he gave a nod of assurance before pulling his hat down over his eyes. Sergeant Brewer knew the conversation was over.

As the sergeant walked away, Sand Burr, who was bedded down three feet away and had heard their conversation, tossed his blanket aside and sat up. He glanced at John, who seemed asleep. Sand Burr breathed in and out in consternation. He began formulating a plan. Just before he lay back down, he turned his head and saw Lambert sitting up five feet downwind from John. He realized that Lambert had heard the conversation as well. He knew the sergeant's talk was working on him too. He did not know what to think of Lambert. He felt a certain kinship with him. He wanted to like him. Lambert had even split his winnings with him fifty-fifty. But he was bothered about a man who apparently was wealthy to begin with wanting to ride with them into such danger without a really good reason except to pay penance for something mysterious. Their eyes locked, but not for long. As if on cue, they both lay down.

Across from them, another set of eyes was watching them. Ollie mulled over what unseen veil had suddenly divided his two friends. He felt he knew. He knew he had to be catalyst to settle the matter between the two men.

The next morning at ten, Sheriff Doby and the stern Roger McFadden arrived with a combined force of fifteen deputies.

Upon seeing the deputies, the troopers had mixed feelings. They were anxious to return to Austin and have their share of the money meted out to them. But on the other hand, it had been an adventure they would never forget, and giving it up was difficult. They loved being around John Lee Johnson. They enjoyed his mystique. It was obvious that he was a once-in-a-lifetime individual.

Sergeant Brewer barked some terse commands. The soldiers shifted John's winnings into one wagon with some water and food. They loaded their supplies into the wagon with the Gatling gun. Without being told, the troopers lined up in a tight queue, walked up, and shook John's hand. He stood humbly accepting their words and handshakes. He watched them mount their horses and ride off with the gun wagon in tow.

John went to the two sheriffs and made small talk downplaying his fight with El Toro. They knew he was in a hurry to get back to Baileysboro. Though the sheriffs had just arrived, they made plans to turn around and head back north. No one complained; all the deputies knew he had been to hell and back.

John saddled up the sturdy claybank. He looked around to make sure his horses and mules were properly tethered. Sheriff McFadden, catching the concerned look of the big man, rode up and assured him that he would personally see to it that they would not lose a horse or mule.

As they were talking, McFadden changed the course of the conversation. He made mention that Turk Larsen had been through his county and that most of his deputies had joined Sheriff French's men and were chasing the devil before he could get to the Nations. He apologized for the shortage of men.

Before John could reply, Sand Burr rode up. Sheriff McFadden held his words when he saw that Sand Burr seemed intent on telling or asking John something. John turned his head to Sand Burr, knowing Sand Burr would not normally interrupt him.

Sand Burr gave a cordial but quick nod to McFadden and uncomfortably fidgeted with his reins; he was looking straight ahead. "Boss, since you got a lot of men to help you get back to Baileysboro, I was wonderin' if you would excuse me for a week or so."

John gave him a questioning look from the corner of his eyes but held his thoughts. Sand Burr knew he needed to keep talking. "I gotta cousin named Connie Jean who lives not too far from here, and well, I'd like to go see her."

John compressed his lips as he digested Sand Burr's request. "You must really like your cousin."

Sand Burr, keeping his inscrutable face straight ahead, dryly said, "Oh yeah."

John nodded sadly. He turned from Sand Burr and stared ahead. "Well, go see Connie Jean." But before Sand Burr rode away, John reached out his strong hand and grabbed Sand Burr's shirt at the shoulder. Sand Burr slowly turned his head, and his eyes met John's. In a low, troubled voice, he said, "Be careful." He reluctantly released Sand Burr's shirt.

Sand Burr slapped his reins and rode out with two canteens bouncing from his saddle pommel. With thoughtful, narrowed eyes, John watched him ride away. He was about to return to his conversation with McFadden when another rider moved up along his side. He turned and saw Lambert on Bobo's three-stocking chestnut. Lambert had a sheepish look on his face.

John sighed. "I got an idea you want to go see Connie Jean too."

Lambert, looking forward, just nodded.

John nodded as well. "Lambert, watch yourself."

Lambert gave him a quick nod of acknowledgement and gigged his horse. He took the same route as Sand Burr had.

John watched Lambert for a long time. He inhaled and turned to McFadden, but he heard another horse ride up beside him. It was Ollie. John said, "Ollie, get the hell to Connie Jean's. Go on. She's probably got supper ready."

He watched a wordless Ollie ride off creating a soft dust cloud.

Sheriff McFadden watched all three men ride away. He rubbed his jaw in thought. He turned to John. "Where does this Cousin Connie Jean live?"

John sighed and looked sadly up to the sky. "Austin."

CHAPTER 15

Sand Burr had not traveled far when he heard hoofbeats behind him. He looked over his shoulder and saw Lambert heading toward him. He pulled up and waited. He was not surprised, but he wondered why. As he turned his mount around to face him, he saw Ollie in the distance on his pinto. That caused him to forgo asking Lambert why he was there. When Lambert had pulled the wad of greenbacks out of his wallet at the Mexican bankers' tent, he instantly thought of him as a duplicitous man who had an ulterior motive he could not fathom. He no longer fully trusted Lambert; he kept wondering what he was up to.

He gave a clipped nod to Lambert as he reined up. Lambert gave him the same curt nod. They remained wordless as Ollie rode up and sat looking from Sand Burr to Lambert. Ollie pushed his black hat up. "Let's get to Austin and do what we know needs doin.'"

Lambert and Sand Burr, grateful for the break in the tension, gave him a small but begrudging grin. Sand Burr turned his horse around, and they took off at a fast trot.

Three weeks later, they pulled into Austin a few minutes past noon. They rode down main street and pulled over at the hotel, which was a block away from the capitol building. Lieutenant Bragg, who was exiting his office's side door in the military building, caught sight of Sand Burr as he and his companions hitched their mounts at the long rail in front of the Texas Hotel. He did not recognize Lambert or Ollie, but he sure knew Sand Burr. He had an uneasy feeling why he was in Austin. He felt that if he were there for what he suspected he was there for, he had to have a quick meeting with him. Lieutenant Bragg purposely moved across the dusty drag with head down but with eyes peeled on the stocky young man.

Sand Burr was lagging behind fortunately for the lieutenant. Bragg hurried his steps, and as he walked closer to Sand Burr, out of the corner of his mouth, he called Sand Burr's name.

Sand Burr turned, and his feathers drooped. Of all the people in Austin, the lieutenant was one of two men he did not want to see. The lieutenant nodded toward a spacious alley. Sand Burr reluctantly waited till the lieutenant broke off and headed toward the space between the hotel and gun shop. He watched Lambert and Ollie enter the hotel. They were unaware that he had been hailed by the lieutenant. He eased to his left from their sight. The lieutenant was out of sight down the alley. Sand Burr ambled toward the alley and saw the lieutenant on his right leaning against the wall of the hotel.

Lieutenant Bragg asked him about the fight although he had already learned of the outcome. A courier from Sergeant's Brewer's group had beaten Sand Burr and his friends by four hours. After a few minutes of small talk, the lieutenant got to the point. "How come you're here, Sand Burr? I know John well enough to know he didn't send you."

Sand Burr hemmed and hawed around and then lied. "We're here to find a man named Smith."

Lieutenant Bragg thoughtfully rubbed his chin. "Smith, eh?"

Sand Burr nodded. He swallowed.

The lieutenant skeptically nodded back. He smirked as he started to turn. "Just make sure Smith stays alive, hear? The sheriff here is named Robert Lang. He is a minion of Judge Roy and on the payroll of Frank McGrew. Watch yourself."

Sand Burr watched the officer briskly walk away. He knew he was hoofing it quickly so no one would see him talking to one of John Lee's men. He waited till the lieutenant was out of sight before making his way to the hotel.

Lambert had rented one room. Lambert gave Ollie the one bed since he was the oldest of the three. The room was austere—the bed, two chairs, and a dinky mirror on the wall above a cheap wooden stand that held a porcelain pitcher and a glass.

Sand Burr had in the back of his mind to go stable their horses with the exception of his, which he planned on leading to Stevens's office for his getaway. But having Lambert and Ollie looking at him for some plan of action, he felt compelled to tell them. Ollie sat on the bed, and Lambert and Sand Burr took the chairs. "Later today, I aim to get me a new suit and clean up. I plan on findin' that Stevens fella's office and wait till T-Dilly shows up. But first, I plan on gettin' me one of them satchels or what some city folks call a portmanteau. I aim to go there pretendin' to contribute money for some cause or another. I aim to shoot the two bastards, get on my horse, and ride like a son of a bitch out of town."

Ollie listened and shook his head. "Where do me and Lambert fit in?"

Sand Burr dropped his head. "I respect you two birds too much to get you in trouble. I'm young and can handle the prairie better than you two can." He stood, sighed, and looked around the small room. "I'm goin' to take care of our horses. I'll be back to spread my bedroll and catch some shut-eye for a few hours."

Lambert and Ollie glancing at each other as Sand Burr left. Ollie listened to Sand Burr's departing footsteps on the hardwood floor of the hotel hallway. His eyes moved to Lambert. "What's the real plan, Lambert?"

Lambert leaned forward with his elbows on his knees. "In a few minutes, I want you to follow Sand Burr and see where he's stabling the horses. Later, I want you to go to the saloon and get a bottle of the strongest bottle of whiskey you can buy, one that'll make flowers wilt when you walk down the boardwalk. We're goin' to see to it that our young gent gets all tanked up later today. Then we're goin' to tie him up on this bed. I'm going to clean up good—real good. Then, I'm goin' to take his carpetbag or whatever he buys and go down and try my best to convince them that I'm a rich donor. I plan on killin' T-Dilly."

"Why are you doin' this, Lambert?"

Lambert was uneasy. He looked straight into Ollie's eyes and broke the stare. His tired eyes moved around. "I made Bobo a promise."

Ollie nodded somewhat satisfied with the answer. "I have high regard for you, Lambert, but I suspect there's another reason."

Lambert frowned and sighed. Troubled by Ollie's trailing remark, he replied stiffly, "You better git goin'. We got things to do."

Later that afternoon, Sand Burr, although he protested, was talked into taking one drink and then another. In an hour, he was wobbly legged and decided to take a catnap before executing his plan. He lay down and fell into a deep sleep. Ollie and Lambert lifted the drunken Sand Burr onto the cheap, narrow bed. Lambert, who had brought a rope for that moment, tied Sand Burr snugly to the bed. He was so well restricted that he would have to have help to get untied.

Lambert, freshly shaven, dusted off his coat and placed his .44 in the flowery decorated carpetbag that Sand Burr had purchased. He gave some final instructions to Ollie, took a deep breath, and left.

Lieutenant Bragg, perched by his second-story window, caught sight of Lambert leaving the hotel. He did not know his name but recognized him as one of the two who had accompanied Sand Burr into town. He watched him intently. When Lambert stopped a passerby on the boardwalk apparently asking directions, the lieutenant felt he was up to something. When Bragg saw the man turn and point in the general direction of Representative Stevens's office, he knew he was up to something. He hurriedly placed on his military holster and left leaving his door open as he did double time down the steps that led to the side door.

Lambert saw two horses tied to the hitch rack that fronted the brick office building where Stevens's office was. He had an inkling T-Dilly was there. Lambert stopped and looked behind himself. He saw nothing to give him alarm. He nervously dusted his coat again. He adjusted his hat and continued walking. He stepped off the boardwalk and crossed the dirt street. He heard some birds chirping and a turtle dove cooing in the distance. He stepped up on the new boardwalk and paused; he was directly in front of the office. Lambert heard a loud argument going on. He did not know whose voice was whose, but he knew that whoever it was, they were not happy with each other.

Lambert did not knock. He opened the door and saw Stevens standing behind his desk with a red, flushed face. He recognized T-Dilly immediately and took silent pleasure in the fact that his left hand was bundled up by a thick bandage.

Stevens, who did not recognize Lambert, barked out, "You ever heard of knocking, you ignorant bastard?"

T-Dilly, still standing with his side to Lambert, focused on Stevens. He did not get a good look at Lambert.

Lambert gave a fake smile. "I can come back later. I just brought this campaign money pledge to you, Representative Stevens."

Stevens, having heard the word *money*, held up his hand as a sign that his discussion with T-Dilly was ending. He tried to fabricate a smile. "Mr. …?" He pointed to a chair.

Lambert filled in the blank. "My name's G.W. Lambert, a big admirer of yours."

T-Dilly, irritated that his argument with the representative had been interrupted, let his eyes briefly move to Lambert, who was seated. He turned to Stevens when it hit him who Lambert was. He quickly turned to Lambert. He started his hand down to his pistol and snarled, "It's you, you bastard."

Lambert's hand was in the carpetbag and grasping his .44. He fired through the fabric. The first shot hit T-Dilly in the right clavicle. His second shot caught the bandit in the top of his chest. He clashed against the wall and slowly began sliding down it.

Stevens, who had his hands out like a schoolmaster dealing with an unruly class, looked at T-Dilly in shock and turned to Lambert. Lambert shot again from inside the bag and hit Stevens between the eyes. Stevens hit the back wall and slid down leaving a trail of brains and blood on the wallpaper.

From a seated position, T-Dilly gritted his teeth and pulled back the hammer of his pistol. He fired a round that caught Lambert in the side. Lambert tried to hold onto the chair he had been sitting. He pulled his .44 from the carpetbag and fired a finishing shot into T-Dilly. "That's for Bobo, you sorry bastard."

Lambert was barely hanging onto consciousness when he saw Lieutenant Bragg breathlessly enter the office. Bragg looked around at all the carnage and uttered a string of cuss words. He stopped briefly as though a revelation had suddenly hit him. He leaned to Lambert and said, "When the sheriff gets here, you tell him it was Pugh Larrimore that shot you and the others."

The lieutenant pulled him closer. "If you care about John Lee Johnson, you better remember what I told you." The lieutenant saw the carpetbag with the burned gunshot holes in it. He scooped it up quickly and stuffed it into his military blouse.

Ollie rushed in behind the lieutenant. His eyes moving wildly around the bloody scene. The lieutenant recognized him as the second man who had drifted into town with Sand Burr. He took Lambert's .44 and then Ollie's. He exchanged them and told Ollie to get the hell back to wherever he had come from.

Ollie did not have to be told twice. He disappeared out the door; the sheriff and two deputies arrived just after that.

Sheriff Lang, a tall, red-headed man with an angular face, wore a black hat with a narrow brim. He entered, looked at the two bodies and the wounded G.W. Lambert, and turned to the lieutenant questioningly. He had seen the lieutenant enter the building after the shots had been fired, so he knew he was not a suspect. He had spotted Ollie too earlier on the street but fortunately had not seen him enter or leave the building. He was looking at the lieutenant for some answers. The sheriff pointed at Lambert, who was still hanging onto consciousness. "I guess this is the bastard who shot 'em." He gave a quick flick of his fingers in the general direction of the two dead men, who had been his friends.

The lieutenant shook his head. He pointed at Lambert. "He was a victim himself."

Lang almost burst a gut when he responded, "Have you lost your mind?" He pointed again toward Lambert. "He's the killer all right."

The lieutenant shook his head. "I tell you it was someone else."

Lang, tired of the see-saw conversation, gave the lieutenant a sarcastic look. Keeping his eyes on the lieutenant, he picked up Lambert's .44. He smelled the clean barrel and then in frustration checked the loads. He looked flabbergasted as he took in the crime scene a second and a third time. He then suspiciously looked at the lieutenant. He held out his hand for the lieutenant's pistol.

"You have to be joshing me, Sheriff."

The sheriff made a compelling wiggle of his fingers for him to comply. Bragg handed over his pistol. The sheriff took a sniff of the pistol bore and checked the loads. He pushed his hat up and scratched his head perplexedly. "Well, who in the hell would want to kill the representative?"

The lieutenant wanted to tell him that half of Texas would have, but he let that go and suggested he ask Lambert while he was still conscious.

The sheriff leaned down as though he were embarrassed but still asked, "Whatever your name is, who caused all this bloodshed?"

Lambert managed to croaked out, "Pugh Larrimore."

When he said that, the sheriff looked at his two deputies, who gave him disbelieving looks. He studied a few minutes on the matter and then unconvincingly shrugged. He turned to his deputies. "Go to the clinic. Have them send a stretcher." He sadly looked at the two bodies in gruesome death postures. "And bring the undertaker too."

He suspiciously turned to the lieutenant. "Do you know this bird?"

The lieutenant said, "I've never seen him before in my life," which was partly true.

The sheriff said, "Pugh Larrimore?" in disbelief to himself as he started to exit. Just before he made his way out the door, he turned once more to the lieutenant. "Did you see Pugh Larrimore?"

The lieutenant shook his head. "I saw someone running but couldn't make him out for sure." The lieutenant was lying, and he was a novice at it, but he hoped the sheriff was buying what he was selling.

Sheriff Lang gave a slow, hesitant nod. He was not convinced, but the possibility of Pugh Larrimore killing the representative was not out of the question. He and his two deputies departed with audible queries going back and forth as they walked away.

Minutes later, a doctor and two hefty men carrying a stretcher arrived. The doctor checked Lambert out and gave a nod for the men to place him on the canvas carrier.

The angular Judge Roy caught sight of Lambert as he was being transported to the clinic. He rubbed his chin in thought. He remembered the face but could not immediately place it. He thoughtfully walked toward the sheriff's office still dwelling on Lambert. When he touched the doorknob of the jailhouse, a sly smile moved across his skeletal features. He gave a knowing nod to himself as he entered.

The judge patiently listened to Sheriff Lang's version of what had happened and how an innocent bystander had also been wounded by the assassin. He gave him a play-by-play description of checking pistols and Bragg's testimony.

When Lang finished, the judge snorted derisively. Lang, puzzled by the judge's attitude, asked, "Is there something I'm missing, Judge?"

Judge Roy stood for a moment basking in his new role as the boss of Austin. With Stevens gone, he was at that point the eyes and ears of Frank McGrew's network there; that knowledge left him feeling smug. His egotistical self-image was overflowing in his body language and his words. "Yes, Sheriff Lang, the man who is currently being taken to the clinic works for none other than John Lee Johnson. As far as Lieutenant Bragg is concerned, he's no friend of ours. He and this despicable Johnson are joined at the hip if you ask me."

Sheriff Lang was taken aback. He thought he had had it all figured out, but the judge had him doubting himself. The sheriff snapped his fingers. "Listen. Lefty and Slick and some of the boys are over at the saloon, and they shore in hell should be able to recognize a John Lee Johnson man."

The judge nodded. "Let's get them and head to the clinic." He superciliously ran his hands up and down his coat lapels. "This will stop this nonsense that Pugh Larrimore pulled this off."

Lang authorized his two deputies to go to the Capitol Saloon and fetch the boys. He told them to bring the gang members immediately to the clinic to identify a John Lee Johnson hooligan.

When Sand Burr awoke, he saw he was tied tighter than a tick. He could barely move. His bleary eyes shot up to Ollie, who stood at the side of the bed. "What the hell is goin' on, Ollie? Get these here damn ropes off me!"

As Ollie was untying Sand Burr, Sand Burr shook his head swearing off whiskey forever. "Where's Lambert?"

When Ollie was slow in answering, Sand Burr's eyes narrowed in thought. Then it hit him—Lambert had taken on the job he had deemed for himself. As the last strand was loosened, Sand Burr threw his legs off the bed and pulled on his boots. "I'm askin' again, Ollie, where's Lambert?"

Ollie sighed and pointed in the general direction of the clinic. Sand Burr, still fighting the effects of too much to drink, shook his head and went to the porcelain pitcher on the crude stand. He drank half of it and poured the rest over his head. He shook the water off like a dog and ran his hands over his face. "Where in the hell are you pointin'?"

Ollie ignored the question and asked Sand Burr to sit. At first, Sand Burr wanted to bolt out the door, but when he heard Ollie speak in such an importuning way, he hesitated. He wiped his face and sat meekly. In a voice modulated with concern, he asked, "What in hell is goin' on?"

Ollie confessed all that he and Lambert had planned. He told about Lambert going to the representative's office and killing Stevens and T-Dilly.

Sand Burr sat there stunned. He leaned forward breathless as he considered Lambert's courage. "Well, he did promise Bobo that he'd take care of matters."

Ollie nodded but looked in the direction of the clinic though he could not see it. "He got shot himself."

"Is he alive?"

Ollie nodded but gloomily remained quiet for a minute. He finally sighed and said that he was alive and that he had been carried to the clinic next to the military building.

Catching Ollie's mood, Sand Burr leaned forward with his hands folded. "I can't figure Lambert out, Ollie. I want to like him, but he ain't square with me sometimes. He got a job as a ranch hand under some kind of pretense, but he already had money and a lot of it. He wanted to ride with me and John to Mexico and wouldn't really tell me why, and that made me suspicious of him." Sand Burr sighed and shook his head as if trying to make sense of the man called G.W. Lambert. He saw that Ollie wanted to talk but was hesitant about doing so. "What do you know about him, Ollie?"

Ollie took in a lung of air. "I ain't shore you can handle it."

Sand Burr considered his words. He leaned back and exhaled audibly. "Hell, I can take it." He shook his head trying to fight the effects of too much alcohol. But he managed to give half a smile. "Can you tell me about what you know without puttin' me to sleep?"

Ollie remained bent over in his chair. He decided it was time to talk. "Do you remember that hombre we buried up to his neck in Lako Springs?" Sand Burr nodded. "Well, it's like this. The first night we spent there after that Austin bunch gave up, I was lyin' in bed thinkin' about that poor turd. I felt bad for him. I remembered being tied to a mesquite tree, and that shore in hell didn't feel too good. So I got up in the middle of the night and borrowed one of the mayor's horses and a shovel. I rode up to the hill and told that feller I was goin' to dig him out. He started cryin' and told me he'd appreciate that. As I was diggin' him out, he started talkin' about Lambert. He said that him and his older brother grew up next to the spread Lambert's father had. He went on to say that Lambert married a pretty girl named Portia Rogers. He said his brother and everyone else liked ol' G.W. He called him a hard worker. He went on to say that Lambert adored his wife ... that he treated her like a queen."

Ollie inhaled, looked into Sand Burr's eyes, and then stared at the floor. "Here's the hard part, Sand Burr. Lambert's wife had a son. But she must have had a hard childbirth. The baby lived, but Lambert's wife died a month later. Lambert couldn't handle the grief of it. He started drinkin,' whorin,' and doin' some crazy stuff. It seems that after tyin' on a bender one night, Lambert shot up his house. He woke up the next day, and there was pistol ball holes just inches from the baby's crib. When he sobered up and seen what he'd done, he got scared and took the child to the orphan home over in Finleyville to protect him.

"Jericho said that his brother told him that Lambert gave the child an unusual name so he could find him later. He gave the child to an orphanage using his wife's maiden name as his surname since he felt unworthy." Ollie wiped his face. "Lambert continued on his wild spree for over a decade until he met a minister named Stan Johnson. He went on to say that Stan Johnson helped him pray his way out of the devil's hand. He has not had a drink in ten years. He did continue to play poker. He won a whole ranch in a poker game in the backroom of a hotel in Hawkshaw. A big ranch too.

"I finally dug Jericho out and gave him a dollar and the horse. Before he took off, he told me that Lambert had recognized him but gave him a look to keep his mouth shut. I don't know if that's true or not. I just know I walked back to Lako Springs feelin' some better about doin' a good deed but burdened with a knowledge I couldn't very well share."

Sand Burr swallowed. He felt dizzy. He looked up and met Ollie's eyes. "What you're sayin' is that he's my father."

Ollie grimly nodded. "Think about it, Sand Burr. Ain't your last name Rogers? Your mother's maiden name was Rogers."

Sand Burr said nothing. His hands shot up to his face to quell the tears streaming down. He stopped and sobbed again. He managed to say tearfully, "He went down to kill Stevens and T-Dilly to keep me alive." Another thought entered his mind. "And he went on that trip to look over my shoulder."

Ollie sighed. "Reckon that's the size of it, Sand Burr."

Sand Burr sat up straighter and looked for his shirt. He wiped his tears. "I reckon I understand things better." He looked at Ollie. "Wonder what my real name is?"

Ollie shrugged and wiped a tear from his own eye. "I'd imagine you're G.W. Lambert Junior."

Sand Burr shook his head as he remembered the day he had met Lambert and telling him ironically that not everybody could be named Lambert.

They reasoned they probably should not venture far from the hotel except at night and separately. They thought that T-Dilly's men were probably in town and that the soldiers who had attended the fight would soon return. They worried that the soldiers might inadvertently recognize them and call them by name causing unnecessary problems. They concluded that they would visit Lambert at night but only with Lieutenant Bragg's permission. Later, they could find a wagon and mules to take Lambert home.

Lambert was lying in a bed at the clinic. A silver-headed army doctor had just extracted a pistol ball lodged deep in his body. He placed the lead ball in a small washbasin filled with alcohol and blood.

At the foot of his bed were Sheriff Lang and Judge Roy. Judge Roy's sagging jaw made him look like a buzzard gauging a promising meal. Lang shook his head as he observed the pale Lambert. "If the boys identify him, he'll shore as hell hang."

The judge nodded rapidly. "There isn't a doubt in mind. He's guiltier than sin."

They heard many boots tromping down the hallway. The door opened, and a deputy led in ten members of the late T-Dilly's gang. Lefty was first in line followed by the rounded, dusky Slick. The sheriff motioned for them to gather around the bed, and he pointed at Lambert. "Is he or not a member of John Lee Johnson's bunch of hellions?"

Lefty leaned in close and carefully examined Lambert's face. He pushed up his hat and looked Sheriff Lang in the face. "I ain't never seen this bird before."

Lambert, who was conscious, viewed Lefty while he was looking at him. Lambert caught sight of a quick wink that signaled that he had just received a receipt for a past good deed.

Sheriff Lang, irritated by that response, went down the line. Each man denied ever having seen Lambert. Slick hooked his hands in his gun belt and stated boldly, "We saw John Lee Johnson's men up close and personal … a bunch of tough lookin' men. Yes siree, we saw 'em all. This man must be a drummer or somethin.'"

Judge Roy look flabbergasted. His venous nose turned purple. He stormed out of the hospital room followed by the two deputies. Lang, satisfied that his assessment of the crime scene had been correct, tipped his hat to the gang members and dismissed them. He turned to the doctor, who seemed mystified by all the cloak-and-dagger stuff whirling around him. "Take good care of him, Doc. He was an innocent bystander."

The following week, several events occurred. Sergeant Brewer's troopers returned and quickly deposited their winnings in the bank. Lieutenant Bragg informed Sergeant Brewer that Lambert was in the clinic wounded. He told the sergeant a rough version of what had gone down in Stevens's office but left out some salient details. The sergeant wisely filled in the blanks. The sergeant, then in confidence, informed his men that they were to treat Lambert, Sand Burr, and Ollie as though they were total strangers if by accident they met them.

Lieutenant Bragg chanced a daytime meeting with Sand Burr and Ollie in their room to bring them up to date about Lambert's improving health. He said that T-Dilly's gang inexplicably did not or could not identify Lambert as being associated with John Lee Johnson. He asked them about how that could have happened but readily saw that Sand Burr and Ollie did not want to discuss the issue. The lieutenant, realizing there was a reason they were being so close mouthed, dropped the subject.

He warned them to never return to work for John Lee Johnson. The lieutenant spoke sharply. "Sheriff Lang is crooked as a goat's path, but he isn't stupid. If you ever return there within two years, he'll know about it." He paused as he made ready to exit. "And that could spell trouble for all you and for John too."

After Lieutenant Bragg's stopover, Sand Burr and Ollie began to visit Lambert at night but separately. After each had spent time with Lambert, they met in the room and compared their thoughts on his progress. They were encouraged that Lambert could talk for lengthy periods and that the doctor had approved of Lambert traveling as long as he went by wagon. He said he would release him at the end of the week. But he strongly advised them that he needed at least a month of convalescing before he could ride again.

Two days prior to their departure, Sand Burr purchased a long-bed wagon and three mules. He tied one mule on the back of the wagon in case one of the others went lame.

On the day of departure, Ollie was seated in driver's box while Sand Burr went inside and assisted Lambert out. Lambert gladly inhaled when he felt the air and looked up at the sun; he sensed the healing powers of the great outdoors. Sand Burr helped Lambert up into the bed of the wagon and onto a thick cotton cushion he had bought.

Lambert had noticed three things about Sand Burr over the previous few days—Sand Burr no longer acted as if he suspected him of anything, he did not call him Lambert or by any name, and he was treating him kindly. He contemplated these changes in Sand Burr's behavior as he stretched out his six-foot frame trying to get comfortable.

They headed out to Roxy; it took them almost three weeks to get there. Ollie drove the wagon pulling the mule. Sand Burr followed on horseback pulling two horses. The last week of the journey, Lambert, feeling stronger, would occasionally sit with Ollie until he grew tired and would return to his bed. When they reached Roxy, Lambert sat up from his bed and directed Ollie to the trading post.

They stopped there, and Lambert with the aid of a cane entered and was hailed by Finley, the owner. Lambert bought a water vase filled with lilies. They had a decent meal and left knowing they were closing in on their destination. They traveled all day with Lambert clutching the vase worried about spilling water; Sand Burr and Ollie saw that he was obsessed about keeping the lilies fresh.

Close to sundown, they found the dusty trail that led over several sandy drumlins. Lambert suddenly had an impulse to ride beside Ollie.

With Sand Burr's aid, he climbed into the driver's seat and directed Ollie down the faded, almost invisible trail until they reached his deserted house and the gravesite of his wife.

When they pulled into the abandoned ranch yard, Sand Burr saw the cross over the grave. That lonely mound of dirt reminded him of all he had missed and how it could have been the key to his future. He knew it was the spot that held his mother's remains. Though he had no memories of her, the grave caused his chest to fill with emotions he did not understand. He wished he had the connection he should have had. But still, it was his unseen mother, who had loved him. He had to inhale deeply to keep from crying. He would have given all he had to tell his departed mother he loved her too.

He watched Ollie stop the wagon and tie the reins around the brake. He watched as his father stepped down holding the vase of lilies and fix his eyes on the grave. Lambert limped to the small mound and knelt. Sand Burr's vision, bleary with tears, saw Lambert's mouth moving as he talked to his wife.

Sand Burr slowly dismounted. He wiped some tears from his eyes but to no avail—others kept coming. He walked with his head down to stand behind his father.

It was emotionally difficult to see his father's body convulse in grief. Sand Burr placed his hands on Lambert's shoulders. He felt his father tremble as he tried to deal with his grief. Sand Burr watched as his father laid out the lilies in an attempt to spell the word *love*. When Lambert felt he had done the best he could, he pulled a handkerchief out and tried to wipe away his copious tears.

Sand Burr, who still held his father's shoulders, asked in a broken voice, "Was my mother pretty?"

Lambert nodded; his son's words had not yet hit him. But as he wiped his eyes again, it occurred to him what Sand Burr had just said. He attempted to rise but could not. Sand Burr grabbed him under one arm and helped him up. "Pa, I think my mother would want us to go home and find peace. Let's make up for some lost time."

When Lambert heard Sand Burr call him Pa, all the pent-up guilt that had gripped him for years took flight and was replaced by a rush of happiness. Lambert slowly turned and embraced Sand Burr in a teary-eyed bear-hug and looked up. He remembered what he had told God months before. Though his thoughts were unspoken, he thanked the unseen God for granting him that day. He pushed back Sand Burr. "Son, we got cattle to sell."

In a tearful and choked voice, Sand Burr replied, "Damn right we do."

Ollie, who had been watching them, wiped tears from his eyes. He was surprised when G.W. Lambert Senior and Junior came over and gave him hugs. The orange sun cast a brilliant ray over the scene. They walked slowly away savoring the moment. They eventually became black outlines as they rode over the sandy rise.

Weeks earlier, Floyd, Seth, and Yvette were taking a roundabout way to Baileysboro. They sat in the wagon seat watching a lot of cattle in the distance among mesquite scattered here and there. As they came upon a clearing, Yvette saw many men constructing a beautiful house on a rise. She heard hammers, saws, and the voices of working men. She admired the house they were building. A porch went around most of the two-story house. She saw a smaller but nonetheless elegant house going up behind the main one.

She pointed to the larger house and sighed. "What a beautiful house, Seth. Can you imagine someone having the privilege to live there and enjoy such a large ranch?" When no one responded, she made mention of the smaller house she had just viewed. "That smaller one looks wonderful to me also." She checked herself. She realized that Seth was a fix-it man and that she should not have praised someone else's good fortune when her husband had no way to match that kind of wealth. She thought it was okay to ask who was going to live in the smaller house, so she did.

Seth looked ahead and casually remarked, "That's goin' to be Floyd's house."

Yvette nodded slowly not sure if Seth was serious. When she saw he was, her hands went to her mouth. Tears began to form. She realized the implications of that statement. Seth turned her to him, put his hands on her shoulders, and said in a loving voice, "You see, Yvette, that other house is yours."

She grabbed Seth by his neck and held on for dear life. Her tearful eyes moved to the sky. "You aren't a fix-it man, are you?"

"Nope."

"Floyd's not a fix-it man either, is he?"

"Nope."

"And that's goin' to be our house?"

"Yep."

Yvette, still hugging Seth, looked up at the azure sky. "Rich or poor, young or old, there is a God in heaven."

Seth nodded. "Yep."

It was August 1, 1865. John Lee Johnson had been home a number of days. But he was uneasy. He had heard nothing from Austin concerning Sand Burr, Lambert, and Ollie. He reasoned correctly that Lieutenant Bragg must be under some scrutiny because he was not sending telegrams or couriers to him.

However, he had had some good moments since he had returned. He met Seth and his wife, Yvette, and had watched as they gathered in the four, happy, young orphan girls in their wagon. He knew they would love their new home, which was the largest in the county. Seth had told him privately that Yvette was carrying his child. They became misty eyed over that announcement. He watched his cousin, a very rich man by all accounts, drive away even wealthier for having a good woman to share his life with.

But that had happened a week earlier. Though John had put on his best face, he felt a keen anxiety about what might have transpired in Austin. John went moodily walking. He was standing supported by his arm on one of the corral posts watching the sun go down. He was looking in the direction of Austin. He was about to return to the house when he saw a chunky rider wearing a high-crowned hat riding down the ranch road. He had seen the man before but could not place him immediately. The rider stopped a cowhand near the bunkhouse apparently asking where John was. After he got directions, his eyes moved up and saw John looking at him.

John saw the rider nod his thanks to the cowhand and ride toward him. He intuitively knew this man was bringing news from Austin. He dropped his arm off the post and awaited him anxiously.

The man rode up and nodded affably. "My name's Fred Malone. I came by here sometime back."

John remembered and told him so.

Fred removed his dusty hat, gave it a whack against his pants leg, and put it back on. "I was sent here by Lambert to let you know what's goin' on."

When he said Lambert, John straightened and inhaled. "Well, what's goin' on?"

"The man named T-Dilly was killed along with that carpetbagger Stevens. The word is that Pugh Larrimore did it."

John's eyes narrowed as he tilted his head to absorb that information. He knew it would have been virtually impossible for the Comanchero leader to have done that.

Fred, seeing the hesitant look on John's face, said, "The boss, er, Lambert, was injured in the fracas. It seems that Pugh shot him too."

John let a small smile move across his handsome features. He knew he was listening to a crock, but he liked hearing it. He asked about Sand Burr and Ollie.

Fred took in a lung of hair making his jaws inflate to control the words he was about to reveal. "Sand Burr is now called Junior. None but a few of us knew Sand Burr was Lambert's son." He smiled. "Junior's runnin' the ranch, and he's one hell of a businessman. Lambert's makin' money, and he and Junior are thicker than thieves."

John stood there mulling all this. He had to admit that he had not seen that coming. He raised himself up on his toes and back down again as he contemplated Lambert and Sand Burr. He shook his head in friendly dismay at himself for not having figured that one out. But the more he dwelled on it, the more obvious it was.

"What about Ollie?"

"He's my ramrod. He's healthy, and he told me to tell you he ain't repairin' roofs and diggin' wells no more."

Fred sighed and told John that the Lamberts, father and son, would love to come and see him but it might be a spell before they would be able to do that. He said they had been advised by the lieutenant to be mindful of the investigation of the murder of Stevens and T-Dilly and keep their distance from John. That confirmed what John had suspected all along— the lieutenant was playing it close to the vest and not putting himself or John in harm's way by trying to contact him.

Just as Fred started to turn his horse to leave, he said, "One more thing. Junior told me to tell you that the success he's havin' now is because of you. Since he now has his daddy back in his life, he wanted to know if he could tell people you was his uncle."

John humbly dropped his head but managed to nod his approval. "Yes, but tell him it was my idea."

Fred gave him a full-faced smile and a friendly wave. He rode away.

John watched him disappear into the distance. He took in a lung of satisfactory air. For some reason, a good reason, he felt better than when he had exited the hell pit in Mexico. He began to hum the church song, "Shall We Gather at the River." He felt at peace at last. He began walking to this ranch house. He knew he could spend some time with the love of his life even if it was a short time. But he was not disillusioned. He knew before long that Frank McGrew would make another move and deal him more misery.

That very day, Judge Harold Roy received a telegram from Philadelphia. The judge, ensconced in the shadows of his office, looked at the large, printed words through his pince-nez glasses perched low on his long, thin, red nose. It read, "Judge, you are now the most powerful man in Texas. If you want to stay that way, you will rid me of you know whom in one year. I expect you to expedite this process immediately."

The judge nervously swallowed as he tossed the yellow telegram on the desk. He eased his hands into his coat pocket, pulled out a small bottle of Tennessee whiskey, and uncorked it. His thoughtful eyes reread the McGrew telegram. He had been a low-level lawyer in Pennsylvania, but because of the fortunes of war, he had more power than he could have ever dreamed of. He took a heavy swallow. He intended to remain the most powerful man in Texas. He would not make the mistake his predecessor had made. He intended to swarm the big Texan. He let a prideful, crooked smile ease across his spare features. He intended not only to keep his power base but also extend it. His new mantra would be, "John Lee Johnson must die."

CPSIA information can be obtained
at www.ICGtesting.com
Printed in the USA
BVHW03*1122200818
525056BV00007B/34/P